The

ANGEL

of

SOLANO

NORMAN HALL

ISBN 9798634868981

In memory of
Major Colin Keartland-Mole
12th January 1921 – 19th October 1997

Harry stood at the open window, staring east over the expanse of barren land that separated the two halves of the city.

Even at 3 a.m. the night air was balmy and humid from the remnants of a scorching hot summer's day with, undoubtedly, another to follow. He'd fallen into bed naked as usual but had felt obliged to put on a pair of shorts before standing by the full-length window smoking his cigarette.

The glow from the street lamp three floors down was yellow and feeble and the street devoid of people or traffic, the absence of human activity at this time of night normal in a part of the city widely regarded as the front line. The silence was almost absolute, punctured only by the occasional and unintelligible shout in the distance and the random barking of a dog paying no heed to protocol.

Bisecting the gloom and darkness that pervaded both sides of the city, the two-hundred-metres-wide stretch of wasteland between the two concrete barriers was bathed in the glare of powerful floodlights emulating broad daylight at its edges, fading to a warm and incongruously sunny glow at its midpoint.

Harry took another long draw, held his breath for ten seconds to allow his lungs time to absorb the nicotine, then exhaled, blowing a dense cloud of noxious chemicals into the night air. The glow from his cigarette would be visible from the watchtowers situated at hundred-metre intervals in the centre of the strip but there was no danger. Not any more. He remembered a time when smoking openly and carelessly was to invite a bullet through the head, but this was no longer policy for the enemy, whoever they were, their restraint pragmatic, understood and reciprocated.

Nowadays, he could smoke with impunity; although he mused they were being told increasingly, it was bad in other ways. Now, apparently, it wasn't the stimulating and life-affirming exercise in social self-expression he'd always been led to believe, and if the newspaper adverts had been accurate, widely embraced by members of the medical profession. It had now become a lethal cocktail of poisonous carcinogens that would rapidly and inevitably result in death by a thousand illnesses.

He'd always smoked, as had everyone else he knew and it had done him no harm and anyway, how could anything that made him feel this good be so bad? One day in the future, perhaps, people would stop telling others what to do and how to live their lives. After all, wasn't that what they'd all been fighting for?

Petra had told him to stop, several times. She said he smelt like a kipper factory and chided him when alone or with friends, tediously reciting an infernal rhyme she knew would cause him maximum irritation.

Tobacco is a filthy weed,
That from the devil doth proceed.
It drains your purse, it burns your clothes,
And makes a chimney of your nose.

He turned to look at her, lying naked, face down on top of the bed covers, arms and legs spread wide, fast asleep despite the heat, her long blonde hair trailing haphazardly across two pillows. She was probably right, and one day he would give it up. For her. But for now, he still needed it.

He watched her slow breathing and his heart filled with warmth and trepidation in equal measure. He still didn't know what she saw in him, this tortured, damaged chain-smoking automaton with his chronic depression, persistent anxiety, crushing self-doubt and multiple inadequacies, real and imagined, concealed within an impregnable shell of diffidence and dispassion.

Woefully mismatched would be his assessment, but he couldn't do without her and by all accounts, nor she him. He'd make an honest woman of her one day, God knows she'd asked him often enough, but he needed to be certain he had given her enough time to come to her senses, realise there were far better options out there. Others of her own age, who were more likely to make her happy, or at least happier than he ever could.

Under mild interrogation, he would have to confess his apparent ambivalence was more to do with a lack of self-worth than any feelings of consideration for the young woman whom he had loved and with whom he had lived for the last eighteen months. The fear of commitment, the antipathy towards stability and the constant urge to get away, to run away, was what drove him. That, and the suspicion that happiness was a cruel deceit, a precursor to disaster.

This was what challenged his thinking and dictated his behaviour, day and night, and to some extent why, as usual, he was awake at 3 a.m., knowing what the night held in store and fearful of what the day would bring.

He raised his cigarette hand up to his right shoulder and without thinking, rubbed the scar above his chest, a reflex action he carried out several times a day. Eighteen years on, it still caused him discomfort: tingling, tickling, throbbing, a constant reminder of the past, as if he needed for one minute any physical evidence of something that to this day continued to occupy his mind in every waking hour of his life. About time it healed, he thought.

The faint howl of a distant dog drew his attention back to the vista across the barren corridor between the concrete Wall on his, the western side of the city, and the barbed wire fence two hundred metres away. The "death strip".

Despite the euphoria of May 1945, the war had never really ended. No sooner had the conflict ceased and the celebrations subsided, another had been contrived to take its place. Former allies, united in a shared struggle against a common enemy and who once had greeted each other with joy, clapped each other on the back and waved to the world in triumph at their wondrous achievement, were soon trading insults and accusations and taking up their respective positions on opposite sides of the power divide. The perpetual power struggle of mankind played out on a new board in a new game. The only difference was that now, for the time being at least, this war was cold and it was Harry's job to try to keep it that way.

He cupped what was left of his cigarette in his hand and put it to his lips for one last draw, and as he inhaled, as he relished the fragrance and his brain embraced the soporific effect of the drug and wound itself down, all hell broke loose.

A blinding shaft of light accompanied by a dull-sounding crump hit him with the intensity of a thousand white suns jolting him back to his senses. He dropped to the floor instinctively, closing his eyes a fraction too late to stop a swirling mass of kaleidoscopic imagery dancing across both retinas, expecting a hail of gunfire to strafe the window while realising at the same time that, whatever the reason for the sudden activity, it could have nothing to do with him. And he was right.

No sooner had the spotlight hit him, it swung away from his position and down onto the death strip. The room went dark again and he squinted to readjust his eyes to the contrast. He flicked his cigarette butt out of the window and crawled forward onto the narrow balcony, straining his still impaired vision to try to work out what was happening.

At the far side of the strip a group of dark figures – soldiers and dogs – lumbered into view, shouting and barking amidst the random crack of handguns and, fifty yards ahead of them, a single bulky figure, running, ducking and weaving, staggering its way towards him, halfway across the wasteland, illuminated clearly in the vector of two spotlights. A runner.

A single crack from a sniper rifle – the new Dragunov, Harry judged from his weapons training – echoed and reverberated in the night and he watched in horror as the running figure threw both arms in the air, its body propelled forward in a wild leap like an acrobat in a macabre circus show. The body hit the ground heavily and bounced once before lying still.

"Harry? What is it?" Petra, suddenly awake, was sitting up and staring at him in shock and confusion.

"Get down!" he hissed at her, gesticulating with one hand. "It's a runner, but I think they got him."

"Oh God."

But as he returned his attention to the death strip where the body lay inert, he saw it magically leap to its feet and resume its crazy trajectory towards the Wall.

"Wait! He's up. My God, how come…?"

He watched transfixed, willing the figure on, and caught a glimpse of the dogs loose at the other end, bounding across the land, vaulting the concrete tank barriers set out across the mid-point, barking and slavering in pursuit of their prey. A bullet would surely be preferable, he thought, to being overpowered and savaged by a pack of Dobermanns. He guessed the sniper must have been caught off guard, assuming his work was done, but the figure had only gone another twenty yards when the Dragunov cracked again, and again, the figure flew forward.

"Shit. He's down again. There's no way he can take two bullets like that."

"Harry! Come away from the window!" screamed Petra.

"They aren't shooting at me."

"Even so, please!"

"My God, he's up again. Go on, man!" Harry shouted involuntarily into the void and waved a fist in the air. "Go on!" He felt Petra behind him, her arms clasped around his chest, her cheek on his back, the heat of her body pressing against him.

"Oh, no, it's terrible. I can't bear to watch."

The sniper had stopped firing. The dogs were getting closer and would no doubt finish the job. Harry clenched both fists and his forearm muscles strained. He desperately wanted to help but there was nothing he could do. The runner was only ten yards from the Wall and would, in an instant, be out of view but Harry knew there was no way to scale its smooth sides and the dogs would be on him within ten seconds.

A roar of an engine and swinging headlights appeared in the empty street below. An open-topped Land Rover carrying four uniformed military police screeched to a halt and the two MPs perched on the back leapt out onto the road, one of them carrying a coiled rope knotted at two-foot intervals. His partner looped the other end over a tow bar on the back of the vehicle before he threw the rope in a lazy arc over the twelve-foot Wall. Both men took up position with their backs to the Wall, one shouting something unintelligible, the words drowned out by the revving engine.

An arm went up, was held for a few seconds and then brought swiftly down. The vehicle spun its tires, its nose lifting momentarily off the ground as it jerked into life, engine roaring, dragging the knotted rope back over the Wall.

Harry watched in astonishment as the end of the rope suddenly appeared over the rounded top of the Wall with the runner attached to its end. The figure released his grip in mid-air and, with arms and legs cartwheeling manically, sailed over the Wall, landing with a hideous thud and a shriek of agony on the road below.

"Holy shit! The guy just flew over the bloody Wall! There are MPs down there trying to pick him up but it looks like he's injured himself."

"He's alive?" said Petra, daring to peer around Harry's shoulder to catch a glimpse of the scene below.

"It's not possible. Two bullets in the back and a twenty-foot drop onto hard cobbles. If he's not dead he's Superman."

Petra kept her body concealed behind Harry, suddenly aware she was naked in front of a full-length window and they both watched in fascination as the MPs roughly hauled the semi-conscious body into the back of the Land Rover, stowed the rope and took off at speed.

"Unbelievable!" said Harry, rubbing his jaw with his left hand, his heart beating furiously. He reached behind him and put an arm around Petra's shoulder. They could still hear the Dobermanns barking on the other side of the Wall, accompanied by a few shouts in German and, in an instant, the dogs fell silent, apart from the odd whimper: the sound of failure. The floodlights went out abruptly and the strip fell back into relative darkness. He turned to her and as she gripped him tightly, he kissed her head. She was shaking.

"What kind of world is this we live in?" she said softly.

"The same as we ever did."

"But when will it end? How long before we see how wrong we all are?"

"I don't know."

"Sometimes I want to get away, Harry. Away from all of this. There has to be something better."

"This is your home."

"And I hate it. What kind of a home is this? For anyone? We had hopes for the future. Hopes that the dark days were gone. But now I can only see hatred and misery."

Harry sighed deeply. He had never heard Petra say anything so pessimistic, so fatalistic. He needed her optimism. Her grounded reality. It was only too easy for him to succumb, to acquiesce in the despondency of his life. It provided him the excuse he needed, to be who he was. But she'd been a beacon of hope and in truth it was what kept him going when, in other circumstances, he might either have ended it, or turned to something darker, submitting to the will of his demons, justification for his own torment. If Petra were to believe herself lost, then surely he would too.

"C'mon. Back to bed."

He picked her up in his arms and carried her to the bed, laid her down and she pulled a single cotton sheet over

11

herself. He reached for another cigarette from the bedside table.

"Please don't."

He sighed again, put the packet down and got under the sheet beside her. She snuggled up closely and he inhaled her scent.

"I love you, Harry Male," she whispered quietly as she dropped off to sleep.

Harry didn't respond. He didn't think he needed to. She knew he loved her. How could he not? She was twenty-eight and he, forty-two. Any man would give his right arm to have someone so beautiful in his bed, in his house, in his life. But he was a man of few words, the fewer the better, he always said. Words mean nothing. Actions speak louder, so when you need words, make them count.

He stared at the ceiling, craving nicotine, and thought again about the runner. Wondered whether he was on a slab somewhere or if, by some miracle, he was drinking hot tea and whisky, exchanging jokes with a bunch of squaddies. He would try to find out tomorrow, but for now, he was left with his thoughts and waited for sleep either to release him or cast him back into the past.

But as ever, and prompted by the drama outside his window, the memory came flooding back, replaying the same events time and again, always with the same conclusion – that being, there was no conclusion at all. An endless loop in which he played out each step, knowing full well how it would end, but hoping perhaps to see something new, something seminal, something that finally might give closure. The darkness and silence of the night slowly enveloped Harry Male and left him alone with his demons.

CHAPTER 2

Italy – March 1944

Dawn was breaking as the convoy of trucks and armoured vehicles crossed the pontoon bridge over the Ambrone River, twenty miles due south of the ancient town of Montellano. Hundreds of bedraggled troops of various nationalities trudged wearily back the way they had come two days earlier, their hard-fought gains squandered in half the time and their strength further depleted. The Allied push for Rome had been halted yet again.

German panzer divisions still occupied the high ground and, despite their overwhelming superiority in firepower and personnel, the Allied armies had failed to break through the extensive fortifications, and when they did, often succumbed to counter-attack. The mountainous terrain not only constituted a natural barrier for the invading forces, it afforded the enemy a natural observation post from which to monitor the advance of the Allies from the south and to direct artillery fire with uncanny accuracy.

Second Lieutenant Harry Male, twenty-four, winced in the chill wind of the winter's morning, pulled his greatcoat collar up around his neck and turned to check on his platoon, whose members followed dutifully behind. They were down to sixteen now, having lost Forbes and Alcott in yesterday's ignominious retreat from the village. His men were subdued and demoralised and would remain that way for a day or so until thrown into action again, when they could vent their anger and possibly exact some revenge on their enemy.

Harry's men knew exactly what lay in store and were battle hardened enough to know it wouldn't be easy. The same thing all over again. He had instructions to brief them once they'd reached their makeshift garrison at Moscuso, by which time the aerial bombardment of Montellano would be well underway. The ancient town stood in the way of the Allied push towards Rome and had so far proven to be impregnable, each assault by ground forces repulsed with ease, such that the military high command had determined Montellano would be completely destroyed from the air.

"Come on, chaps," said Harry, "another couple of miles and there'll be hot tea, bacon sarnies and most important of all, clean socks."

"It's not me socks I'm worried about, sir," offered Sergeant Bill Fraser, twice Harry's age and veteran of Ypres.

"Thank you, Sergeant, we don't need to know about the state of your nether regions."

"Hey, Sarge," piped up Corporal Joe Fleming, "maybe you should march at the back. Me and the boys are finding it a bit whiffy back here."

"Shut it, Fleming."

"Told you it was horse that geezer was flogging. And it was well dead." Corporal Fleming laughed at his own joke and one or two of the others joined in, which only encouraged him to continue. "I reckon it'd been dead a month. Weren't no rump steak, that's for sure."

"I ain't telling you again, Corporal."

But Fleming fancied himself as the joker in the platoon and he was on a roll.

"Every time you fart, the rest of us duck thinking it's another one of them Stukas comin' over."

Fraser stopped abruptly and turned to confront his junior NCO, but he was interrupted by a familiar whistling noise that grew rapidly to a crescendo and they all looked to the sky. There was a whoosh over their heads.

"Down!" shouted Harry and the entire platoon dropped to the ground like synchronised acrobats. The shell landed with a deafening explosion in the field fifty yards behind them, throwing up a plume of grass, soil and stones that slowly fell back to earth, pummelling their backs and helmets like giant hailstones. They lay still for a second expecting another, but as was often the case, it was a random attack.

"Bloody hell, that was a close one," grunted Fraser, but to his intense frustration, Fleming, face down in the dirt, was still chuckling.

"Blimey, Sarge. That was a ripper!" Some of the others chuckled with him.

"Enough, Corporal," barked Harry, getting to his feet, though he too thought it was funny. "C'mon, let's get going before the bastards get their eye in."

They trudged on and Harry noticed a church a half-mile distant, its steeple standing tall and proud amidst the devastated olive groves and vines that surrounded it. He wondered fleetingly whether God was choosy about which house of worship took a hit from one of his creation's creations, but dismissed it as pure luck. He had no time for religious mumbo-jumbo; you just had to look around to see how pointless it all was, how deluded his followers were.

The road curved to the right and they came to a lop-sided road sign that forlornly announced their arrival in Solano. Harry remembered passing through a couple of days ago, noting at the time there were few buildings or features to suggest it had a population of any size or that it was indeed a village at all. But his attention was drawn to a commotion up ahead where a small group of soldiers appeared to be in heated debate.

An elderly man in saggy black cord trousers, crumpled brown jacket and waistcoat, cloth cap gripped in both hands, was gesticulating and jabbering incoherently in Italian at the men and they were doing their level best to ignore him. He seemed particularly agitated with one of them, who lifted his arm as if to swat him away like a fly, before another interjected and pushed the old boy to the ground. Harry frowned and broke into a run.

"Oi!" he shouted and the soldiers turned to look back at him in disdain. He reached them in seconds. There were four of them and they looked surly and disinterested, bodies slouching, weight on one leg, defiant. "Who's in command here?" The silence betrayed a semblance of guilt. "Well? Speak up!"

"No one. He's dead," said the largest of the four, a tall, thickset private with three days' stubble, insubordination clearly on display.

"Stand to attention!" Harry barked and the four soldiers snapped out of their torpor as his own platoon caught up behind him. He took a step towards the large one.

"What's your name, Private?"

"Dawson, sir."

"Okay, Dawson, what's going on here?"

"Crazy old Eyetie," said Dawson, gesturing to the prostrate figure. "Been pissing us off."

The man tried to get up but was clearly having difficulty, panting and mumbling incoherently in Italian.

"Sergeant. Help the gentleman."

"Yes, sir!"

Fraser knelt down and put a hand under the old boy's arm and lifted him to his feet. He resumed his animated babbling.

"Signore, signore, per favore aiutatemi… per favore."

"Momento, signore," said Harry in his best Italian, holding a palm up at the man, who was now hopping from one foot to another, still wringing his cap. Another whistle, another whoosh. "Down!"

The ground shook as the shell hit, this time in the field to their left and when Harry lifted his head, he saw all the men flat out except for the old boy, who was still on his feet, seemingly unperturbed by the explosion, still agitated and pleading.

"Per favore aiutatemi…"

Harry got up and brushed some mud from his coat.

"Dawson!"

"Yes, sir."

"Signore, per favore…"

"Momento!" shouted Harry at the man in irritation. "Take your men off. At the double. I'll talk to you later."

"Yes, sir!"

Both he and Dawson knew this was an idle threat. There was little or no chance of them meeting up again but it wasn't the time or place for any dressing-down and the incident would be forgotten in no time. Dawson and his colleagues didn't hesitate, turning on their heels and jogging away, one hand instinctively on helmet, rifles drooping. The man grabbed Harry's arm.

"Signore, per favore…"

Fraser stepped in, raising the butt of his rifle. "Oi! Let go of the officer, you grubby old wop." The man flinched, cowed in fear.

"Sergeant! That's enough!" shouted Harry, increasingly frustrated. Fraser lowered his rifle and the man looked back at Harry. His eyes were bloodshot and tearful, his lips quivering and his body shaking in desperation, but for what, Harry could only guess. He'd learned all his Italian from the last three months in Sicily and it still amounted to little more than a couple of pleasantries and the ability to order two beers. He rustled up enough to ask him what the problem was.

"Cosa c'è?"

"Mia figlia sta molto male."

Harry shook his head. He had no idea what the man was saying and realised they were not going to have a sensible conversation in Italian. Harry looked the old boy up and down. He was probably only in his late fifties, but the terrors and hardships of the last four of years of war had clearly taken their toll.

"Wilkins!"

"Yes, sir!" Private Marco Wilkins, nineteen, pushed his way forward. Yorkshire dad, Italian mum.

"What's this man saying?"

"He says his daughter's ill, sir."

"What does he mean, ill?"

Wilkins translated and the man responded anxiously.

"Sta per avere un bambino."

"She's having a baby, sir."

"Oh, is that all?" Harry sighed in relief but also in frustration and turned away. "C'mon, let's go."

The old boy grabbed his arm again. *"Signore, per favore… sta per morire!"*

"He says she's dying, sir."

Harry stopped and turned to look into the man's eyes. The whites were yellow and rheumy, criss-crossed with tiny spider webs of blue and red, the irises grey and colourless and his pupils black as bottomless wells, yet the emotion and terror and honesty they portrayed somehow reached deep down into Lieutenant Harry Male's heart and twisted it till it hurt. Three fully loaded transport trucks rumbled by, each towing a howitzer, men crammed in the back swaying and bumping together as the wheels bounced over the potholed road. It had given him time to think.

"Where is she?"

"Dove'è lei adesso?" said Wilkins. The man jerked his head and gestured behind him, pointing to a small farmhouse nestling in a field two hundred yards up a rutted track.

"A casa mia. Vieni subito."

"Farmhouse, sir. He wants us to hurry."

"Dammit! We're not bloody medics or midwives!" shouted Harry to no one in particular but he knew inside he was committed and that the frustration he felt was directed more at himself.

"Signore?" pleaded the man again.

"Okay. Okay. Tell him we'll take a look. Fraser, Wilkins and I'll go up to the house and see what's up."

"Sir! You can't!"

"Take the rest of the men, carry on up to Moscuso and get the bloody kettle on. We'll check it out and then we'll be right behind you."

"Sir! What if it's a trap! What if there's a bunch of Jerries up there?"

"Doubt it, Sergeant. Bit too subtle for your average Kraut, don't you think?"

"But, sir?"

18

"Fraser, do as I say. Wilkins. Come on, I need you to translate."

"Sir!"

Harry waved towards the farmhouse and the man, who had been watching the exchange in confusion, looked first relieved, then reinvigorated.

"Grazie, grazie! Grazie mille!"

He stumbled off up the track and into the field, hobbling from one leg to the other, continuing his agitated discourse while constantly looking behind him to ensure the soldiers were still there. Lieutenant Harry Male and Private Marco Wilkins followed, trepidatious and wary.

"Keep your eyes open for trouble, Private."

"Yes, sir!"

Harry looked up at the ever-lightening sky. He knew the bombardment of Montellano would soon be underway, and as he picked his way amongst runnels and puddles and the ice-capped mini craters of the muddy field he thought he could hear, between the random thud and crump of German artillery, the distant drone of heavy bombers.

***

Two hundred miles to the southeast at Foggia airbase, First Lieutenant Mitch McLennan of the United States Army Air Force took one last draw from his Havana and tossed the still glowing butt out of the open cockpit window onto the tarmac twenty feet below.

The Boeing B-17G bore a painting on its cheek of a fantasy goddess with long blonde hair and curls. She had white teeth and deep red lipstick, impossibly long legs and large breasts that burst out of her skimpy pink swimsuit, and she rested one hand on her hip, her other arm reaching up to the cockpit in a provocative pose. Above her, in flamboyant and garish script that traced the contours of her voluptuous figure, was her name: *Nora Desirée.*

Mitch stretched a hand out of the window and slapped palms with Nora before sliding the glass shut and securing the catch, instantly dulling the rumble and snarl of engine noise that pervaded the cockpit. He reached for the mouthpiece that dangled from one side of his flight mask, hooked it over the other side and turned to the co-pilot on his right. Second Lieutenant Carl Withers slid his own window shut and flicked the catch.

"Let's go, *Nora*!" said Withers with uneasy enthusiasm. Twenty-eight-year-old Mitch knew it was forced and served only to hide the young man's fear. He winked at his young first officer and spoke into the intercom.

"You guys strapped in back there?"

Tail gunner Fred Sherman, waist gunners Brent Morris and Mickey Flanagan, ball turret gunner Cody Fisher and radio operator Ben Kravitz, staff sergeants all, sat in a huddle amidships, ready to take their respective positions straight after take-off.

"Secure, Cap'n," replied Kravitz. Mitch could imagine their faces: jaws set, a mixture of insouciance and defiance concealing the crushing weight of terror that accompanied every operation.

"Balatelli?"

"Check," responded the flight engineer seated above and behind the cockpit just ahead of the bomb bay.

"Rosenberg, Kovacs?"

"Check," came the joint replies from the navigator and bombardier from the nose compartment ahead and below the flight deck.

"Wagons roll," shouted Mitch into his mouthpiece, "let's do this. When we get back, coffee and doughnuts are on me."

The B-17 ahead of them was barrelling down the runway a mere two hundred feet away but there was no time to wait for it to get airborne. There were eight more in the squadron lined up behind him and all would be anxious to get on their way.

Mitch gripped the underside of the two pairs of throttle levers and Withers placed his own behind the pilot to steady the vibration that fed through the controls. He edged the levers forward and wound the engines up to a roar. *Nora Desirée* shivered and hesitated, then lurched into motion as both pilots pushed hard on the throttles until the rev counters read twenty-five hundred.

Four thirty-litre radial engines, each packing twelve hundred horsepower, bellowed their rage in response and dragged *Nora*, shuddering and lumbering down the runway carrying her full eight-thousand-pound bomb load.

"Shalom," he heard Manny Rosenberg mutter softly over the crackle and pop of the intercom.

"Don't be a smartass, Manny. We ain't carrying a shitload of peace to them Krauts."

"No, sir!"

Withers cast a sideways glance at Mitch and caught his wry smile, but the pilot was staring straight ahead, both hands gripping the shuddering yoke. Withers held the throttles and the rhythmic thump-thump of the wheels on the runway seams came faster as the plane gathered speed.

"Sixty, seventy, eighty…" called out Withers, reading the airspeed indicator as the tail wheel lifted off the ground. "Ninety, ninety-five, one hundred."

Mitch hauled back on the yoke, the vibration subsided and *Nora Desirée*, engines roaring like a thousand lions, hoisted her thirty tons into the morning sky.

***

Harry and Wilkins tentatively followed the man up the muddy pathway that led to the farmhouse. Wilkins scanned the field left and right for movement while Harry stared ahead, both weapons at the ready. But the man had neither hesitated nor acted suspiciously which gave Harry some comfort there was nothing sinister in his intent. He stopped and looked skywards.

A squadron of B-17s droned overhead at about ten thousand feet. Harry guessed they would be about twenty miles and less than ten minutes' flying time from Montellano and, assuming they dodged the flak, he wondered what manner of hell they'd unleash on the town. The old boy reached the front door of the farmhouse, stopped for a second, then turned to Harry.

"Momento, signore."

He opened the door tentatively and stepped inside, closing it behind him. Harry was confused and mildly irritated. The man had been very anxious and in a desperate hurry to get them there as soon as possible and now he was making them wait. What for? To tidy the house for visitors?

"What's he doing?" said Wilkins, equally puzzled and now doubly alert. "I don't like it, sir."

"Nor me, Private."

Harry dropped to his haunches to the left of the door and pressed his back against the wall, gesturing to Wilkins to do likewise on the opposite side. They waited a minute, listening for any sign of danger above the drone of another squadron of aircraft drifting in from the south. The farmhouse door opened again with a loud creak. The man appeared, cap still in hand, looking at first confused and worried, but then noticed the soldiers crouched down either side of his front door.

"Ah, per favore, entrate…"

"Stay here, Wilkins."

Harry got to his feet and lifted his Sten gun to waist height. Keeping low, he ducked into the gloomy farmhouse after the man, swinging the gun from side to side, his eyes struggling to adapt to the darkness.

A stone staircase rose on his right to a landing that was bathed in the yellow glow from a first-floor window. A threadbare rug lay incongruously in the alcove beneath the staircase and to his left, an open fireplace burned brightly, its orange flames casting flickering shadows on a shiny stone floor worn smooth by decades of footfall. A single rocking chair with moth-eaten cushions sat to the left of the chimney breast, one side scorched and blackened by permanent exposure to the heat, and nestled against the front wall of the house behind the open door was a battered oak table with three chairs. Straight ahead, set against the far wall between the chimney breast and a second doorway, was an iron bedstead where a slight figure lay under heavy blankets and thick eiderdown.

"Prego, prego," intoned the old boy, gesturing his visitor forward, inviting him to approach the bed. Harry relaxed and stood to his full height, a good six or seven inches taller than his host.

"All right, sir?" came the call from outside.

"It's clear, Private. Stay there and keep an eye out."

"Yes, sir!"

The faint popping of anti-aircraft fire sounded like mini claps of thunder on a distant horizon; the B-17s would soon be over their target. Harry lowered his gun, removed his helmet and stepped tentatively towards the bed.

"Prego, prego..." repeated the man. *"Mia figlia. Si chiama Isabella."* His voice had softened, his anxiety supplanted by a wistful melancholy, a mixture of love, pride and wonder at the sanctity of the scene. He kissed two fingers, made the sign of the cross on his chest and forehead and knelt down next to the bed, reaching across to take his daughter's hand.

"Isabella. Isabella. Ho trovato aiuto."

"What's he saying, Wilkins?" said Harry to the open doorway behind him.

"He's telling her he's brought help, sir."

Harry groaned. He had no idea what to do and even if he did, was ill equipped to do it. He leaned over the kneeling figure of the old man and looked down at the young woman.

She was eighteen or nineteen and beautiful, her long dark hair spread haphazardly on either side of a dirty pillow. Her eyes were half-closed, sunken in pools of dark shadow above prominent pasty cheeks and her grey lips mumbled a mantra, incoherent and repetitive. Beads of sweat glistened on her forehead and neck, flowing in rivulets down her chest onto a gold chain and crucifix before disappearing into a heavy cotton nightdress.

She was slight in build, but the bulge in the bedclothes was unmistakeable, pronounced and disproportionate to her size and the blankets stretched up and over legs that were bent at the knee and splayed outwards.

"Wilkins?"

"Yes, sir!"

"Did you do medical training?"

"No, sir. Well, I'm handy with a bandage, sir."

Harry sighed again, but his mind was racing. He heard two thunderous explosions from miles away and then twenty seconds later, two more, interspersed with myriad small pops that sounded like fireworks. He rubbed his chin, seeking inspiration, guidance, or even divine intervention. But he was lost. He was, however, an officer and it was his job to make decisions.

"Wilkins, come in here!"

"Yes, sir!"

Marco Wilkins stepped into the room.

"She needs a medic. Nothing we can do here except hold hands and mop fevered brows. Go on after the others. I saw a radio truck pass us an hour ago so if you catch up with it, radio ahead to the field hospital and tell them we need a medic here on the double. If not, brief them when you get there."

"Yes, sir!"

"What's his name?"

"*Lei come si chiami?*"

The man stood up, still gripping his cap. "Alfredo. Alfredo Girardi."

"Tell Alfredo what we're doing, Private."

Wilkins explained and Alfredo Girardi nodded in understanding. Harry held out a hand.

"*Mi chiamo Harry.*"

24

Alfredo looked at it dumbly then took it, turned it palm down and pressed his forehead to the back of Harry's hand as if in supplication. Harry drew it back, embarrassed at Alfredo's show of humility, but squeezed one of his shoulders and nodded an acknowledgement, of sorts. He had no idea what he would do next. He simply prayed Isabella would hold on until proper help arrived.

"Where's his wife?"

"Dov'è sua moglia?"

Alfredo's face fell and he fidgeted with his cap again, seemingly unable to find the words. He shrugged.

"Morta."

Wilkins looked up at Harry. He didn't need to translate. Harry cursed himself for his stupidity and squeezed Alfredo's shoulder again, nodding sombrely, trying to avoid his eyes.

"Okay, Private, good luck and God speed."

"Same to you, sir."

Wilkins saluted and went out into the chill morning as the sky above them filled inexorably with the sights and sounds of war.

***

Mitch levelled the B-17 at ten thousand feet. The temperature was a mere 10 degrees Fahrenheit, well below freezing and only the cockpit was heated. The rest of the crew wore electrically heated suits, which although crude and unreliable, took the edge off the cold. They were all used to it and once the action started, they'd be oblivious to any discomfort.

Nora Desirée settled into her cruising speed of one hundred and sixty. It was a mere hundred miles to the target with a flight time of just forty minutes. Mitch kept *Nora* within two hundred feet of Squadron Leader Enders, with the rest of the squadron assembled in loose formation behind.

The men aft had assumed their gun positions, constantly alert to fighter attack although little had been reported. Kravitz had relayed intel from the first wave that they should expect heavy anti-aircraft fire over the target and Enders would break up the squadron ten minutes before the bombing runs commenced.

Nora flew on steadily, engine revs throttled back to eighteen hundred to conserve fuel. She carried only enough to get them there and back, the weight saving given over to maximise the bomb load. Six squadrons in the first wave carried a pair of two thousand pounders. The remaining eight squadrons, including Mitch's, would follow with their sixteen five-hundred-pound ordnance to carpet bomb the resultant rubble and surrounding areas. One hundred and forty planes in total: four hundred tons of high explosive.

Mitch couldn't help wondering how many of his comrades had been lost to fighters or ack-ack. It was something never revealed during a mission and unless they witnessed a downing themselves the final reckoning would only be done when the last plane returned home. He was a veteran of thirty-six sorties, and apart from some strafing and minor damage had always got home in one piece, testament to the inherent strength of the B-17. He wasn't a statistician or a gambler, but instinct told him that one day, his luck would change and, as he mused every time he went up, it might be today.

He had every reason to remain optimistic. Following the Italian capitulation six months ago, the Krauts fought alone and with the Allies now on the offensive, maybe the war would end before his luck ran out. Maybe. The speakers in his earphones hissed.

"Twenty minutes to target," announced Rosenberg, hunched over his table in the nose. In front of him and surrounded by a Plexiglas bubble, Lukasz Kovacs sat on his stool peering into the gyroscopic bomb sight, computing height, air speed, wind speed and drift on his slide rule.

"Check," said Mitch. "Kovacs. You set to arm?"

"Zgoda!"

"English, you dumb Polack!" Mitch was not in the mood for fooling around, but he knew Kovacs was in high spirits. There was nothing the Pole liked more than killing Germans.

"Check," mumbled Kovacs, compliant, but unrepentant.

***

The Girardi farmhouse was comfortably warm thanks to the fire in the open range. Alfredo threw on a few more logs and adjusted two cast-iron cooking pots that rested on a metal rack. Harry could see steam escaping from the lid of one and for the first time sensed the aroma of food.

He laid his helmet on the floor along with the Sten, took off his greatcoat and tunic, folded them neatly and placed them next to the hardware. Finally he took his standard issue jackknife out of his pocket and laid it on his tunic. He ran a hand through his thick shock of dark hair wondering what he could possibly do before help arrived. The body on the bed suddenly convulsed.

"Papà...!"

Alfredo rushed to his daughter, leaning over the metal frame to take her outstretched hands and kiss her glistening forehead.

"Isabella!" he cried and Harry stepped forward, fists clenched by his side, embarrassed and frustrated by his own impotence. He'd never felt so useless and lost.

"Fa così male, Papà..."

The girl's cry pierced his heart and he dropped to his knees beside the bed, but he had no idea what to do. Another shell landed close by and Isabella shrieked again in pain and terror as debris clattered on the roof of the farmhouse like it was raining pebbles.

Harry reached across and put his hand on her forearm. It was pointless and pathetic, he knew, and she ignored it, instead gripping her father's gnarled and bony fingers, the knuckles white on her tiny shaking hands. He looked down at the bulge in her middle and without thinking, rested his hand on top of the eiderdown. Even through the thick layers of blanket he sensed movement and his mouth dropped open in shock. A tiny human being was in there and seemed ready to come out.

Harry turned his head. Alfredo was looking at him, grim and earnest, and for the first time, Isabella's eyes were open and through her tears they were imploring him to save her.

"Hot water! *Acqua calda,*" he heard himself say and Alfredo sprang into action. Harry could have laughed at himself. He'd heard childbirth always involved hot water, but he had no clue what to do with it. Was it for hand washing? *One step at a time*, he told himself. *It will all become clear. What the hell will become clear?*

He took Isabella's hand and she gripped it fiercely, gritting her teeth between spasms of pain and throwing her head back in a screeching wail that drowned out the distant sounds of war building up outside.

Alfredo returned from the fire with a tin bowl of steaming water and a coarse towel and laid it on the stone floor. Harry let go of Isabella's hand, rolled up his sleeves and plunged his hands into the water, gasping at the heat but feverishly scrubbing his filthy hands and fingernails with a bar of brown pungent soap until they were cleaner than he had seen them for weeks.

"Pronto," said Alfredo. Harry looked up at him in fear. He knew it meant *Ready*. He gulped deeply and moved slowly to the bottom of the bed as Isabella cried out again, her body heaving upwards, the bed springs creaking and groaning with her shifting weight. *"Vai avanti,"* pleaded Alfredo. *Go ahead.* *"Per favore…"* Then resumed his position at the head holding his daughter's outstretched hands.

"Scegli il nome per il bambino."

Harry had no idea what he was saying. *"Non capisco."* I don't understand.

"Il nome!"

28

Harry shrugged.

"Il bambino, gli dia un nome," Alfredo shrieked, pointing at Harry in frustration.

"Name?"

"*Sì!* You name!"

Harry could do without this. He had better things to worry about than thinking up a name, but it was charming of Alfredo to consider him. It didn't matter. If they all got out of this they'd forget each other and Isabella would think of one for herself. He shook his head, trying to make his brain work. His parents were Reginald and Kathleen.

"Reg!"

"Ah, sì! Reggio! Bravo! E se fosse una bambina?" If it's a girl?

"Kathleen?"

"Catalina? Sì."

Harry thought to correct Alfredo's pronunciation, but the old boy was nodding enthusiastically and decided it wasn't worth the effort. Anyway, "Catalina" sounded better.

Harry wiped an arm across his brow. He was sweating profusely and he felt his heart racing, the beat pounding in his head so that he didn't flinch as another shell landed, throwing grass, mud and rocks against the back wall of the farmhouse.

He cast an eye over the foot of the metal bed frame, which extended from floor level to fifteen inches above the mattress. He examined the frame and noticed on each side a spring-loaded clip and hinge mechanism halfway up its height. He wrestled with the clips until they moved with a metallic screech. The end frame swung down and he was able to place one knee on the mattress.

"Avanti," urged Alfredo, but it wasn't Alfredo's encouragement that spurred him on, it was Isabella's latest cry of anguish. She flung her upper body forward and snarled at him in a terrified rage before slumping back on the bed, panting, her chest heaving. Harry rolled his sleeves up further and took another a deep breath. He gripped the

29

bedclothes in both hands and in one slow but determined movement pushed them back over her legs.

***

"Ten minutes, Cap'n," crackled Manny Rosenberg through the headset.

"Kovacs?"

"Set, Captain. Going in at five thousand. Air speed, one forty. Head wind ten."

"Roger," said Mitch as he pushed the controls gently forward and *Nora Desirée* began her descent to the target zone.

The squadron had already broken formation and four miles ahead he could see their buddies in the twelfth spread out in a wide line below, the sky around them peppered with black puffs of anti-aircraft fire.

Withers took his eyes off the gauges to survey the land as the target came into view: a hilltop dead ahead marked by flashes of fire and palls of black smoke that rose into the morning sky. To the east, the advance squadrons were heading back, mission accomplished, and despite standing orders to concentrate on his own mission, he couldn't resist counting, hoping they were all there.

"Eight thousand," called Mitch. *Nora* was descending at twenty feet a second. "Two and a half minutes to drop height."

"Check," called Kovacs, still hunched over his sight in the Plexiglas nose, oblivious to the black puffs of smoke that burst in the sky ahead and increased in size and intensity as they flew on.

"Bandits?" called Mitch to the five gunners behind him.

"Negative," came the collective reply.

"Just a bevy of beautiful B-17s coming up our ass," said Sherman from the tail.

"Okay. We're gonna get some ack-ack, so start prayin' to your God, whoever the hell that might be."

On cue, they felt the first shockwaves as anti-aircraft shells exploded in the sky above and below them, buffeting the airframe and causing *Nora* to rattle and shake as if her screws were working loose.

"Six thousand," announced Withers. "Forty seconds to release altitude."

"Roger," said Kovacs, totally absorbed in his task. Rosenberg stood behind him, a hand on each nose gun, navigation duties suspended now they had visual contact. Kovacs reached behind to his left and pulled a lever on the bomb control stand. "Bomb doors opening." Beneath the fuselage, two electrically operated bomb doors swung slowly open, sending an icy blast of air through the aircraft.

"Five thousand," said Mitch, his hands and feet taut on the controls, adjusting to the altered aerodynamics, determined to keep *Nora* steady in the turbulent air. "It's all yours, Lukasz. Give 'em one for Warsaw."

Kovacs pulled back a second lever from the "Safe" position to "Select".

"Bombs armed, Captain."

Mitch saw Squadron Leader Enders' airplane unload its ordnance a hundred yards ahead and then bank sharply to the east. He wanted to watch them fall but steeled himself to concentrate on the instruments.

"Steady, steady," muttered the Pole softly, one hand steadying his head on the bombsight; the load would release automatically when the bomber reached the point computed by the sight.

In the cockpit behind him, Withers' left hand gripped the throttle levers tightly, four fingers working in tiny independent movements to maintain their air speed at one forty.

"Steady… steady…"

They all held their breath. Soon, they could go home.

***

31

Harry stared down between the legs of the young woman, a sight he had only ever imagined before. He was woefully ill-educated in the anatomy and physiology of the opposite sex and barely more experienced when it came to matters of the flesh.

He'd lost his virginity at seventeen to the form master's libidinous wife, as had one or two of his classmates, or so he'd discovered, but he remembered little of the encounter, had simply done his best to avert his eyes and do as he was told.

At twenty, a grope and a fumble in the back row of the Coventry Picturedrome had provided him at least with a tactile sense of what to expect but the relationship with Mary Scott had been short-lived and never developed any further.

The memory of the middle-aged tart in Plymouth before embarkation in '41 was clouded by the excessive amount of alcohol he'd consumed beforehand, and latterly, in Messina, he'd had his most fruitful encounter yet, although for the signorina concerned, time was money and she made sure it was all over in a flash.

But this was different. Here in this hellish place, this utilitarian farmhouse, exposed to random attacks on their very survival from casual and indiscriminate acts of terror, he saw nothing other than a vulnerable and desperate human being in need of help. And notwithstanding his profound helplessness, the young woman needed what little he had to offer.

He had already seen death and mutilation – the bodies of men, women and children, friends, enemies and innocent strangers, physical remains of former lives cut short by senseless violence – and despite the horror, he had been able to shrug it off, accept it as the norm, a grim and inevitable consequence of war.

But right here and now, alone with these traumatised people, a caring father, his beautiful daughter and her unborn child, he held their lives in his hands and he would do whatever was necessary to preserve them. *But how?*

The sheets were soaking. *Her waters!* As if for a moment he knew what that meant. *It means the baby's arrival is imminent. Does it? Does she not need to push?*

"Push! Push!" he shouted. *What's Italian for push?* He gasped at his own ignorance, his absolute stupidity. *Dammit!*

"Per favore... mia bambina," moaned Alfredo, holding his daughter's hands as Isabella writhed and screamed below him.

"Papà!" she wailed and the tears came like torrents. A random shell landed close by, the explosion so deafening the whole house shook and loose plaster fell from the ceiling coating them all in a fine mixture of dust and grit.

Isabella coughed between her cries and Harry shook his head to clear the dust from his eyes, putting his hands on her knees to press them further apart. A bloody red and angry gap opened up between her legs and a pink dome shape appeared, an object impossibly large to fit the confined space, never mind exit from it. Harry's eyes opened like saucers. He had never seen anything like it before.

"Push! Push! *Poussez!*" *That's French, you damn fool!* "*Bambino! Bambino!*"

"Madre di Dio, Santa Maria Madre," prayed Alfredo, eyes closed tight, held tilted up towards his imaginary heaven. Isabella screamed again as another explosion rocked the house. Harry let go of her knees and touched the smooth slippery dome, but there was nothing he could grab hold of. He pressed her inner thighs even further apart and the gap widened, the dome expanded in size.

"Bambino! Bambino! I can see it coming."

He knew they had passed the point of no return, that there was no chance now of any medical help before something either wonderful or catastrophic happened, that it was all or nothing and he prayed again and implored Mother Nature to take care of things and do what was right.

Isabella screamed again, long, agonised, visceral and loud. Loud enough to drown out the distant rumble of thunder from the faraway bombing and plenty loud enough to mask the whistle and whoosh that rose in a crescendo in the sky above them until eventually it drowned out her cries and was itself too loud to bear.

Then, the world as they knew it ended.

The seventy-five millimetre shell hit the roof of the farmhouse at the apex of the side wall, blowing the entire roof into the sky; slates, trusses and cross members flew upwards, reached their zenith, then sailed lazily back to earth, crashing through the floorboards above and bringing down the giant oak beams that supported them, while the top half of the two-foot-thick side wall collapsed inwards and tons of stone, bricks and mortar fell into the room.

Harry was thrown backwards by the blast and lumps of flying masonry collided with his temple, knocking him off the rear of the bed onto the floor where his lower legs were first pummelled then buried by rubble.

Everything went black and silent.

***

Twenty miles north and five thousand feet above the farmhouse, *Nora Desirée* flew on doggedly to her assignation as yet impervious to the anti-aircraft shells exploding all around.

Kovacs felt his heartbeat loudly in his ears. He tightened his grip on the sight, while silently mouthing the countdown.

"Three, two, one…" would be his last words.

The anti-aircraft shell scored a direct hit on the B-17's nose, smashing through the Plexiglas, filling the entire space with white-hot shrapnel that ripped apart everything in its path, severing arms, legs and heads, the penthrite and white phosphorous explosive material vaporising whatever fragments were left of its occupants. The entire nose compartment evaporated and although the two pilots were protected below the neck by the armour plated bulkhead, a hot metal fragment smashed through the right side of the cockpit window, penetrating Withers' brain through his left eye, ramming his head back in the seat and killing him instantly. Another blade of shrapnel hit Mitch, ripping through his leather jacket, piercing his upper right arm and spraying his own blood onto his right cheek, the force of the impact loosening his grip on the flight control wheel.

Within a second, another shell exploded in the air alongside engine three, piercing the nacelle, severing the fuel lines and blowing a hole in the high pressure oil tank that fed the propeller feathering pump. Mitch reached instinctively for the fuel cut-off switch and the feathering control, for unless he altered the aspect of the blades, the unpowered propeller would spin out of control. But without the oil, it was useless. The propeller on engine three, fuelled by the momentum of the plane and the outside air, freewheeled uncontrollably until, finally, the gearbox tore itself apart in a screeching orgy of self-destruction. The propeller shaft snapped and four hundred pounds of blade detached and cartwheeled into engine four, obliterating both propellers. Stricken by the loss of two engines, *Nora* banked sharply right and pointed what was left of her shattered nose down towards earth.

Mitch felt the adrenalin flood his body and he fought to regain his grip on the controls as a chorus of shouts and expletives from the crew filled his headset. He cut the fuel to engine four and prised Withers' dead hands off the throttles, hauling back on one and two to reduce the push to the right. He gripped the yoke, using all his strength to steer left, and pushed hard against the left rudder pedal to arrest the relentless swing right, otherwise he knew *Nora* would spin out of control. *Nora* screamed with agony as her engines kept pushing her right while the rudder and ailerons pulled her left and although Mitch was able to slow her turn, she kept falling relentlessly. He had already done the math and it didn't add up.

"Balatelli? You there?"

"Yes, sir!"

"Sherman?"

"We hit, sir?"

"Wadda you think, Sergeant? Fisher?"

"Aye aye."

"Morris?"

"Sir!"

"Flanagan?"

"Sir!"

"Kravitz… Kravitz?"

"Flesh wound, Cap'n!" But Mitch could tell from his agonised tone, Kravitz was suffering.

"How bad?"

"Left arm, sir! Still attached… sir!"

"Radio in our position. We're three men and two engines down with a full payload."

"Transmitter shot to pieces, sir."

Mitch would have slapped the wheel with his left hand in rage but he was wrestling with the shuddering, creaking aircraft as it continued to drop out of the sky, sweeping in a long downwards arc to its right. He continued to wrestle with the yoke but it really needed two pilots with two good arms and even with the left rudder pedal to the floor he knew it would make little or no difference to their lop-sided trajectory.

"We bailin', Cap'n?" shouted Fisher. It was an option Mitch had considered and rejected, for now, but before he could reply, he heard Flanagan bellowing from the starboard waist gun position.

"Bandits! Three o'clock!" He swung his fifty-calibre Browning right, but as *Nora* continued her turn, they disappeared out of view before he could pull the trigger. "Cody! Me109s, two from the west."

The ball turret beneath the fuselage swung upwards as the plane banked and, now lying on his side, Cody Fisher let off a three-second burst as the fighters came into view. One exploded.

"Fuck you!" shouted Fisher in triumph as he tried to track the second but he'd lost the angle and the fighter pulled a sharp turn and fired back, strafing the bomber's fuselage aft of Morris's waist gun position, penetrating the thin fuselage skin and slamming a hail of bullets into Flanagan on the opposite side.

"Micky's hit, sir!" screamed Morris.

Sherman picked up the Me109 as it circled behind them and he pulled hard on both triggers as he tracked it across the sky. He held the burst as long as he could, knowing the barrels would melt after ten seconds' continuous fire, but it was only six before the fifty-calibre shells found their mark, blowing off one wing, the fighter cartwheeling out of sight in a smoke-trailed death spiral.

Mitch used all his strength to pull the yoke back to the stop but though he'd managed to arrest the turn, *Nora* continued her relentless descent. The altimeters read two thousand and falling. If they didn't lose weight, they'd hit the ground in three minutes. He'd already gone through the options and there was only one. With little strength in his right arm, he leaned forward and hugged the yoke with his body so he could use his left and reach down towards his left foot for the emergency bomb release. He yanked the handle and held his breath. Nothing happened.

"Shit!"

He grabbed the yoke again with his left hand and hung on, watching the altimeter slowly spiralling backwards.

"Balatelli!"

"Sir!"

"Bomb release is shorted. Get your ass down to the bomb bay. We need to lose the payload."

"Sir?"

"Controls are shot. Go to manual," he shouted above the din of the engines and the incessant rattling of an airframe that was now shaking itself to pieces.

"Cap'n, we're way off target. Our guys are down there!"

Mitch clenched his teeth; they had no time for a debate. "Now listen up, Sergeant. This baby's carrying eight thousand pounds of high explosive on two engines. She ain't going nowhere but down. We bail, she goes down, we do nuttin', she goes down, we release and I find a quiet field that needs ploughin', then maybe, just maybe, we can all get home. So you get down to the bay or else we all go down with those mothers strapped to our ass. Which is it gonna be?"

There was silence for a second, but only a second.

"Yes, sir!"

Mitch stared grimly out of the cockpit window. He knew what Balatelli was saying but he had already assessed the risks even though he had no real knowledge of who or what was down there. The Allies may still be coming up from the south from all directions: Brits, Poles, New Zealanders, Indians, as well as his own 8th Army and of course civilians. It was unthinkable any might get hit by friendly fire and he prayed to God to guide him to the right place. But he had no choice. If they bailed or did nothing, *Nora* would hit the ground with one almighty bang. If she held together and if he could stay above a thousand feet, and if he could keep her steady, then maybe he could pick a safe spot to release and maybe she could fly them home. There were too many ifs and maybes for his liking, but it was all he had.

***

Harry lay on his back, staring out at a grey sky where the roof of the farmhouse used to be. The side of his face felt wet and when he reached up a hand to wipe it away, it was sticky and gritty and he winced in pain. He tried to move his legs but he couldn't feel his right and his left was weighed down by a pile of masonry. He thought he could hear the sea, but it was just his eardrums slowly recovering from the shock of the blast. He twisted his body sideways and onto his front so that the bricks and stones fell soundlessly from his left leg onto the floor and then managed to push himself up with his arms onto one knee.

He tried again with his right leg and it responded but when he put pressure on the knee, he collapsed again in searing pain. It subsided after a moment and he was able to sit up. The right leg was bloody below the knee but straight, which suggested no break, but he couldn't be sure.

The bed lay at a crooked angle, supported by a single buckled leg that was bent almost in two. At the far end, the wall had gone, replaced by a view of open countryside and there was a pile of rubble where Alfredo had been sitting. At the head of the bed an eight-inch square oak beam and slabs of ceiling plaster lay where the pillows had been. He dragged himself across the floor over the debris of slates and tiles and bricks, gasping from the exertion, knowing what he would find.

Mercifully, Isabella's face and head were hidden, but she was dead, crushed under the oak beam that straddled the bed, her arms still raised up behind her where she'd been hanging on to her father. Alfredo's body was behind her, buried under the rubble of his own home, a single lifeless protruding hand the only visible evidence.

Harry broke down. He threw back his head and let out a primeval scream of anguish and rage and when the air in his lungs had gone, he sucked in more and did the same again. He lowered his chin to his chest, shaking and sobbing like a baby. *A baby!* He wiped his face and eyes, smearing blood, sweat and tears into one gooey mess and, dragging his right leg behind him, crawled back to the foot of the bed, peering over the edge, desperately afraid of what he would find.

The dome shape had gone, replaced by a sphere. A filthy, dusty sphere with slits and orifices where eyes, nose and ears would normally be. He breathed deeply and stared at the object in wonder, assuming it too was dead. Then it moved.

Shocked, he blinked and hoisted his body onto the bed, thrusting his face between Isabella's lifeless limbs until he was just inches away. It twitched again and he slowly and carefully put one hand under the baby's head.

"Catalina," he whispered, pressing his cracked and bloody lips to her tiny skull without questioning his own assumption that the baby was a girl. "Oh, my Catalina."

But the moment of euphoria was short-lived. Catalina's head was moving, her tiny body struggling, but making no progress. *You have no mother to help you now. You will have to do this all by yourself. This grown man staring lovingly at you is weak, pathetic and useless.*

He wanted to pull her head to help her and he touched the sides but they were so soft and delicate, he would surely hurt her, or worse. He was racked with indecision, oblivious to the pain of his own injuries that nevertheless conspired to cloud what little judgement he had. But he felt certain that time was running out for the baby girl and if he didn't do something quickly, he would watch her die like her mother and grandfather, and that would be worse than dying himself.

He watched her twitch again, her eyes pressed shut, and he saw Isabella's abdomen expand and contract briefly, which made him think for an instant she was alive after all, but then quickly realised it was the baby's legs kicking, trying to free herself from the prison of her mother's womb. He put his head in his hands and moaned, despair growing that for no other reason than his own incompetence he would watch Catalina die.

"God! Help me, you bastard!" he screamed at the sky, but there was no response from above.

Then he gasped involuntarily, shaking his head in denial.

"No," he muttered to himself, trying to block the thought that had just formed in his mind, an abominable crime emanating from some dark perverse corner of his psyche that he was being urged to commit. He dismissed it.

"No. I can't," he blurted out, but he was talking to himself and there was no one to answer him other than the evil conscience that persisted and dominated his brain. It was a crime, yet it was as much a crime to let her die than do as his diabolical instinct now demanded. The devil had come to his rescue. He had nothing to lose but his soul.

***

Nora Desirée had descended to fifteen hundred feet and with her airspeed down to one hundred and three, she was clinging to the air by her wing tips. The needles on both oil temperature gauges were red-lining and she was losing manifold pressure on engine two; the supercharger was failing. She was losing altitude at the rate of ten feet per second so she would be at the minimum drop height in one minute forty, two point four miles away.

Flight Engineer Giorgio Balatelli had slid, fallen and tumbled from his lofty position in the roof turret, down the steps and onto the bomb bay catwalk, his passage interrupted and impeded by violent shakes in the airframe. His head had collided with a horizontal support strut, hanging loose from its bullet-shattered mounting, and he sported an ugly gash above one eye. The catwalk shook and moved under his feet like a wave-tossed surfboard threatening to throw him off into a giant breaker and he gripped the slanted frames of the bomb racks with both hands for support. On either side of him, eight fully armed five-hundred pounders rattled and swayed in their cradles.

"In position, Cap'n!" he shouted above the cacophony of grinding, clattering metal and vibrating high explosive.

"Sixty seconds," came the reply from the cockpit.

Balatelli could see the ground coasting by through the bomb doors and there were no roads full of foot soldiers and trucks, just green fields and, mercifully, no sign of life other than a random farm building. He reached for the screwdriver mounted in a pouch on the bulkhead wall, but the catwalk was shaking so hard he lost balance and had to grab the bomb rack again to steady himself. He tried again and this time managed to extricate it, wedging his knees between the bomb racks to brace. He knew what he had to do. He'd pry over the release lever on each bomb release control box. There were sixteen.

"Captain!"

"Yes, Sergeant!"

"It's gonna take time. How much we got?"

"Just do it, Sergeant. Go starboard. Four thousand pounds off the starboard rack will help the trim."

"Yessir!"

Balatelli swung his body around, steadied himself with his knees and leaned over the first release box, screwdriver in both hands, waiting for the order.

"Sherman?" came the call from the cockpit.

"Sir!"

"Abandon station. Get the hell outta the tail. When those babies hit the ground they're gonna send up a pile of shit and slap *Nora* in the ass."

"Sir!"

"Balatelli?"

"Sir!"

"On my count."

***

Harry found the jackknife on the floor under some roof slates and pulled out the blade. It was sharp and it glistened and it filled him with terror. *A finger to save a hand, a hand to save an arm, a foot to save a leg, a leg to save a life.*

He pulled himself back onto the bed and felt a stab of pain in his right knee, but he ignored it. It was of no consequence. Baby Catalina's arms were still inside with only her head showing but she moved it slowly from side to side, losing strength with every passing second. He sensed his heart beating in his chest and despite the cold that pervaded the room, now open to the air, his shirt was wet with sweat. He felt the perspiration from his forehead run into his eyes, carrying dust and grit with it and making them sting. He blinked and shook his head to try to clear it.

His knife hand hovered over Isabella's abdomen but it was shaking uncontrollably and he looked at it dumbly, willing it to stop, but it refused and he used his left hand to steady it. It made little difference, the vibration, transferring through both arms to his body until he screamed in frustration. *Deep breaths, Harry!*

He filled his lungs and exhaled deeply, once, twice, three times, then kept going until he had achieved some semblance of control over his tortured mind and his trembling hands. He put his left hand on the dead woman's belly and felt the movement inside, weak but persistent, but he was racked with indecision. He couldn't decide where to cut, where to be sure he wouldn't hurt the baby, or was it simply that he didn't have the courage to violate the dead? *To save a life!*

He slid a shaking left index finger inside the dead woman above the baby's neck and pulled the already stretched and tightened skin upwards and as the tears streamed down his face and he sobbed with grief, self-pity and self-loathing combined, drew the tip of the jackknife across her belly.

The skin parted easily and as her bloody flesh gaped open, he continued to slide the knife upwards while he wept and his body shook and his eyes and nose streamed tears of shame for being the hideous monster that he was, eviscerating a corpse.

Catalina's legs appeared and he reached his hands inside and pulled her back out through the birth canal, and she slipped from his hands and tumbled out onto the bedclothes. He recoiled in horror and choked on the bile in his throat, but then gasped in awe and wonder at her tiny wriggling form, her minuscule arms, legs, toes and fingers reaching out in desperation to grab hold of her new world. He laid the bloody knife down on the bed, carefully lifting the shivering, slimy, blood-smeared baby, umbilical cord trailing, and held her in his hands as she cried. He gently touched her forehead with his lips and when he drew back, he watched as his own tears fell on her tiny cheek. Tears of joy.

***

Mitch squinted, his eyes scanning the ground ahead, looking for any signs of activity; seeing none. Fields of olive groves and vineyards flashed by, the landscape scarred and peppered with craters. Random farm buildings, barns and sheds were dotted around and stray cows, horses, sheep and goats fled in panic at the sight and sound of the infernal monster roaring over their heads. He watched the altimeter breach five hundred feet and although he was worried about the concussive effects of the exploding ordnance on the shattered airframe, he wanted clear space ahead, and found it. There was no more time for hesitation.

"Three, two, one, release!"

He heard a metallic bang through the headphones, then a cacophonous rattle as one after the other, eight starboard bombs clattered down their guide rails and tumbled out into space.

"Going to port, sir!" shouted Balatelli and the banging recommenced. From only a thousand feet, the bombs had little time to reach terminal velocity; the first hit the ground eight seconds after release, the remainder following at one-second intervals. But four thousand pounds in weight had been jettisoned and as Mitch had predicted, *Nora*'s attitude changed. Dramatically.

The right wing swept upwards and *Nora* lurched drunkenly left. Mitch wrestled with the controls to try to straighten the shuddering, creaking aircraft while watching the altimeter needle slow but continue to creep anticlockwise. *Nora Desirée* continued to drift left and then into Mitch's line of sight loomed a farmhouse, a smouldering wreck with half of its roof missing. He saw a shambling figure outside, limping and staggering up the path towards the front door, its stumbling and erratic gait clearly indicative of injury and distress. They were right in *Nora's* flight path.

"Balatelli! Abort!" But the order was countermanded by fate. Before the flight engineer could react, the electrical short, now jolted free by the sudden lurch of the aircraft, reconnected the bomb release, and all eight bombs on the port side fell as one, the second one severing Balatelli's arm on its way out. He staggered backwards off the catwalk and fell through the open bomb bay doors into space.

***

Harry laid Catalina down on the bed and steeled himself to cut through the umbilical cord, when he heard eight massive explosions in quick succession, but they were some distance away and his first thought was simply that his hearing had returned. But then he frowned. *Bomber?*

His instinct was to protect the baby, so he scooped her up in his left hand and stepped off the bed, but when his right leg touched the floor, his knee gave way and he fell onto his left. Catalina's slimy little body slipped out of his hand but he caught her by the foot before she could hit the stone floor. She dangled upside down in his hand, the severed umbilical cord trailing, and she continued to cry, but he smiled at the sound, relieved, exhausted and vaguely euphoric. But the moment was quickly shattered.

The farmhouse door burst open; a figure limped into the room, the door slamming shut behind it. Harry looked up in surprise, full of hope. *Medics!* But then his mouth dropped open and in an instant, his joy turned to fear.

The grey tunic and black leather boots were unmistakcable, as was the Luger drooping in the right hand. The left arm hung limply, the entire left side of the uniform was blackened and blood streamed down one side of its face onto more blood that seeped out of a smouldering left shoulder. What may have been blonde hair stood proud from the right side of its head, the other side matted black and glistening red. The *SS* motif was clearly visible on the collar.

The figure lurched across the stone floor, dragging its left leg behind it and stopped, face set, emotionless and cold. Harry didn't move, but the baby still wailed and wriggled in his left hand, his right still turned upwards holding the bloody jackknife. The German erupted.

"I am Obersturmbannführer Ernst Kessler!" He screamed each word with a visceral rage and streams of phlegm spewed out between his blackened teeth, his body shaking uncontrollably as he struggled to lift the Luger to a firing position. "I have come to kill you!" But his diabolical rant was drowned out by the thunderous, monstrous roar of the fire-breathing dragon that swooped over their heads, the deafening volume surpassed instantaneously by a huge explosion.

And although the devil's lips moved and his face contorted and his gun arm shook as if it were possessed, he didn't flinch as, at half-second intervals, seven more, ever-louder, ear-splitting explosions followed, the eighth and final bomb landing ten feet from the farmhouse door.

The blast blew the heavy oak door off its hinges, propelling it into the room at the speed of sound, where it slammed into the back of the German like a runaway train. Harry saw the muzzle flash before Kessler hit the floor, the combination of bomb blast and nine-millimetre round hitting him in the shoulder flinging him backwards against the wall, the collision breaking his collar bone and delivering him a stunning blow to the head.

He slid to the floor as, in slow motion, the chimney breast collapsed around the open fire and toppled into the room, falling on top of the body of the German, which finally lay still and lifeless.

***

Nora Desirée, finally lightened of her load, crawled her way back up to two hundred feet where she limped slowly home, tacking across the countryside in the clear crisp air of an Italian winter's morning.

Mitch McLennan stared grimly ahead out of the cockpit window. Provided *Nora* held together, he and what was left of his crew would be all right. He turned his head to look at the body of Second Lieutenant Carl Withers, peaceful in death, skin already turning blue with the cold, and he thought of Kovacs, Rosenberg, Flanagan, Kravitz and Balatelli and the words he'd use when he wrote to their loved ones. *They died bravely for their country, doing their duty.*

But it wasn't just the death of these brave men that grieved him deeply. They knew the risks; they accepted the danger and embraced it willingly in the name of freedom and righteousness. It was the others.

He was wholly to blame for a deadly attack of friendly fire. He'd seen the figure and the farmhouse and he had, in all probability, delivered death to the door of the most vulnerable – non-combatants, women, children, civilians, innocents all, the very people he was pledged to serve and protect. Despite all his experience, his skill, his intentions and his best efforts, when it came down to it, he had come up short. And that fact would stay with him for the rest of his days.

***

Harry Male's body lay propped up against the wall of the ruined farmhouse. He was barely conscious. The baby lay motionless in his lap, supported by his left arm – an arm he could neither feel nor move any more than he could feel or move any other part of his body.

His hearing had gone again but in his clouded vision he sensed a flickering light dancing amongst the shadows and, after a while, his addled brain worked out it was the remains of the fire, from which a whisper of smoke floated upwards and into the open sky. The flames slowly came back into focus and he tried to familiarise himself with his surroundings.

Death and destruction lay everywhere: Alfredo, Isabella, their home as well as some crazy German called Kessler who was buried under most of it, their lives ended in the most violent and horrific way imaginable.

He forced himself to look down at his lap. Catalina no longer cried and wiggled her arms and legs, her filthy little body apparently uninjured yet still and lifeless. The most innocent of victims. The cruellest blow of all. There was nothing and no one left alive apart from him and the flames of the fire and he knew that very soon, they too would both be extinguished. Yet he felt neither pain, nor anger, nor hurt, nor regret, simply an overwhelming weariness and a desire to get on with the inevitable. *If this is dying, it's not so bad. I'm ready.*

The rising sun projected a beam of light through the remnants of the front wall of the ruined farmhouse and Harry closed his eyes and felt its warmth. A flicker of a smile crossed his face and he allowed his senses to drift, a delicious light-headed contentment taking hold of him as, little by little, his vital functions began to close down.

And as he awaited his final breath, his eyes half-opened one last time and through his delirium, out of the misty haze of sunlight and wispy smoke, an ethereal spirit swathed in a diaphanous cloak rose up before him and hovered in front of his clouded eyes. A young girl of extraordinary beauty with long reddish-brown hair, a face with skin so pure, eyes so deep and brown and an expression so inscrutable, he recognised her at once. *An angel. An angel has come.*

The angel came closer and he could smell the fragrance of divine purity and he bathed in it as she leaned over his body and took baby Catalina from his arms.

Oh yes. Please take Catalina and take Isabella and take Alfredo and if there is room for me, please take me too.

The angel dissolved into the smoky sunlight and Harry Male, finally peaceful and content, laid back his head and died.

CHAPTER 3

West Berlin – August 1962

Harry woke with a start and stared at the ceiling of his apartment, blinking as his eyes adjusted to the light. His body was drenched in sweat but he felt cold as the moisture evaporated in the cool air of a Berlin morning. He shivered and instinctively pulled the single sheet over him while he gathered his senses. He'd eventually fallen asleep just before dawn and in his deepest slumber he'd relived the events of eighteen years ago as he did almost every night.

In the dream, he died again. He always died. The outcome was always the same and in the dark hours of the night when he lay awake, fearful and apprehensive yet knowing what sleep would bring, he wondered whether in fact life was the illusion, a cruel deceit visited on him by some force of evil, intent on retribution.

Through the open window, he heard the first sounds of morning emanating from the street below and he turned his head. Petra, the only constant and reliable thing in his life, lay face down, breathing gently, her beautiful slim body curled up under the fine cotton sheet. He rubbed a forearm across his brow and felt the familiar stab of pain in his shoulder, a cruel and constant reminder that part of the dream at least was real, or had been real. Once.

He threw the sheet aside and sat up on the edge of the bed, reaching for his cigarettes, already hearing Petra's rebuke in his subconsciousness. He slipped on a thin dressing gown and took the cigarette packet through the double doors into the sitting room, then plodded barefoot into the kitchen area. He filled the coffee pot, put it on the stove and lit a cigarette from the gas burner.

He felt drained, as ever, from reliving the events of the past and habitually tormented himself with futile thoughts of what might have been, what he could have done to make things different and what would have happened if he had.

But today, mercifully, he had other things to occupy his mind. He looked through the kitchen window down at the street below; at the growing volume of trams, cars, delivery vans and pedestrians going about their business; at the Wall and beyond it, the desolate death strip, weirdly calm and benign, devoid of any activity.

Escapes from the east were not new, but last night was the first time he had seen one with his own eyes and he wondered whether he'd be in line for the debrief. He hoped so, assuming of course the guy was still alive.

Major Harry Male had worked for Military Intelligence for five years, the last three stationed in West Berlin, where his department specialised in monitoring, intercepting and deciphering coded transmissions from "the enemy" in East Germany. The innocuously titled Department for International Policy Development was also responsible for receiving and debriefing "runners": the ones who were not only brave enough to run the gauntlet to freedom but lucky enough to succeed. Each escapee was assigned a debrief officer and Harry was one of three in the department.

He thought it iniquitous that, having risked their lives in a bold bid for freedom, these poor souls should be subjected to any sort of interrogation. Most of them were nobodies, ordinary individuals seeking to throw off the shackles of tyranny, or who, having been stranded when the Wall went up, were simply driven to re-join their families in the West.

He saw the irony that, before the Wall had forcefully curtailed freedom of movement between one sector and another, there had been neither the need nor the desire to interrogate those entering the western sectors and failing to return home. But the Wall had changed the rules of the game and it was becoming apparent that people who took such great risks probably had good reason beyond a simple urge for freedom.

The Western powers had found that they were able to garner useful information from academics, scientists and government officials, and in return, they could assist their integration into western society, offer them roles in equivalent disciplines and most important of all, provide sanctuary.

But naturally, they had to be sure that those who appeared to have escaped under the most difficult and dangerous circumstances were indeed who they said they were, neither servants of the communist regime nor agents bent on infiltration and espionage.

Harry poured himself a black coffee and sat down at the kitchen table, taking in the view across the death strip, reliving in his mind the previous night's events. He took a long draw from his cigarette, savoured the drug for a while and blew the smoke into the air. Last night's incident was a welcome distraction from his normal train of thought and he would look forward to finding out who the runner had been and whether indeed he was okay.

"Ugh! What a stink!"

Petra came up behind him, wafting her hands in the air, and slid open the kitchen window to let out the fumes.

"Tobacco is a filthy weed—"

"I know. I know," he said irritably, interrupting her before she got into her stride.

"Then why don't you stop?" She was barefoot, wearing one of his old shirts with the sleeves rolled up, the shirt tails extending to her thighs offering a tantalising glimpse of buttock whenever she stretched. Even in her dishevelled, just-got-out-of-bed, tangled-hair state, she was beautiful, vibrant and feisty.

"I will," he sighed. "I just need it at the moment."

"You're always saying that. You don't need it." It was well intentioned as always, but it sounded like a nag and he wasn't in the mood.

"How do you know what I need?" he snapped at her, suddenly angry. She had touched a nerve and it was the same nerve as always. Her face dropped and she pursed her lips, then turned on her heel and stomped off towards the bathroom, bare feet slapping on the tiled floor. She slammed the door behind her.

Harry cursed under his breath, wallowing in a cloud of anger and contrition. He hated himself for the outburst and wanted more than anything to rewind the last few seconds and live them again. As soon as the words had come out he'd regretted them, knowing immediately what he'd said was wrong and insensitive and that he'd gone too far.

But just as ever, he couldn't rewind the past, however recent or distant. He had to live in the moment, cast aside any regrets and move on. Despite having again hurt the one he loved, and hurting himself in the process, he knew he'd be able to make it up to her and they'd forget about it in no time. He scratched his head, took a long look at his smouldering half-cigarette and angrily stubbed it out in the ashtray.

***

They sat quietly across the kitchen table, picking at their *Brötchen* and coffee, having hardly exchanged a word since their little spat, which was over, if not yet forgotten.

Harry craved another cigarette, but it was out of the question. He'd have to wait till he got outside before he lit up again. Petra was engrossed in some papers, pen in one hand, scribbling and scoring in red, the other hand alternating between bread roll and coffee cup. He watched her work and marvelled at her concentration, her focus on the task at hand, something he'd always struggled with. He was forever distracted, wary and watchful, anticipating the next interruption and when it came, knowing it was usually self-induced. They would give it a name one day; it would be a syndrome or a condition or something, but for now, he was content to put it down as a character defect.

If Petra was aware of his attention, she showed no sign of it, her brow furrowed and pen poised over a student's thesis. A graduate in international politics from the University of Bonn, fluent in English and French, competent in Russian and Czech, and now lecturer in philosophy and humanities at the Free University of Berlin, Petra was fourteen years his junior. Beautiful, intelligent, gregarious and light-hearted, a glass half full of a woman bursting with enthusiasm for everyone and everything and the myriad possibilities and opportunities that life and the future held. That she made him feel inadequate and undeserving was no fault of hers, nor a consequence of anything she said or did, just another example of his own insecurity. Another character defect.

"Busy day today?" he ventured, not wishing to disturb her, just wanting to break the ice. She looked up and smiled at him, the earlier incident now forgotten, her natural warmth preventing the formation of any ice.

"Nothing special. Second year student lecture on Leibniz and analytical philosophy, followed by a tutorial on Nieztsche and the influence of the *übermenschlich* on the Third Reich. Spot of lunch, first year lecture on humanistic theories and practices then it's head down in the office to finish marking these dissertations."

He nodded knowingly as if, other than the stuff involving the red pen, he had any clue what she was talking about. As usual, her answer to his simple question made him feel stupid and inadequate in equal measure. But that was his fault, not hers; she didn't mean it and he didn't love her any less.

"Oh, I forgot to say," she went on, "we've got a management meeting at five and it'll probably go on a while so you go ahead and have something to eat." It sounded like an afterthought, which was unusual for Petra, so organised and precise about everything.

"What, again?"

She gave him a patronising look that compounded his feeling of inadequacy. "We have one every month?"

"Oh yes. Of course. Just came around quick, that's all."

"Go to the Kronestube and have some dinner. You like it there," she said, brightening. She was making the event sound like an opportunity for him, encouraging him to socialise a little, and not for the first time.

"By myself? No thanks."

"Can't you get someone from the office to go with you?"

"Maybe." He shrugged, but even if he'd been enthusiastic about the notion, he didn't want to show it. He didn't need any help organising his social affairs because he never had any so they didn't need organising. He knew he looked and sounded disgruntled. Petra sighed and changed the subject.

"Wonder what happened to that guy?"

Harry would have been on safer ground with this subject, but Petra had no idea what he did at work. He couldn't tell her and although she'd asked way back when they first met, she'd learned not to ask again. She knew he was a civil servant and that was all, but she was far from stupid, had probably drawn fairly accurate conclusions and decided long ago it was futile to probe any further.

"No idea. I still can't believe he took those bullets and survived. Unless of course he didn't."

"Didn't take the bullets or didn't survive?"

Harry shrugged. "Either. But if he's still in this world, I'm sure the MPs will hand him over to the right people." That was as far as he was prepared to go. Petra, without her knowledge, had been vetted right at the beginning and he'd been given the all clear to continue the relationship. But her professional and private life would be subject to routine review so the less she knew, the less she could say. Better for them both.

He had a feeling this job would come his way, especially when they found out he'd witnessed the entire incident, and he regretted he couldn't share it with her as he knew she'd be interested. He looked forward to jobs like that. He was always intrigued to find out what story the runner had to tell and if he were being honest, he liked best the task of separating the truth from the lies. It was one thing he knew he was good at, spotting duplicity and deceit, seeing through half-truths and embellishments, and that was the reason he enjoyed doing it.

Petra shuffled her papers together. "Must be off."

"Yes, you go. I'll deal with these," he said and reached for her cup.

"No. Leave them. Helga's in today."

He had forgotten it was Thursday. The apartment and most of its contents belonged to the MoD and they lived rent-free for as long as he was posted there. The weekly houseclean was all part of the package so every Thursday Frau Leitner would arrive after they'd left for work, beaver away for as many hours as it took and disappear before they got home when they would find the whole place restored to pristine condition.

They walked down the stairs together and out into the street, exchanging brief kisses and wishing each other a good day before setting off in opposite directions.

Harry lit a cigarette and sucked in the poison with relish, the dark memories of his dream dissipating, at least for now. He slung his jacket over one shoulder and crossed the cobbled street, striding out on another warm summer's day in West Berlin with a spring in his step. *Tobacco is a filthy weed...*

CHAPTER 4

At 7.15 a.m. in the basement of the five-star Hotel Regent on Kurfürstendamm, activity in the kitchen service area was beginning to build. Breakfast had just begun and there would be no let-up until ten thirty, when most of the tourists would have gone sight-seeing and the few remaining businessmen had concluded their breakfast meetings.

At peak times, the ground floor kitchen with its complement of twenty chefs was supplemented by up to twelve kitchen porters, support staff who toiled one floor down in the bowels of the hotel. In sharp contrast to the tranquil and serene ambience of the restaurant, both departments were subject to a relentless barrage of heat, steam and noise that would challenge the sanity of any man. Nowhere were working conditions more arduous than in the pot-wash, where, round the clock, thousands of items of dirty crockery, cutlery, glassware and cooking utensils were cleaned, dried and returned to service with military precision.

Karl Schneider stood hunched over the giant stainless-steel trough, hands immersed in the caustic soapy water, scrubbing burnt sugar from the inside of a twenty-six-millimetre copper using a steel-wool pad. Alongside him, four of his colleagues stacked and then emptied an array of industrial-sized dishwashers, sorting and sending the clean items back upstairs in one of four dumb waiters.

Schneider had never seen inside the Hotel Regent in all the five years he had been there. He came and went by the staff entrance in the basement and had never once clapped eyes on the marble floor in the entrance lobby, the magnificent reception desk hand-carved in the finest German oak, the glittering French chandeliers, the nineteenth-century gilded portraits that lined the walls of corridors carpeted in the finest Italian wool. But he had seen photographs in a magazine and that was enough for him. He knew his place and his place was here doing what he was doing.

"Here you go, Quasi." Section leader Helmut Fuchs dumped four more copper pans into the water, taking little care, as usual, to avoid splashing his junior colleague who, as usual, ignored the taunt. His ten-hour shift would be over in fifteen minutes when the rest of the day staff arrived and he'd be spared, for fourteen hours at least, the jibes and bullying tactics of Fuchs and the other morons.

It had started almost from day one. For many years, Schneider had suffered with chronic back pain, which along with a badly deformed left leg gave him an inelegant gait, both afflictions permanent souvenirs of a past conflict most of his colleagues knew little about. The hotel gave him the job as a concession, so they'd said, an act of charity towards the disabled, although his disabilities, such as they were, had no bearing whatsoever on his punctuality, his efficiency and his reliability. It had just been an excuse to pay him less.

As a second-class "retard" pot-washer-gofer with physical deformities, he was the obvious candidate for bullying, exacerbated by his refusal to respond, complain or react to the bullies in any way. He barely spoke to any of the others unless absolutely necessary; he just turned up on time, worked hard and went home when the night shift was over and the cycle would begin again.

Morons would come and go, each new one rapidly conforming to group pressure, consolidating the isolation of "Quasi" by their physical and verbal abuse, or else risk isolating themselves. He didn't blame them for being weak and he actually preferred it that way. Once a spotty teenager arrived straight out of school and made an attempt to befriend the hapless "Quasi" before his advances were soundly rebuffed and he joined the pack. Schneider was and would remain in a minority of one and that was the way he liked it.

In the absence of idle banter or any rational discourse with his fellow workers, he whiled away the working hours, amusing himself with fantasies of how he would despatch each of them in an entertaining fashion: Fuchs, drugged then squeezed into No.1 dishwasher with the dial turned to "steam"; Müller, his arch-nemesis, dismembered and fed through the mincer to emerge as *"Müllerwurst",* a speciality of the house; and Ziegler the queer, his dick amputated in a freak accident involving a meat cleaver and the butcher's block. He had a final solution for them all. *One day, perhaps.* He looked at the wall clock. It was time.

"Oi! Quasi, you retard." Müller as usual, with the last word of the day. "What you got on today then? Spot of bell-ringing?" He turned to his cohorts to check they'd heard and they all laughed dutifully. Müller slapped Schneider on the back of the head when he didn't respond. "You listening, you deaf old git?" Schneider rested both hands on the edge of the trough and stared down into the soapy water. *Acid bath – even better.* "Retard," scoffed Müller, turning to Ziegler, who was grinning foolishly so he slapped him too. "What are you simpering for, Nancy? A bit of retard arse?"

Schneider removed his rubber apron, exchanged it for a shabby jacket that hung on a hook on the wall then slowly headed for the door, limping heavily.

"Give Esmeralda one for me!" He heard Müller's shout and imagined the hip thrust being performed behind his back. Karl Schneider left the building with the sound of raucous laughter ringing like bells in his ears.

***

Schneider climbed the wrought-iron staircase out of the bowels of the Hotel Regent and stepped into a shady side alley, hobbling seventy metres to emerge onto Kurfürstendamm, his eyes squinting in the bright morning sun. He stopped by Rudi's newspaper kiosk as he did every day, exchanged perfunctory pleasantries with the owner and collected his *Berliner Zeitung* before limping along the street to the tram stop, amused as ever by the discomfort on the faces of his fellow travellers as they noticed that unprepossessing character who shuffled towards them.

He rode the fifteen stops to Bornstraße and stepped carefully onto the pavement. He watched the tram roll away, put both hands on his hips and straightened his back for the first time in ten hours. His left leg would always give him pain to some extent but the alleged deformity was not nearly enough to affect his gait. Karl Schneider, now tall and erect, ambled casually along Bornstraße towards his apartment.

CHAPTER 5

Major Harry Male swung open the double doors of the Department for International Policy Development and strode confidently into the outer office, jacket still slung over his shoulder, smouldering cigarette between two fingers.

"Morning, ladies!" he announced without breaking step to the pool of sixteen typists who sat eight on each side, hammering away on their machines in synchronised word-bashing.

"Morning, Harry," came the similarly synchronous reply, although only one or two deigned to look up from their work which carried on unabated. Through another set of doors, he entered Operations, an oak-panelled room containing a dozen desks arranged in facing pairs, each with its own lamp, filing cabinet and telephone. Metal-framed windows and venetian blinds ran along the entire length of the right-hand side of the room, the left filled with an array of filing cabinets topped with stacked wooden trays. The wall ahead of him sported a number of maps in varying levels of detail of East and West Germany as well as Berlin. Most of them were new, recently redrawn to accommodate the physical separation of the city. The same wall had windows into the radio room where several men wearing headphones sat in front of consoles and continuously rotating tape recorders. Another door led through to the conference room and the directors' suites.

Johnny Bristow was in his usual place, poring over a sheaf of papers, sleeves rolled up, jacket slung over his chair, cigarette in one hand, its smoke wafted away by one of six ceiling fans working at full speed to compensate for the heat.

"Morning, old man," he said without looking up.

"Morning, Johnny, what news from the Oval?"

"Fifty-three for six at close. Chasing three hundred and five on the last day. We're getting a right kicking from the Windies." Harry wasn't really interested in cricket but he knew it was a religion to Johnny and always made for a good opener, so to speak.

"Ah well, all to play for then? Anything interesting happen overnight?" he ventured innocently.

"Nothing I know of, a lot of hubbub from the other side, so I understand, but it's still being transcribed and translated."

Harry's phone rang before he could sit down. "Male," he answered, stubbing out his cigarette. He recognised Cynthia's voice immediately. "Yes of course, be right there." Johnny looked up from his papers, interested. "I'm wanted in the nerve centre."

"Good luck."

***

Cynthia showed Harry into the opulent room that served as an office for Commander Eric Laughton. Whenever he entered this room, he couldn't help imagining its previous occupant: a Wehrmacht *Feldmarschall* perhaps, surrounded by his *Generals* and *Obersts* poring over military maps, watched over by a giant portrait of *Mein Führer* framed between two leaning flagpoles bearing swastikas.

Commander Laughton was sitting behind a magnificent oak-carved, leather-topped desk, an antique that had survived both wars but from which all traces of Nazi insignia had been judiciously and subtly removed. He looked up briefly when Cynthia announced Harry's presence.

"Ah, Male, come in." Harry took his cue to walk the thirty feet from the door to the desk and cleared his mind of past imagery. *Mein Führer* had long since been replaced by a coronation portrait of Queen Elizabeth, flanked on her right by a brooding, cigar-smoking Winston Churchill and on her left, a proud and imperious Harold MacMillan, looking every inch the man who'd never had it so good. "Take a seat."

"Thank you, sir." Harry sat on a rigid unpadded seat as Laughton removed his glasses and leaned back in his plush leather swing armchair.

"We had an incident last night. At the Wall." Laughton wasn't much on pleasantries and it suited Harry just as well but he had to stifle the urge to jump in. Laughton didn't like clever dicks and anyway, the "incident" he was referring to could well be something entirely different, so he kept quiet and let Laughton finish.

"Chap called Klaus Bergmann. Assistant to a junior minister in the East German politburo. We already have a thin file on him. Came over the Wall last night, er" – Laughton replaced his glasses and leaned forward to point at a spot on a map in front of him – "fairly close to your apartment, I believe?" The question was phrased as if Laughton was simply curious at the coincidence, but they were both professionals and took nothing and no one for granted. Harry didn't hesitate.

"Yes, sir. Heard the commotion and saw the MPs take him away right beneath my window." He knew being deliberately economical with the truth put him on dangerous ground but he wanted to avoid mentioning why he'd just happened to be staring out of his bedroom window at 3 a.m. He didn't want to get into a discussion about insomnia, recurring dreams or anything that could possibly be construed as psychological. If Laughton wanted to know exactly what and how much he saw, he would of course respond in full, but for the moment, he judged a brief acknowledgement would suffice. He felt four pairs of eyes on him, intimidated not only by his boss, but also by the reigning monarch, a national hero and the current prime minister, and he had to concentrate on returning Laughton's stare.

The pause was no more than four seconds, but he knew Laughton. It was stage-managed to keep a professional distance between them and to confirm, as if Harry needed reminding, that Laughton assumed nothing. In this business, no one could or would be trusted.

Laughton sat back. "We knew he was coming. It was set up a few days ago but we only got confirmation last night that it was on. He made a remarkable escape."

Harry saw an opportunity to expand a little on his testimony. It gave nothing away but eased his conscience a little. "Yes sir. I heard the shots. I can't believe they missed him."

"Well they didn't actually. Took two rounds in the back but he had some sort of bullet-proof vest on under his coat. The boffins are examining it now. Much better than anything we or the Americans have, so if nothing else, we'll benefit from that."

Harry was feeling more comfortable now and dipped a toe in the water. "I, er, presume he didn't come across to show us their fancy new body armour?"

"No, indeed he didn't." Laughton paused for effect. "You were at Montellano, weren't you?" The question sounded superfluous, the tone academic. Laughton was already fully aware of his service record and had probably examined it again before their meeting. Harry tried to keep his answer neutral and his face impassive but his damned left eye betrayed him, blinking once of its own volition.

"Yes, sir."

"But you were badly injured."

"Yes, sir."

"And never returned to active service."

"No, sir."

"How much do you remember?"

Harry frowned. *Remember what? The bombing? The filth and the squalor? The freezing cold? The corpses? The rats and the lice and the cockroaches? The utter incompetence of those in command? The obscene and universal disregard for common humanity? What I was having for breakfast during a mortar attack or the entire bloody fiasco? How long have you got, sir?* And for the most part, he'd forgotten all of it, expunged it from his memory or at least given it the rose-tinted treatment and moved on. It seemed such a long time ago. But Alfredo's farmhouse, young Isabella and tiny Catalina, their misery, torture and murder? That was only last night and it was raw, visceral and only too real.

"I'm sorry, I don't understand, sir."

"Do you remember a place called Santa Cristina De Lago?"

Harry thought for a moment. It was one of many villages they'd encountered on the outskirts of Montellano. They'd had barracks there. Together with New Zealanders, Indians and Gurkhas, they'd taken it from the Germans and it put them within striking distance of Montellano. The villagers had welcomed their liberators and although they had little food, shared it as best they could until supplies could be brought up through the mud.

But within days, before the next push could begin and just as had happened elsewhere in that god-forsaken country, the Germans had counterattacked, the Allies had been pushed back, forcing them to regroup and try all over again. Hundreds of lives wasted, zero ground taken.

"Yes, sir. I do."

"Bergmann claims to have amateur film footage of a massacre. He says when the Germans retook the village they rounded up the men and butchered them all for collaborating with the enemy. The wives and children had other uses, apparently."

The wives and children did what they needed to do to survive… sir.

Harry could have wept. He'd never gone back. His war had ended at Alfredo's farmhouse, so he hadn't returned to the village. He just had vague memories of humility, gratitude and euphoria; of smiling people, women holding babies and men throwing their hats in the air.

The war may have ended but had never gone away. Stories like this had surfaced time and time again over the years, before Nuremberg and after, and the hunt for the

Nazis who perpetrated such crimes continued all across the world to this day. Their frequency was diminishing, but somehow took on a greater significance as time passed, even more heinous than they had seemed at the time, incomprehensible in this modern age. They would never be allowed to forget.

"And has he produced this... footage?"

"He brought with him a single nine-and-a-half-millimetre film reel, sewn into his coat. Lasts about four minutes. The tech boys are working on restoring it because it's fairly poor quality, but already they're saying it contains some horrific images. About a hundred and fifty men and boys shot dead in front of their families."

Harry bristled, the anger and dismay he felt at the alleged atrocity magnified by Laughton's air of insouciance.

"So what does Bergmann expect in return. A medal?"

"Hardly. He got the film, or rather stole it, from one Gustav Klein, the junior minister for whom he worked. He says Klein was planning to use it to advance his career and get into the politburo."

"Not sure what you mean, sir."

Laughton paused. "Because the SS commanding officer back in forty-four, the one who ordered the massacre and who, he says, is clearly identifiable in the film, is now a senior member of the politburo."

"Blackmail," said Harry, thinking out loud. "Who is it?"

"It doesn't matter for now." Harry's first instinct was to protest and probe further, but he recognised Laughton's tone. No need to know, just yet. "Bergmann says he was horrified when he found out about the footage and decided it needed to be in the hands of the Western powers."

Harry looked dubious; his default position was always scepticism. "So he sacrificed his cosy career, his luxurious apartment and his all-expenses-paid lifestyle amongst the communist elite, abandoned his family and risked his life dodging bullets on a mission to bring a Nazi war criminal to justice."

"Apparently."

"Bullshit. Er, sorry, sir."

"Quite. There's no doubt he decided there was commercial value in the material, but we've only had a preliminary chat with him and haven't interrogated him in depth. There's been no time and he's still rather shaken up, having fallen badly. Broken arm, I think. We need the full story, Harry."

"Yes, sir."

"First, we need you to confirm if you can, that the place in question is indeed Santa Cristina De Lago. German military records, assuming they weren't destroyed, will show which officers were there and we should be able to establish from the film the identity of the man in charge."

"That could be dynamite, sir."

"I wouldn't bank on it, Harry."

"A senior politburo member indicted as a war criminal?"

"I'm more interested in what other use Bergmann can be to us. If he's expecting to emulate his comfortable lifestyle here in the West and for us to keep him out of harm's way, then he should be able to provide plenty of juicy detail about the inner workings of his erstwhile employers. We haven't had such a high-profile defection for a while. We should be able to use it against Klein as well. Once he realises we know what he was up to we should be able to put pressure on him and, who knows, maybe turn him as well." Laughton sat back with a look of satisfaction. The possibilities evidently pleased him.

Harry felt his anger rising and couldn't stop himself. "Surely, sir, if we can bring a war criminal to justice, and he happens to be a member of the communist regime, we win on both counts?"

Laughton's smile dropped and Harry knew straight away he'd gone too far.

"Let's leave politics to the politicians, Male." The reversion to surname was deliberate and pointed. "Our job is to find things out so others can decide how best to deal with them." The reprimand was thinly veiled and unmistakeable.

"Yes, sir."

"Put your arm round Bergmann. Tell him what a hero he is, that we're extremely grateful for his sacrifice and that he's most welcome here in the free West. Find out as much as you can about his background, who and what he came into contact with and tell him he'll stay under our close personal protection until we find him a new name, a nice place to stay and a full-time job."

"Where is he now?"

"He's still in the army hospital with MPs on guard but I'm told he'll be out in a couple of days when he'll be moved to a safe house. I'll let you know." Laughton passed two manila folders across his desk. "This is as much as we have on him at the moment. And this is Klein." The intercom buzzed and a light came on. Laughton leaned over and pressed a button.

"Yes, Cynthia."

"It's raining heavily at the Oval, sir."

"Excellent!"

***

Harry sat on a bar stool in the Kronestube, cigarette in hand, sipping a Weißbier. He'd ordered a wiener schnitzel and potato salad but wasn't much looking forward to it. What he really craved was fish and chips or bangers and mash – proper food as he called it – but despite the preponderance of British ex-pats the Germans had never made much of an effort to cater for their customers' dubious culinary predilections.

After seventeen years of occupation, he wouldn't be surprised if the locals were wondering when they would get their country back, if ever, so he guessed they persisted in serving up foreign muck to encourage the Brits to go home. He knew there were plenty of burger joints in the American sector and fancy French restaurants to keep the frogs happy in their own little patch of Berlin, so why not us?

The pretty blonde barmaid with pigtails and breasts that threatened to burst out of her dirndl offered to refill his glass and he nodded. Despite the food there were some consolations at the Kronestube.

He'd spent the afternoon examining the files on Bergmann and Klein and, as Laughton had alluded, they were short on detail, but had references to their military service and several photos. There were official mug shots and service IDs and a picture of Bergmann as a twelve-year-old in the Hitler Youth dated 1943. There were also group shots of East German officials at political rallies or meeting their Soviet masters, fuzzy images of Klein and Bergmann circled in red, the former in the second rank, the latter, one row behind.

He'd then gone into the basement archives to bring up maps of Central and Southern Italy, particularly the mountains and villages around Montellano and photos from the Italian campaign. It was a sobering experience and by the end of the day, he'd decided he needed a drink. He'd taken Petra's advice and casually suggested to Bristow that he join him, but Johnny had had other plans and that was fine by him. They were prohibited from discussing work outside the office and Johnny would just go banging on about the bloody cricket so it was hard to see what else they could discuss that was of any interest. At least he could tell her he'd tried, but the fact was he was perfectly content with his own company.

He was in two minds about Bergmann. He always looked forward to quizzing a runner and the guy certainly wasn't a nobody, but he'd already proven his treachery and given his history, Harry would take some convincing his motives were honourable. He'd be no pushover either. Anyone who held a reasonably senior role in the upper echelons of the East German regime and managed to execute a highly perilous escape, surely had a trick or two up his sleeve. But the circumstances of his defection were also disturbing and brought back memories Harry would rather have left buried.

The schnitzel arrived: a plate-sized circle of fried veal in breadcrumbs with the appearance of an Olympic discus and a texture like leather, with a dollop of slimy, pungent potato on the side. Harry thought twice about staying, but stubbed out his cigarette, picked up his knife and fork and went bravely in to bat.

***

He was in bed when Petra got home and he heard her tiptoeing around the apartment as if to avoid waking him, but he was already wide awake, his mind buzzing with Nazis, massacres and communist infiltrators as well as anticipating the recurrence of his own dream.

"How was the meeting?" he said as she climbed stealthily in beside him.

"Oh. Sorry, did I wake you?"

"No. You're a bit late?"

"Yes, sorry. Some of the girls wanted to have a drink and then we had some food and then, well, you know how we girls like to chat. Forgot the time completely." Her hair smelled of someone else's tobacco and made him want a cigarette, but he dismissed the thought.

"How was your day?" she asked.

"Oh. You know."

"Yes I know." He would never answer other than in generalities, they both knew it and that fact alone would always put distance between them. "Wonder what happened to that guy who came over the Wall?"

"Don't know."

She kissed his cheek and turned over. "Night."

One week later Karl Schneider ended his Friday shift at 7.30 a.m. as usual and stopped by Rudi's kiosk.

"Morgen," grunted Rudi. Schneider nodded in acknowledgement as Rudi retrieved a folded *Berliner Zeitung* from beneath the display in front of him and handed it over. "News from the East today," he muttered without emphasis. Schneider nodded again and without uttering another word, headed for the tram stop.

He chose not to read his newspaper on the tram, keeping it folded and secure on his lap as he watched the bustling activity of a Berlin morning through the window. He arrived at his apartment block at eight and met Frau Brucker locking the door of her ground-floor flat dressed in hat and coat, clearly on a mission.

"*Morgen*, Herr Radler." She seemed uncharacteristically jolly and emitted a pungent scent that reminded him of the Paris brothels during the war. *An important assignment indeed.*

"*Morgen*, Frau Brucker," replied the agreeable gentleman she knew as Heinrich Radler. "Are you going somewhere nice today?"

She made a poor attempt at appearing casual, lifting her chin and touching the back of her hat in an affected manner. "I'm going with a friend to the Reichs Gallery. They have a new exhibition of Kirchner. Do you know him?"

"I'm afraid not," he lied. He knew Ernst Ludwig Kirchner's work well. An anti-Nazi expressionist who shot himself in 1938 because the Nazis judged his work "degenerate" and by all accounts made his life a misery. A natural draw for a fat old Jew like Frau Brucker, notwithstanding the artist's tendency towards risqué and controversial. But Schneider/Radler never expressed an opinion on any subject, made comment or revealed anything of his knowledge, interests or background. It served no purpose.

"Oh well, you should go. You'd love it!"

Hardly. He indulged himself in a brief moment of entertainment.

"Rather early for the gallery, isn't it?" The question sounded innocent enough.

"Oh well." She blushed and giggled coquettishly. "We're meeting for breakfast at the Café Royal. Then we shall visit the gallery and perhaps have a spot of lunch afterwards." She preened with delight and for no other reason than his own amusement, he decided to probe further.

"You do have a busy day ahead of you. Have I met your lady friend?"

"Well actually, Herr Radler, it's a gentleman. Herr Warburg is in banking, but loves the arts."

It fired his imagination. Two fat ugly old Jews lying naked on their backs in post-coital ecstasy, satisfied expressions slowly turning to horror as he sits astride them and presses a pillow over each face.

"Really. You are well connected. Do have a lovely day." He bowed almost imperceptibly and brought his heels together, careful not to make a noise. She smiled nervously at him and trotted out into the sunshine.

Once in his apartment, he made some coffee, put some pumpernickel and cheese on a plate and opened the newspaper. It revealed a brown envelope containing ten thousand Deutschmarks, a large black and white photograph and a single sheet of paper. He studied the photo carefully and spent the next hour reading the information on the page, repeating it out loud until he had memorised it perfectly. He placed the documents back in the envelope and put it under the doormat. He would repeat the exercise later and then burn the papers before returning to the Regent for his shift.

In the bedroom, he closed the curtains and set his alarm for three hours, although he rarely needed that long and was usually awake before it went off. He lay back on the bed and closed his eyes in silent contemplation. *Tomorrow. Before the evening shift. It is a matter of some urgency, apparently.*

***

The disappointment in Petra's voice was evident.

"I was hoping we might go for a walk in the park. Take a picnic. Get some fresh air for a change."

"I'm sorry. Something's come up at work and I have to deal with it. Maybe we can go tomorrow afternoon?"

"Don't you remember? We're going over to Gisela and Conrad's for lunch."

Harry looked up from his Saturday paper, and felt the colour rise in his neck.

"Oh damn. I forgot about that. Sorry." He returned to his paper to avoid her steely look.

"You don't sound very upset about it, Harry."

"I am. It's just that they're your friends, not mine."

"Well, you don't have any."

"No, what I mean is," he continued, ignoring the jibe, "I probably forgot because I don't know them very well and I didn't make the arrangements. That's all."

"What are you saying?"

"I may have to work Sunday morning too."

"Oh, Harry!"

"I'm sorry. I can't help it. These things come up."

"What things?" She was angry and frustrated and he knew it was partly because he would never explain. "I mean if I knew a little about what you got up to, I might find it easier to understand."

"What I get up to?"

"You know. Your job. All I know is you work for the government."

"Civil service."

"Whatever! But I don't know whether you're a pen-pusher or an assassin."

"Neither."

"I don't need you to tell me any state secrets. I just want to share it with you a little, like we share everything else. It would make life a lot easier."

Harry puffed his cheeks and blew a long breath and then rubbed his forehead. He didn't look forward to socialising with her friends or anyone else for that matter, which is probably why he'd put it to the back of his mind. He had nothing interesting to say to them; he had no hobbies, no interests, had nothing in common with them and couldn't discuss his work. He could only nod and smile and look interested while everyone else had a good time. He was probably just an embarrassment.

She was waiting.

"I can't."

"Okay! Fine! You go and do whatever it is you do and let me know when you're available." She was on the verge of tears and he reached out to touch her arm but she pulled it away and stood up.

"Petra!"

But she was gone. He heard the front door slam. He smashed his fist down on the table in a rare moment of rage. He hated himself just like he hated everyone and everything else. Everyone, apart from her.

CHAPTER 7

The taxi dropped Harry in Judenstraße in the old Spandau area in the west side of the British sector. A handful of pedestrians were out doing their weekend shopping and there was light traffic on a street that bustled with all manner of small shops, restaurants and coffee bars.

He found the coffee shop he was looking for and, alongside it, the red door with two buttons fixed to a panel on the wall. He pressed one labelled "Richter, J." and stood back, casting an eye in both directions as he waited. The intercom crackled.

"Richter."

Harry stepped forward and spoke into the grille. "*Morgen*, Johannes, it's Bertie. Fancy a coffee?"

"One minute," came the reply. Harry stared at the peephole in the centre of the door. After a few seconds he heard footsteps from the inside and caught movement through the lens. He lifted his ID card up and held it still. He heard a key turn in a lock and the door opened revealing a heavy-set, unshaven guy in a crumpled grey suit and loosened tie, the cut of the jacket barely concealing the bulge inside the left shoulder. The man stepped back and let Harry pass into a dimly lit corridor with another door on the left and a staircase straight ahead.

"Morning, Frank."

"All right, Harry?" Frank Boyd made no attempt to conceal his boredom.

"How's the babysitting?"

"Getting a bit stressed."

"He's only been here twenty-four hours."

"I think he expected the red-carpet treatment. A dingy flat up a back passage is not what he's used to, I guess."

"I'll put him straight."

"Better still, get him some proper digs, then me and Nigel can get back to our day jobs."

It was typical Frank. It was probably not very interesting sitting around a flat all day and night trying to ignore the rants of a truculent guest, but then whatever Frank did, he found cause to moan. Harry winked and patted his friend's extensive gut.

"You could do with a bit of exercise, me old mate. Too much strudel."

"Not much else to do."

"I expect we'll have him off your hands in a day or two, if we don't ship him back to where he came from."

Frank led the way up the stairs and turned onto a small landing with a single door. He stood in front of a tiny lens and tapped rhythmically on the door – a preconceived sequence. The door opened and Nigel Dennis let them in. He was in shirtsleeves, leather shoulder holster and Beretta in full view. Each man tilted a head in silent greeting.

Harry stepped into a large sitting room, lit dimly by the glow of table lamps and wall lights. Curtains were drawn across the only window, a crack at the top allowing a sliver of sunlight to project onto the heavy brown patterned wallpaper on one wall. A small kitchenette was arranged in one corner with sink, kettle and coffee pot on a two-ring electric hob. Two sofas faced each other across a coffee table beside a dormant electric fire.

A sole figure sat at a table in one corner under a standard lamp, flicking a newspaper with his left hand, his right encased in a plaster cast. He glanced over at Harry.

"Sir?" Nigel was looking at Harry dispassionately.

Harry opened his jacket and raised his arms. Nigel frisked him from top to toe. "Thank you, sir."

"We'll go into the cooler."

Harry approached the seated figure, who'd now returned his full attention to the newspaper. *All part of the game.* He waited until Bergmann could no longer stand the silence.

"Who are you?"

"Shall we go somewhere private?" Harry gestured towards a doorway and after a second or two, Bergmann made a tired show of closing and folding the newspaper and got to his feet. He was wearing a black polo-neck sweater over grey tracksuit bottoms and black sneakers, all presumably borrowed from the MPs. He had three-day stubble and his hair was unkempt, but apart from the plaster cast on his arm, appeared to be in reasonable health.

Nigel led them through the doorway and down a short corridor with two further doors. The walls were papered in thick stripes, vertical wooden battens fixed at three-foot intervals creating a panelled effect. He stopped halfway and turned to face a section of wall where a cheap landscape painting hung above a heavy steel radiator. He put both hands on the radiator and tugged and, with a loud click, a section of the wall between two battens together with the radiator swung outwards.

He felt around inside and turned on fluorescent strip lights that blinked into life, revealing a room that was bare apart from a large table and four chairs. The table bore a water jug with two glasses, a notepad and pencil, a compact reel-to-reel tape recorder and small TV screen. All four walls were covered in a padded and quilted brown fabric that extended to a door on the opposite wall. The room was comfortably cool compared to the stuffy atmosphere of the apartment.

"Please, take a seat," he said to Bergmann.

"Just buzz when you're done, sir."

Harry nodded as Nigel left, pushing the radiator-door to behind him.

"What's with the sound-proofing? Is this where you carry out your torture and beatings?" Bergmann sat back in his chair and put his good hand in his pocket. Harry sat down opposite, smiled pleasantly and extended a hand across the table.

"Harry Male, Major."

Bergmann looked at the outstretched hand for a moment, then took it without expression. "Klaus Bergmann."

Harry flicked a switch on the TV and after a second a fuzzy black and white image appeared showing Nigel moving around the sitting room.

"Do you mind?" Harry pointed at the tape recorder.

"Do I have a choice?"

"You're not a prisoner here, Mr Bergmann. You can leave whenever you want." Harry detected a flicker of a smile across Bergmann's face. "It's just easier than taking notes." Bergmann nodded.

"Nice to have a name. Your friends out there are not very communicative."

"They don't need to know who you are and you don't need to know them."

"But their job is to protect me, is it not?"

"A precaution only, until we establish whether you're at risk."

"Or whether you are."

"Indeed."

Harry pressed a button on the tape recorder and the reels started to spin slowly. He kept both eyes on Bergmann, sensing the man's initial truculence was beginning to wane.

"First interview with Mr Klaus Bergmann conducted by Major Harry Male at" – he looked at his watch – "eleven thirty-four on Saturday the fourteenth of August nineteen sixty-two. Safe house zero five, location classified, West Berlin." Bergmann fidgeted in his chair and then sat forward, suddenly looking less sure of himself. "Can you please confirm your full name, nationality and occupation?"

Bergmann cleared his throat. "Klaus Friedrich Bergmann. I am a citizen of the German Democratic Republic and I am, er, was, personal assistant to Dr Gustav Klein at the Ministry of Culture."

"Dr Klein is a member of the politburo?"

"No, he is, shall we say, one level below."

Harry already knew the answer. It was just a simple test to see if Bergmann was prone to embellishment or felt the need to aggrandise his position. Harry fished his cigarettes out of his pocket and proffered the open end of the box to Bergmann who shook his head. "I don't smoke."

Harry nodded and reluctantly put them back in his pocket. "Neither do I. Do you have any family?"

Bergmann's eyes dropped. It was the reaction he wanted.

"I have a wife and two children."

"How old?"

"Five and three."

"May I ask their names?"

Bergmann hesitated as if searching for the answer, but Harry could tell he was composing himself. He cleared his throat.

"Claudia, my wife, Thomas and Sabine."

"And where are they now?"

"Prague, visiting her sister."

"Did she know you were going to defect?"

"Yes."

"Are they safe?" Harry knew Bergmann could have had no contact and couldn't therefore be certain. It was cruel, but a necessary test to see if he was human. Bergmann would have to be a good liar if it wasn't uppermost in his mind. His eyes went moist.

"I think so. I hope you can help me."

Harry studied the dishevelled young man in front of him. His initial self-assurance and defiance had crumbled at the first mention of his family and he seemed to shrink visibly in his seat, shoulders drooping and head down. The body language of submission and self-doubt. He offered him a crumb.

"Let me have some details later and I'll make sure the right people know."

"You have people in Prague?" It sounded natural, an innocent expression of hope, a glimmer of optimism in a situation he couldn't control, something Harry the human being would like to encourage. Harry the professional overruled it and ignored the question.

"Why did you defect?"

Bergmann shrugged. "Freedom?"

Harry let out a sigh. *Another deluded soul.*

"What makes you think you're going to be any freer in the West?"

"You don't know what it's like."

"No. But depending on how much of an embarrassment you are to your bosses and how upset they are at your betrayal, you and your family may spend the rest of your lives in hiding, looking over your shoulder. That your idea of freedom?"

"It's a price I am prepared to pay."

"And if we are going to help you, you'll have to help us."

"Of course. I brought you the film."

"The film is worthless." Harry hoped that was untrue but he needed to establish whether Bergmann had a conscience or was just a mercenary. His look of angry surprise confirmed neither.

"But it clearly shows a war crime, committed by a senior government official. A member of the politburo of the DDR!" He prodded his index finger on the table for emphasis.

"Is that why you risked your life and your family? To bring a war criminal to justice?" He was trying to wind Bergmann up and it was working as his eyes narrowed, a vain attempt at stifling his rising anger. Before he could reply, Harry decided to push a bit harder. He wanted to gauge where Bergmann's sympathies really lay if they weren't with the communists any more.

"You were in the Hitler Youth, weren't you?"

Bergmann blinked. "What do you mean?"

"You wore the brown shirt and the corduroy shorts and the armband and you raised your right arm like all the others."

"We had no choice!"

"And you knew what was being done in the name of the German people."

"No, of course we didn't!" The rising pitch of Bergmann's voice betrayed a mixture of anger, frustration and fear.

"Or did you just turn a blind eye to what Charlie Chaplin was doing because he made you feel good about yourself?"

"I had no idea. I was too young to understand, but Germany had spent so many years in the gutter no one cared why we became so powerful so quickly. They had no desire or incentive to question."

"The ends justify the means." Harry made it sound offhand to see if Bergmann would take the bait and his colour indicated the screws were tightening.

"I was only a boy. I am not a criminal!"

"You just work for them."

"My family died at Dresden!" spat Bergmann, pointing at a wall he presumably thought faced east. "They were among the two hundred thousand people murdered by your bombs. Where is the criminal who gave that order?"

Harry's first instinct was retaliation. His mother had died in Coventry at the hands of the Luftwaffe so he was not in the mood to be lectured. But he didn't answer questions; he asked them. In any event, he had no need nor any desire to debate anything, especially not with an ex-Nazi turned commie sympathiser, even if he was beginning to like him. As to the man's veracity, he had still to make up his mind.

Bergmann went on. "Unlike you, Major Male, I am not partisan when it comes to what is a war crime and what is not a war crime."

Harry kept his expression neutral and impassive, determined to let nothing rile him. Something else he was good at. The number of civilians killed at Dresden had been widely disputed but by any measure they had run to the tens of thousands, so in terms of innocents killed, whatever was on the film paled into insignificance compared to the levelling of Dresden. But it had been said the crime lay in the intent, the purpose. Innocent lives to save innocent lives as opposed to wilful aggression and gratuitous

81

extermination. *The ends justify the means.* Either way, if Bergmann's primary motivation had been to bring a criminal to justice, why would he seek justice from those he believed had committed even worse crimes, crimes in which he had a personal interest? He would have to explain.

"So you went from Hitler Youth to Bolshevik apparatchik."

Bergmann shook his head and gave a wry smile at Harry's apparent insouciance. His voice turned sober and measured. "We were all at the mercy of the Russians. I was an orphan – used as slave labour to clear up the mess made by the warmongers. We did whatever we had to do to survive."

"And you survived by climbing your way up the greasy pole in the party machine all the while thinking, *One day, I'm going to wander over and say hello to those good people who murdered my family*?"

"Not all the while. For many years I swallowed the lie: believed the propaganda, bought into the socialist ideal of a classless society owned by and governed by the proletariat. But I began to see the corruption, the hypocrisy, the inequality and I could smell the stench of evil. It was no place to bring up my children."

"But you benefited from the corruption and the inequality, did you not? Nice apartment, good salary, private car, all the perks of the ruling elite? Dacha in the country, perhaps?"

"And I gave it all up. I risked my life, so that my family would be free, so my children would not be slaves of the state. Is that not what you promise in the 'free world', Major Male?"

Harry let the silence hang for a moment. He didn't answer questions.

"How did you get the film?"

"It was handed in by a woman clearing her father's loft after he died. He was an amateur photographer and had taken

82

many reels of film, mostly family but some taken during the war."

"Did she know what it contained?"

"No, she just wanted rid of it. Thought it may be of interest to the Culture Ministry."

"And you identified the officer in charge?"

"Yes. I took it to Klein and he said he'd deal with it."

"And?"

Bergmann shrugged. "Nothing happened. I should have known. Klein tried to use it to further his own career, threaten exposure, demand promotion in return for his silence."

"So what did you do?"

"I was naïve. I argued with him and he threatened me and my family."

"So your career was over anyway?"

"There is no such thing as a whistle-blower in the DDR."

"But you had no choice but to leave. You said you wanted justice and freedom, but all you really wanted was to save your own skin."

Bergmann dropped his head. "I want all of those things. For my family."

Harry was beginning to form a picture of the sad and lonely Klaus Bergmann, on a mission to save the world but instead destroying himself in the process. Would anything different have happened here? He couldn't say. But he'd been told in no uncertain terms he should forget about the contents of the film. It was classified and would remain so until people far more important than him decided otherwise.

The silent TV screen in front of him drew his attention. Nigel had walked out of shot earlier and a static image of the sofas had been all that remained for a while. But now there was movement. Nigel stepped into view and fell backwards onto the floor. It was vaguely comical as he struggled to get up but was then thrown back by an invisible force. Harry frowned and watched, incredulous, as a pair of legs appeared and straddled the motionless body. A hand holding a gun swung upwards, pointing at the head, two soundless jerky movements leaving no doubt.

Harry leapt from his chair, knocking it over, and raced for the door internal door.

"Out!" he shouted at Bergmann, pointing to the door opposite. He pulled down a thick metal bar from the side of the door to rest horizontally on a latch, preventing it being opened from the other side. Bergmann hadn't moved. He was frozen in shock.

"What is happening?"

"Move! Now!"

Harry grabbed Bergmann's arm and hauled him out of his seat, dragging him to the door opposite. He fumbled with a latch and two bolts then heard a commotion behind him as the radiator door rattled and shook on its hinges before it was punctured by four holes of light, two, three and four accompanied by the popping sound of a silencer. The external door swung outwards onto a spiral staircase and he pushed Bergmann out into the warm sunshine.

"Move!" he shouted again, but Bergmann's brain had finally caught up and he needed no encouragement. They flung themselves down the narrow metal fire escape two steps at a time, descending thirty feet to the back yard, then raced down the path to a fence and gate that separated it from a side road. Harry looked left and right, judging the distance to the main road. He chose left.

"This way! Run!"

Bergmann was ten years younger and despite his broken arm put on a turn of speed that left Harry, hampered by a sudden resurgence of pain in his right leg, struggling to keep up. Bergmann reached the main road in thirty seconds and stopped, waiting for Harry to catch up. His leg ached and he gasped for breath, lungs burning, a legacy of years of smoking.

"Where to?"

"Right. Look for a taxi!"

They set off, Bergmann taking the lead again. Within fifty yards he saw a cab coming the other way and waved. It turned in the middle of the road and stopped by the pavement. They threw themselves in the back.

"Reichstag building. Hurry!"

***

Schneider stepped over the body of Frank Boyd in the hallway and exited the safe house the way he came in, by the front door. He wanted to hurry – he knew he'd have to be quick if he were not to lose his target – but it might attract attention. He looked left and right. He had a fifty-fifty chance.

He went right, walking briskly and then broke into a shuffling run towards the main road. He reached the corner and looked right, seeing two men running away a hundred metres distant then watched as they flagged down a taxi. He was lucky: another pulled up beside him. He wrenched open the back door and dragged a bewildered old man out of the back, throwing him onto the pavement.

"Fahren Sie los! Schnell!" he shouted from the back seat, ordering the shocked driver to get going, but the man hesitated and began to protest. Schneider had no time. He put the gun to his neck. *"Schnell!"*

CHAPTER 8

They got out of the cab at the Reichstag and walked the three blocks to Harry's apartment by a convoluted route. Bergmann had been highly agitated, almost frantic when they first set off, and Harry had slapped him down immediately. The back of a taxi was no place to discuss defections, security services or assassins. Bergmann had spent the rest of the journey looking mournfully out of the window, ducking his head whenever another vehicle came alongside, while Harry's attention had been given over to the rear window, turning his head every few seconds to check if they were being followed.

His mind was buzzing, trying to work out what to do next. He'd never been in this situation before – *I'm just a bloody analyst* – and struggled to recall standard procedure in such an event. He couldn't go to his office. The department already operated undercover so regardless of the circumstances, he couldn't just stroll in with a defector, especially one whose security clearance had not yet and might never be issued. It could compromise the entire operation and put other people's lives at risk. He'd be court-martialled and rightly so.

He knew there were other safe houses but not their current status and there was no way he could find out without going through Control, and that meant going through the department. He'd also come to the grim but obvious conclusion they had someone on the inside. There was no way Bergmann could have been targeted so soon or so accurately without inside knowledge. There was nothing more corrosive or destabilising than a breach of security that placed everyone and everything under suspicion and cast a dark shadow over the entire operation. On a practical level, and until it was resolved, no one could be trusted, rendering it virtually impotent.

There was one obvious solution and he tried to resist it, but he couldn't think of an alternative. He had a secure phone in his apartment – a hot line to Control, standard issue in government buildings occupied by security personnel. To be used only in an emergency. Well, if this wasn't an emergency, he couldn't think of one even though harbouring a communist defector in a government-owned residential apartment would never have been sanctioned. He'd make the call and, provided he issued the correct codes, the boys in suits would be round within the hour.

But first he had to be sure they weren't being followed. He'd fought off a creeping paranoia that made the cab driver, every man in the street, even Bergmann himself, the enemy. He dismissed the latter. The guy was unarmed, under-dressed, debilitated by a broken arm and, until the moment the assassin had struck, merely a victim of his own misfortune.

He'd had to consider Petra too. She couldn't be exposed to this madness, but when he'd told her he was working that day she'd decided to jump on a train to Hanover to see her mother. By the time she got back, Bergmann would be long gone and she'd never know.

When they'd reached the Tiergarten he'd abandoned the cab and they'd walked across the park to the Hofjägerallee. It was open space and they'd be easy to spot by anyone who knew what they were looking for but then the same applied to any pursuer and he'd decided it was worth the risk. They'd picked up another cab on Tiergartenstraße that took them to the Reichstag. It was one forty-five when they arrived outside Harry's apartment door.

He was acutely aware he was unarmed and however unlikely he thought anyone might be waiting inside, he couldn't be certain. If they had inside knowledge of the safe house, they would probably know who'd been sent to interrogate him and by extension where he lived. Whoever was coordinating the attack could not yet know their operation had failed so it would take time for them to formulate a new plan. He had an old Enfield service revolver hidden in the back of a cupboard in the study but he hadn't fired it in over ten years so it offered little more than a confidence boost, and not even that if he didn't get to it first.

He examined the door and saw no evidence of tampering but that did nothing to reduce his anxiety. He'd said little to Bergmann in the last hour other than to issue curt instructions and Bergmann had followed him dutifully in silence.

"Wait here," he whispered as he turned the key gently in the lock and pushed the door open. In an instant he was back in the farmhouse, stepping again into the unknown, but back then he'd been battle hardened, young and armed with a machine gun. He felt his heart beat in his chest and strained his ears to detect any unnatural sound, but the apartment was silent and gloomy, the window blinds still in place just as he'd left them. He ventured slowly down the short hall and into the sitting room then checked each room and, as he did, his confidence grew. He retrieved the Enfield, loaded the cylinder with six rounds from a battered box of nine and returned to the sitting room.

"Bergmann?" he called and the German appeared in the hall, looking worried and helpless. "Shut the door."

"What are we going to do? I thought you people would protect me and instead you're going to get me killed."

"Stay calm, Klaus." It was the first time he'd used Bergmann's first name. "Help will be here soon." Harry brushed past him and locked and bolted the front door.

"What help? If the Stasi can find me that easily what chance do we have?" Bergmann appeared panicky again but Harry had no time for histrionics.

"Shut up and sit down. I need to make a call."

Bergmann sat nervously on the end of the sofa, hands between his legs, rocking gently back and forth. Harry went back into his study and laid the Enfield on his desk next to two telephone handsets: one black, one white. He dropped to his knees in front of a small safe and twirled the dial back and forth until he heard a click, gripped the handle and twisted it to the right. The door emitted a satisfying clunk and swung open. The safe contained cash in various currencies, three passports, a photograph of him with his platoon in Sicily in '43, a number of maps of Berlin in different scales and a small ring-bound notebook secured by a rubber band.

Harry flicked through the notebook until he found the page he wanted and picked up the black phone. He dialled a four-digit number and waited. It was answered after three rings. He listened for a moment then spoke, reading from the codebook the responses to each question.

"Capricorn, Milkmaid, Albert, Concubine. Zero two four zero… Code ten… Safe house zero five. Two down… Terminal… Five zero nine seven… Immediate… Two chickens, one fox… Imminent… Roger, out."

He replaced the receiver and put the notebook back in the safe, then returned to the sitting room.

"Let's have some coffee."

"Have you nothing stronger?"

Harry had a bottle of Johnnie Walker in the kitchen and he was tempted but dismissed the idea. He had to stay alert and didn't feel inclined to mollycoddle Bergmann, who, after all, had got them into this mess in the first place. "'Fraid not."

"You don't smoke and you don't drink? Admirable."

Harry ignored the sarcasm and went over to the shutters but then thought twice about opening them. Better they stay in the gloom for the short time it would take for the experts to arrive. "I think you may have a security breach." Harry ignored the taunt as he walked over to the stove and filled the coffee pot. "What makes you think this house is any safer than the last? Or the next?"

"Black?"

"White."

"There are no guarantees, Klaus. You should know that. And there's no going back. You made your bed and you have to lie in it."

"You're calling me a fool?"

"No. Just trying to manage your expectations."

"I have no expectations. Not any more."

"Good." Harry leaned on the kitchen counter, waiting for the pot to boil. He craved nicotine, but it would reveal to both of them how weak he really was. He desperately tried to remain focused on the present, the task at hand, but the past was ever present. Bergmann no doubt wished he'd kept his mouth shut, abandoned his naïve notions of freedom, his quest to right the wrongs of others and just made the best of what he had. If he and his family got out of this alive, it wouldn't be much of a life. He probably wished he could turn back the clock and have another go. Harry knew only too well what that felt like. What would have happened if he had made different decisions?

But there had been no other possible decisions. No other outcomes. He'd been through it time and time again. There was nothing he could have done, but it made no difference to the crushing weight of guilt that ate away at his soul, dragging him down little by little, day by day. *When will it end? It'll end when you're dead.* But then he was already dead. Dead a hundred or a thousand times. Dead every night and finally, mercifully at peace until he woke up and then he had to live through the nightmare all over again.

The coffee pot gurgled just as he heard the key in the lock and he snapped his head towards the sound. Bergmann got to his feet.

"Stay there," hissed Harry moving swiftly towards the hall, Enfield in hand. *Petra? No, too soon. Experts? No, they don't have keys, or do they? Even if they do they'd either knock first or else break the door down, not casually let themselves in.* The door shook, held by the bolts, and the lock rattled as whoever it was on the other side persisted with the key. Harry tiptoed silently up to the door, staying low, listening for any sound that might identify the caller. The noise stopped. He raised his body slowly upwards until his head was level with the peephole, feeling an ache in his chest from holding his breath. He stole a quick glance through the lens and pulled his head back sharply. He frowned in confusion. He took another look and breathed out. Frau Leitner.

She looked puzzled, examining the key in her hand. Harry relaxed and unbolted the door. Saturday wasn't her normal day and he didn't know why she was here but he didn't care. He was just relieved it was nothing sinister. He opened the door and she looked up, equally surprised to see him, then, as if suddenly distracted by something, turned to her right.

Her head exploded, brains, teeth, hair and blood expanding in all directions, colliding with his face as if someone had thrown at him a bucket of hot steaming offal: warm, wet, slimy and repugnant. Frau Leitner's body crumpled to the floor and Harry bent double, blinded, coughing and retching while instinctively reaching out to slam the door shut.

***

Schneider leapt over the old hag and burst through the closing door, crashing into the blood-soaked body of the man inside, catapulting it down the hall. The body twisted and writhed on the slippery wooden floor in a desperate attempt to recover and got to its knees only to meet the swing of a right leg, the boot landing a vicious kick to the head without having to break step. The man flew backwards and landed heavily, his head striking the floor with a satisfying thud and forcing him to release the antique revolver that clattered down the hall.

Schneider walked briskly into the sitting room and stopped in front of a paralysed Bergmann, who was still glued to the sofa. Schneider's head twisted left then right, quickly taking in his surroundings, eyes checking for danger. There was none.

"Klaus Bergmann?"

Bergmann gave an imperceptible nod. Schneider raised the silenced Makarov and shot him in the chest. The impact of the soft-nosed bullet threw Bergmann backwards against the arm of the sofa, exiting his back, ripping foam and feathers from the sofa's insides and spreading blood, muscle and fabric in a wide arc onto the wall. Bergmann looked down at his own chest, bemused by the rapidly expanding, saucer-shaped patch of red and coughed blood as it filled his lungs. He was as good as dead, but Schneider stepped forward to within thirty centimetres and shot him again between the eyes.

Noise on the stairwell: multiple boots on stone steps. They were coming. He glanced around the apartment. There was nowhere to go – three floors up, one way in and one way out. He'd have to fight. He expelled the clip from the Makarov and loaded a full one from his pocket. Eight rounds. One for the guy on the floor plus seven *Polizei*. Or one for himself. He strode over to the moaning, twitching figure lying flat on its back, face and chest caked in blood and gore, eyes closed. He raised his arm and pointed the weapon at the head, finger tight on the trigger

But his brain had stalled, refusing to issue the instruction to pull. A tornado-like rush of air followed by the distant rumble of thunder filled his head and his gun hand began to shake uncontrollably. He stopped breathing and his vision blurred. He felt detached from the scene, a third-party observer of a hideous show, an audience of one at a gruesome play. He had lost himself in the moment and it was too late.

"Halt!"

He stood, rooted to the spot, incapable of voluntary movement. The Makarov wobbled in his grip as his arm lowered itself to his side and his head turned robotically to the door. Two uniformed *Polizei* crouched in the open doorway in front of two men in suits and fedoras who stood behind, all four of them with pistols pointed at him.

"Waffe weg!" He heard the shouted command telling him to drop the weapon echoing through the roar in his ears. Schneider/Radler – their lives were over. They were no more. He breathed in the scent of life reborn.

CHAPTER 9

The apartment had turned into a busy crime scene. Police standing by the door, police searching every room, opening drawers and cupboards, rifling through possessions, photographers with flash-popping cameras, two men in suits and fedoras in muted discussion, two ambulance men lifting the plastic bag containing the body of Frau Leitner onto a stretcher, Bergmann's corpse lying under a white sheet, patiently waiting its turn.

Harry sat at the kitchen table holding an ice pack to one cheek, being ministered to by two pretty *Fräuleins* in nurse's uniforms, one of whom dabbed a cut on his chin with antiseptic-soaked cotton wool. He took a sip of Johnnie Walker from a china cup and stole a puff from his cigarette each time a *Fräulein* foraged in her medical bag for new supplies. They'd cleaned all traces of Frau Leitner's body parts and fluids from his eyes, face and hair, but his shirt and trousers were splattered with ever-blackening stains, some spreading as far as his shoes and socks. His blood-soaked jacket hung on the back of the chair.

He had a thumping headache and his speech was slurred not so much by the whisky but, given the throbbing pain, by a jaw he knew must be broken even if the experts insisted otherwise. He was still numb with shock but it didn't stop him reliving the last few hours, looking for the fatal errors in the operation, in particular, his own. But it was too complicated; there were too many variables, the adrenalin had long since worn off, the alcohol and aspirin were taking effect and his brain was telling his body to rest. One of the suits came over to inspect as a nurse applied a sticking plaster to his cut.

"Are you ladies almost finished?"

"Just about. Keep taking the aspirin, Harry. Go easy on the whisky, please."

They packed up their bags and left.

"Major, we need a preliminary statement from you now, and as soon as you're ready, Commander Laughton will want to see you. Tomorrow if possible." Harry took another swig. "We're going to take you to the Excelsior. The apartment is now compromised and out of bounds. We'll have to find you something else, but until we do, you and your, er, girlfriend can rest easy. You'll have protection."

Harry raised an eyebrow. He'd suddenly lost faith in the value of protection, but then again, he was not nor had ever been the target. Like the others, he'd just got in the way. Systematic elimination of British government officials on their own territory by the Stasi or anyone else would be a declaration of war and whatever the state of diplomatic relations between East and West, they did not yet amount to that. But as regards moving out of the apartment, he'd come to the same conclusion for different reasons. He and Petra couldn't live here any more. Even if the place were gutted and redecorated, it would always be the scene of two murders, forever in their minds, forever damned, a place visited by evil.

"But you got him?"

"Yes. Wasn't difficult. He gave up without a fight. The police took him to go through the formalities and then lock him up. We'll send a team in. We need to know if he's just a hired hand or if he's better connected than that. If he has a network."

"He was certainly well informed."

"Yes, it appears so. But he was totally calm when we arrived, almost a zombie."

"A well-informed and very clever zombie."

"You were lucky."

Harry's analytical mind saw the trap immediately. He regularly used the same technique himself. The suit's tone was conversational rather than inquisitorial – an innocuous throwaway remark made simply to test the reaction, lay the ground for the lie, if there was to be one. No one was trusted. Everyone was under suspicion. He knew the assassin couldn't have done what he did without inside information and at this precise moment, he was first in the frame, not least because he was the last man standing.

Why didn't he kill Harry when he had the chance? He'd simply disabled him, shot Bergmann, then returned to deliver the coup de grâce. But he'd hesitated and left it too late. It made no sense to Harry or, by inference, the suits and it worried him. Only Harry knew Harry was innocent.

But then if the assassin had pulled the trigger, he would have condemned himself to die in a hail of police bullets. He wouldn't have been the first to sacrifice himself for his profession or his love for the motherland. But maybe he thought he could bargain his way out of it, do a deal, or a swap, even? He'd be taking a big risk. He risked being left high and dry by his masters depending on how useful he was, how much he knew himself and whether or not his side had anyone they were prepared to trade. What he'd done was a hanging offence on either side of the Wall. The stakes could not be higher. For them both. *Someone's shouting. Petra!*

"Get out of my way! I live here!"

She's early. He stood up abruptly and his head swam for a second. He steadied himself then tottered to the front door followed by a suit. Petra was gesticulating with two *Polizei*.

"What the hell is going on?" She saw Harry and her mouth dropped open in shock. "Harry? *Oh mein Gott!* Harry?" She pushed between the policemen and rushed up to him, stopping to take in the sight: the black and blue cheek, the plaster on the chin, the blood-spattered shirt. "Oh my God, Harry. What the hell happened?"

"It's okay, sweetheart."

She looked at him as if he were an alien.

"It's not okay! What happened? Oh my God, you're hurt! Is that your blood?"

She dropped her bag and flung herself at him. He winced in pain from several places at once and wrapped his arms gently around her. She hung on as if for dear life. Behind

96

him she would see the sofa and the white, bulging, blood-stained sheet, the blood on the floor and the sofa and the walls, and she'd watch as two ambulance men walked casually past them with a stretcher and a black body-sized plastic bag. "Harry?" She was on the verge of breaking down.

"Come on."

He shepherded her over to the kitchen and turned her so her back was to the sitting room. He held her at arm's length. She had tears in her eyes and it broke his heart to see her so upset and afraid.

"There's been… an incident. Two people have been killed" – she gasped and put a hand to her mouth – "and the man who did it is in police custody." He tried to say it as calmly as possible but his speech was impaired. He sounded like someone just back from a major session at the dentist. She shook her head in confusion.

"What man? Who's been killed? What were they doing here?" Her eyes pleaded with him for answers to questions beyond her comprehension. "Who are these people?" she said, looking at the suits.

"These men are colleagues of mine. They're here to help us." The suits were watching the exchange but made no attempt to acknowledge their introduction.

"Help us do what?"

"We're going to stay in a hotel for a few days, to let things settle down."

"Settle down what? What? Tell me!" she shrieked, her fear turning to anger. He held her by the shoulders.

"Petra. Go into the bedroom and pack a bag for a few days. I promise I'll explain everything to you later. Okay?"

She flashed a glance at the suits and then back to Harry. She wiped a hand across her face and moved unsteadily towards the bedroom as they all watched. One of the suits followed her. The other turned to Harry.

"You're still bound and will always be bound by the Official Secrets Act, Major."

"I know that," he said icily. "Have the good grace to let me handle this. I know what I'm doing." The suit nodded but in a way that made clear he was not convinced.

***

The porter showed them into their room at the Excelsior, placed their bags on a stand and bowed as he backed out.

Harry had spent an hour with the suits giving them a blow-by-blow account of the last three days' events, from the time he was briefed by Laughton, the research he'd done and where, the places he'd gone, the people he'd met, what he'd said to them and, in particular, what happened from the moment he stepped into the safe house earlier that day.

Petra had spent the time locked in the bathroom, largely of her own volition, but she was not cleared to hear what they had to say and Harry didn't want her to anyway. He would tell her in his own way in his own time regardless of OSA considerations. He owed her that.

"We'll be right outside, Major," said a tall guy with a crew-cut, a chiselled jaw and a sharp suit, "round the clock." He pulled the door shut behind him. Petra sat on the bed, still apparently in a daze. They hadn't said anything on the ride over from the apartment.

"Major?" she said at last with heavy irony. Harry sighed. He had so much explaining to do and even now, he couldn't tell her everything. It wasn't that he didn't trust her; it was just that she didn't need to know. Or maybe she did? He was still confused himself and not sure what on earth he could say that would calm her, which was all he really wanted. But what could he possibly say to reassure her that, despite being chased by a professional assassin who'd shot dead four people in cold blood, two of them in their own home, there was nothing more to worry about?

"More of a formality than anything."

"Your work gives you a rank?" she said in disbelief.

"I work for the secret service…"

"Jesus!" She stood up and stomped across to the window, which, he judged, was about as far away from him as she could get. She crossed her arms and stared through the glass, keeping her back to him.

"Don't tell me it comes as any great surprise."

She put on a mocking voice. "How was your day at the office, dear? Ooh, a couple of people got their brains blown out, nothing special."

"It doesn't happen to people like me."

"Nor me!" She whirled around, stabbing her chest with one finger.

"Petra, I know it sounds sinister but really, most of the stuff I do is boring and mundane."

"How can I be sure of that? You never tell me anything. If it's so boring and mundane why couldn't you tell me? Why did you have to wait for something hideous and awful to happen before you mention anything?"

Before he could answer there was a tap on the door. He found it a welcome relief. Maybe it would give her a moment to calm down.

Chisel-jaw's head appeared. "Major? Can we have a moment, please?"

Harry stepped into the corridor. The suits were back. They looked awkward and serious.

"Did you forget something?"

"They lost him."

"Who?" But he had no doubt.

"Your assassin. The *Polizei* lost him."

"Oh Christ. How?"

"He shot them. Three of them."

"No! That's not possible. Wasn't he cuffed?"

"Apparently."

"Well then…?"

"Look, we don't know all the details yet and I doubt there'll be many witnesses to exactly what happened. The car mounted the pavement and crashed into a phone box.

99

People saw a big guy with a gun crawl out and run off. Three dead coppers inside. Thought you should know."

Harry's head began to throb again. It had to be a macabre joke, a ruse just to watch his reaction or trick him into saying something incriminating. He didn't trust the suits any more than they trusted him. There was no room for trust in their game.

"Look," said Senior Suit. "I don't think you've got much to worry about. You were never the target; he already had a chance to finish you off and didn't" – *Why do you keep mentioning that?* – "so he's got nothing to gain and everything to lose by trying to hunt you down again." *Hunt me down again? Thanks, pal!*

Harry thought about it. It was logical. Boyd and Dennis were in the way and would have tried to stop him. There would have been no other way to immobilise them. Frau Leitner too. She would have screamed or struggled, an obvious impediment. Harry'd had a gun but he was already on his knees and maybe it was quicker to kick him in the head and save a bullet than break step. Whatever the reason, the target had been reached so there was no further need to clear a path. But the guy had come back for him, so they'd said, and hadn't pulled the trigger. *Because I wasn't the target, the police had arrived, he was outnumbered and he wasn't ready to die just yet.*

Senior Suit was talking. "The *Polizei* are pulling out all the stops. Different when it's one of their own, never mind three, but my bet is he's already back on the other side. Get some room service and have a rest. You've got a meeting with Laughton on Monday at ten. We'll pick you up."

Harry watched them turn and go. No pleasantries, no concern, no grace, no humanity. What a miserable world they lived in, he thought to himself. *The same one as you, Harry.* They still believed he was guilty. That was the default position, guilty until proven innocent. That was the way it worked in their world. Justice turned on its head. He went back inside, unsure of what he was he was going to say

100

to her. He'd have to tell her. He'd have to tell her everything, including the gory details. He had one chance to finally be honest with her and he would leave nothing out or else he'd lose her and that was unthinkable.

She was standing by the bed, looking at her unopened suitcase, arms folded, biting a nail. He took a deep breath.

"Er, that was the guys in suits again."

"Laurel and Hardy?"

"I don't know their names."

"Of course you don't!" she snapped at him. This was not going to be easy.

"The guy who killed, er… the killer, is on the loose. He got away." She threw her head back and exhaled, long and deep. "But he's not considered a danger, not to us anyway."

"He's murdered two people and he's not considered a danger?" The words came out slow and measured but the look said it all. He was not credible. None of them were. *Tell her everything.*

"Seven."

"What?"

"He's killed seven."

She slowly sat down on the bed and put both hands to her head as if to steady her brain, force it to compute the irrational nonsense she was being told.

"Seven? Why stop at seven? Why not nine?" she simmered, challenging him to dispute the obvious.

"Because I was never the target. The guy had a job to do and the people he killed got in the way of him doing that job. He's a professional, he doesn't do it for fun."

"Listen to yourself! You actually admire this guy? He's a professional? He has principles?"

"No!"

"What kind of a world do you live in, Harry? I have no idea who you are."

"Petra. They think he's already back in the East."

"Think!" she screamed. "They think? What do I care what these people think? What do I care what you think?"

101

She stabbed a finger at him. It hurt but it was true. He may as well be a stranger to her. "What if I'd been at home?"

It had already crossed his mind and if he thought there had been any chance she'd been there he would never have taken Bergmann. Never in a million years. He would never knowingly put her in danger. *Knowingly? But you have put her in danger, Harry.*

"I'll look after you. I'll make sure we're okay and soon things will get back to normal and…"

"I'm pregnant."

The mini-fridge in the corner of the room kicked into life, the rattle and hum of the condenser incongruously loud in the silence that suddenly engulfed them.

"Oh," he said, lost for words. For a moment, he saw a glimmer of hope, a ray of optimism, a feeling of release and escape and the stirrings of joy tempered by the fear of a new unknown. But like the fragments of a dream you try so hard to remember that it dissolves into fairy mist, the moment came and went. They had not had sex for a long time and she showed no signs.

"It's not yours."

They stood in silence, heads down, unsure of what to do next. Her belligerence had gone; her body language spoke sadness and regret and his, desolation. He wanted to be angry. He wanted to berate her for betraying him, for the lies she must have told: the monthly meetings that went on late, the drinks with friends, the weekend conferences, visiting her mother. The deceit and the cruelty and the utter selfishness of it all. But he knew he was to blame. He knew it was all his fault and any anger he felt should be directed, as usual, at himself. He had form, and it was inevitable. *I don't know what she sees in me – I'll make an honest woman of her one day.*

"May I ask…?"

"A friend from university." She sniffed. She was crying and he wanted to hold her, but he felt awkward. It would be impolite. She'd suddenly become as much of a stranger to him as he appeared to be to her and it wasn't the done thing to cuddle a stranger.

"May I ask why?"

"Why do you think, Harry?" She wiped the tears from her cheeks and stood up, her anger returning to counter the anguish. "I don't know who you are. You never talk to me. We never go anywhere together. I don't know what you do or what you have done or where you came from or where you're going or whether you have any family or where they are."

"I have no family."

"Well, it really doesn't matter now."

"You're all I've got."

It was someone else speaking his words. Harry Male never said anything that revealed his emotions or his feelings. His innermost thoughts were private, not for public consumption. Articulating his inner thoughts served no purpose other than to trivialise their essence and demean the speaker. That had always been the case before. The dubious justification.

Her face creased in frustration. The anguish was back. "I'm just someone who shares your apartment. Nothing more."

"Tell me what you want, Petra."

"What do I want? I want to love someone. Someone who loves me. Someone to share my life with. I want children. I want a family and a nice house and a good job and I want to go on sunny holidays and swim in the sea and have picnics in the park and go to the Christmas markets and play in the snow and sit indoors in front of a roaring log fire when the rain is falling outside. I want a puppy dog and cosy slippers and a soft bed with a hot-water bottle. I want a real life, Harry. I want a normal life. With someone I can trust."

"That's what I want too."

"You don't know what you want, Harry. That's your problem."

103

"My problem?" She was slipping away from him now. His instinct was to lash out, react to her hurtful criticism, tell her she was the one who'd been unfaithful to him, she was the one who'd slept with someone else and kept it a secret and lied to him. But he couldn't, because he knew she was right and if he were really honest with himself, it was too late. She'd already gone.

"You're trapped alone inside this shell, wrestling with whatever demons are tormenting you, hoping that one day it will all be okay, that one day it won't matter any more, that time will have healed the wounds and you can move on. Yet somehow you stay, wallowing in the past, in your self-pity. You won't talk about it, you can't forget about it and you can't deal with it. Unless you do something to break free, you're doomed to spend what's left of your life in this living hell."

"Then help me."

"I've tried, Harry. But you always push me away. Sometimes I think you don't even know I exist. You have to do this yourself."

She picked up her case and jacket.

"Wait. Where are you going?"

"To stay with a friend."

"Who?" She didn't answer but they both knew. "But you can't. Not yet. Wait till it's all died down."

"You said there was no danger. Laurel and Hardy said there was no danger."

"I know. But I just don't like the idea of you going alone."

"I've been alone for a long time and so have you. I hope it all works out for you, Harry. Please ask your colleagues to let me into the apartment tomorrow so I can collect the rest of my things?"

It was over. There was nothing more to say or be said.

***

The man known to Frau Brucker as Radler got back to his apartment block just before 6 p.m. as a tall, well-dressed gentleman was closing her door behind him. He was in his sixties, sported a grey goatee, a few strands of wispy hair and wore a striped three-piece suit. He positioned a black homburg on his head, but frowned and looked furtive when he saw the dishevelled figure approaching him. Radler guessed the man's demeanour was more dirty secret than disdain and he'd be too conscious of his own indiscretions to notice the splashes of blood on Radler's clothing.

"Abend," the man known as Radler said without stopping and carried on up the stairs.

"Ah, guten Abend, mein Herr." The tone was too casual, affected normality.

He dismissed any thought of the filthy assignations of two old Jews. On another day he'd have stopped and had some sport at the old boy's expense and maybe even knocked up the old hag Brucker to see how quickly he could make her blush, but the man known as Radler had a lot to think about. He had much on his mind and it needed planning. He'd terminated seven today, all but three collateral damage, some of which was to be expected, but three *scheiß Bullen* was a bonus he hadn't anticipated.

He let himself into his apartment and stripped off his jacket and trousers which were speckled with blood – whose he couldn't say, but imagined most of it had been acquired within the confined space of the police car. Those amateurs had cuffed him with his hands in front, the young pig next to him in the back seat holding a gun. A moment's distraction and he'd pounced, twisting the handcuff chain around the pig's wrist and forcing it upwards. The gun had gone off, shooting the driver in the back of the head, causing the car to veer across the road. The other pig in front tried to grab the wheel while he struggled with the pig in the back and they'd put two holes through the roof of the car before shooting the passenger too. He'd then smashed gun and handcuffs into the face of the young pig, twisting the gun round and firing into his left eye before the car mounted the pavement and rammed a phone box. He'd used the gun to shoot through the handcuff chain and then tumbled out on the pavement amongst a number of astonished pedestrians, who panicked and scattered at the sight of the armed assailant who walked briskly away and disappeared up a side alley.

But the man known as Schneider had had a long day. He was fatigued and he was due back on duty at the Regent at nine thirty so he needed food and rest. He'd already decided the best place to hide was in plain view, which meant not deviating from his schedule. He could have a couple of hours' sleep, pick up a bratwurst from a stall and eat it on the way to his shift.

He drank deeply from the tap in the kitchen then used a bolt cutter from his toolbox to cut through each handcuff and, along with his clothes, stuffed them in a box which he slid under the bed. He didn't have to go to great lengths to conceal evidence; by the time anything was found he'd be long gone. He took a hot shower, washed the brown colouring out of his hair and fell into bed. He set the alarm but although he was desperately tired, his mind would not let him rest. The moment he'd dreamt of all his life had actually arrived and it had come in the most unexpected way. Now everything had changed and both Schneider and Radler would soon disappear without trace.

He felt a surge of energy course through his body, a renaissance of spirit and a rekindling of purpose long since lost, he'd thought never to regain. It was like being reborn, being given a second chance to achieve the only objective he'd ever had and now better equipped than ever to succeed. He felt the pride once more, the burgeoning ferocity and the uncompromising determination to do what he had to do and this time, he would not fail.

CHAPTER 10

The Kronestube was relatively quiet but then he rarely came on a Monday. He recognised one or two regulars, old guys who probably came in every night for their daily dose of beer, stodgy food and some semblance of social interaction. Old guys who probably lived alone in grubby apartments, living off their meagre pensions, eking out what few pfennigs they had left, awaiting their time to shuffle off. Guys like him, just older.

Harry poked at his goulash with a fork, moving chunks of gristle around the plate, hungry but not hungry, tired but restless, isolated but not alone, perched on his bar stool, head propped up by one arm. Suit Number Two sat in a booth to the side watching him, neither blinking nor diverting his gaze, it seemed, a feat he'd maintained for over an hour. Harry drained his glass. The barmaid was on him.

"Another?"

She wasn't wearing her dirndl tonight but somehow the paucity of exposed flesh made her slightly more alluring. Maybe it was the beer. Maybe it wasn't.

"Why not?" he said wearily.

Within seconds the empty glass had turned into a full one and he dived into the thick head of creamy froth to locate the cool amber liquid lurking beneath. He glanced at Suit Number Two sitting motionless in the booth like a mannequin and raised his glass in an attempt to provoke a reaction, but there was none. He pushed his plate away and lit a cigarette from a packet that lay on the bar next to a full ashtray.

At the debriefing that morning, Laughton had been joined by a suit from compliance, who, naturally, had not been introduced and had said nothing while Harry reiterated the events of Saturday. The suit had glanced repeatedly at a sheaf of notes, presumably checking the story had not changed. Harry knew the score. They'd been to the same school and been through the same training so he knew how to behave: *don't protest innocence or challenge the relevancy of any question, don't try to steer the conversation, don't try to embellish the facts with opinion or supplement them with thoughts you didn't have at the time and, above all, don't, under any circumstances, get riled.* All those behavioural characteristics he would look for. The complications and inconsistencies that would ultimately undermine the lie, because the truth, however implausible it may sound, was always pure and always the simplest.

Laughton had listened intently while the tape whirled, allowing him to speak freely and only interjecting to clarify rather than challenge a remark. They were going through the motions and they all knew it. There was nothing on Harry, but he knew that alone might not be enough to save him and it was highly unlikely he could just slip back into his old role, put it all down to experience and carry on as if nothing had happened. Anyway, he was not the only one on trial. Someone had totally misjudged the operation, sending an analyst into a situation so profoundly dangerous that even the two guys with field training had been unprepared. Furthermore, someone had betrayed them and that someone had to be found. He judged that Laughton's subdued and benign demeanour reflected perception of his own vulnerability in the wake of the Bergmann fiasco.

And the film that he'd told Bergmann was worthless even though they both thought otherwise? Now Bergmann was dead, it was the only thing they had of any value, provided it could be leveraged. It was the only crumb of comfort to offer those caught up in the violent deaths of another seven people, the violence revealed by the film begetting violence in its revelation. In the end, he doubted whether natural justice would prevail over diplomatic pragmatism or political expediency and it depressed him.

A new apartment had been found three streets away. He should stay at the Excelsior tonight and tomorrow and arrangements would be made to move his belongings. Petra was staying with a friend, he'd told them, and she'd moved out yesterday, as requested. Just as a precaution. He would clear it with them before she moved back in, he said. He wasn't going to engage in any discussion about his private life even if he knew that part of it was over. But he knew she would be watched for a while and he thought of warning her but decided against it. It would be like adding fuel to the fire.

He would stay away from the department for the rest of the week; take a rest, Laughton had said. He'd be assigned protection until he returned to his desk next Monday. Just as a precaution. He glanced at the suit in the booth and saw surveillance rather than protection, but he had no choice other than to cooperate for the time being. It would all become clear if and when they found the mole, and in time, everything would settle down and they'd be back to normal. *Normal?*

Petra's words were still ringing in his ears. He bitterly regretted deceiving her, if only by omission, but what choice did he have? That was a consequence of the career he'd decided to follow and it was incompatible with all the aspects of the normal life she craved. But he'd deceived her on a personal level too and that was a choice he'd made. He'd never discussed his experiences with her, never explained why he was who he was, never confided in her or succumbed to the self-indulgence of admitting he had a problem, his excuse being he believed that in time everything would be all right.

But time alone would not heal his wounds unless he allowed it to and he didn't know how. He didn't know why the memories persisted, why he couldn't consign them to history and put the past behind him, but he did know that it had cost him dearly. His failure to break free from his own cycle of misery and self-destruction had destroyed the only thing he held dear and would go on destroying everything until he did. He needed her more than ever now, but it was too late.

He took another swig and, leaving his glass half-full, got to his feet, stubbing out his half-smoked cigarette and throwing a handful of marks onto the bar. Time to go. He stepped out onto the pavement and a car pulled up. The suit opened the door and they both got in without speaking. Tomorrow would be another day, a new start perhaps? Tonight, the dreams would be the same.

CHAPTER 11

A spotty, twenty-two-year-old technician with glasses showed Harry into the small windowless projection room. A twin-reel projector mounted on a stand threw a white square of light onto a wall-mounted screen fifteen feet away, three rows of empty chairs on either side of the projector affording the audience an uninterrupted view.

He'd only been back in the building ten minutes when Laughton's replacement had summoned him into his office to tell him of the changes that had occurred while he'd been "on leave". Investigations were ongoing, he'd been told by Admiral Sir Aynsley Webb KCB, a former navy supremo and acting head of department, whose retirement to Eastbourne had been temporarily postponed while the department's *modus operandi* and security were reviewed and assessed by internal affairs.

Admiral Webb's demeanour had scarcely concealed his irritation at this unexpected posting following the sudden retirement of Commander Laughton and offered up his own selfless devotion to duty as an example everyone should follow, which Harry of course had concurred graciously.

"You're in the clear, Male," he'd declared in portentous manner. "Never in any doubt as far as I was concerned, once I'd read the files. I mean, what sort of chap is going to take the trouble to set up an assassination in his own living room? It's just not conceivable." Harry had quickly concluded that Admiral Webb needed little encouragement in portraying himself as an expert in matters of intelligence, even though his initial assessment amounted to no more than a statement of the bleeding obvious.

"No, sir," Harry had replied.

"Trouble with you spook chappies is you overthink it, can't see the wood for the trees, try to complicate matters when the answer's right there in front of your face," he'd puffed.

"Yes, sir. Sorry, sir."

"Not getting at you, Male."

"No, sir."

"I think you did your best in very difficult circumstances."

"Thank you, sir."

"I mean, you can't expect a mere analyst to cope in a situation like that. Lamb to the slaughter, that's what I call it." Harry the lamb hadn't been sure how to respond to the combination of sympathy and belittlement implicit in Webb's last pronouncement but it hardly mattered as the admiral had been in full flight. "Bergmann was always going to be a target, given his profile. Should have kept him under armed guard."

"He was, sir."

"Well, it wasn't good enough, was it?"

"No, sir. Sorry sir."

"Not getting at you, Male," he'd grumbled again.

"No, sir."

Harry had had an irresistible urge to look at his watch. The conversation, if that's what it was, had been at risk of going round in circles. Webb didn't want to be here, that was clear, but Harry had no time to listen to the old fart moaning on about the perceived inadequacies of others. The sooner he was pensioned off to Eastbourne the better.

"Still haven't found the blighter on the inside, either."

"No, sir."

"Any ideas, Male?"

Harry had ideas. They were looking in the wrong place. They were looking for some low-level flunkey who either needed cash for a gambling problem or on whom the enemy had some serious dirt, when, given the profile of the target, this went much higher up the pay grade.

"No, sir."

"Well, keep an eye open."

"Yes, sir." *Keep an eye open?*

112

Every member of the department had been interviewed, and none had mysteriously disappeared or acted strangely before or after Bergmann had been shot. There was no way a mole in their own department could tough this one out.

"Look out for strange behaviour. You know what I mean." Webb had waved a hand in the air, dismissing the subject as if he'd been wafting away a nasty smell.

"Yes, sir."

"Now. I understand you're the man to identify the location on this film Bergmann smuggled out."

"Yes, sir. I know the village where the incident is alleged to have taken place."

Webb had put on his glasses and consulted some notes. "Santa Cristina De Lago."

"Yes, sir."

"And what were you doing there?"

Harry blinked. *What do you think I was doing there, you pompous old git? "I thought I'd take my platoon to the local ristorante where I heard the tortellini was particularly good. Sir."*

He tried to keep his voice neutral.

"We were trying to take Montellano, sir. We drove the Germans out and set up divisional barracks there, but they counterattacked a few days later and we had to pull back."

"Retreat, you say?"

"Yes, sir."

Webb had grunted. Harry wasn't sure whether the admiral had been expressing disdain or disinterest. *I wonder from which cosy desk you directed naval operations?*

"And the Germans took reprisals."

"So I'm told, sir. I haven't seen the film."

"No. Quite. Neither have I, nor do I wish to. But you're wanted in the projection room. Take a butcher's, old chap, then finish your report and we can close the file."

Webb may just have been suggesting the department's role would then be complete, but it sounded to Harry like the decision had already been made. War crime or no war crime, it was clear the evidence would simply be filed away until such time as there was some political imperative to use it.

The kid in the projection room was fiddling with the controls on the projector.

"Do you know how to use one of these, Harry?"

"Major." Harry wasn't in the mood to be pally with a spotty kid straight out of university.

"Er, Major."

"Show me."

"On-off button here. One main dial; just twist it forwards for forwards, backwards for backwards. I've spliced in ten seconds of blank film to the end so you can stop it before it runs off the reel. Otherwise, you'll need to rethread it." He thumbed over his shoulder. "Light switch is at the back."

"I'll call you if I have a problem."

The kid grinned at him. "Hope you've got a strong stomach. It's pretty grim."

Harry looked in disdain at the smirking, bespectacled young technician that slouched before him: stripy sleeveless pullover, hands in the pockets of his brown corduroy trousers, tousled hair looking like it hadn't seen a comb in a week. The kid thought this was all a game.

"What's your name, son?"

"Roger."

"Roger... what?"

The smirk evaporated and he removed his hands.

"Er, Roger, sir."

Harry looked straight at Roger until Roger knew he was in trouble and one eye began to twitch.

"When were you born, Roger?"

"1940, sir." He'd missed National Service, never worn a uniform and seen and learned everything he knew from Hollywood and war comics. A bit of discipline and some extra training at the university of life was in order.

"I was about your age in 1940, bit younger even. I remember it well. Me and thousands of lads the same age on a beach in France getting dive bombed by Stukas and strafed

114

by Me109s. I saw my mates blown to hell – legs and arms shot off, decapitated, blood everywhere, blood on the sand, bodies floating in a blood-red sea, and I remember trying to grab hold of a poxy, blood-smeared little pleasure boat full of holes, waiting for the bullet with my name on it, the smell of smoke, fire and death, the screams for help, boys shouting for their mothers and their wives and their girlfriends as they lay dying and you know what, Roger? Even then, I knew I still had a chance." Harry stabbed a finger at the humming projector. "Those men and boys in that film had no chance. They knew exactly what was about to happen to them and so did their mothers and their wives and their girlfriends who watched and listened as their loved ones were murdered in front of their eyes. And all so that spotty little pricks like you can play with your toys in peace." Roger swallowed, his eyes wide with terror. "And the best you can come up with is… 'grim'? Go back to the safety of your little cubbyhole, Roger, and stay there till I tell you it's safe to come out."

"Yes, sir."

Harry watched the boy slope off and he took a deep breath, feeling instant remorse and a rush of self-hatred. The lad wasn't to blame; he was just a product of the times and he'd come down on him like a ton of bricks for nothing other than making a flippant remark. He knew no better but nor did Harry. Harry always wanted to lash out at everyone and everything even though he knew it made things worse, not better. He couldn't help it either; he was a product of his own times and Petra had lashed out at him for the same reason: that his behaviour was incomprehensible and destructive and it made her angry and frustrated that he wouldn't let her help him. The only difference between him and young Roger was that he no longer had any excuse.

He switched the lights off and sat down next to the projector so he could easily reach the controls. He let out his breath and turned the dial. The reels spun slowly as the projector chattered into life, the white square of light on the screen flickering with black spots and scratches for a few seconds until a chillingly familiar image appeared and the years rolled away.

***

German soldiers standing around in heavy coats, smiling and joking, smoking cigarettes and waving at the camera; a village with houses and people and dogs milling around, the camera panning upwards to the church steeple; a crowd of villagers looking pensive and subdued despite the sunshine, mothers holding babies, men wearing cloth caps, smoking pipes; a Panzer tank rolling into the market square, followed by a column of soldiers marching in time; a swastika unfurled from a balcony in the town hall. Santa Cristina De Lago. He recognises the buildings and the church and the fountain and even some of the residents. They've been very happy to see the Allies, but now they're back where they started. He watches, transfixed, his heart rate beginning to climb, heat spreading up his neck.

Three officers in peaked caps, two of them facing the camera, Waffen SS motifs on the tunic collar, chin up in the typical style of the arrogant strutting fascist, nodding at each other in self-congratulatory pose; an old man kicked and beaten with sticks; a group of soldiers eating from mess tins, swigging wine from tankards, laughing and shouting in the silence; then local residents, all men, some as young as twelve parading into the square under guard; close-up of three bipod-mounted machine guns, MG42s he can tell, one man squatting behind, the other holding the trailing ammunition belt. Long shot, and in the eerie silence the smoke billowing from the muzzles, the guns dancing, panning left and right and the men and boys falling where they'd stood, piling up on each other like sacks of coal.

Harry wipes his eyes and exhales deeply again. He's been holding his breath for the last thirty seconds, as if he's forgotten how to breathe, perhaps in harmony and respect for those whose last breaths he's just witnessed.

116

Close-up: mangled twisted corpses, lifeless limbs entangled in a grotesque display of camaraderie, posing in still life, a static dance of death, some eyes open, some closed, black blood on white shirts. Medium shot: one officer strolling alongside, pistol drawn, examining the pile of human flesh, pointing and shooting intermittently as he walks, snuffing out any flicker of life that dares persist. He reaches the end of the mound and retraces his steps, shooting once or twice more. He wears long, shiny, black leather boots, and bears the SS motif on his collar and in his hand, a Luger.

Harry fights back the wave of nausea threatening to overwhelm him. He leans forward in his seat, eyes glued to the screen. He stands, unsteady on shaky legs that somehow drag his kicking, screaming body towards the face that's coming slowly into focus, the brief look into the camera, the image from hell. Finally, the walk out of shot. The screen goes white and the chatter of the projector is accompanied by the rhythmic slap-slap of untethered celluloid.

Harry stares dumbly at the blank white screen, looking but not seeing, the last image burned into his brain. He senses a cool wetness at the side of his mouth, wipes away a slimy trickle of saliva and swallows deeply, having lost the ability to control more than a couple of bodily functions at once. He turns and reaches out for the chair like a blind man and manages to lower his aching body to rest.

He doesn't know how much time passes, minutes or maybe only seconds, but the lights come up and the slap-slap stops and there's a new silence to break.

"Major?" He doesn't hear the first time, but his brain registers movement. It's Roger the kid. "Major. I've brought you a brew."

***

Harry looked up and saw the tousle-haired technician holding out a cup and saucer, initially unsure of what to do.

117

Then the power returned to his limbs and he took the cup to discover, miraculously, his hand wasn't shaking. He cleared his throat.

"Thanks, Roger."

"Do you want me to run it again, sir?"

Harry took a second or two to think and sipped the tea. It was hot and sweet and milky and not at all the way he liked it, but it tasted of life itself and he felt his numbed senses recharging.

"No. Thanks, Roger. I've seen all I need to see, except…"

"Yes, sir?" Roger seemed to have suffered no ill effects from his earlier lambasting, now eager as a puppy.

"The very end. Where the SS guy looks into the camera. Can you print that out on a still photo?"

"Yes, sir!" said Roger with glee. "Within the hour." He unhooked the reel of film, affected a clumsy amateur salute and trotted out of the projection room.

CHAPTER 12

Harry sat at the bar of the Ostenkeller, picking at his knockwurst and potato salad. The sausage contained too much garlic for his liking and the potato was slimy and weirdly tangy as usual. *Foreign muck.* But it was no worse than the Kronestube and had rapidly become his venue of choice now he'd moved apartments. The beer, as always, was good, at least as far as cold fizzy beer went.

He often fantasised about being back home in an English country pub with real ale and fish and chips but convinced himself that, however pleasant he may recall the experience, it would, in reality, fall short of expectations and was certainly not worth abandoning his career for. Maybe he could get some leave and go home and see his father; after all it had been three years since he'd been back to Coventry. He could do his duty and salve his conscience and also indulge in his misguided culinary fantasies.

He'd told Petra he had no family and to all intents and purposes, that was true. His father Reg had been living in a veterans' home for almost thirteen years and had slowly descended into the darkness of dementia, such that he could barely function unassisted. The letters had long since ceased and on Harry's last visit, he'd hardly recognised his son. By all accounts he was little more than a vegetable. Harry felt guilty about his lack of attention, but the fact was there was nothing he could do about it. Reg was being looked after as well as possible and had been on borrowed time for a while.

He had never been particularly close to his father and believed Reg's military background was probably responsible for his stern manner and disciplinarian streak. Harry could never remember having a laugh with Reg and had always assumed his father's hideous experience in the trenches had affected him so profoundly he was incapable of levity or showing affection. Life for Harry as an only child growing up in Coventry involved endless streams of instructions and orders both at school and at home. He was subject to the constant threat of corporal punishment, which was routinely and regularly administered, deserved or not.

They'd drifted further apart when his mother Kathleen had been killed in the Coventry blitz of November 1940. Harry had been given leave to attend the funeral and been shocked to find his father reduced to a hollow shell from which he would never emerge. Harry returned to active service and apart from infrequent letters, never saw or spoke to his father again until he was invalided out in 1944, by which time Reg, singularly incapable of looking after himself, had deteriorated further. Within five years, he had moved into a home.

Harry took a swig of beer and burped loudly, the stench of garlic sausage making him wince, but he had no need to worry about his breath any more – one of the few advantages of living alone. He missed Petra greatly, for her beauty, her charm, her gaiety, her intellect and most of all her company. But Petra needed more than company and, as she'd made clear, better company than Harry could offer. He wanted to see her and wish her well and say he hoped they could still be friends, but he persuaded himself to leave her be. It was the least he could do.

He'd written up a report about his role in the Bergmann affair, had it typed and re-typed until he was happy there was no room for misinterpretation or doubt and appended his unequivocal opinion that the crime portrayed so graphically in the film had indeed taken place at Santa Cristina De Lago. He knew it was academic. The main objective had been proving Bergmann's veracity in order that further use could be made of him, not necessarily identifying the perpetrator of a crime so that charges could be brought. Now Bergmann was dead, the main objective had died with him. But even though Webb had thanked him for his thoroughness and diligence in producing an "excellent piece of work", he did so unaware of something Harry had omitted to mention.

Identifying the perpetrator had never been part of his brief; that had been left to others. One of the three SS officers in the film had been identified as Horst Engel and, although he'd not been seen to pull any triggers, the iron cross with the SS symbol at the throat marked him out as the man giving the orders. Engel was indeed a senior member of the politburo, for what it was worth.

The image of the third SS officer and the subject of the photograph Roger had given him had not featured in his report because it wasn't relevant. Harry had compared the image with stock photos of all the members of the East German politburo, already knowing there was no conceivable match, nor could there be, because only Harry knew who he was and only Harry knew he was already dead.

Revealing another connection between himself and Bergmann apart from his knowledge of the location where the crime was committed served no purpose, would unnecessarily complicate matters and raise questions he didn't want to answer. He had never spoken to anyone about what happened to him in Alfredo Girardi's farmhouse; it was too painful. He had never even told Petra so the last people to whom he would confide something so personal were idiots like Webb and the suits, notwithstanding any professional duties or obligations.

He'd spent the last eighteen years hoping the memories would simply evaporate or at least dull with time, but having seen the film and its images of appalling barbarity, looked at the photograph of the man who'd so casually demonstrated such obscene cruelty, he'd been plunged deeper into the abyss. He knew the man with the Luger. It was the man who killed him every night. It was Ernst Kessler.

***

That evening, alone in his new apartment, he lay in bed, listening to the sounds of the night, smouldering cigarette in hand, postponing the moment he had to shut his eyes and visit the other place.

He resolved to approach Webb and ask for some leave. He'd already had a week off, but that had been forced on him by circumstance and he'd have much preferred to have been at work than fester in a hotel room with nothing to think about other than the Bergmann debacle and his own problems. He'd delivered his report; the case, according to Webb, was now closed and unless there had been any other dramatic developments overnight, the workload had eased.

He'd ask for a fortnight and take unpaid leave if necessary, citing "personal reasons". If pressed he'd refer to his recent life-threatening experience, coupled with the break-up of his relationship. He could not in all honesty blame the department exclusively for Petra's departure but the Bergmann affair had been the final straw, the catalyst for their separation, however inevitable it might have been. He would disappear for a while, maybe even go to England, visit his father and have some proper food, take another look at his life, his career and his future.

He heard dogs barking in the distance. The death strip was no longer in sight but its presence cast a sinister spell, symbolising everything that was wrong with the world. Something had to change, that was for sure.

CHAPTER 13

The next day, he felt more relaxed and at peace with himself than he had for a long time. Miraculously, he had slept well, and had no recollection of dreams, good, bad or otherwise. He still missed Petra's comforting presence, but he knew in his heart it was for the best and he would get over it.

When he got to the office, activity in the typing pool was as frenetic as ever and he greeted the girls cheerily.

"Morning, ladies!"

One or two murmured something in return but it felt unusually restrained, forced somehow, but he thought nothing more about it and pushed the swing doors open. Johnny Bristow was in his usual place, hunched over a transcript, cigarette in ashtray, sleeves rolled up, tie askew even though it was only eight forty-five. The heat was getting to him.

"What's the latest, old man?" Harry said, removing his jacket and slinging it over his chair.

Johnny continued to run his pencil along a line of text and spoke without looking up.

"Don't ask. It's going to be a whitewash."

"Damn," said Harry although he didn't really care one way or another about the cricket. He noticed a white envelope on his desk and picked it up. It was postmarked Coventry.

"Oh, that arrived at your old flat. One of the suits brought it in," said Johnny.

"Suits?"

"Yeah. They're back."

"Oh, really?" Harry frowned. This was far more important than cricket. "I thought they'd finished."

Johnny looked up. "So did I. It's really putting a dampener on things. Everyone's looking at everyone else. Looking over their shoulder. I found them going through your desk when I got in. Probably been snooping through mine…" He trailed off and Harry noticed Johnny's attention had shifted. He turned around. The two suits, minus overcoats and hats, had come up behind him.

"Major Male. Can I ask you to step into Admiral Webb's office for a moment?" Suit Number One – no greeting, no pleasantry, no grace.

"Yes, of course."

The Queen, Churchill and MacMillan eyed him intently as he followed Suit Number One into Webb's palatial office and approached his ornate desk. Suit Number Two followed closely behind. Suit Number One took a seat next to Webb.

"Please sit down, Major." An instruction, not a courtesy. Webb remained silent, relegated to observer on this occasion, but Harry guessed that alone didn't explain the surly Churchillian countenance. "We've read your report and it concurs with the two previous interviews you've given on the matter, with the sole addition of the information regarding Santa Cristina De Lago." Suit Number One laid a thumb and two fingers on a manila folder in front of him as if it might blow away. "Is there anything else you'd like to add?"

Harry knew it was a leading question but he could answer it truthfully. There was nothing he'd like to add. There was always something he could add if they insisted but it would be of no use to them. He hadn't told them what he'd been wearing that day, nor what he'd had for breakfast, nor how he felt about the Bergmann affair in general, nor how he felt about Petra leaving him, nor, indeed, that he recognised a dead Nazi from way back. None of it was relevant. He dealt in facts. The rest of it was personal, no one's business but his own.

"What kind of thing?'

"Answer the question, Major," Suit Number One said with barely concealed irritation. Harry would have been irritated too had he been on the other side of the desk. It sounded like evasion and it always happened when the one being questioned needed a clue so he could be sure what to lie about. But he wasn't going to play that game. Not any more. Somehow, something made him feel emboldened and if his request for leave was denied and it turned into something more permanent, so be it.

"I'm sure you have something in mind." It was totally out of character, but it made him feel good. "It will save us all a lot of time if you just come out with it."

Webb's jowls twitched. "Now look here, Male…"

"Thank you, Admiral, but I think Major Male is right. It will save time."

Webb gave a mild harrumph and sat back in his capacious leather armchair, chin raised in defiance. Suit Number One opened the folder, pulled out the picture of Kessler that Roger had printed for him and slid it in front of Harry.

"Do you know this man?"

Harry looked into the face of evil one more time. There was no doubt. It was Kessler, minus the blood and the blackened face and the lame leg and the broken arm and the rage and the rabid hatred he'd exhibited that day in '44 in the farmhouse. This was Kessler, calm, collected, smart in his crisp uniform, enjoying a good day at the office in the sunshine, murdering a few hundred innocents and revelling in the attention and the admiration for his professionalism.

"Yes, I think I do."

"Do you or don't you?"

"I don't know him. But I know who he is."

"What does that mean?"

Harry hesitated, trying to find the right words. He really didn't want to relate the whole ghastly episode, not to these people.

But Suit Number One had smelt blood. "Why didn't you say anything?"

"It wasn't part of my brief to identify the perpetrators of a war crime. I was asked to confirm the location."

"Then why did you ask for the photo?"

"Because I thought I recognised him and I wanted to be sure."

"Sure of what, Major?"

"Sure that I recognised him." Harry saw Suit Number One's patience ebbing away. Obfuscation was not his intention, but he would have to concede that was how it looked. "I wanted to check he wasn't the official Bergmann was talking about. The guy in the politburo." It seemed perfectly simple to him but Suit Number One's face betrayed only confusion and bewilderment.

"Why?" He spread his hands wide.

"Because if he were the politburo official Bergmann was talking about, I'd have been wrong about recognising him."

"I'm not with you, Major."

Harry's temperature was rising too. It was none of their business but they would drag it out of him eventually. He couldn't bear to go there, revisit the scene, but he had no choice.

"Because the guy I know is dead. His name's Ernst Kessler and he's dead, crushed under a chimney stack. I saw it happen." They looked at him blankly. He fumbled with his shirt buttons while Webb and the suits watched in mounting consternation. He pushed back his shirt to reveal the scar in his right shoulder. "He shot me. Here. With that bloody Luger, no doubt." He poked at the photo angrily.

"Major!" Webb was out of his chair again. "I strongly suggest you temper your language and your behaviour!"

Harry took a breath and slowly buttoned his shirt. "Sorry, sir."

Suit Number One waited a second or two. "So you wanted to confirm to your own satisfaction that Kessler, or whatever he calls himself these days, is not a member of the politburo, and that's the end of it?"

"More or less."

"And you decided he isn't?"

"Yes… I mean no."

"Which is it, Major?"

"I mean yes, I decided he's not the guy Bergmann was talking about."

"And why is it so important to you?"

"I wanted to be sure he was dead."

"I'll ask again. Why is that important?"

Harry had no answer to this, either for himself or the others. When he'd seen the image in the film he'd had a horrible thought that somehow, Kessler may have survived and was now a high-ranking member of the East German government. It made his war crimes no less heinous, just personal. Too personal.

"How do you know he's dead?"

"I told you. A chimney fell on him."

"And then what?"

"What do you mean then what? I don't know. He shot me, the chimney fell in and the next thing I know I wake up two weeks later in a field hospital miles away."

"So you never examined the body. Took a pulse?"

Harry shook his head in dismay and had a sudden urge to laugh. They had no idea. He wanted them to understand, to know what he'd been through but without having to tell them. He could not and would not relate the sorry, hideous episode. It was far too painful, and even if he tried, it would sound so far-fetched as to be too incredible for words. It even seemed incredible to him every time he thought about it, which was maybe why he had never been able to put it out of his mind. To him, it was still a bad dream and as in all dreams, the things that happened in it were unreal. But Kessler had been real and the shock of seeing him again was real. He'd come in today filled with purpose, enjoying a flicker of optimism about the future and a hint of self-confidence that he hadn't felt in a long while, despite being reminded of the evil Kessler. He'd had the satisfaction of knowing what a criminal Kessler had been, that he'd met his end and that justice had somehow been done. But now felt profoundly subdued again. He offered another crumb of testimony, hoping but not expecting it would satisfy them.

127

"No, I didn't examine the body. I passed out."

Webb's intercom buzzed – a welcome distraction. He picked up the handset rather than talking into the speaker.

"Webb." He listened for a second or two and looked at Suit Number One. "Thank you," he said, replacing the handset and nodding at Suit Number One. "They're here." Suit Number One sat back in his chair.

"It's out of our hands now, Major. It's a police matter."

Harry heard the click of a door opening and twisted his head around. Cynthia was showing two new suits flanked by uniformed *Polizei* into the office.

"What's going on?"

"The police are investigating the murders of seven people and they believe you may be able to help them with their enquiries in identifying the murderer."

"Everything I know is in my report!" he protested and hated himself for sounding weak.

"We believe you know who he is."

"I never once saw him."

"Maybe. But we did. We saw him stand over you with a loaded gun and fail to shoot and we saw him being taken away by three police offers whom he subsequently murdered."

A chill went up Harry's spine as the penny dropped. He whispered the name.

"Kessler."

"Indeed. Not quite as dead as you thought, Major."

CHAPTER 14

The cell was a mere ten feet by five with a twelve-foot high ceiling and no windows. The only way in or out was a narrow, barred door that at least gave him a view out into the corridor. It contained a bed but nothing else. If he needed the lavatory, he was escorted to a single cubicle along the corridor by an armed *Polizei* and twice he was given food on a tray together with a bowl of warm water, soap and towel. The cell wasn't intended for long-stay prisoners, just those in temporary custody pending a decision on whether or not there was a charge to answer.

He'd been interviewed twice by two plain-clothes detectives – yesterday, when he'd arrived and again earlier that morning, both times in the presence of a solicitor appointed on his behalf who took copious notes but said very little. Harry had been struck by the irony of the whole affair. The detectives were, like him, in their forties and would have played some part in the greatest conflict of all time. He mused whether they'd been SS, Gestapo or just plain *Wehrmacht*; how many Allied soldiers they'd shot and whether he might have known any of them; how many civilians they'd murdered; whether they had been or still were fanatical Nazis or whether they had just been ordinary guys "following orders". He felt angry about his treatment and made no attempt to conceal his bitterness that the roles seemed to have been reversed. *Who won the fucking war anyway?*

The *Polizei* seemed particularly wound up by this one, probably because they'd lost three of their own. They were less concerned about Bergmann – a foreign national – and not at all about two British field agents who knew the risks and had no business being in their country anyway. They'd ranted over British incompetence which had led to the murder of poor Frau Leitner, but glossed over their own in letting Kessler out of their grasp.

They had nothing on him. They'd examined the safe house, seen the "cooler" and the locking bar over the internal door. If he'd been an accomplice to Kessler, he would have simply let him in, shot Bergmann and disappeared. He had given them a name, which ought to be of some help, but beyond that, there was no conceivable connection between him and Kessler other than the one he'd already explained.

Harry had found the two interrogations surprisingly cathartic. Both the detectives and solicitor Goldschmidt – *probably not a Nazi* – were, of course, complete strangers, and as such he felt relaxed about retelling the story of the farmhouse, his role in providing humanitarian assistance to civilians while under constant bombardment from Nazi artillery. He took a perverse pleasure in describing the appearance of Kessler, the archetypal rabid Nazi, but watched in vain for any flicker of discomfort or embarrassment from the two policemen. They were either in denial or maybe it was just possible that, in the past, they'd been "good" Germans.

But he had no reason or desire to give them the benefit of the doubt. As far as he was concerned, they owed their jobs and their lives and their freedom in a western democratic society to people like him, yet here they were giving him a hard time, *ungrateful bastards!* He had every reason to help them bring Kessler to justice, not only for crimes he'd committed in the present, but also for those of the past. Yet he could do no more than he'd already done.

He sat on the bed and waited. Goldschmidt's view was that there was no case to answer and since they had either to charge him or release him, he would be out by the end of the day. He guessed it was around 3 p.m. but he couldn't be sure as he had no watch; it had been taken along with his belt and his wallet, a fountain pen and some loose change.

He thought of Petra, how he'd shut her out of his life and as a consequence put her own in danger, and he shuddered. She at least had been brave enough to confront the inevitable and if any good had come out of this ghastly business, it was

130

that she could now go on to live a normal life. He wanted to see her and say how desperately sorry he was, but dismissed the idea. It was pointless and counter-productive.

And he thought of Kessler. Where was he? Who was he? What had turned him into the monster he'd seen in the film and the monster he continued to be to this day? Not for the first time, he wondered why this guy had stumbled into Alfredo Girardi's farmhouse that horrendous day in 1944, bloodied and battered, screaming for murder, hell bent on killing everything he could. His performance in the film provided a clue, but it wasn't enough.

Why hadn't he pulled the trigger in the apartment when he had the chance? He'd casually despatched four people already so another would make no difference. He'd been cornered by the enemy and chosen not to fight his way out. Why? Because he was confident that later, he could effect an escape, or because he was genuinely ready to give up? Neither made any sense, especially not the latter. Kessler was and always had been a fanatic and would have relished the chance to kill a few more of the enemy even if it meant him going down too. The Makarov was fully loaded, apparently, his victim was on the floor, stunned, blinded and helpless. It was point blank, yet…?

He shuddered again, this time at his own mortality, yet in his head he'd died so many times he was beginning to think nothing of it. He took every day one at a time. He had no plans for the future; every day was just another in which he could think about and relive the past, neither a fresh start nor a step towards a new goal. Petra had shown him that he had to take a step in a new direction or else the past would eventually consume him. A rattle of keys broke his concentration and the door swung open. It was a uniformed *Polizei*, one he had hadn't seen before.

"You are free to go," he said curtly and turned back into the corridor. Harry followed him meekly to the front desk where he retrieved his belongings from a wooden box. They included the white envelope he'd picked up in the office and he realised he hadn't opened it yet. He signed a piece of paper and, without a further word, stepped out into another warm Berlin afternoon.

He slung his jacket over his shoulder and watched the people of West Berlin walking in the sunshine: women pushing prams, men in suits carrying briefcases, van drivers unloading supplies, all going about their daily business. He watched the cars and the trams and the taxis carrying their passengers on their journey to somewhere, every one on their way to a predetermined destination, each of them, presumably, having some expectation of what they might find when they got there. All moving forward, none looking back.

He ripped open the envelope and pulled out a letter that bore a fancy letterhead in fine script: Rowland, Jarvis & Stroud, Family Solicitors. He scanned the text and although it told him something he'd been expecting for years, he felt a wave of sadness. He tilted his face to the sun and felt its warmth. It lifted his spirits and cleared his mind, making way for new thoughts. This was the final spur. He would move forward, not back, but not from here. He needed to start again from a different place and he knew exactly where that was.

CHAPTER 15

The weather in Coventry was much cooler than West Berlin, low clouds casting gloom over the crematorium, and spots of rain threatening to dampen an already sombre occasion.

When he'd read the letter, Harry had thought twice about coming back, but during the telephone conversation Arthur Rowland had left him in no doubt he had a duty and it was the least he could do. Harry had been mildly irritated by the rebuke from his father's solicitor but concluded his mother would have wished him to be there and in any event, it had provided him with an opportunity to take some time to think through his plans and defer any arguments with Webb over his future. Rowland had insisted that, as the last surviving member of the family, Harry should be briefed on the contents of Reg's will, without actually revealing whether or not he was a beneficiary or indeed whether there was anything left in the estate of any value. Harry had never considered what would happen in the event of Reg's death. He had no perspective on his own future. But even now he harboured no illusions that his father's estate amounted to much, especially not after twenty years living off an army pension, the last thirteen in an expensive nursing home.

There had been no church service; Reg had never been a religious man and nor was Harry, and Rowland had kindly made what few arrangements were necessary to deal with Reg's body and give him a respectful send-off.

Harry, Rowland and Reg's friend Eric, medals on show, regimental beret in place, standing as straight and rigid as his withered body would allow, listened to the resident vicar saying a few stock words about the afterlife and then, to the accompaniment of mournful music, they watched as the casket, lying unadorned on the plinth, was slowly enveloped by red velvet curtains. Harry noticed Eric's crisp salute and felt a wave of remorse that he'd not made a greater effort to see his father in his final years or tried to mend bridges. But then emotion and sentimentality had been strangers to him for a long time and had never featured in his father's life.

On the way out, Harry shook hands with the vicar and Eric and watched the old soldier hobble off down the driveway to the bus stop where he'd catch a bus back to the veterans' home. A return journey for Eric this time; both would be wondering how many more of those there'd be.

"Thank you for all you've done, Arthur. I appreciate it."

"All part of the service, young man." Harry guessed Arthur was around seventy but old enough, on a day like today, to be feeling his age. "How long before you have to be back in Berlin?"

"They gave me a week although to be honest, there's nothing much for me to do here." Harry knew it was unusual for the department to grant as much as a week in circumstances such as this. More likely, Webb had already decided on a period of suspension while he worked out what to do with him and Reg's death had been a useful excuse. "Can I buy you some lunch?"

"Thank you but no. I need to get back to the office. Would you be able to pop by tomorrow, say about ten, and we can go through the paperwork?"

"Yes, of course."

"Can I drop you somewhere?"

"No, thanks, Arthur. I could do with a walk."

They shook hands and Rowland headed off to the car park. He climbed into a claret-coloured Bristol and waved as it trundled down the driveway. Harry looked up at the crematorium chimneys, expecting to see wisps of smoke, but there were none. He felt a few drops of rain and immediately his leg began to ache. He pulled up his coat collar and put his hands in his pockets. Maybe a walk was not such a good idea after all.

***

He'd checked into his accommodation at The Red Lion Inn the previous night but had arrived too late for dinner.

"Chef goes off at eight thirty, but I can do you a cheese sandwich and a packet of crisps?" The buxom landlady Veronica had made no attempt to make it sound appealing so he had no expectations and it was just as well. A thin slab of Kraft processed cheese between two slices of soggy white bread slathered with margarine made him yearn for the Ostenkeller or even the Kronestube but he was hungry and didn't complain. Compensation came in the form of two pints of Everards ale and the pretty young waitress in tight trousers and a low-cut blouse who brought him the curled-up sandwich, garnished with a single leaf of limp lettuce and a segment of orange tomato.

"Cook, more like," she'd sniffed. "Fat old bastard. Ex-army catering corps. Does bangers and mash and fish and chips and that's about it."

"Sounds wonderful to me," he'd replied and just to provoke a reaction "as an ex-army type".

"Ooh, you don't look like him, that's for sure," she'd said. He'd spotted the flirtatious tone immediately and any lingering doubt had been dispelled when she'd leaned over his table and given him an eyeful. "Staying here, are you?"

"Yes, just for a couple of nights, then off back to Berlin."

"What? Germany?" It would have sounded exotic to most people around here. "Ooh, I bet that's exciting," she'd said, swaying like a fashion model and touching a hand to the back of her beehive.

"Not really, just a desk job. But someone's got to do it."

"I'd love to go to Berlin," she'd gushed. "Anywhere other than this dump. Maybe you could show me round?" They'd been interrupted by a shout from the bar.

"Mandy!"

"Strewth!" Mandy had raised her eyebrows, shrugged and trotted off. "Yes, Mum."

Mum? He'd been letting his mind run away. Regrettably he'd had to concede that inviting the landlady's daughter into his room was crossing a line, however keen he might imagine her to be. He'd swiftly decided Veronica was not one to be trifled with and Mandy, therefore, definitely off limits. But he felt an urge he hadn't experienced in a while and the indecent thoughts gave him a frisson of pleasure.

He got back to The Red Lion at four, having had lunch in a greasy spoon café full of leather-clad bikers and then taken a walk in the park, but the rain had started in earnest and he spent the rest of the afternoon reading in his room. He came down for dinner at six thirty and was delighted to find Mandy behind the bar.

"What can I get you, soldier?" she said with a big smile, thrusting her uplifted pointy breasts in the direction of his eye line.

"Pint of Everards please, Mandy, and can I order the fish and chips?"

"Course you can." She winked at him and he smiled sheepishly. "Brian!" she hollered over her shoulder while pulling his pint. "Fish and chips!" And then, as an afterthought for her customer: "Do you want peas with that, darlin'?"

"Yes please."

"Peas an' all!" she shouted and then quietly, "I'll put it on your bill, shall I?" She winked again.

***

The fish was fresh from the freezer, shaped like a small brick and tasted of cotton wool wrapped in a greasy brown overcoat. The chips were soggy and cold in the middle and the peas, fresh out of the tin. He doused the lot with ketchup and washed it down with three pints of Everards. One of the dishes he'd craved the most while perched on a bar stool in West Berlin, bemoaning the lack of "proper" food, had been a bitter disappointment. Either his memory had played cruel tricks or he'd just been unlucky in his choice of hostelry. It didn't matter. He'd check out tomorrow, go and see

Rowland and get on the next train to London. He'd be back in Berlin by Friday and he could make plans.

**

A secretary showed him in.

"Good morning, young man." Rowland got to his feet and proffered a hand, peering over the top of his glasses.

"Morning, Arthur." Harry laid down his small suitcase and overcoat.

"Are you heading back then?"

"Yes. Provided there's nothing else you need me for. I've checked out of the inn and was hoping to get the two o'clock to London."

"Yes, quite. Won't take long, just a signature or two so I can get probate underway, then it should be three or four weeks before I can distribute the estate." Rowland lifted a file from a stack and placed it in front of him. "Your father was not a wealthy man," he opined and Harry shrugged.

"I don't doubt it, Arthur."

"You may recall we sold the house back in fifty-one. Needed cash to fund the home." Harry didn't recall, but then why should he? He hadn't been consulted, and even if he had he wouldn't have raised any objection; it was none of his business. "It was sold for just over nine thousand pounds. Of course, his living expenses exceeded his pension so that pot of money reduced over time. But your father was also fairly active in stocks and shares." Harry frowned in surprise. Reg had never said anything to him, but then why would he? They barely knew each other. "A little here and a little there, starting just after the war. He built up a tidy little portfolio, mostly blue chip, reinvested the dividends and at current values we're looking at around twelve thousand after fees and commission."

"Wow," said Harry, genuinely surprised. *The dark horse.*

"I estimate that after death duties we are looking at a net value for the estate of around fifteen thousand."

Harry nodded his understanding but suddenly felt compelled to ask. "And who are the beneficiaries?"

Rowland looked up as if startled and removed his glasses.

"Why, you are, my boy. You are the sole beneficiary."

"Oh, my goodness." He did some mental arithmetic. *That's about four years' salary!*

"What did you think? Do you think I'd have dragged you out here otherwise?"

"I didn't think. I suppose I imagined he might have left it to the Veterans' Association or the Masons or something like that."

"He was very proud of you, Harry. He told me so, on many an occasion." Harry's heart sank. His father had been proud of him? Reg had never said and he never knew. Reg had concealed his true feelings behind a façade of restrained belligerence, the innate disciplinarian in him precluding the demonstration of sensitivity towards his family, forbidding any show of weakness. But how he felt and how he behaved were two different things. Harry could empathise with that. Maybe they were not so different after all? He felt himself welling up then stifled it quickly; his father would have gone berserk. He struggled to find the right words.

"Right. Okay. Thanks, Arthur. Oh, by the way," said Harry, suddenly remembering an important detail. "I've moved apartments." He retrieved a slip of paper from inside his jacket. "Here's the new address."

***

He watched the English countryside flash by through the train window, but he didn't see it. He was far too preoccupied with his own thoughts: the surprise revelation of Reg's will, memories of childhood tinged with guilt for what he had or hadn't done, had or hadn't become, opportunities squandered, deferred or postponed until ultimately lost. Memories of his parents, young people themselves once, living through the most difficult of times, raising their son

138

the best they could. Memories of birthdays and Christmases, hardly celebrated, and his father refusing to take him out on Bonfire Night. Memories of being eight, saving up his pocket money for Guy Fawkes and bringing home a small box of fireworks, wanting to set them off in the back yard, his father shouting at him, and throwing the box in a bucket of water and him crying and screaming *"I hate you!"* and his father slapping him. His father disappearing upstairs on Guy Fawkes Night and his mother looking mournful – *"Your dad doesn't like the noise"* – but the following year going looking for him and finding him, curled up under the bed, sobbing and shaking as the rockets, bangers and jumping jacks went off in the street outside. Memories of presenting himself in uniform for the first time; his father shaking his hand, his mother weeping – *"Control yourself, Kathleen"* – and the relief he felt at finally getting away and the shame he was made to feel getting back from Dunkirk – *"We didn't have the luxury of retreat"*. Memories of his mother's funeral, his father stiff and silent, the suppressed rage and fear threatening to blow at any minute. *Where did our lives go?*

Whatever was done was done. He was looking to the future now and although that involved revisiting the past one last time, his father had made sure his son was equipped for the journey.

CHAPTER 16

The troika stared down at him, foreboding as ever, yet Harry felt neither intimidation nor nervousness, just a quiet confidence about the way forward and a sublime certainty of purpose.

"Now look here, Male," blustered Webb, "I think we've all learned a lot from this caper." *Caper?* "Time to let sleeping dogs lie, hoist the mainsail and set course for new horizons, don't you think?"

"Yes, sir."

"You're a good operative, Male," he blundered on. "Even if you have made your fair share of mistakes, you're not entirely to blame."

"Thank you, sir."

"I told the powers that be I wasn't prepared to lose you. I can tell you they were after a scalp. To show an example to the rest, you understand."

"Commander Laughton, sir?" Harry ventured.

"Yes, well, him too, poor chap. Mind you, he was only two years off retirement so he gets his pension early and it won't get in the way of his gong. Landed on his feet, lucky devil." The Churchillian bulldog expression said it all: envy. "No," he boomed, suddenly brightening. "I said the department could ill afford to lose someone like you, so I went in to bat and hit them for six." He sat back, satisfied with himself and his analogy.

"Thank you, sir. Any news on finding Kessler?"

"Police matter" – he waved a hand dismissively – "best left to them I think."

"And the informer?"

"Drawn a blank, but he's out there somewhere and he'll slip up one day. Between you and me, Male" – he leaned forward conspiratorially – "I'd hazard a guess the suits are looking in the wrong place."

"Really? I hadn't thought of that, sir."

140

"You mark my words. There's a chance this goes all the way to the top." *All he needs is the cigar.* "Never mind. Let's get on with the job. Is there anything you'd like to say?"

"Yes, sir." Harry pulled a brown envelope out of his pocket and slid it across the desk. Webb frowned.

"What's this?"

"My resignation, sir."

"Your what?" Webb fumbled with the envelope and ripped out the paper, scanning it quickly. "What's the meaning of this?" he barked, the colour spreading rapidly from his neck to his face.

"I think you'll find it's self-explanatory, sir."

***

There were no goodbyes, no well-wishers, no leaving party and no speeches, just a surrender of his ID and an escort off the premises. He could stay in the apartment for the duration of his notice period and within the week he should expect a visitation from the suits bearing documents he'd be required to sign under pain of immediate internment. He'd be assigned a liaison officer through whom all communications between him and the department in the next four weeks would be channelled and to whom he would hand over the keys to the apartment on the appointed day. Thereafter and until the end of his natural life, he remained bound by the provisions of the Official Secrets Act, any transgressions of which would be dealt with in the harshest possible way. *HMG thanks you for your service to your country and wishes you well in your chosen career, if you're able to find one. We'll be watching you.*

***

Harry had no difficulty spotting the suit. He was sitting at the opposite end of the island bar with a half-glass of orange juice, the grey jacket, shirt and tie together with the omnipresent fedora, standard attire.

The Ostenkeller was busy and vibrant, packed with off-duty workers celebrating the start of the weekend, waited on by dirndl-clad maidens swooping from table to table balancing overloaded trays of glasses above their heads. He moved his head to catch a glimpse of the suit partially concealed behind two voluble customers and watched with amusement as, to his evident surprise, a waitress deposited a stein of beer in front of him. He made to protest but she pointed across the bar to Harry and Harry raised his glass. *Prost!*

They hadn't warned him he'd be followed because they didn't need to; it was a given. He found it tedious although probably not as tedious as the suit doing the following. It had been going on since he left the department three weeks ago, during which time he'd been busy organising his affairs, finalising his plans and preparing for departure. He had precious few belongings and owned none of the furniture in the apartment so there was not much to do other than thin out his already sparse wardrobe and go shopping for new – a novel experience he found curiously enjoyable. The suit had kept a discreet distance although not discreet enough to avoid detection, which was probably his intention.

They'd made him surrender his service revolver. The Enfield was an antique, unreliable, had little value and was impossible to take with him, so he hadn't protested. He'd been to the bank and arranged to close his account, withdrawing most of it in traveller's cheques together with a substantial wad of foreign currency.

He'd called Arthur to explain his change of circumstances and that he'd be at his new address for only a short time as he was leaving Berlin.

"Holiday?" Rowland had asked.

"Not quite," he'd said. "I'm going to revisit an old haunt."

"Well, call me when you get a chance, so I know where to contact you." They agreed the proceeds from the liquidation of his father's estate would be held in Harry's client account at Rowland, Jarvis & Stroud pending further instruction.

He planned to leave Berlin the day after his notice expired and although he knew exactly where he was going, he had no idea how long he'd be there and no expectations of returning; that part of his life was over and the last ties he had with it would be cut next week.

The beer slipped down effortlessly and with barely a nod and a wink it was instantly replaced. He was reminded of the old days in a crowded pub at home, desperately waving a ten-bob note in the air, trying to attract someone's attention before he died of thirst, and he marvelled at German efficiency. *How the hell did we win the war?* He'd miss that.

The aroma of tobacco filled the room. It pricked and taunted his senses, but he hadn't had a cigarette since he'd got back to Berlin and he was resolute. Furthermore, his taste buds had enjoyed a renaissance and he revelled in a sudden appetite for food he didn't know he'd lost.

The wiener schnitzel arrived and he tucked in, waving his fork at the suit, who remained impressively inscrutable despite the provocation. *Guten Appetit!*

CHAPTER 17

Colonel Lance Travers liked Berlin. Unlike his compatriot at the DIPD, the fifty-year-old military attaché to the British Embassy liked the food, the beer, the bars and the restaurants. He also liked the nightclubs, the art galleries, the museums, the parks and the architecture, at least that which had survived destruction in 1945.

He liked his three-storey government residence with private garden in the affluent suburb of Charlottenburg and his chauffeur-driven Mercedes-Benz. He liked a diplomatic status that provided him with four live-in staff: personal assistant Caroline; French chef Gaston; Gertrud, his German housekeeper; and Bogdan, his Polish gardener.

He liked entertaining the ambassador, friends and foreign dignitaries at home along with his socialite wife, Antonia, eldest daughter of Lord and Lady Bascombe, and when they weren't being ferried to an exclusive restaurant or the opera he enjoyed playing his extensive collection of classical music on his Grundig high fidelity stereophonic radiogram.

He loved his teenage children, George and Annabel, going for walks in the park with them and their German shepherd, Lilli, closely but discreetly shadowed by their personal security escorts, Trevor and Martin.

But he especially liked being at the epicentre of world affairs: the stand-off between four nuclear powers, who, like pumped-up boxers standing nose to nose in the biggest arena, traded insults, threats, abuse and relentless provocation in preparation for staging the biggest event in world history. World War Three would surely start where World War Two had ended, here in Berlin, the final frontier. Best of all, as the ambassador's representative on the Joint Intelligence Committee, he was at the cutting edge of international diplomacy and privy to all intelligence and counter-intelligence matters.

He'd had a routine and superficially constructive meeting that morning with his opposite numbers from the French and US Embassies at which they'd exchanged titbits of useless intelligence. The tripartite occupiers of West Berlin were always keen to show off their intelligence prowess and demonstrate their unwavering commitment to the joint struggle against a common enemy, but that didn't extend to sharing sensitive information because anything remotely useful they always kept to themselves.

So the diplomats played out their monthly charade for an hour or two and then, at the invitation of Monsieur Gaillard, whose turn it was, retired to lunch at *Le Papillon*, a three-Michelin-starred restaurant in the French zone. Five courses, two bottles of vintage claret and three cognacs later, the American made his excuses and left his European cousins to spend the afternoon at the sauna in the basement of the Kolonial Kavalier Klub.

Alone in the sauna, Gaillard and Travers were able to speak freely about the vulgar and uncultured American and go on to exchange "classified" information they'd withheld from their supposedly unreliable opposite number.

Gaillard could not resist having a dig. "I understand you lost Bergmann before you even got started."

Travers didn't care to take lessons from the French. They had never thanked the British properly for saving their backsides. *Twice!* And anyway, it wasn't his department.

"Bloody spooks. Should have kept him in jail, put the thumbscrews on him instead of moving him around their little network of burrows and hidey holes."

Later, when the pompous frog Gaillard had left, the philistine rosbif retired to his private dressing cubicle and Colonel Travers was finally free to indulge in the thing he'd been looking forward to most: sitting naked on the wooden bench with his back against the wall, legs akimbo, being fellated by Kristof, the eighteen-year-old pool attendant. It would have been the highlight of his day had they not been so rudely interrupted.

The door to the cubicle opened with a click, the unexpected sound breaking Travers' enrapt concentration and causing him to open his eyes and glare at Kristof. *Lock the door in future, you stupid bitch!* Kristof got to his feet, wiped the back of a hand across his mouth and, as he left, took a handful of notes from the tall stranger standing by the open door, naked but for the white towel around his waist. Travers sat up, confused and annoyed and suddenly conscious of his own nakedness.

"Who the devil are you?"

The stranger closed and bolted the door behind him and walked over to the bench, reaching behind his back to extract a pistol tucked into the towel. He pointed it at Travers' head.

"I am your humble servant, Colonel. You are my master."

It took a while for Travers to make the connection. The guy was no member of his household nor was he employed at the embassy, so 'servant' meant nothing. But "master"? Through an intermediary, he handled three operatives. To each he was known uniquely as "overlord", "sovereign" or… "master".

"Kessler?" he hissed. Travers had never seen the guy before. Not in the flesh. He'd seen an old picture and knew his name and that, through his intermediary, he was the ultimate recipient of assignments passed to the newspaper kiosk owner in Kurfürstendamm and, somehow, the job got done.

"What the hell are you doing here?" he snapped, attempting to exert his authority while fully aware that he was, at this particular moment, powerless and extremely vulnerable. "We can't be seen together."

"I want a name and a location."

"Who, what? What do you mean?"

"Bergmann's handler."

"What about him?"

"I want to know his name and where he is. We have unfinished business." The tone of Kessler's voice said it all, leaving a chill despite the heat.

146

Travers thought for a moment, trying to quell the panic he could feel building inside. He had a gun pointed at his head by a trained and highly experienced assassin, someone who had no compunction about murder. He'd eliminated Bergmann successfully but he'd wasted six others, including three cops. That made him a fucking psychopath and that made him unpredictable. He took a chance.

"You did a good job, my friend. You know you're held in high regard." He thought he sensed the gun hand relax a little and although it may only have been his imagination he clung on to it. "You did extremely well to complete the assignment so swiftly and the target got what he deserved, but I confess our superiors are a little perturbed about the, er, collateral damage. A bit too messy for their liking," he ventured. The wrist holding the gun tightened at the implied criticism and Travers' heart skipped.

"They were in the way. It was necessary."

Travers breathed again. "Yes, I'm sure it was. But the job's done now. Mission accomplished!" Travers managed a weak smile. "There's nothing to be gained by going after a low-ranking civil servant. It'll just cause us all a load more aggro."

"Name and location."

Travers wasn't making it up. The incident had been turned from a political assassination into a routine murder investigation, and that was far preferable. The target had been silenced; that was all that was required. Pursuing and murdering another incidental player would be counter-productive, probably lead to reprisals and make them think again about using the film. They'd discussed the entire operation in the JIC and he knew the film was of less importance than Bergmann himself. He took another chance.

"You're in the film, you know. A starring role." He saw Kessler blink and he felt further emboldened.

"What film? What nonsense is this?"

"Bergmann brought with him a film, taken in '44. Nazis shooting a load of Italian civilians. Engel was in charge. You

147

were there too, doing your bit for the Fatherland." Kessler's eyes strayed a fraction. Travers was feeling more confident now. "They won't use it. They've got skeletons of their own we already know about, but if you waste another one of their flunkeys, they might think twice. Out of spite." He watched Kessler. Remembering 1944, perhaps? Considering the options? It lasted only a second.

"Name and location."

Travers sighed. "Who is this guy anyway?"

"It's personal."

Personal? Travers shook his head. Kessler had lost it.

"Look, Kessler —" he started, but didn't finish.

Kessler grabbed a handful of hair and pulled the naked, shrieking Travers off the bench and onto the tiled floor. He lifted him onto his knees and held his face down on the tiles with his buttocks in the air and his legs spread wide.

"You will find out and you will tell me. You are a British traitor. You have no choice." He pressed the muzzle of the Beretta against Travers' anus and prodded it. "And in case you are not sure, that is the gun."

"Don't be a fool. If you do this, you have no country left." The words were strained and distorted, squeezed out of one side of his compressed mouth. "They'll come after you and kill you."

"I am already dead. But you will also be dead and then I will go to your house and I will torture and murder your family, chop up their bodies and flush the pieces down the toilet."

Travers wasted no more time. "Harry Male."

"Repeat!"

"Harry Male, he's in a civilian role but technically he's a major."

"Where is he now?"

"I have no idea. Even I don't know where these guys live. All I know is he moved out of his apartment after you redecorated it with blood and bullets."

148

"Your house will look the same if you don't do as I say. I want to know where he is!" he shouted, increasing the pressure on Travers' neck and poking the gun even harder.

Travers whimpered. "I don't know. I'll find out."

"You will find out and send me a message by the usual means. You have two days!"

"Okay. Okay!"

Kessler removed the gun from Travers' anus and pressed it against his jaw instead. Using his free hand, he unfastened his own towel and let it drop.

"What are you doing?" asked Travers, suddenly alarmed, but the question was stifled as Kessler clasped his free hand over Travers' mouth and pulled back his head, pressing himself against his buttocks. Travers moaned in fear and a sense of foreboding.

"That is not my gun. So, in case you have any doubt. This is what I will do to your wife and children, before I kill them." He thrust steadily and Travers' muted cries turned into a rhythm of muted screams that continued for three whole minutes.

***

Kessler had watched the apartment on and off for two weeks. The day after the kill, he'd seen a young woman assisted by a tall, bearded young man with spectacles and sandals remove several boxes and load them into a small van. But he'd had limited time to conduct surveillance between shifts at the Regent and was also faced with two difficulties: the apartment was so close to the Wall there was no convenient vantage point, and he had to contend with the continuous presence of the police, to whom he was now public enemy number one.

According to the posters he'd seen, the man they were looking for was aged between forty and forty-five, one metre ninety in height with dark brown hair and athletic build and had been wearing a leather bomber jacket over a cotton button-down shirt, khaki trousers with leg pockets and stout boots. The man known as Schneider was five to ten years older, thirty centimetres shorter due to his stoop and walked with a pronounced limp, had grey/blonde hair and was only ever seen in a threadbare tweed jacket, creased black trousers and scuffed sandshoes. Even so, the man known as Schneider would be conspicuous in his own right if seen regularly passing a crime scene.

He'd made the assumption the target would have moved out of the apartment and although he'd thought twice about blowing his cover with Travers, the fact was, his life was over and there was no going back. They could send whomever they wanted; they would fail. He alone would succeed and he didn't care who he took down with him in the process.

He finished his shift each day and picked up the paper. There was no news from the East or anywhere else. He concluded he would have to pay a visit to the Travers residence after all and it frustrated him. He had no qualms about carrying out his threat; it was just that he couldn't understand why Travers would not take the easy course and give him the information. He had nothing to lose by complying, everything to lose by not.

On the third day, Rudi engaged him in conversation and the envelope appeared inside his paper. He now had an address as well as a name. But there was more. Major Harry Male had resigned his position and would be required to leave the apartment by the end of the week. It meant the plan had to be brought forward. Soon Kessler, along with Schneider and Radler would disappear forever. But first, he had business to conclude at the Regent.

***

The man known as Schneider was able to watch the main entrance of Major Harry Male's new apartment from a coffee shop on the opposite side of the street but as yet there had been no sighting of the target. He checked his watch. It was almost time to leave for the Regent. He couldn't possibly be late for his final shift and, for the first time ever, it would be foreshortened.

The timing worked quite well. By the time he got back to Radler's apartment early the next morning, collected his weapon, some tools and his few belongings and returned here it would be around eight a.m. He and the target, once suitably restrained, could spend a couple of hours discussing old times, during which he would conduct a range of minor medical procedures, including one or two amputations and when either he got bored or the target was no longer responding satisfactorily, he would terminate the meeting and take his leave. But he wanted to be sure – sure he had the right place and the right man, because by the time he returned, he would have burned bridges and it would make his job all the harder. He had already considered the possibility Travers may have misled him and if that were the case, retribution would be swift. Travers was a coward but he was no fool; the target meant nothing to him and he should be in no doubt about Kessler's sincerity and his ability to carry out the threat. He would do anything to avert danger to himself and his family now he'd experienced first-hand what would follow if he didn't comply.

Kessler allowed himself a wry smile. He'd known many queers in his time, most of them of rank, and he hated them all. Perverts; he'd have had them all shot. But the stimulation and pleasure he'd got with Travers was born out of something else. It was the humiliation, the domination and the violent oppression that turned him on, his uncompromising show of omnipotence and unassailability, the ultimate aphrodisiac.

Movement across the road caught his eye. It was him: casual clothes, back from a night out somewhere, putting a key in the lock and entering the apartment building. He waited and watched and counted the steps in his head. The lights would go on in two minutes on the third floor. It took

151

fifteen seconds longer, but a figure appeared at the window. The panes were unlocked and pushed open and the inside shutters closed to leave a vertical sliver of light. *See you at eight, Major Male.*

***

The man known as Schneider resumed his station at nine thirty, hunched over the steaming, foaming trough, scrubbing at the soiled pans and baking trays in between loading and unloading the industrial dishwasher. The headcount in the basement would reduce as dinner service ran down until by 1 a.m. only he, Ziegler the queer and the new arrival Dulka, a filthy Slav, were on duty.

"Quasi" brushed off the usual jibes from his work colleagues as they reached the end of their shifts. They were always worse in the evening; the morons were in high spirits and looking forward to getting off and having a couple of beers and his butt was the obvious one to kick. He was sorry he couldn't say goodbye to them all, but maybe by tomorrow they'd learn and for a short while afterwards at least reflect on their shortcomings. On the bright side and barring any unforeseen events, he would be able to bid farewell to Müller and Fuchs, who would arrive at 4 a.m. in order to prepare for and supervise the morning deliveries. It was cutting it a bit fine but it was doable.

Once the last load had been sorted, stacked and sent back upstairs to the kitchen, Schneider filled his bucket with hot water, splashed in some detergent and pungent disinfectant and started mopping the floor. Ziegler and Dulka left him to it as usual, retiring to the staffroom for a cigarette.

He worked methodically, going over the entire area twice, and it took him an hour to finish. He emptied the dirty water down the drain and wiped down the stainless-steel surfaces before heading into the staffroom to tidy up. Ziegler and Dulka were nowhere to be seen but the stink of tobacco smoke lingered and he masked it by spraying air freshener around the room. He swept the floor, rearranged the chairs and emptied the ashtrays then hobbled off towards the staff toilets.

Inside, he heard a rhythmic grunting from one of the cubicles and stood by the door, listening; the queer had obviously made a new conquest with the Slav, or maybe it was the other way round? He dropped to the floor and peered through the fifteen-centimetre gap under the door. Two pairs of shoes, one behind the other, pointing the same way towards the back wall, trousers and underwear round the ankles. He pondered leaving them to it, but they were annoying him and he had nothing better to do for a while. He decided he was due a bonus.

He took a step back then launched himself at the cubicle door. The flimsy catch broke easily and the door flew inwards, smacking into Ziegler's backside and ramming him and the conjoined Dulka against the back wall where they uncoupled and collapsed over the toilet pan in a tangled heap.

The Slav was the first to try to recover but Kessler grabbed a handful of hair and thrust him face-first against the wall, breaking his nose and leaving a bloody smear on the tiles as he crumpled and fell on top of Ziegler. The queer started screaming, unable to move, pinned down by the Slav, squashed in the corner between the toilet pan and the cubicle wall. Kessler hauled the Slav off him and flung him out into the wash area, then stepped back in and stomped on Ziegler's genitals. The queer screamed again, face contorted in agony. He leaned over and grabbed the queer's tunic at the throat, lifted his head up and punched him once in the forehead. He fell back, unconscious.

Kessler gathered his breath. The Slav was still semi-conscious so he gripped his shirt collar and dragged him backwards, trousers still around his ankles, out of the washroom and across the floor to the walk-in freezer where he released his grip, kicked him in the ribs for good measure and opened the door. He threw him onto the floor of the

153

freezer then went back for Ziegler. He was back in thirty seconds, by which time Dulka was already on his knees trying to get out, so he kicked him in the head and he toppled back inside.

He dragged the groaning queer inside the freezer and threw him on top of the Slav like a sack of potatoes, then snapped off the inside door handle, slammed the door shut and turned the temperature dial to blast-freeze. They would be solid within forty minutes. Kessler looked at the trail of bloodstains on the floor that stretched from the washroom and considered cleaning them up, but decided it wasn't worth the effort. No one would have time to notice.

He looked at his watch again: three forty-five. Müller and Fuchs would be here soon. He returned to his wash trough and filled it with steaming water and detergent. He put on his elbow-length rubber gloves and waited. Within minutes he heard chatter from the corridor: Müller and Fuchs, bellowing with laughter about something, swaggering into the wash area, looking for sport. He buried both hands in the water up to the elbow and Müller slapped him on the head as he walked by.

"Morning, retard."

Fuchs looked around. "Where's the other two?"

"I believe they are locked in the freezer, Herr Fuchs."

The two men looked at each other in surprise, as if trying to see the joke, then back at the hunchback stooped over the trough. Quasi never uttered more than the odd grunt, so to hear him articulate an entire sentence was a novelty indeed. They were further surprised when the retard removed his hands from the water and turned to face them, making eye contact for the first time ever. And their surprise turned first to astonishment then alarm as the freak straightened his back and stood to his full height, seeming to tower over them. So gripped were they by the transformation, they failed to notice the kitchen knives in his hands, or resist as they watched him slide one into each of their bodies, just below the ribcage.

154

Kessler watched each face contort in confusion and terror as reality took hold and then used all his weight to push forward, pinning each of them against the high-sided dishwasher. Müller let out a scream of horror and Fuchs grabbed the knife hand in desperation but Kessler was strong and proceeded to work both knives up and down until both men were screaming and their bodies convulsing, their heads bobbing up and down like they were on springs. Then after only a few seconds, Müller went limp and he let him fall to the floor. But Fuchs was still resisting, so he twisted him around until he was facing the trough, reached down and grabbed both feet and tipped him in. Fuchs' face came to the surface, arms flailing, knife still embedded to the hilt as the water and foam turned red; Kessler casually held him under until the writhing and splashing stopped.

Kessler removed his rubber apron, and with the muffled sound of desperate wailing and banging coming from the freezer, put on his crumpled jacket and left the Regent for the last time.

***

The man known as Radler didn't bother to tell Frau Brucker he was leaving. He regretted she would find a sizeable sum of money in his apartment but he had taken all he could squash into his rucksack and if he needed more later, there was no shortage of ways in which to get it. It pained him to think another fat ugly Jew might benefit from a windfall and he had considered knocking her up and strangling her, but dismissed it as a self-indulgent distraction and he didn't want to take any unnecessary risks, not now he was so close.

The alarm would have been raised at the Regent for sure and they would be in no doubt as to the identity of the murderer: a deformed hunchback retard with a pronounced limp called Schneider. They knew his address, too, but they'd find it was three kilometres to the north of Radler's apartment and inhabited by an elderly couple called Schmidt.

155

He'd changed into clean clothes because he wanted to look his best: a white shirt, navy cotton drills and black leather bomber jacket. His black leather boots were polished and he wore a dark green Tyrolean hat with an eagle feather in the band.

His rucksack contained all he needed: electric hair clippers, a pair of pliers, a small bolt cutter, a junior hacksaw, surgical scalpel, three metres of electrical flex with a plug on one end, two clamps on the other and a light switch in the middle, a fifteen-centimetre metal spike, a Swiss army knife and some nylon cord. His new Makarov nestled in its holster under his arm.

He had breakfast in the coffee shop and surveyed the entrance to the apartment from a seat by the window. The windows were still open and the shutters still closed on the third floor which meant the target was still in bed. The only person to leave so far had been a woman and her small dog. He checked his watch: 8 a.m. It was time.

He slung his rucksack onto his back and crossed the street. There were six buttons on the panel outside the building – two apartments on each floor, the button second from top bearing the name "Male, H.". He pressed the named button at the bottom.

"*Ja.*"

"Parcel for Stümmer."

The front door clicked open and he made his way swiftly along the hall and up the stairs. At the top, he chose the door to his left, the one facing the front of the building. He reached inside his jacket to retrieve the Makarov and screwed on the silencer he'd taken from the opposite pocket. He had no intention of shooting the target, at least not immediately. First, he had work to do with his set of tools, but he wasn't sure how much initial resistance to expect and the gun was a necessary precaution to ensure he could take control of the situation quickly.

He put his ear to the door but could discern no noise from within the apartment. He tried the doorknob with little expectation, but was surprised to find it turned easily and he braced himself. The door opened silently and he stepped inside, senses taut and alert to the slightest sound or movement. But the apartment was gloomy and the only noise was that of traffic three floors down filtering through the gap in the shutters.

He reached the sitting room, moving silently, gun arm extended, sweeping left and right, past the kitchenette, into a carpeted corridor to an open door: a bedroom with a freshly made bed. He felt a prickle in his neck. He turned and opened the door opposite: empty. He increased his pace, his heart beginning to pound. He kicked open a third door: bathroom, empty. He whirled around and strode back into the sitting room. There were keys on the coffee table on top of a handwritten note.

Arrivederci!

He lowered his weapon. Harry Male had gone.

CHAPTER 18

Harry sat under an umbrella outside the Ristorante Umberto and watched the world go by. The centre of the Piazza Navona teemed with tourists, street traders, artists and performers, encircled by anarchy on wheels: an endless stream of angry cars and weaving scooters hooting and tooting impatiently as they tried to circumnavigate the square, getting nowhere fast.

He took another sip of his Chianti Ruffino and loosened his tie, basking in the warmth of a sunny autumnal afternoon in one of the world's greatest cities. The *linguine alle vongole* had been superb and had dispelled any residual craving he'd had for fish and chips. This was the place to be for food and wine and pretty much everything else, he'd decided.

He was struck by how much had changed in the short time since the war, how quickly life had got back to normal after one of the darkest periods in world history, as if it had never happened. Rome had been liberated a mere eighteen years ago and had escaped much of the destruction heaped upon other capitals. With most of its exquisite architecture still intact, there was little evidence to suggest it had ever been involved. Furthermore, German, British, French and American rubbed shoulders with Italian, enjoyed the peace and took pictures of each other by the Fiumi fountain, preserving fond memories that would stay with them forever. *Eighteen years.*

He hadn't been here before. He hadn't been back to Italy at all since 1944 – since that day. After two weeks in a military hospital, he'd been shipped back home to a desk job to live out the rest of the war from a distance. It hadn't taken long. The Allies had landed in northern France that June, blazing relentlessly south-east while the Russians came from the east, charging west. The army of which he'd been part had eventually broken through Montellano from the south, racing to Rome and beyond, destination Berlin. The Russians had beaten them to it, but by May of the following year, the Third Reich would finally implode.

He resigned his commission in late 1945 and joined the post office, hoping to find stability and peace in civilian life but he was never happy. It was as if he had work left undone, hadn't completed the job. The war had finished prematurely, without consulting him, without allowing him to participate in the dénouement, without him properly seeing the fruits of his labours. But when he looked around here now, he could see in the faces of the people the results of their sacrifices – sacrifices made by him and men like him, many of them gone but hopefully not forgotten.

The people here lived life to the full, brimming with optimism and joy. Much more so than in Berlin, which remained a smouldering cauldron of tension, a ticking time bomb for which no one admitted responsibility or took ownership; no one knew how it had got there and no one knew how to defuse it. In Rome, the war was over; in Berlin, the ashes were still warm and ready to reignite.

He'd read the news reports about the Russian blockade of West Berlin in 1948 and he thought of re-enlisting, but his injuries had never fully healed and it was made clear to him that his days of active service were over. Undeterred, he applied to the Ministry of Defence and in 1952 secured an administrative job in Whitehall. Within five years, he was in Berlin, working for an administrative offshoot of MI6.

And now, he was a civilian again and this time he wasn't looking for a change of career. He was looking for something else. If he were religious he would call it absolution, and without it, there was no future, at least none he could see. Yet there was no one to exonerate him because no one knew and no one could possibly know. He had to find it for himself. He was going back to where it all started.

***

159

The train from Rome to Montellano took almost four hours, snaking its way through the Liri Valley in the shadow of the vast Apennine mountain range that formed the 750-mile backbone of the Italian peninsula. The landscape bore no resemblance to that he remembered, but then he had never travelled north of Montellano and didn't know what to expect. But by the late afternoon the extraordinary sight of the abbey perched on a hilltop above the town hove into view and the train pulled into the ancient town.

Back in '44, he'd experienced no more than a glimpse of the old town and that from a ridge to the north-east, but it had been completely destroyed by the Allied bombing and now revealed itself to be a modern but drab town with street upon street of homogenous, uniformly constructed four-storey apartment blocks.

A handful of cabs waited outside the *stazione* but the afternoon sun was warm and he preferred to walk into town to find a hotel. He removed the jacket of his cream linen suit and tossed it over a shoulder, adjusted his panama and set off along the Viale Dante, clutching his rigid leather suitcase. He hadn't been sure what to expect, but it soon became clear that nothing of any historical interest remained and he felt an irrational sense of guilt that he'd been indirectly associated with the wholesale destruction of a medieval town that had stood for a thousand years.

He checked into the Hotel Abruzzi and was welcomed warmly by the owner, Fabrizio, and his wife, Carla.

"*Signore* is English?" he said with a beaming smile. "*Benvenuti a Montellano.* How long is your stay?"

It was a matter he hadn't given much thought. It rather depended on what he found, if anything. He had no firm plans other than to take each day as it came.

"Two, maybe three days."

"*Prego.* We can recommend a restaurant for you. It is owned by my brother Angelo."

"Of course," said Harry. "Thank you."

160

"*Prego.* Perhaps you wish to visit the abbey? My brother Giuseppe can take you."

"I'll let you know. Is there anywhere I can hire a car?"

"*Certamente.* My cousin Silvio will bring. When would you like?"

"Tomorrow morning."

"I will arrange."

"May I make a telephone call to England?"

"But of course, *signore*."

He spoke to Arthur Rowland, told him where he was and that he would be staying for a couple of days.

"Well, have an enjoyable holiday, young man,' he said. "I'll let you know the minute I have some news."

***

The room was modest and simply furnished, but clean and boasted a private bathroom. That evening at the Ristorante Chimera, he ate spaghetti carbonara with a carafe of the local red wine and was generally fawned over by its corpulent host, Angelo.

"I was a partisan," said Angelo proudly. "It was big mistake joining with the Nazis, but Mussolini was a fool. He pick the wrong side, eh?" He laughed and slapped Harry on the back. There were obviously no hard feelings that the Allies had bombed his town to hell in order to beat the Germans. "I was very happy to kill Nazis." He grinned, but then turned serious. "We have some Germans who come here." He shook his head. "I try to see if I recognise them. There are some things we will not forget."

"Do you know of a village called Santa Cristina De Lago?"

Angelo thought for a moment then nodded. "*Sì.* I think it is about twenty kilometres from here."

"I wondered if it had been destroyed."

"No, is not destroyed. You wish to go there?"

"I was there during the war. Do people still live there?"

161

"*Sì*. I think so. You know some people there?"

"I doubt they would remember." Harry thought twice about continuing but he told himself he had to face up to reality. After all, that was why he had come. "There was a massacre. The SS murdered all the men."

Angelo nodded sombrely and made the sign of the cross. "I think this happened a lot. Many, many people were killed. It is not unusual."

Harry was taken aback by his composure. He hadn't wanted to provoke Angelo into a rant about the Nazis, but he was surprised he seemed so matter of fact, almost sanguine about it. He couldn't imagine such an unspeakable horror like that ever happening in England but perhaps it was different here. What had happened in Santa Cristina De Lago had probably happened elsewhere. The Italians had capitulated as soon as Sicily had fallen. Their army had crumbled and they preferred to surrender to the Allied forces than stick with the Germans, who naturally took reprisals.

"I know who did it," he said absently and his mind suddenly filled with a heady cocktail of thoughts and memories and fears.

"Then you should kill him. Or you tell me and I shall kill him."

Harry smiled inwardly. It sounded naïve, but it was not just a show of bravado on Angelo's part. If Engel or Kessler strolled in here for dinner and they were recognised, they'd never be seen again. Summary justice; perhaps that was the only way? He'd said enough. He didn't want to prolong the conversation.

"I don't know where they are."

"There are many of these people out there," said Angelo, waving a hand at the window, "all over the world. They run and hide, but God will find them and punish them." Harry wished he could share Angelo's optimism, but unlike the Italian, he had no God.

Angelo turned away but he was back within seconds carrying two shot glasses and an unlabelled bottle of clear liquid. The restaurant had been busy earlier but apart from Harry, only two couples remained.

"My best grappa," he announced with pride, pouring a shot into each glass and sitting down facing Harry. "*Salute.*"

"*Salute.*" They knocked back the fiery liquid and Angelo immediately refilled the glasses.

"Why do you come here, Signore Harry?" It was a good question and he didn't really have an answer. "You do not look like a tourist to me. There is nothing to see here but the abbey."

He took a breath; he had never mentioned the place or the name in eighteen years, but the grappa had had an instant effect. "Do you know a village called Solano?"

Angelo's nose twitched as he thought. "No. I do not think I know such a place."

"What about a man by the name of Girardi? Alfredo Girardi?" He watched Angelo's face for a flicker of recognition but there was none. He shook his head and shrugged.

"No. I have heard the name, but it is common in Italy. There are many Girardi. Are you looking for this man?"

"No. I am afraid to say he's dead." Harry knocked back the grappa and Angelo refilled his glass without touching his own. "I did something terrible." The spirit was taking over and he fought its effects, but he was losing the battle, wrestling to conceal a conscience that refused to stay hidden.

"Terrible good, or terrible bad?"

"Both." He looked Angelo in the eyes, a priest to his confession.

"And you think that if you come here, Alfredo Girardi will forgive you?"

"He can't do that."

"Then who can forgive you, Signore Harry?"

CHAPTER 19

"Your car is ready for you, Signore Male," Fabrizio called from the doorway of the dining room as Carla cleared away the last of the breakfast dishes. The freshly baked panini with prosciutto and *formaggio* and black coffee had been a delight and had set him up for the day.

"*Grazie mille,*" said Harry in his best Italian.

"*Prego.*" Carla scuttled off through the kitchen door and Harry wiped his mouth on a napkin.

He'd slept well thanks to the grappa and despite his proximity to the scene of his nightmares, or perhaps because of it, he'd been spared a repeat. He felt more relaxed and confident as each day passed and the awful memories of his time with the Girardis were gradually taking on a new perspective, evolving in a positive way as, little by little, flawed recollections and suppositions were superseded by reality. Increasingly, the Girardis were ceasing to be ghostly figments of his tortured imagination, becoming real people again, real victims caught up in a conflict not of their making.

He stepped into the reception area and Fabrizio led him out into the morning sunshine, holding a car key aloft. His heart sank.

"*Prego, signore.*" Fabrizio beamed, gesturing to the diminutive vehicle parked outside the hotel. It was a white Fiat 500, a Cinquecento as it was known locally. It had red leather upholstery and sported a part-sliding black canvas roof that was already open. Harry cursed himself for not enquiring about or specifying anything bigger, but Fabrizio seemed so pleased with himself he didn't have the heart to say anything.

"*Grazie mille.* How much do I owe you?"

Fabrizio shook his head. "Later, later. I put it on your bill. *Si?*"

"Do you want to see my driving license?"

"No."

"Do you want me to sign anything?" He made a writing impression in the air.

"No." Fabrizio shook his head and handed him the key and a folded Michelin map. *Welcome to Italy!*

"Do you know a place called Solano, Fabrizio? It was a very small village in 1944."

Fabrizio thought for a moment, but the answer was the same. "I do not think so, *signore*. I know of no such place."

Harry thanked him and slid into the driver's seat, the backward opening doors facilitating his entry, and examined the few controls, then turned the key and the twin cylinder engine behind him rattled into life like an angry lawnmower. He slipped it into gear and pulled jerkily out into the quiet street.

Within fifteen minutes he'd got the hang of the gears and left Montellano behind, exploring the countryside with the wind in his hair. He was soon beginning to enjoy the little car. It handled like a go-cart and was perfectly suited to the narrow country lanes. He stopped to consult the map and after a few detours found a sign that sent him on a winding route up the hillside towards his destination. The Cinquecento responded like an eager puppy, its engine singing operatically as it propelled the miniature car and its full-sized occupant up the steep, bendy road.

An hour after he'd left the hotel, he came across the village sign: *Santa Cristina De Lago*. He slowed down, partly from a sudden sense of deference but also from hesitation, a fear that he was intruding. The tarmac gave way to cobbles and the deserted streets narrowed as he steered the Fiat at walking pace towards the village centre. The buildings were old and despite the many bullet holes that peppered the walls of the houses, clearly hadn't suffered the same destructive fate as those in Montellano, but most of the window shutters were closed and there was no one about. The place was eerily quiet and he struggled to recognise anything until the street finally opened out into a piazza dominated, like many such villages, by a large church.

He stopped the car and took in an image as familiar to him as any, but which he'd seen only twice before, once in March 1944 when his brigade had briefly been resident and again, a few weeks ago in a scratchy, black and white horror film. A number of people were moving about the piazza: old women in headscarves hobbling bow-legged with heavy shopping bags, children playing with hoops and ropes and chasing stray cats, dogs lying comatose on the cobblestones or else standing motionless, bored and lethargic. A small number of open carts loaded with fruit, vegetables or flowers were on display, the vendors' horses still attached, waiting patiently alongside, chewing hay, their owners haggling and gesticulating with customers. A fountain stood in the centre, topped with a statue of Santa Cristina herself, harp in the crook of one arm, the other holding a tilted urn from which fresh water tumbled into the circular base. The women wore black; there were no old men.

He parked the Fiat behind a van, took the keys out of the ignition and put them in his pocket, having no urge to close the canvas roof or lock any doors. He retrieved his panama from the rear seat and stepped out into the square feeling instantly conspicuous in his linen suit, but no one paid him any attention. The sun beat down into the piazza and he reluctantly placed the hat on his head, as if doing so conveyed a lack of respect.

"Buongiorno." An old woman passed him without looking up, taking him by surprise.

He turned swiftly, fumbled to remove his hat and mumbled in return, but she was already gone. He felt like he was intruding in a private place, somewhere he didn't belong and hadn't been invited, but one whose residents had never forgotten how to be civil.

He crossed the piazza, passing in front of the steps that led up to the entrance to the church, doors open and welcoming, forever at the disposal of those who needed succour and sanctuary. He wandered over to the far side of the piazza and found a brass plaque affixed to the wall. He removed his hat and loosely translated the inscription in his head.

This is the place where 143 sons of Santa Cristina were murdered by the Nazis. May all their souls rest in peace.
14th March 1944

Harry gripped his panama, feeding it through his hands as if it were too hot to hold, recalling the images in the film and imagining the sound of gunfire and then turning to look down at the cobbles, expecting to see a river of blood. They were dark and smooth and shiny, all traces of death long since washed away and consigned to history.

"Americano?" The sound startled him, but he was relieved by the distraction. A young woman in her twenties was watching him, leaning her weight on one leg, supporting a small boy on her hip. The child eyed him coldly, lollipop stick protruding from stained lips.

"No. Inglese. Buongiorno."

"Buongiorno. Giornalista?"

"Oh, no. I'm not a journalist. I'm just… er…" Her gaze was unwavering and it unnerved him. "I came here once. Many years ago." He examined her face, wondering if he had seen her before. She would have been six or seven years old. She glanced at the plaque.

"They killed my papà," she said without emotion, "and my two brothers."

"I know. I'm sorry."

The woman shrugged. "Is not your fault."

"I wish we could have stopped it."

"We wish many things."

He felt awkward – the need to explain, but it was too difficult. They had fought their way up the hillside, lost many men along the way and believed at last they were making progress. But then the Germans had come back at

167

them and they'd been driven out, back to where they started, more men lost, no ground gained. They'd retreated and left the men of Santa Cristina to their fate although they could not have known and anyway had no choice.

"We wish the men who did this could be found and punished," she said. "But they are probably enjoying their life somewhere."

The lump that formed instantly in Harry's throat threatened to choke him. He already knew the names of two of those responsible: Engel and Kessler. They were free to do as they wished, Engel to strut about the world stage gorging on the trappings of luxury afforded officials of a Soviet puppet regime and Kessler, to murder anyone the likes of he, Engel or his cronies chose as well as anyone else who got in the way or just took his fancy. He knew who they were and others knew who they were and he was filled with shame that neither he nor his erstwhile superiors had the balls or the morality to speak out. His silence made him an accomplice to the crime, but he knew, sadly, there was nothing to be gained by breaking it. It was a burden he would have to bear. He cleared his throat and changed the subject.

"And who is this?"

The young woman softened and ran a hand through her son's curly hair. "This is Alan."

"Alan?"

"I give him *nome inglese*" – *an English name* – "to remind me that you help us."

Harry felt humbled beyond measure, her gratitude a further twist of the knife in his conscience. Despite the human cost, evil had finally been vanquished – a community destroyed to save a country. Yet she would never know how unworthy he felt; she even had good cause to despise the British and the Americans and the New Zealanders and the Poles as much as the Germans for the terror they'd unleashed on their village. But redemption and justice? They were at the mercy of only those brave enough to offer it.

168

"My name is Harry." He held out a hand. She took it without hesitation and to his surprise, pulled him towards her and kissed his cheek. It was not just a courtesy; it was more than that.

"Adriana."

Harry felt charmed, flustered and broken all at once, but her expression remained neutral. He took a deep breath to clear his head.

"Adriana? Do you know of a village called Solano?"

She shook her head. "There is no place with that name... *Addio*."

Adriana walked off with her son Alan under her arm and Harry watched her go as the church bells chimed eleven.

***

He could only guess which way to go. He spread the map out on the bonnet and ran a finger over it for several minutes searching in vain for the name. The landscape had changed completely and back then, he and his men had stumbled and staggered chaotically down the rugged hillside, not effected an orderly retreat down a winding tarmac road. All he remembered was that it had taken two or three hours dodging snipers and artillery fire before it got dark and they were able to dig in, create some shelter from rocks and stones and hunker down for the night. He tried to rationalise the distance, but it was impossible and if Solano no longer existed, there was no map that would indicate where he wanted to be. After an hour pottering along country lanes between endless vineyards and olive groves, he remained totally disorientated and increasingly despondent, starting to believe the village of Solano was a figment of his imagination.

The Fiat reached the brow of a hill and he stopped. He stood on the seat, poked his head out of the sunroof and scanned the landscape. It all looked so different: green and peaceful and ordered. Nature had repaired the damage

169

wreaked by man. Then, just as he decided to turn the car around, a church steeple caught his eye. It was three or four miles away, but it stood proud on a hillock to the east. He tried to plot a route but there were only two choices, forward or back, and as he didn't remember passing any turn-offs along the way, he continued on.

Galvanised with hope, he gunned the little Fiat forward, repeatedly looking left to try to catch a glimpse of the steeple. Within a mile, he came across a narrow track on the left and turned in. The car bounced and shook on the dirt road, its tiny wheels pelting the underside with small stones and kicking up a cloud of dust behind. The track swiftly deteriorated and he feared he might have to turn back, lest the Cinquecento shake itself to pieces. Mercifully, after five minutes, he reached the safety of tarmac.

The church was clearly visible now, and within five minutes was just a half-mile distant, the orientation of the steeple just as he remembered. He parked the Fiat at the side of the road in front of a gate, switched off the engine and opened the door, which sounded loud and harsh in the relative silence. He stood in the road, rolled up his shirtsleeves and stared up at the deep blue cloudless sky, soaking up the warmth on his face. The air was devoid of any wind and the buzz of insects and the occasional twitter of a bird competed with the pinging and popping of contracting metal emanating from the back of the Fiat. He retrieved a pair of sunglasses from his jacket, slung it over his shoulder and positioned his panama. He set off on foot.

He found it within two hundred yards. The contours of the ground on either side gave it away despite the camouflage afforded by orderly rows of vines that now carpeted the fields. There was no track and no farmhouse but he picked his spot, stepped off the road into a field and walked up a small incline between two vines, counting the paces. A voice from the past echoed. *Keep your eyes open, Wilkins… Yessir!* There were no explosions, no gunfire, no

170

droning aircraft, no cries for help, just an exquisite tranquillity that soothed his senses.

He came to a small clearing with an open-sided wooden shed. A pile of metal supports and several reels of plastic-coated wire were stacked under its sloping roof: hardware supplies for a vineyard that stretched out in all directions. But around him on the ground where he now stood were the remains of a building. There was virtually nothing: a few fragments of brick, a few shards of roof tile, a short section of rusty drainpipe and some splintered wood. But he could visualise the door, the window, the staircase, the fireplace, and the room where lives had been lived and lives had been ended.

He sat on a boulder and removed his panama. He ran a hand through his hair and wiped the sweat from the back of his neck with his handkerchief. He tried to think of something to say and if he were religious, a prayer would have come, but that was all just mumbo-jumbo and talking to himself was not something he did easily. *What are you doing here, you fool? What did you expect to find? Peace. That's what I expected.*

He ran through the events again, but this time he felt somehow detached – casual observer more than participant. A place damned by violence, death and destruction was now an oasis of peace and beauty. The place of his nightmares had moved on and the example it set just might convince him to do the same.

"Buongiorno."

"Christ!" He jumped to his feet, startled by the sound. A man wearing a long black cassock and a wide-brimmed hat was watching him, smiling broadly. Harry's shock was quickly subsumed by embarrassment. "Sorry, Father."

"I regret, I am not he. Merely a humble servant of our Lord." The smile remained inscrutable, but he'd clearly enjoyed the irony.

"I was miles away. I mean, I was thinking of something else."

171

"I am sorry if I disturbed you. I saw the car and then spotted you up here. I wondered if I could help?"

Harry shrugged and fiddled with his hat. There would be no confession, at least not to a priest, but the Father appeared benign and clearly had a sense of humour so there could be no harm.

"This place is called Solano, is it not?"

"I am not aware of the name."

Harry looked around him. There were no other buildings nearby. He guessed they had suffered the same fate. Solano had been wiped off the map.

"I'm probably trespassing here."

"I do not think the farmer would mind. You do not look as if you have come to steal his grapes."

"No." Harry couldn't resist asking, "Do you know the farmer's name?" The question was put tentatively and he felt the priest's eyes on him. He feared the pause might signify suspicion, but the priest was only searching for an answer.

"I think this land belongs to Signore Cavallaro. Do you know him?"

"No. Not at all. I just wondered." He saw the raising of a priestly eyebrow and he took his cue. "I once knew a family called Girardi. They lived here. They had a farmhouse, right here." He pointed to the ground.

"You were a soldier?"

"Yes. I tried to help them... the Girardis, but..." He shrugged. "It wasn't possible."

"I see. We have a grave bearing that name. In the churchyard. Would you like to come and see?"

Harry swallowed. He hadn't thought where the bodies might be, nor once considered what might have happened after he'd passed out. Someone had found him and carried him to a field hospital; his own troops, he'd assumed, but no one there remembered who'd brought him in and he never found out. Perhaps the same guys dealt with the bodies of Alfredo, Isabella and Catalina? Possible but unlikely. And how the hell did Kessler get out alive? His mind raced. In his

172

mind the world had ended for them all when the last bomb hit and the last bullet was fired, but of course, it went on, for some of them. *What happened afterwards?*

"I would like that very much. Can I give you a lift?

***

Father Giorgio Benelli had taken over the church of San Dionisio ten years previously following the death of his venerable predecessor, Father Aiello. He said the church had suffered extensive damage during the war but had been fully restored and it now gleamed white in the autumn sunshine. The graveyard, in contrast, had escaped and still bore headstones dating back five hundred years. They strolled amongst the graves on the exquisitely kept grass between beautifully maintained flowerbeds.

"I think we will find them here," said the priest, directing Harry to a modest headstone of grey granite. He felt the hairs go up on the back of his neck as his eyes fell on the inscription.

GIRARDI
Maria, 6 marzo 1898 a 22 febbraio 1943
Moglie di
Alfredo, 11 agosto 1890 a 14 marzo 1944
Madre e Padre di
Isabella, 18 ottobre 1925 a 14 marzo 1944

"Is there something wrong?" Father Benelli was looking at him curiously. Harry's face had betrayed his confusion.

"I never knew Maria, but I knew Alfredo and Isabella. She had a child. A newborn baby. There is no mention of her here."

"Are you sure?"

"Yes, there's no doubt. I was holding her myself when she passed away." The words sounded alien to him, as if he were talking about someone else and in a strange way he was.

"We have records inside. Maybe they will show some more light?"

They stepped into the cool entrance to the church where a table bedecked with lighted candles greeted them. Father Benelli made the sign of the cross and led the way up the central aisle.

"The church records are kept in the sacristy," he said, indicating a door in the corner to the left of the altar where an elderly woman was swabbing the tiled floor with a mop. She was short and stout, with silvery grey hair and wore a floral housecoat over her green woollen sweater and heavy tweed skirt.

"Buongiorno, Rosa. Come stai?"

"Bene, Padre."

He stopped and turned to Harry. "Rosa has been here forever. Maybe she knows something?"

Harry watched as Benelli launched into a long and apparently involved explanation of the stranger *inglese*, how they'd met and his connection to the Girardis. Rosa leaned on her mop and listened intently without interrupting, casting a glance or two at Harry but maintaining a severe expression throughout which he could only assume was her natural demeanour.

Rosa began slowly but as she spoke she gradually became more animated and vociferous. Harry couldn't understand the words she was using but got a hint of the meaning through her increasingly aggressive tone and whatever she was saying, it wasn't complimentary. She flashed a look of anger at him and gesticulated with her free hand and although Benelli nodded sagely, Harry could tell the priest was uncomfortable and like him, had not been expecting a tirade. Harry wondered if Rosa was ever going to stop and he felt embarrassed, wishing he were somewhere else. Benelli tried to calm her by raising his hands.

"Si calmi, signora." He asked her something else presumably to clarify, Harry thought, but she launched into her diatribe once more until she finally ran out of steam and

waved a hand in dismissal. Harry was grateful for the silence but one word rang in his ears and seemed to echo round the hallowed walls. *Prostituta!*

Rosa resumed her mopping with a vengeance, transferring what remained of her aggression to the eight-hundred-year-old floor tiles while muttering under her breath. Benelli turned to Harry, looking subdued and apologetic.

"She say the Girardis were a good family..." *But?* "She say that Maria and Alfredo were good parents... but... maybe..." He stopped to consider his words carefully and Harry decided to help them both out of their misery.

"She called Isabella a prostitute."

Benelli nodded sadly. "Yes. I don't know if this is true or just gossip. But she says that the Germans went to the Girardi house a lot, and the Girardis always had food and they never suffered like other families." Benelli shrugged. It was the least explicit he could be in the circumstances. This was not a subject normally debated in a house of God.

Harry sighed. He didn't know if it was true and he didn't care. He thought no less of Alfredo and Isabella. What were they supposed to do? They did what they had to do to survive and what Isabella may or may not have done against the backdrop of war was of no consequence and paled into insignificance compared to the crimes of others. If it were true then baby Catalina was probably a consequence of her actions, but the absence of any mention on the gravestone disturbed him. It pained him to know that even the most innocent of all had been denied the basic show of respect and dignity she deserved. It was as if Catalina had never existed.

"So they all died and that was the end of the Girardis."

"Oh, no," said Benelli. "You may not have understood. Rosa said Isabella had a sister, Lucia."

"What? A sister?"

"*Sì*. The sister was younger, maybe four or five years."

"But I never saw anyone else."

"I can't explain this."

175

Harry was now agitated himself. He needed to know more. "But where is Lucia? There's no grave. Is she still alive?"

Benelli turned to Rosa. *"Rosa, Lucia è ancora viva?"*

Rosa muttered something without looking up and Harry looked expectantly at the priest.

"Dov'è lei?"

Asking Rosa where Lucia was set her off again, but the rant was short-lived.

"She says she went missing for a few years, then, after the war, she married a local businessman in Montellano called Luigi Barone. He was much older. Not a good man according to Rosa. But then they moved away from Montellano."

"Prostituta! Mafioso!" Rosa shouted, waddling off in disgust with her bucket and mop.

CHAPTER 20

He had no idea how he was going to find Luigi or Lucia Barone, whether they were still together and, indeed, still alive, but over dinner and grappa, Angelo had been able to provide him with some interesting background.

He knew nothing of Lucia Girardi but remembered Barone and in less than complimentary terms. Old man Riccardo Barone ran a fruit and vegetable business before the war, but son Luigi was a natural *imprenditore* and when the Germans arrived he quickly saw an opportunity to service the demands of the occupying forces as well as exploit the privations of the local populace.

Luigi had boasted of his daring adventures in a partisan brigade although his primary allegiance was to money and after the town had been destroyed and the Germans driven out, he'd plied a lucrative trade providing luxury goods to the liberators, such as cigarettes, liquor and soap. He'd then started a construction business, jumping on the bandwagon to rebuild the town, exploiting the desperate need for new homes and made his money building shoddy apartment blocks. As his influence and wealth grew, he opened a restaurant and hotel and, it was rumoured, dabbled in prostitution.

But he was a small fish swimming in an increasingly murky pond and eventually he was driven out by Mario Coppola, another local villain who regarded the upstart as a threat to his own expanding empire. Coppola still operated in Montellano and Angelo had no idea where Luigi Barone was now, but he'd ask around.

***

Fabrizio greeted him at reception with a smile and a bill, which he paid using a traveller's cheque.

"Your stay was very short, Signore Male. Maybe you come back one day and visit the abbey?"

Harry had done all he needed to do in Montellano and there was little likelihood he'd return, but he was grateful for the hospitality and didn't want to offend.

"Perhaps, but there are many places in the world to visit first."

"Now you are going back to Roma?"

"Yes, that's the plan."

Fabrizio handed over a slip of folded paper. It bore a single word: *Casavento.* Harry looked at the obsequious owner, who was grinning at him knowingly as if begging to be asked what it meant, but he didn't need to, as Fabrizio couldn't resist.

"My brother he telephone me. He say that the man you are searching for is in this town, Casavento. Or perhaps it is the lady that interests you?" he said, barely able to conceal his delight at the intrigue. Harry had obviously had too much grappa last night and now Angelo, Fabrizio, Carla and the entire family were in the know. He ignored the question.

"That's very kind. Can you thank Angelo for me?"

"Certainly." The grin was fixed and annoying, not least because they both knew what Harry's next question would be.

"And, where is Casavento?"

"Is a town about eighty kilometres north of Roma. In the mountains."

"I see. I am most grateful to you."

"Prego." Fabrizio's grin dissolved and he suddenly turned serious. *"Signore… be careful."*

***

He dozed on the train back to Rome. He'd got little sleep that night, notwithstanding dinner at Angelo's followed by several shots of grappa. He'd been offered another dimension to the story of the Girardis and his thoughts were

178

consumed with speculation and hypotheses about Isabella and the enigmatic Lucia, such that he lay awake until the early hours thinking about it. He'd worked out Lucia would be in her early thirties by now. Alfredo had never mentioned her. Isabella hadn't either but then she'd been delirious with pain.

Her connection to Luigi Barone was tenuous even though Rosa had sounded unequivocal. Angelo could not remember her name and nor could Fabrizio or Carla, so it was entirely possible that he was off on a wild goose chase going to Casavento. He tried to manage his expectations, but he was excited. He was on a voyage of discovery and he had no idea where it would lead.

The path was clear. There had been nothing left for him in Montellano or Solano, no more memories he wanted to rekindle. He could still feel the warmth of the life-giving sun, smell the vines, hear the sounds of the birds and the bees in the countryside under an azure sky and he had seen where Alfredo and his family had been laid to rest. The terrible images that had plagued him continuously since 1944 had been replaced by images of hope.

***

Back at his hotel in Rome, Harry asked the concierge if he could make an international call to England. Arthur Rowland was in good spirits.

"Good morning, young man, or should I say *buongiorno?*"

"Hello, Arthur. Are you well?"

"Yes indeed. And I'm pleased to report all the funds are in and lodged in a client account to your order. The balance is twelve thousand one hundred and twenty pounds plus a few shillings and pence."

Harry was pleasantly surprised. "Oh, well done. That was better than I thought."

"And our fees come to one hundred and seventy-five pounds, four shillings and sixpence." Harry had to laugh. He should have known better. "May I settle them from your account?"

"Of course, Arthur. Go ahead."

"Thank you. Now do you have enough funds to continue your little expedition?"

"I expect so, but I'm not sure how long I'll be out here. I'm off to a place called Casavento tomorrow."

"Well give me a week's notice before you need more. We can arrange a foreign telegraphic transfer pretty much anywhere in Europe these days."

"Okay, Arthur, thanks. I appreciate it."

"My pleasure, young man, you are paying for it after all!"

***

He decided to hire another car and because he was now feeling suitably flush, to treat himself to something more substantial than a Cinquecento, not least because he felt he needed a car with the power to tackle eighty kilometres of winding mountain roads. The brand-new red Fiat 1200 Spyder coupé fitted the bill perfectly and was sleek and stylish too, even though it was outrageously expensive.

IIc droppcd thc roof and navigatcd his way out of Rome heading northeast, crossing the River Tiber twice before beginning his ascent into the mountains. The map indicated Casavento would be found in a valley on the other side of a small mountain range that peaked at fifteen hundred metres. According to the guidebook, the town enjoyed an elevated position overlooking the River Galliano, its main industries being ceramics, wine growing, agriculture and tourism. Casavento attracted thousands of visitors each year to the vineyards and the mediaeval architecture typical of an ancient hilltop city.

The Spyder swallowed up countless hairpin bends with ease as the road snaked its way up the mountain before descending into a lush valley and after a journey that lasted three hours, Harry finally crossed the Roman bridge over the Galliano and entered the city walls through a triumphal arch.

The streets of Casavento were narrow, many of them cobbled and unsuited to heavy traffic. A one-way system was in force where they were not wide enough to allow two vehicles to pass and myriad pedestrian alleyways snaked off in all directions, hosting an endless array of shops selling ceramics, clothing, souvenirs and general provisions. He ticked the Spyder along at little more than walking pace, navigating around carefree tourists and shoppers and hundreds of scooters, which appeared to be the preferred method of transport. For a while he felt as if he were going around in circles as he inched his way upwards towards the epicentre of the town dominated by the Gothic cathedral of San Giovese in the Piazza di Duomo.

The piazza was pedestrianised so the road veered left down a steep hill that widened out into two-way traffic. He spotted a small square with parked cars and scooters and after some intricate manoeuvring pulled into a space in front of the Hotel Garibaldi.

The narrow six-storey building was ancient but well kept and the Italian *tricolore* dangled lazily above a revolving entrance door that sported etched glass and polished brass handles. He was lucky. They had one spare room and although it had no view, it was close to the fire escape, which, insisted *proprietario* Alfonso, would be handy in the event of an emergency. Harry was tempted to ask how often they had emergencies at the Garibaldi but was simply relieved he'd found a place to stay.

He retrieved his suitcase from the car, secured the canvas roof and locked both doors before being taken up in a rickety elevator to the fourth floor by Alfonso's daughter Cleo. They alighted into a gloomy, carpeted corridor that featured five doors and she showed him through one at the end, predictably close to the fire escape. The room was spacious and clean and perfectly adequate for his needs. The bed was

181

a double, had tables and lamps on either side and there was a double wardrobe and a separate sitting area with a writing table and two chairs. The bathroom was functional, the walls tiled in white and navy with dolphin motifs.

"I hope you enjoy your stay, Signore Male," said the young girl. Harry guessed she was no more than sixteen and wondered why she wasn't at school or college. "Are you wishing to have lunch? There are many restaurants we can recommend."

"Thanks, Cleo. I think I'll just go for a walk for now."

"Prego." She smiled and closed the door behind her.

He opened a full-length window that opened onto a Juliet balcony but the only view was of another building immediately opposite. He looked down to a narrow alley where people meandered while scooters weaved between them and then up to the adjacent rooftops where he caught a glimpse of the cathedral cupola.

He unpacked his belongings and hung up his linen suit and clean shirts. For the journey, he'd dressed simply in a white polo shirt with blue denim trousers and black sneakers and decided that, along with his lightweight jacket and panama, he was presentable enough for a stroll around the town. But where to start?

He decided just to wander, familiarise himself with the topography of the town and have a bite to eat. He kept a look out for the name "Barone", imagining he might strike lucky and see it in a shop window, or on a restaurant sign. But he'd read that Casavento had a local population of around ten thousand, so the chances of bumping into the man were negligible. However, both Rosa and Angelo had described Luigi Barone as a businessman, an *imprenditore.* He would probably be in his fifties and it seemed unlikely that a man motivated by money would have retired and disappeared from view.

He strolled gently along the back alleys and passageways, peering into shop windows, gazing in wonder at the ancient buildings that locals took for granted, and becoming slowly intoxicated by the aroma of coffee, cinnamon and garlic emanating from the hundreds of *caffetterie*, *pasticcerie* and *ristoranti* whose tables and chairs lined the pavements. He could resist it no longer.

He picked a table at random and within an instant, the waiter was there, with a paper tablecloth, linen napkin, condiment set and menu.

"Buongiorno, signore. Il piatto del giorno è il polpo."

He knew it meant octopus and although he was a fish and chip man, he was not averse to something slightly more exotic. But instead he ordered penne arrabbiata and a beer.

He watched the people go by, taking note of women who looked under forty – a pleasurable pastime in itself – wondering if any could be Lucia Girardi. He'd formed a picture in his mind but it was based on his limited recollection of Isabella. There had to be some family resemblance, but even if there were, Isabella had been under great strain, her features distorted by pain. Isabella had never smiled; she'd only screamed in anguish. He hoped Lucia, wherever she was, was blessed with a more peaceful existence.

The pasta was unassailable and the beer, crisp and cold. He had another, remembering the day not so long ago he would have had a couple of cigarettes for dessert. No more. Another Italian siren strutted by like a model on a Milan catwalk. There was no doubt the Italians could put the Berliners to shame when it came to style, but then he had to admit they could do the same to the British.

He had to conclude that barring the unlikely event a thirty-something woman came along wearing a name badge, he would have to make enquiries. He paid the bill and continued his exploration of the town. He reached the Piazza di Duomo, a typical Italian square with the Cattedrale di San Giovese taking up one side, the other three sides lined with restaurants. In the centre, locals and tourists congregated around an ostentatious marble fountain that featured gods on horseback slaying tigers and bears while being serenaded by nymphs playing flutes and harps.

He circumnavigated the square, reading the restaurant names one by one but none bore any resemblance to "Barone", and why should they? He'd been told Barone once had a restaurant and a hotel in Montellano, but that was back then; there was no reason to assume he was in the same business now even though from the look of them all it appeared to be a lucrative trade.

He went into the cathedral and put some money in the donations box, then sauntered around marvelling at the exquisite stained-glass windows, the priceless artworks, the gilded dome roof and the extraordinary carvings. It never ceased to amaze him how much wealth the Catholic Church had; God was big business once upon a time and in Italy probably remained so.

But it was time to do some work. He strolled along a side street and into a souvenir shop. He waited until the young woman behind the counter had finished with a customer and approached her, removing his hat.

"Do you speak English?"

"Yes, of course, *signore*. Can I help you?"

"I'm looking for someone. A Signore Barone. Luigi Barone. Do you know him?"

Her face barely flickered and she hadn't even had time to think before she replied.

"No. I'm sorry, *signore*. I don't know him."

The immediacy of the response struck him; Harry hadn't been interrogating people for the last five years without picking up the signs, but there was nothing to be gained by pursuing it and he simply smiled and shrugged.

"Grazie mille."

He left the shop and tried another whose window was adorned with exotic and expensive ceramics. Inside, he made a show of examining a figurine of Madonna and child. He had the look of an affluent tourist and was not surprised when one of the sales assistants approached him.

184

"It's very beautiful, no?" said an imperious middle-aged man in a smart three-piece suit wearing a name badge: *S. Moretti.*

"Yes, it is."

"It is made by the finest craftsmen in Italy."

"Really? How much is it?"

"It is two hundred and twenty thousand lire." Harry tried not to react while he did the maths but the assistant helped him before he could work out the answer. "Is about one hundred and twenty-five of your pounds." *Two weeks' pay!* Harry nodded sagely but there was only one thing on his mind.

"I wonder if you can help me?"

The imperious Signore Moretti tilted his head and smiled condescendingly.

"I am looking for a gentleman; a Signore Luigi Barone."

The same speed of the response was telling. "I can't help you, *signore*, I don't know anyone with that name. Does he work in ceramics?" He spread a hand to indicate the contents of the shop, the words and gesture strangely revealing.

"I'm not sure. He's a businessman."

Signore Moretti sniffed. "Is there anything else I can show the *signore*?"

He was being dismissed. The conversation was over. Harry bowed slightly and looked Moretti in the eye.

"You've been very helpful. *Grazie.*"

He tried twice more, once in a delicatessen and once outside a café where he ordered a cappuccino. The woman in the deli was more credible and tried her best by asking further questions – *how old was he? what did he look like? what's his line of business?* – before finally giving up. But the waiter's response in the café was the same as the others: polite, but unhelpful and dismissive. There was a pattern to their behaviour, without doubt.

***

Alfonso was in reception when he came down for dinner dressed in his linen suit, pale blue shirt and regimental tie.

"*Buonasera, signore.* Have you had a good afternoon?"

"Yes thank you, Alfonso. Perhaps you can recommend a restaurant?"

"Oh there are many, many restaurants here in Casavento. All of them very good."

"How about one of those in the Piazza di Duomo?"

Alfonso shrugged. "*Sì.* They are also good but maybe the price…" He rubbed two fingers together. "The tourists like them for the position, but the best ones are hidden away." He winked at Harry and unfolded a street map. "You can go here, here and here" – he marked several crosses with a black pen – "and here. The prices are very good and the food is *magnifico!*"

"Thank you. I'll try one." He picked up the map and folded it around the crosses.

"*Prego.*"

"By the way. I have come here to find an old friend, but I don't where he is." Alfonso was still smiling, apparently eager to help. "His name is Luigi Barone." The mouth stayed the same but Alfonso's eyes gave him away. He blinked twice.

"You are a friend of Signore Barone?" he asked hesitantly, his scepticism evident.

Harry felt his pulse quicken and he tried to sound casual. "Well, we have a mutual friend, shall we say. I haven't met him before but I promised myself I would look him up if ever I came to Casavento."

Alfonso nodded in understanding but it was clear he was analysing Harry's words, trying to gauge the correct response.

Harry pressed on. "Do you know him?"

Alfonso was looking uncomfortable now. "I know the name, but I, er, do not know the man."

"Oh. I see. Is he important?"

"Signore Barone has many businesses in Casavento."

Harry nodded. He could be a dog with a bone when he wanted and he'd learned over many years to be subtle and go slowly, but he felt like he was in control here.

"I understand he may have a restaurant?" He understood nothing of the sort, but it was worth a try. Alfonso was non-committal.

"As I say he has many businesses. But he is, shall we say… a private man. He may not wish for someone to call on him unexpectedly."

"No, I understand."

"May I?" Alfonso took the street map and unfolded it again. "You may after all like to try a restaurant in the piazza?" He marked four crosses around the perimeter. "You can try here, here, here" – he paused for effect – "and… here."

***

The Ristorante Quadrifoglio was teeming, as were all the others in the Piazza di Duomo. He had no reservation and it was impossible to accommodate a single diner who would take up a table for two. Instead, he made a reservation for lunch the next day.

"Uno?" said the harassed waiter, trying to mask his irritation and then held up a finger, "One person?" in case the customer was mistaken. Harry nodded and the waiter tutted.

"Grazie."

"Prego," said the waiter without humour.

He found one of the restaurants Alfonso had first recommended in a back alley. The tables on the street were tiny and the slatted wooden seats uncomfortable, but all the diners appeared to be locals, which he took to be a good sign. He wasn't disappointed. The waiter seemed as welcoming and attentive towards his single guest as he was to larger parties and the food and local Montepulciano was superb, the meal rounded off with complimentary grappa.

Harry resisted the temptation to mention the name "Barone". Results had been mixed and he didn't want to spoil the evening.

**

The next morning, he had time to kill, so he visited the Museo Civico, but his mind was restless and he couldn't concentrate on ancient Roman artefacts. There was no evidence the Quadrifoglio was connected to Barone, but even if it was, that didn't mean he would necessarily see him there, and even less likely he would find Lucia. He was also wary of making further enquiries given his experience of the previous day, so he hoped the restaurant would be a step in the right direction.

He announced himself to the waiter at twelve-thirty, fifteen minutes early, because he could wait no longer. He was shown an outside table for two, and sat at the edge with his back to the adjoining restaurant so he could see everyone coming and going. The piazza was full of tourists and peddlers and the restaurants were already getting busy. Two waiters were serving the outside area and he strained to look through the windows but could see little inside the restaurant. He'd go to the toilet at some stage and take a look.

He opened the menu and examined the inside cover, which featured ancient photographs of the Quadrifoglio and a brief history, but it made no mention of the owner. Nor was there any clue in the signage and he began to wonder what his next move would be if, as he was beginning to realise, Barone was indeed as private a man as Alfonso had suggested.

A waiter balancing three plates on one arm passed by and cast him a glance. He deposited the plates on an adjacent table, took further instructions from the diners and turned back towards the door. Harry raised a finger but the chap was clearly in a hurry.

"Uno momento, signore," he said, and as he passed the open doorway Harry heard him shout, "Lucia!" Harry tensed.

A young woman appeared within seconds clutching a notepad and pencil. She wore a green apron over a white dress with a floral print that flared out from her slim waist, her short reddish-brown curly hair giving her a boyish look. Harry watched her approach and felt his heart begin to race. She barked something in Italian at another waiter, pointing to an empty table, and flipped a page on her pad before looking up.

"Prego, signore."

He looked at her dumbly, gripping the menu, unable to speak, seeing the mist come down over his eyes and sensing a distant rush of sound in his ears. He slowly got to his feet. She tilted her head back as she took in his full height and she looked perplexed, not sure what to do. He heard himself speaking.

"Lucia? Lucia… Girardi?"

She stared at him for a moment and then her bewilderment turned slowly to fright. She dropped her pad and clasped both hands over her mouth. She gasped and stepped back, colliding with a waiter carrying a tray of glasses that fell to earth with a crash. Then she was gone, fleeing inside the restaurant as if in a panic, the waiter dropping to his knees trying to rectify the damage while all the other diners turned to see the commotion.

"Mi dispiace, perdonatemi! I'm sorry, forgive me," said the waiter.

But Harry wasn't listening or hearing or seeing or breathing.

He had just stared into the eyes of an angel.

CHAPTER 21

Within a minute or two, the mess had been cleared up, diners had returned their attention to their plates and the Quadrifoglio was back to normal.

Harry looked blankly at the menu in front of him, reading the words but seeing nothing, unable to focus his attention on anything other than the image that still burned in his consciousness. There was no doubt. The young girl was now a woman, the long hair shorter and curlier and redder in colour but he had known her for as long as he could remember. Lucia Girardi had knelt before him as he lay dying in the ruins of her home next to her dead father and her dead sister and she'd taken from him the body of baby Catalina. Another scene in his interminable nightmare had been rewritten and represented as an episode of reality.

But once the shock faded and realisation began to dawn, he became confused and disturbed by her reaction. He wanted to go after her and hold her and express his deep sorrow at her loss and tell her that he'd never forgotten what happened and never would. Seeing her again had been an almighty shock to him and it could be no different for her, but he couldn't let it rest there. He couldn't simply go back to Berlin or Coventry, or wherever his new life might take him and forget about it. He needed to know more about the Girardi family, a family to which he felt more connected than his own. They'd shared the most intimate and traumatic moments of their lives and he needed her help to finally come to terms with it, to make sense of it. He wondered whether she needed the same.

He glanced at the door, but there was no sign of her. He needed to go inside and look for her. He'd apologise for frightening her and they'd have a chat and a coffee and he'd explain what happened in the farmhouse, what happened to him during and after and she'd explain where she'd been and

190

what happened to her and they'd lay all their ghosts to rest and everything would be fine. He pushed himself to his feet.

"Signore Male." A rotund middle-aged man in a white, open-necked shirt was standing by his table, blocking his way. A substantial gut hung over the belt around his black trousers and shiny black hair was slicked back over a high forehead. His upper lip was dominated by a fulsome black moustache and around his neck dangled a gold chain and medallion, nestling amongst a forest of chest hair. "Please, be seated." The man snapped his fingers in the air and a waiter appeared with a bottle of grappa and two glasses. Harry slowly resumed his seat and the man pulled up a chair alongside. His shirt sleeves were turned back, revealing dark suntanned forearms covered in a carpet of black hair. He held out a hand and Harry's attention was drawn to a vulgar gold ring on his small finger, a diamond-studded Rolex on his wrist.

"I am Luigi Barone."

Harry shook a big hand that was soft, fleshy and warm. Barone poured two shots of grappa.

"I seem to have caused a fuss. I apologise."

He was handed a glass. They chinked, knocking it back in one, and Harry relished the burning sensation and the instant hit of alcohol. He noticed Barone looking at him as if he were carefully considering his next statement or more likely sizing up his customer. Either way, if it was intended as a form of intimidation, it was working.

"I hope I haven't upset the young lady."

"My wife" – he paused for effect – "is how you say, highly strung. Maybe it's the time of the month, eh?" He grinned and poured two more shots and Harry was relieved that Barone, despite his intimidating manner, seemed to be loosening up. "Are you married?"

"No. I haven't found the right girl yet." He put on a weak grin in an attempt to complement Barone's benign expression but it didn't last long.

"What is the purpose of your visit to Casavento, Signore Male?" It was more than curiosity – inquisitorial, not conversational.

Harry was a useless liar; he'd seen too many in his time to know that the average liar gets lost in a maze of deceit and eventually reaches a dead end. But there was no way he could or would explain the whole truth, certainly not to Luigi Barone.

"I was in Italy during the war, in Montellano, and I came back to take another look. I have memories, good and bad and I had friends who fell and I wanted to pay my respects. I was told Casavento was an interesting place to visit." It was all true. *Even the last sentence.*

Barone shrugged. "And how can I help you?" The emphasis was on the "I".

Harry decided to continue the dumb tourist act for a while. "Well, I came in for a spot of lunch. Your restaurant was recommended."

Barone nodded. "I see. Then why have you been making enquiries about me?"

He should have known better. The guy was no pushover. He was a "businessman", a euphemism for something else in this part of the world and whenever his name had been mentioned, there had been some reaction, however infinitesimal, that should have warned him to be careful. Fabrizio had warned him to be careful. And he'd just been careless. "Or maybe your interest is my wife?"

Harry tried to draw a line. "I knew her father, that's all. He died during the war."

Barone sat back and rested his hands on his ample girth. A man like him would have only two objectives: seek an opportunity to exploit or eliminate the possibility of any threat. Harry couldn't see how he fitted into either but the guy was looking for an angle and having presumably finished his assessment, sat forward and leaned in closer. Harry caught a whiff of Old Spice.

"I think my wife does not want to remember things like that. It is distressing for her."

"It was not my intention to cause distress."

"I am a private man, Signore Male. I don't like surprises and my wife does not like surprises." He'd lowered his voice, affording a sinister gravitas to an otherwise innocuous comment.

"I don't wish to cause offence and I am sorry if I upset your wife."

Barone sighed. "Your apology is accepted."

"Perhaps I can talk to her and apologise to her directly?"

He knew it was provocative, but he wanted to know whether Barone was just playing at being the hard man or was genuinely concerned about Lucia's welfare. But most of all, he also wanted to speak to her, very much. The answer was direct and unequivocal.

"I suggest you return to England, Signore Male."

"I will. Soon."

Barone put a chubby hand on Harry's arm and squeezed it. "I suggest perhaps tomorrow."

He guessed the conversation had been terminated and lunch would be out of the question. He stood up and offered a hand but Barone turned and walked back into his restaurant. The message was clear.

He sauntered across the piazza, considering his options. He was no longer hungry but he wanted some coffee and he wanted time to think. He sat down in a café on the opposite side of the piazza and ordered a panino and Americano. He could see the Quadrifoglio seventy metres across the square, his view obscured intermittently by people wandering back and forth and he watched and waited, hoping to catch another glimpse of Lucia. He knew it was dangerous, but he had no choice. A hole was burning inside him as intense and painful as any he had felt before. He had come looking for answers to questions that had tormented and almost consumed him; he'd come to seek admonishment, or at least

193

justification and, above all, closure. But instead he'd opened up a new chapter that prompted more questions than ever.

Lucia had looked shocked and terrified, that was for sure. What could she be afraid of? He had no memory of anything after her apparition apart from a sublime peace and finally the comfort of darkness. He'd passed out; he'd died, so he thought. Maybe he'd attacked her in his delirium? Maybe she thought he'd killed the baby? Maybe she saw what he'd done to Isabella? The thought gave him a chill and not just at his own recollection of the horror, but at what she may have witnessed: her sister's body ripped open, her blood and insides spread over the bed. Or maybe it was just the explosions and the bombs and the destruction and the death of her loved ones? *She was only a child, for God's sake!* And if she had ever been able to forget, then his reappearance would have brought it all back. What was she supposed to think? How was she supposed to react?

He desperately wanted to talk to her and he tried to convince himself that it would be helpful to her too when, deep down, he knew it was he who needed it most. But the questions kept coming. How did she get out of the farmhouse? What did she do with Catalina's body? Did she know her father and sister were buried in the churchyard? And what was she doing with a second-grade middle-aged *mafioso* like Barone? Maybe she was so unhappy with her life this had tipped her over the edge? Maybe she wanted to get away from the oaf? *Stop it, you fool!*

He rubbed his forehead. The need to meet her again was driving him insane, and the more he thought about it, the more certain he was he couldn't let go. There was nothing more important to him, not even life itself, life which would have no meaning unless the truth was clear. He'd learned that lesson the hard way. He would no longer run and hide and hope everything would be all right in the end. *You don't have the luxury of retreat!*

But there was a complication and he was called Luigi Barone. He had been warned off and although he believed

194

the guy could be dangerous, he could not be sure how dangerous. In any event, he wasn't sure Lucia would want to see him again. Both were risks, but risks he was prepared to take. If he wasn't going to bow to Barone's implied threat and leave Casavento, he would still have to move out of the Hotel Garibaldi. If Barone were Mister Big in the town, then he would know if Harry was still there and that would make life difficult. He had lots to think about and not much time to do it in.

An image caught his eye. *Lucia!* The white floral dress was unmistakeable, but she wore a bright yellow headscarf and black sunglasses and carried a black handbag. She walked briskly out of the restaurant and turned right, heading away from the cathedral. Without further thought, Harry fumbled for his wallet and threw some money on the table.

He took a parallel route on his side of the piazza, looking up to catch a glimpse of her between the crowds while dodging pedestrians and scooters. He saw her reach the edge of the square and turn left. She was walking with purpose, breaking into a trot from time to time, crossing the road between the traffic. She was in a hurry, either to get somewhere or get away from something. He increased his pace, wary that in the maze of streets and narrow alleyways it would be very easy to lose her, all the while wondering what on earth he was doing pursuing the wife of a local hood.

She turned right, out of sight, and he sprinted to the corner to close the distance. He didn't want to catch up with her just yet; he wanted to pick the right moment, whenever that might be. Not so long ago, his lungs would have protested the exertion but he covered the ground with ease and although he felt a twinge in his leg, his chest was clear. He followed her down a narrow cobbled street, only fifty yards distant, but he was reluctant to run to catch her up. The last thing he wanted was to frighten her again; she might scream and cry for help, or worse, outrun him. She reached a T-junction at the bottom and he could tell she was going to turn right. He took a chance and turned right down a parallel alley, hoping he could take a left further along and intercept her.

He broke into a run and took the second left. He arrived ten feet in front of her. She stopped abruptly.

"Lucia, please." Now he really was short of breath. He held up a hand and clutched the other to his side. "I just want to talk to you." She stayed silent, rooted to the spot, clutching her bag to her middle, the body language of self-defence, but he could see she was breathing deeply too.

"I can't."

"Please, there are things I need to ask you."

"I can't."

"It's okay. Please. I mean you no harm. I promise." He sounded pathetic and weepy but that was how he felt.

"Is there a man behind me?"

He frowned and looked over her shoulder. A guy stood at the junction of two streets fifty metres away, neither coming nor going, just loitering and observing.

"Er, yes," he said, confused and concerned at the same time.

"Wine-coloured jacket, yellow shirt."

He checked. "Yes."

She walked up and thrust her face at him aggressively, eyes hidden behind dark sunglasses.

"I can't talk to you now," she hissed, pointing a finger at his chest. "He will know and he will tell my husband. And my husband will kill you."

"Why?"

"Because he can," she whispered through bared teeth then stabbed a finger in Harry's direction three times. "Chiesa di San Pietro. Tomorrow. Twelve o'clock," she said, gesticulating theatrically in the air with one hand. "Now, when I push you, walk away. The way you have come." She shoved him hard in the chest and carried on up the street, swinging her bag. He watched her go, and then, understanding he had a role to play, hung his head and trudged up the alley, hands in pockets, dejected.

***

He went back to the same restaurant for dinner but he couldn't concentrate on anything or anyone else. He couldn't stop thinking about her, how she looked and how she'd behaved towards him and whether her aggression was real or born out of fear. If she'd thought he was harassing her, all she'd had to do was whistle for the goon in the red jacket, but she hadn't, which suggested he wasn't there for her protection, he was following her to see where she went. The theatricals were for his benefit, there to create the illusion she was disturbed by the Englishman's presence and evidently rejecting his unwanted advances.

He kept telling himself that if she didn't want to see him or talk to him, then she would never have given him a time and a place to meet. Luigi Barone had made it clear his wife was off-limits and he should leave town tomorrow. The accompanying threat was clear; Barone had probably threatened her too and he felt an urge to protect her, but there was nothing he could do for now. He thought about Barone's instructions and his instinct was to ignore them, not be pushed around by an ugly Italian and he fought the craving to go past the Quadrifoglio in case he caught a glimpse of her but decided it was too dangerous for them both. He would wait and meet Lucia tomorrow, as planned.

It was after ten when he pushed open the revolving door of the Garibaldi and found Alfonso on duty at reception.

"*Buonasera.* How was your meal?"

"Very good, thank you, Alfonso." he said, but had no desire to chat and kept walking. *"Buonanotte."*

"*Buonanotte, signore.* I understand you are leaving tomorrow?" Harry stopped in his tracks. He hadn't mentioned it to anyone because he hadn't made his mind up, yet it seemed the decision had not only been made for him, it had been communicated to others. He turned slowly to face Alfonso and then approached the desk. The *proprietario* projected an air of inscrutability, but Harry saw something others would miss. It was in the eyes and the posture and the positioning of the head.

"Word gets around." Alfonso gave an imperceptible nod. "I'm not sure. There's something I would like to do tomorrow."

"I see."

"Would that inconvenience you?"

Alfonso shrugged. "May I suggest the *signore* check out tomorrow and, er, if maybe he changes his mind and wants to stay one more night I am certain I can find him another room?"

"I don't want to cause you any difficulty... or embarrassment."

"No no, it will be my pleasure." The smile was warm and genuine, Harry judged. The chap had been put under pressure but he'd worked around it despite having no obvious incentive.

"I'm very grateful to you."

"I trust you found the gentleman you were looking for, *signore*?"

"Yes indeed. He gave me some... helpful advice."

"Then you are even wiser than before." He laughed and Harry nodded in agreement. He trusted Alfonso for some reason and it broke all his rules. Trust was never taken for granted; it had to be earned and that took time. He'd known the chap for less than two days, not time enough, but he needed to know something else and the mere fact of his asking could put them all at risk. He trusted Alfonso.

"Where would I find the Chiesa di San Pietro?"

"Ah, *sì, signore*. The church is easy to find. If you drive down to the river and turn to the right, it is maybe five kilometres away."

"Thank you."

"Prego. Buonanotte."

CHAPTER 22

He fired up the Spyder. It burbled and snarled like a tame tiger and he was pleased to be back behind the wheel with the wind in his hair. He'd checked out as agreed and his suitcase was in the boot, but thanks to Alfonso, his options remained open. His instinct had been to ignore Luigi Barone's threat, but he had to consider others too. Whatever happened, he'd be leaving Italy soon but Casavento was Alfonso's home and life and he had his wife and daughter Cleo to think of. It wasn't right to make life difficult for them, especially after he'd been so hospitable and helpful.

Harry didn't know what would come out of his meeting with Lucia, whether she would castigate him for his crime, demand explanations of her own or simply send him away with a flea in his ear. Any of those would mean his scuttling off back to Rome and from there, who knows? Whatever happened, it was unlikely he would need to return to the Garibaldi, so he may as well be prepared to depart for good.

The late summer sun continued to shine, although the trees were turning amber and the lack of rain meant the Galliano meandered calm and serene on its way to the Adriatic.

He found the church easily. It stood alone on the riverbank, its whitewashed walls gleaming in the morning sun. He pulled the Spyder off the road into a rough, dusty car park devoid of vehicles other than a single scarlet-coloured Vespa parked by the open church door. He sensed a mild attack of nerves and a vague nausea in his belly. There was so much he wanted to say to her but he couldn't shake off the fear she would be angry and resentful. But most of all, he just wanted to see her again.

He parked the car, leaving the roof down, and stepped tentatively inside the church, the warmth on his back giving way instantly to cool, his eyes adjusting to the sepia light, the aroma of candles, incense and old oak filling his nostrils.

It echoed from the faintest sound and for a moment he thought he was alone until a slight figure appeared from behind a pillar to the right of the altar carrying a mop and bucket. He was instantly reminded of Rosa, the truculent old bird he'd met with Father Benelli, and he hoped not to have a similar conversation. He walked up the central aisle towards her, the sound of his footsteps on the ancient stone reverberating around the holy place. She laid down her bucket and stood the mop inside, staring up at a giant gold crucifix that dominated the space behind the altar.

She wore a simple, white, short-sleeved blouse over pale blue slacks that were short in the leg, exposing her ankles. A shaft of sunlight from a stained-glass window illuminated the back of her head, endowing her auburn hair with a golden aura. He saw her make the sign of the cross and then she turned to face him. He approached to within a few feet and she crossed her arms across her chest as if to say "no further", her face set and expressionless. He was lost for words, struck again by her beauty, as struck as he had been eighteen years ago and again yesterday, when their shock encounter had momentarily paralysed them both. She bore a faint shadow above her left cheekbone, her left eye puffy and red. The bruise had been covered, painted over with some substance that had been only partially effective. Without thinking, he put a hand to his own cheek and he felt a sudden rage that made him clench a fist.

"Did your husband do that?" She ignored the question. It needed no reply but he felt responsible. "I'm sorry, it's my fault he—"

"I am glad you survived," she interrupted. "I always wondered what happened to you. I thought you would die too."

She'd lifted a huge weight from him, more than she could possibly imagine, except that now he felt guilty all over again – guilty that he'd survived and her family hadn't.

"I never knew you existed, other than in my imagination. I have dreamt about you almost every night since then, this apparition that brought me peace in my final moments." She shifted her body and relaxed her arms, her face betraying some discomfort and he feared he'd said something disrespectful. "I dream the whole episode. Your father and Isabella and the baby. I have lived through it time and time again, wondering how much of it was real and how much a cruel fantasy."

"I don't know your name."

"Oh, no. Of course not. It's Harry Male."

She thrust out a hand. "Hello, Harrimale," she said, stringing the names together as if they were one, and as if any confirmation were needed, "I am Lucia, Isabella's sister."

He took her hand and it was small but strong, just like she was. He was entranced in the same way he'd been entranced back then when the explosions had finally stopped and the dying embers of the fire were about to expire and all that was left was the vision of hope from the angel now standing in front of him.

"Lucia, there are things I need to ask you, lots of things about you and your family and—"

"Wait." She held up a hand to stop him. "This is not the place. There are things that cannot be talked about in the house of God. We will go somewhere else. Please." She gestured towards the door.

"Yes, of course. I understand."

She slid past him and he caught her fragrance, which prickled his senses. She picked up a black linen matador jacket that was hanging over a pew and set off down the aisle.

Their eyes squinted in the sunshine, her bruise glowing purple under the make-up.

"Follow me. It is a few kilometres." She pulled a pair of black sunglasses from inside her jacket, stepped onto the Vespa and kicked it into life. He hastily climbed into the Spyder, afraid he would lose her, but she waited at the side of the road for him and then gunned the engine, leaving a cloud of pungent blue smoke billowing in her wake.

The roads were empty of traffic as he followed her along the riverside, her jacket flapping in the breeze, until after a few minutes, she turned off to the right and sped up a winding road. They passed a village sign that read *Monte Galliano* and she led him through a maze of narrow deserted streets then through a tiny piazza to a small car park. She dismounted, propped the Vespa on its stand and was running both hands through her windswept hair as he pulled up alongside.

"Come, Harrimale, we can talk in the piazza."

She walked briskly away and he followed her dutifully back to a piazza that featured the ubiquitous fountain at its centre and a number of small shops and cafés, clearly the hub of the tiny metropolis. She strode across the square and up some steps to a café with wooden tables and chairs outside. She took off her jacket and sat down. Four old men in caps and heavy tweed jackets were playing cards on a nearby table, brandy glasses and espresso cups in evidence, but they didn't look up once, neither at the beautiful young woman nor the handsome young man who cautiously sat opposite her. A waiter appeared.

"Due cappuccini," she ordered, without reference to Harry. The waiter swivelled on the spot and disappeared inside.

"No men in red jackets today?"

"Paolo has a job to do. Just not today."

"What is his job and why not today?"

She sighed. "I have one day off each week from the restaurant. I go to the church and do the cleaning and dusting and tidy everything and replace the candles and polish the silver and brass. You know." He didn't know but he nodded anyway. "And I have a place to myself. Where I can think and pray and make my peace with the world." She shrugged.

"And Luigi is happy for you to go alone?" It sounded impertinent, but it was meant to express concern and he

202

wanted to understand her relationship with him. "I mean, he seems very protective of you, even though... ". He gestured to the bruise on her cheek.

She let out a puff of air. A snort of derision. "He protects me like he protects his money and his property and his business. I am a possession. He does what he likes with me."

"But not today?"

"No. Today he is busy. Today he has a council meeting at the town hall with the *sindaco*, that is the mayor, and also the chief of police and the *sacerdote*, who is the priest of the cathedral. Then they have a long lunch at Ristorante Santi Divini and then they go to the Hotel Alba to play cards and get drunk and fuck some whores and then he comes home."

Harry closed his open mouth, but just to open it again.

"The priest...?"

She laughed but it was mirthless. "Maybe he goes home before the whores. I don't know."

Harry shook his head in dismay and the waiter brought two cups of coffee.

"Prego."

"But on other days Paolo is your chaperone?"

"No. Just yesterday. Luigi thought you might be a threat."

"A threat to you?"

"No! Of course not – a threat to himself."

"I'm not a threat to him, or you."

"I know that," she said, and he thought he saw a flicker of compassion behind the frosty exterior, a softening. "It was just a shock, you understand. I was confused."

"So was I."

"How did you find me?"

"I went back to Montellano. I had to. Something happened to me in Berlin; that's where I live and work, though not any more. It made me think again about what happened, at your father's house, in Solano. The nightmares have been with me ever since and I thought perhaps if I looked at it again, it would be different."

"And is it?"

"Well, I didn't expect to meet you. In the flesh. Oh, what I mean is…"

"I know what you mean." She was smiling at him now, laughing at his discomfort, and it was alluring, more so than anything he had experienced in a long while.

"I found the place where your house used to be."

"It was demolished after the war ended. There was nothing left and no one left to rebuild it."

"And I met the local priest, Father Benelli, who didn't know your family but his cleaning lady Rosa remembered you all."

Lucia took a sip of her coffee and then nodded.

"Ah yes. Rosa Agnelli," she scoffed. "I remember her. She probably had a few choice words to say about me." Harry wanted to tread carefully, but he believed she wasn't one to be embarrassed so neither should he.

"She said you had married Luigi Barone and left town."

Lucia gave another hollow laugh. "She said I was Luigi Barone's whore! But then being his wife is not so different."

The old men in caps burst into a heated debate that involved various hand gestures and a fair amount of complaining until another hand was dealt and they fell silent again. Harry turned his head to the piazza and watched a bulky black motorcycle with leather-clad rider rumble slowly by, heading in the direction of the car park. He gave it only a cursory look; he had other things on his mind.

"I saw your sister's grave. And your parents'." She looked away abruptly, avoiding his eyes. She was strong, but not that strong. "I asked around and someone said Luigi had moved to Casavento…"

"Chased out of town."

"… but I wanted to see if I could find you."

"And now you have found me?" The truculence had resurfaced but he could see it was just a defence mechanism. "What now, Harrimale?"

He struggled to pose the question. He now knew what had happened; there was no doubt. The answer would be simple and as expected and she would confirm it for him and they would wish each other well and go on their way. The last piece would fall into place and it would finally all be made clear. But he didn't want the last piece to fall into place; he didn't want this to end with a chat over a cup of coffee.

"There was a baby," he ventured softly.

"Yes, there was a baby. Her name was Catalina."

CHAPTER 23

Little Lucia kneels by her sister's bed, gripping her hand in hers, trying to wish away the pain, afraid Isabella will die before their father gets back. If he ever gets back.

"Papà will be here soon. He will bring help and then soon we will have another member of the family. You will have a baby boy or a baby girl and I shall be an auntie!"

"Oh, Lucia! It hurts. Why does it hurt so much?" Isabella's face is twisted in agony and it breaks her heart to see her beloved sister suffer, but she has to remain calm.

"It always hurts when a woman has a baby," she says with all the authority of a fourteen-year-old. "Mama said it hurt when she had you and it hurt when she had me; it's normal." Isabella arches her back and screams and another explosion rocks the house, sending flakes of plaster and dust down on their heads.

"Make it stop, Lucia!"

"I can't. It will stop when they are ready to stop."

She wipes Isabella's forehead with the sleeve of her dressing gown. Isabella pants as the contractions come and she writhes and twists her head on the filthy pillow and Lucia tries to contain her rising panic. She hears the latch of the door and turns her head towards the sound.

"Papà," she whispers.

Alfredo Girardi hobbles into the room and closes the door behind him, gasping for breath. "Papà?" She looks expectantly at her father as he approaches the bed.

"How's my little girl?"

"Papà, where is the doctor?"

"They are here, Lucia. They are outside. But you must go upstairs."

"But why?"

"Please! Lucia." He gives her a look that alarms her. "They are soldiers. English soldiers. I don't know them. I don't know what they might do. I can't take the risk."

206

"But, Papà..."

"Go now. At once!" He pulls her to her feet and pushes her towards the staircase. "Go!" She runs up the stairs. She's always obedient towards her father. Always.

She kneels on the landing at the top of the stairs as her father opens the door and then she sees a soldier come in behind him, crouching, moving slowly and carefully, swinging a big gun from side to side. His uniform is greenish brown in colour, different from the grey and black ones she's used to and he looks wary, not angry like the others. She ducks into the landing corridor in case he sees her. She sits on the floor with her back to the wall, listening, but the sound is muffled and he speaks a language she doesn't understand. All she recognises are Isabella's screams amidst the explosions that happen at random intervals and make the house shake and she puts her hands over her ears because being able to hear but not see makes things worse.

Isabella screams again and she hears her father.

"You can name the baby," and then, "Reggio, yes, or if it's a girl? Catalina. Yes, Catalina." Then the soldier is asking for hot water and there is another big bang outside and then there is quiet and after a while she dares descend a stair or two and peek between the uprights of the balustrade. The soldier is bending over Isabella, looking between her legs and then there's an almighty explosion outside that rocks the farmhouse again and Isabella is screaming and her father's shouting and praying, "Mother of God, Holy Mother Mary!" and the soldier is shouting, "Baby, baby!" and she scuttles back upstairs and onto the landing, shaking with fear.

And then a whistle approaches from the distance, rising like a banshee until it hurts her ears and she pulls the dressing gown over her head until there's a deafening boom and she feels the air being sucked out of her lungs as the roof above her head flies off into the sky. The wall at the end of the landing disappears and she tucks herself into a ball on the moving floor in case it tips her backwards and she has to

207

grab hold of the doorframe to stop herself falling into the room below and then the roof tiles fall back to earth through a hole where the floor used to be.

And then there's quiet again, apart from the odd piece of loose brick and creaking beam yielding to gravity, settling in its final resting place.

Her hair and dressing gown are covered in a thick layer of dust, and she rubs her arms and chest to shake it off and after a moment or two ventures a little way down the stairs and peers through the broken balustrade. The room is open to daylight and the fire continues to flicker in the chimneystack and the floor is covered in rubble. She inches further down the staircase and lets out a whimper. Her father is gone, and a huge wooden beam lies across the top of the bed. Only Isabella's lower half remains visible, knees bent upward, legs wide apart. The soldier lies partially covered by rubble, moaning but moving. She freezes and she watches him as he drags his broken body over to the bed and tries to help Isabella. She watches him howl like a wolf and cry like a baby. What kind of soldier cries? A good one. She cries too but she can't move. Her family is gone but the soldier is back behind the bed, kneeling over her dead sister's body and he's muttering to himself and still sobbing and then he has a knife! He has a knife and he's cutting her open and she gives out a silent scream and she can't watch so she scurries back up the stairs and rolls into a ball and cries.

More explosions, a distance away; she counts eight in succession and then she hears a baby cry. A baby? She opens her eyes, straining to hear but there are more explosions now and they are coming closer and closer and then the devil himself is shouting and the roar of a thousand lions is above her head and the stampede of a thousand elephants is at the door and she screams and she screams...

***

It's quiet now. It's been quiet for hours or maybe it's only minutes or seconds, but the devil and the lions and elephants have all gone and she stirs and moves down the staircase on her bottom: one, two, three steps. The chimneystack has fallen into the room, the last flames of a dying fire weak and withering. The soldier is sitting on the floor with his back to the wall. She crawls towards him on all fours over the stones and the bricks and the wood but he looks dead and blood oozes red and glistening from his shoulder. He's holding a baby. Isabella's baby! Then he moves his head and his eyes open and she stares at him but he looks blind because he's smiling stupidly through her and his lips are mumbling something she can't understand. She looks down at the baby lying still in his lap and she picks it up and holds it to her chest. Catalina. The soldier closes his eyes and his head lolls to one side. He looks peaceful, sleeping.

***

The old men in caps had reached the end of a round and kicked off again. The sudden noise broke Harry out of his trance and he saw Lucia looking at him closely.

"So you see, Harrimale, I am no angel. I am just the one who was left alive and at the time, I didn't even want to be alive. I saw what you did. I saw what you did for my sister before she was killed and what you did to her afterwards and I thought, this man has died trying to help her and her baby."

He was profoundly moved by her testimony. His own horror had been bad enough, and the re-telling of the hideous drama by someone who observed it, sobering beyond measure. But he could not imagine how a child could possibly have witnessed such carnage and yet survived mentally; go on to live some semblance of a normal life, however challenging and distasteful. He had never coped with the aftermath and he wondered how she had.

"Where did you go?" he asked, but his voice quavered and he had to clear his throat.

"I wanted to get away as far as I could, but I had no shoes and I had only a nightdress and dressing gown and there was still ice on the ground. I heard soldiers coming and I was frightened and ran away across the field."

"Where did you bury her?"

"Who?"

"Catalina."

The smile dropped and her gaze shifted to somewhere over his shoulder. He turned his head. A black Mercedes-Benz pulled up outside the café and two men jumped out, leaving the driver, engine running: Paolo in his red jacket and sunglasses and another in a grey suit, faces grim and determined.

CHAPTER 24

Lucia stood up, suddenly anxious and wary and Harry got to his feet with her. Paolo and Grey Man took a step forward. The old boys in caps had gone suddenly quiet, but kept their heads down, staring at their hand of cards.

"Lucia. You should go now and wait for Luigi. He say you must return home immediately."

Lucia glowered at him then looked at Harry, but he knew there was danger and wanted her to leave even if it meant going back to her oaf of a husband. He gave her an almost imperceptible nod. Paolo removed his sunglasses.

"Signore Barone would like to have a talk with you. Please. We take you." He gestured towards the car, courteous, non-threatening. Harry hesitated, but knew they were serious when Grey Man opened his jacket, revealing a glimpse of shoulder holster. Grey Man opened the back door of the Mercedes and Harry climbed in with Grey Man alongside. Paolo got in the front and the driver gunned the engine, spinning the tyres on the cobblestones.

They drove at speed back down to the riverside then turned right, away from Casavento, and Harry realised it was unlikely he was being taken for a pep talk with Luigi Barone. It was far more serious than that. Neither Paolo nor the other two goons said a word, which was also significant and fairly indicative. The executioner keeps a mental distance from the condemned; engagement of any sort weakens resolve and makes the job harder. They crossed the river over a single-track bridge that led uphill into a forest. The bumpy dirt road narrowed and after a few minutes, they pulled up. The car was blocking the road, but it hardly mattered as there was no one around.

He tried to recall his field training but it was a long time ago and he'd never had to use it. In any event, hand to hand was all very well provided you had a weapon of some sort – a stick even – but he had nothing other than his fists. He'd made a quick assessment of the opposition. None of them were athletes, clearly. Paolo was forty-something, skinny, had yellow, drawn skin and, between coughs, had smoked all the way. The driver was older and short, carried a few stone more than necessary and had a florid complexion. Grey Man with him in the back was in his fifties, grey hair and stubble to match his suit and looked the most dangerous.

"We get out here," said Paolo as he and Grey Man opened the doors and beckoned him out. He thought a chat with Luigi Barone was probably not on the agenda, but couldn't decide whether he was in for a beating or something more terminal. Given the remote surroundings and the general appearance of his captors he thought it unlikely they'd risk a bout of fisticuffs, even if it was three to one. But any doubt was dispelled when Grey Man opened the boot and extracted a large shovel. Paolo reached inside his jacket and pulled out a Beretta. He waved it towards the trees.

"Walk!"

Fat Man stayed with the car, which was good because this reduced the odds, but only from bad to poor. He knew Grey Man was armed too but he was carrying the shovel over one shoulder and that would impede sudden movement. Paolo's latest cigarette dangled from a lower lip when it wasn't in his hand flicking ash, and Harry noted each transition put him at his most vulnerable. They arrived at a small clearing between pine trees, a hundred yards from the car.

"Stop!" Grey Man threw the shovel down at Harry's feet and pulled out his gun, pointing it at his head.

"Now you dig," said Paolo, waving his gun at the ground.

Harry was pleased to have a weapon, even if it was only a shovel. On the bright side, nothing would happen until he had finished digging a big enough hole. The goons were obviously too lazy to do it themselves and had watched too many gangster movies. The longer it took the harder it would be for them to maintain their concentration, but unless they came within striking distance, he wouldn't be able to wield the shovel effectively. The ground was soft, decades or more of fallen pine needles producing a rich mulch that was perfect for breaking down organic matter. It wouldn't have to be deep, just enough to cover a body with a thin layer, then nature would do the rest, unless, of course, the bears got there first.

He was running out of time and he felt a sadness wash over him. He'd been in dangerous and difficult situations before, but had never been confronted with an inevitability like this. Even in war, he'd never had time to contemplate his demise, apart from his last moments in the Girardi farmhouse and, in their own way, those moments had become precious. He thought of Lucia, alone with her vile and repulsive husband, and wanted more than anything to see her again. He'd had nothing left in his life until he'd met her and now, unexpectedly, he did. He made a decision.

He stopped digging and leaned on the shovel. The mulch had ruined his brown loafers and smeared his pale trousers with dirt and he was angry. He'd had enough. He climbed out of the hole and Paolo and Grey Man both took a step back.

"You finish!" said Paolo, waving the gun again.

"Finish it yourself," he said wearily.

Paolo looked at Grey Man then back at Harry. He blinked, which was never a good sign for a pro, but then Harry had already come to the conclusion these guys were amateurs. They should have shot him first and then dug a hole. There was nothing to be gained by postponing the act and everything to lose.

"Drop the gun!" The amateurs froze and looked at each other. "I'll kill you both!" They turned their heads slowly. Lucia was only ten feet away, swinging a gun nervously from one to the other and back again. Paolo looked at Grey Man and they both sniggered, their gun hands still outstretched, weapons still pointed at Harry. She gripped the gun with both hands and tried again with more intensity.

"Drop your gun, Paolo Barone or I promise I will shoot you. You too, Franco." But her hands were shaking and she was trembling. Paolo spread his arms.

"Lucia. My brother will be a very unhappy man," he said with a mischievous glint and Franco chuckled with him. "We only come to frighten the *inglese* and now you spoil the joke!"

"I mean it, Paolo. This man is worth more than the two of you."

Both men shrugged. She fired two shots over Paolo's head and he ducked, taken completely by surprise, humour evaporating instantly.

"Hey! Okay. Okay." Both men lowered their guns. Franco turned to look at Harry, who'd raised the shovel to shoulder height in case it were needed. But before Harry could move, another shot sounded. Franco's body suddenly jerked as a red flower blossomed in his chest and they watched, as if in slow motion, he toppled forward into the hole. They stared down at him in confusion when another shot made Harry duck, then look back at Paolo, who'd gone cross-eyed and now sported a red hole in the centre of his forehead. Paolo's knees buckled and he crumpled to the ground, rolling into the hole on top of Franco.

"Sniper!" yelled Harry. He dropped the shovel and dived forward, taking Lucia down in a rugby tackle, grabbing an arm and dragging her on her back behind a pine tree. "Give me the gun!" She handed it over, gasping, the wind taken out of her by the fall. Another shot and splinters of bark flew from the trunk near his head and he felt the tree shudder against his back. He looked up to the track and saw the Mercedes roaring away uphill; Fat Man had seen what was going on and was making his escape.

"Who's shooting at us?"

"How should I know? Not friends of your husband, that's for sure. What are you doing here?"

"I followed you. My scooter is on the track, out of sight," she said, breathless and terrified, her chest heaving.

"Look, we have to make a run for it. There's plenty of cover. I'll stay behind you." He pointed to a thick pine fifteen feet away diagonally to their left. "When I say go, go for that tree and don't look back, whatever happens. Okay?" She nodded, terror in her eyes. He peered around the tree and there was a shot and bark splintered again with a dull slap. Whoever it was hadn't moved position; the sight was centred on the hole he'd been digging and the aim had swung left to the adjacent tree. It would be a good sniper that could hit a moving target, especially if the target was shooting back. He was transported back to Sicily and Southern Italy. He was commanding his platoon again, pinned down by a sniper, again, except that this time he was poorly equipped. Conventional strategy, and the safest thing to do, was to split up and go in different directions because then the shooter would have to choose. But he wouldn't risk it; he had to cover her.

"Stay as low as you can, hands and knees. Ready?" She nodded again and he saw the beginnings of panic. He pulled her towards him and kissed her forehead. He wasn't sure why; it just seemed the natural thing to do. "Go!" She went left and he let off three shots in the general direction of the sniper, then followed her, scrabbling on all fours, keeping their heads below some ferns, and reached the next tree. He sat with his back to the trunk, pulling her close with a hand wrapped around her chest and he felt her heart beating furiously. "That one," he whispered in her ear, pointing left again where there was a cluster of ferns and shrubs that would inhibit line of sight. "Go!" She dived forward and he followed immediately behind, shielding her from the estimated trajectory of any bullet, but there were no more shots. *Maybe he's on the move too?* That would be logical. He'd have to reposition in order to get another shot and that would take precious seconds. But they couldn't afford to give him the luxury of time. He pointed again. "Go!"

This one was further away, a giant eucalyptus with a metre-wide trunk, and they stopped again, huddled together.

He risked a peek around the trunk, but there was no reaction. They were fifty yards from the track and soon they'd be running across the line of sight behind dozens of trees, making them impossible targets. "Go!" Still no shot or slap against bark, so he made a decision. "Keep going!"

They reached the dirt track and sprinted downhill the way the car had brought him and there, around the first bend, sat the red Vespa. She jumped on top and kicked the starter. He swung a leg behind her, she twisted the throttle and the little red scooter leapt off its stand and careered down the track. She drove just like an Italian and the scenery blurred but he caught a flash of light, a glint of chrome in the bushes to his right. *Another bike?* He wrapped an arm around her waist and pressed against her back, fearing he'd be thrown off but she twisted the handlebars left and right and weaved the Vespa expertly between potholes and ridges until they hit the narrow bridge across the river and were back on tarmac. The engine buzzed like a demented bee as she cranked up the speed and he had to shout to be heard.

"Back to the car!"

***

She guided the Vespa through the piazza and into the car park and he was relieved to see the Spyder still there and apparently intact. He dismounted and opened the boot: his jacket and suitcase were still there too. Lucia sat astride the scooter, engine still running, holding the handlebars, but she looked distraught. In the ten-minute journey he'd been working out a plan.

"What do we do now, Harrimale?"

"We need to get away from here. Away from Casavento."

"Where?" She sounded angry but he knew it was just fear. He stepped forward and put a hand on her arm. She looked straight ahead, unable to make eye contact.

"Just do as I say, Lucia. I promise I won't let anything happen to you."

She turned to look at him and her eyes were moist. "You said that yesterday."

He'd said he wouldn't harm her and it had been true, *never in a million years*, yet indirectly, his persistence had put her in harm's way. She was his responsibility now, unconditionally.

"You saved me just now," he said, trying to make light of dark situation. "It's my turn and I'll say it again. I won't let any harm come to you." She looked unconvinced. "Get in the car. Now."

***

She argued but he insisted. There was no alternative in the short term if he was going to keep her safe. Sooner or later, Fat Man driving the Mercedes – Bruno, she called him – would get word back to Luigi about what had happened. As far as Bruno could tell, Lucia had shot Paolo and Franco and run off with the *inglese.*

"What were you doing with a gun?" he asked her as they hit the riverside road and sped back towards town.

"There's a compartment in the scooter. I have it for protection when I am alone. Parts of Italy are still like the Wild West."

"So I can tell. What made you come after me?" He cast a glance at her. Her arms were folded across her chest, eyes staring ahead.

"I know what Luigi is like. I tried to warn you. Lives mean nothing to him. People who invade his territory are warned once, then they pay the price."

"But you said he was friends with the mayor and the police chief. And the priest!"

She gave him a look of disdain. "Exactly. How else can he do what he does? They have control over everything and everyone." He'd been naïve. He'd worked in the shadows for so long he'd forgotten that out here in the real world, bad people still did bad things on a daily basis. The Wild West indeed.

They reached the Ponte Galliano and he turned right to cross the river. He saw her looking at the mediaeval arch into the town as if he was going the wrong way, but she stayed silent and just stared through the windscreen. Her world had unravelled at lightning speed and at this precise moment she had nothing other than the clothes she was wearing. He couldn't know what was going through her mind, but he cared deeply.

The Spyder reached the opposite side of the river and began its winding ascent up the mountain on the road to Rome. Harry drove at speed and had to concentrate, especially on hairpin bends and places where there were no protective barriers, while his mind wrestled with random thoughts. He didn't care one way or another what befell the foot soldiers of a second-rate *mafioso*, but he was still puzzled about the sniper. Yes, she'd said, Luigi had enemies; a rival had driven him out of Montellano all those years ago and he might at some stage have come up against competition in Casavento.

But it made no sense that a rival's hitman might be hiding in the woods just in case Barone's flunkeys came wandering by. Maybe it was some weirdo with a sniper rifle shooting at anyone and everyone, just as a form of entertainment? And why did Franco and Paolo get shot first when he was the closest and easiest target? Why did the shooter then fire off a couple of rounds at them but then stop? Just to scare them? It troubled him because there were no obvious answers.

Speculation was one thing, but he had to deal with realities. Two of Barone's men, one of them his brother, were dead and his wife had gone missing with the *inglese*. There was no way she could go back home and convince him it had all been an innocent misunderstanding, even though, until somebody began shooting, that was exactly the way it had been. Harry and Lucia shared a tragic history of which Barone knew little or nothing and none of it was a threat to him. Maybe, as Lucia had tried to explain, Barone was simply the type to see a threat in everything; absolute power and control was his religion and would not be compromised. But there was still a shooter out there who might be in pursuit and soon Barone's army of goons would be joining the chase. He had to get her away from Casavento.

He had no idea of the scope and scale of Barone's network, whether it was confined to the area around Casavento or extended further beyond, and nor did she.

"Luigi makes many trips out of town, sometimes to Rome, but I don't know where he goes or why. Whores, I suppose."

"Does he ever go back to Montellano?"

"I doubt it. The town belongs to someone else now."

Whether Luigi had already been alerted to the crisis or was still lying drunk and sated in a brothel, he would at some point give chase. He'd get straight on the phone and mobilise his troops: *find her and kill him.* Harry couldn't know how quickly things might happen, but within minutes, he found out.

A black Mercedes-Benz careered around a hairpin bend ahead of them, its rear end askew, sliding across the road and almost colliding with the Spyder. Harry wrenched the wheel right to avoid it and narrowly missed the barrier but caught a glimpse of the corpulent and sweaty Bruno, twirling the wheel in panic, desperate to get back and report the debacle to his master. Bruno's face confirmed instant recognition of the Spyder and its occupants, his expression feverish, eyes wide in triumph. Harry kept his eyes on the rear-view mirror, expecting to see brake lights and a car in pursuit, but there was nothing; Bruno was outnumbered and, for all he knew, probably outgunned too. The danger had passed for now.

"Where the hell did he come from?" said Harry in exasperation, but Lucia's anxiety had returned.

"The forest track leads to a main road and circles round to join this one."

Harry considered the options. They were only ten minutes out of Casavento on the road to Rome and that was almost three hours away. It would not take long for Bruno to alert Barone and get reinforcements. There was no guarantee he could outrun them, but now Barone would know their general direction was south-west and that was a matter of grave concern. He looked at Lucia. She was rubbing her upper arms, possibly from fear but just as likely cold. The temperature had dropped steadily as they'd ascended and the sun had dipped behind the mountain.

They reached a plateau and a fork in the road. He pulled the car over to the side.

"What's happening?" she said, suddenly alert.

He jumped out and grabbed the canvas roof that was folded behind the seats, pulling it up and over her head, then retrieved his jacket from the boot and climbed back into the driver's seat. He leaned over to her side, snapped down the roof retaining clips and wound up the window, then spread his jacket over her chest and arms.

"Thank you," she said, smiling weakly.

He looked at the road sign and made a decision. Rome was to the right. He slicked the car into gear and steered left, towards Montellano.

CHAPTER 25

Harry watched her from the chair by the window, wondering how long he should let her sleep. Lucia lay curled up on the bed, covered by the blanket he'd laid over her. The last few hours had been traumatic and he guessed her fatigue was as much a reaction to the day's events as a genuine desire for sleep. But they'd had nothing to eat and it was now six thirty. He was hungry and even if she wasn't, he couldn't just go off and leave her alone, so he'd have to wake her at some point.

They'd arrived at the Hotel Abruzzi just before five and been warmly welcomed by Fabrizio and Carla, who were effusive in their greetings towards their repeat guest and his delightful young companion.

"You come back to visit the abbey, *si?*" he'd said.

"Something like that."

Lucia hadn't protested when he'd asked for a double room and, in contrast to the reaction he might have expected in a provincial hotel in England, no eyebrows had been raised either. Carla had put an arm around Lucia and kissed her when she saw how drained she was.

"Ah, ha un aspetto stanco. Prego." She'd insisted Fabrizio give them the best room and, of course, he'd obeyed without question. They both looked dishevelled with dried mud and mulch stains on shoes and trousers; they needed to shower and change. Harry had clean clothes in his suitcase, but not so Lucia, who had nothing but the clothes she was wearing.

"Signora Carla, are any stores still open?" he'd asked her. No, they would be closed now, she'd said but she knew the *signora* who owned and lived above a ladies' clothes shop and because it was an *emergencia* she'd go and get her to open up and bring back a selection of garments. But as soon as they got into the room, Lucia had crashed out, shutting out the world and, presumably, any residual thoughts she'd had about the day's events.

Harry had contemplated their situation on the journey to Montellano. He expected Luigi and his goons to come after them but hoped they'd head to Rome and waste time looking there. Perhaps he would send his people to search both simultaneously; the *inglese* had confessed to visiting Montellano and his wife might still have connections there. He cursed himself for hiring such a distinctive car, but then he'd never imagined his self-indulgent adventure, his harmless trip down memory lane, would turn into such a nightmare. While Lucia was sleeping, he'd had a word with Fabrizio.

"I wonder if your cousin Silvio can look after my car for me?" He'd dangled the keys. "Maybe swap it for the little Cinquecento? Just for a day or two."

Fabrizio had looked perplexed. "*Signore...* you have not... stolen this car?"

"No, no, of course not. The hire papers are in the glovebox. I just want him to keep it safe in a garage."

"Ah, I understand."

"There's one other thing, Fabrizio."

"Sì, signore."

"It would be better if you and Carla call me Signore Harper." He'd slid a green, Republic of Ireland passport across the desk and Fabrizio had examined it briefly, preparing to ask a question before grinning with intrigue. "*Sì,* Signore Harper! I change the register."

Lucia snuffled and he turned to look at her. She was beautiful, even in her bedraggled and unkempt state. He remembered how struck he was with her sister Isabella, whose classic Italian beauty had shone through even in her own pitiful condition. Mr and Mrs Girardi had done well and would have been very proud.

He was responsible for Lucia now, just as he had taken responsibility for Isabella and her baby; *yeah, and look how that turned out, Harry.* He saw no way he could reason with

222

Barone nor any way he could let her return to him, now he knew his true character. Ultimately though, it would be her own decision; he hoped she'd be able to make the right one. He looked at his watch: almost seven. He got up and walked over to the bed.

He knelt down, reminded of the moment he'd knelt down in front of Isabella, and hesitantly touched her arm. She was sleeping, breathing steadily, and half of him wanted to leave her alone, but the other half made him squeeze her arm and she awoke suddenly and let out a gasp, eyes wide and anxious. To his surprise, she threw both arms around his neck, gripping him fiercely and he felt the warmth of her body and the beating of her heart against his chest.

"I didn't mean to frighten you," he said, gently touching her back and shoulders with fingertips as if she were made of glass. "I'm sorry." Her breathing steadied but she maintained her grip for a few seconds, then released him and rubbed her eyes with one hand.

"I was dreaming."

He had an idea what she might have been dreaming about, but thought twice about asking. "You can tell me about it later. Carla brought you some clean clothes. Maybe we should get cleaned up and then I'll take you out to dinner?"

She looked up at him, embarrassed, but smiling. "I'm a mess. I'm sorry."

"Not at all. I'm a mess." *If only she knew.* "Take a shower, the stuff's over there on the sofa. I'll be outside."

"No!" she said, instantly alarmed. "You can stay here."

He helped her up and she went into the bathroom, locking the door. Within seconds he heard the sound of the shower and he felt a rare comfort.

***

Angelo greeted him fondly with a crunching handshake, a slap on the back and a bear hug that so surprised and

223

bemused him, he was unsure how to respond. The Italian bowed solemnly when introduced to the *bellissima signorina* and kissed her hand.

"Lucia Girardi? Ah, this is the young lady you were seeking? Please, I have a lovely romantic table for you. *Prego!*" Harry and Lucia studiously avoided each other's eyes and followed him to the back of the restaurant, where he seated them at a table for two in a corner alcove.

She'd chosen a white long-sleeved blouse with patches of lace on the front and close-fitting black trousers. Carla had even got her some new shoes. Her short auburn hair shone in the candlelight and although her face was free of make-up, she didn't need it. He kept stealing a look whenever he could.

"Are you hungry?" he asked as they examined the menus. "I'm starving."

"Yes, I can eat something," she said, sitting on her hands, understandably still nervous and unsettled. The wine helped. She was halfway down the first glass when she began to mellow.

"I'm sorry I got you into this," he said, picking his moment. "I didn't appreciate how serious you were when you warned me about Luigi."

"You made me realise how much I am a prisoner. I have been a prisoner for many years and I did not have the courage to break free."

"Do you have the courage now?"

Her eyes went glassy and he wanted to hold her again.

"I am not sure. I don't have anyone else. I have no family or friends, not even here in Montellano. I am not sure what I am going to do now."

"You won't consider going back?" It was half question, half statement.

"To Casavento? No. Never. I have to go far away, where he will never find me."

Harry was relieved. He'd feared she might have second thoughts and that he'd be forced to talk her out of it. It was

224

inconceivable to him that she'd ever contemplate going back, but at the same time, he was concerned she had no natural place of refuge. He was also relieved because he wanted to stay close to her and it wasn't just out of some sense of duty or responsibility. She was an intrinsic part of his past and he wanted her to be part of his future. She'd been there with him in his darkest hour, seen the things he'd seen and suffered just the same if not more. They had both suffered again in the aftermath, directly or indirectly – she by falling in with a villain like Barone and he because his fractured, uncontrollable mind would not leave him in peace.

He would happily whisk her away to England or Berlin, but he had to rein in his desires. The angel of Solano had been in his mind for as long as he could remember, but he had only known Lucia Girardi for two days. It was too soon to be formulating life-changing plans for either of them, despite the drama of their situation and while she'd been sleeping, he'd had time to analyse their predicament and it wasn't good.

But he also had unfinished business and he wanted to try to conclude it before they made their next move. He wanted to know what happened to her and the baby after he'd passed out, and was about to ask when she got in first.

"Tell me about yourself," she said, taking another sip of her wine. The bottle would not last the evening. "Where did you go, afterwards? You said you were in Berlin. What do you do there?"

"Nothing now. I left my job and my apartment."

"You are homeless too, then?"

"Yes, something like that." He laughed. He didn't feel homeless but then there was nowhere to go back to. Home could be wherever he wanted it to be. At this precise moment, right here and now, being with her, felt like home.

"I woke up in a military hospital. They said I'd been there for a few days. Then once they'd fixed me up, I was sent home to a desk job. Not fit for active service, they said. That was the summer of forty-four."

225

"You were bleeding a lot. I thought you would die."

"Yes, well, one leg got a bit mangled and I suffered a blow to the head, but I was also shot by a crazy German – up here." He indicated his right shoulder and he felt it twinge in agreement. "Lost a lot of blood."

"A German?"

"Just before the place got bombed, this SS guy kicked the door down. He was badly injured himself and delirious, waving a gun around, screaming and shouting. He shot me but then the chimney fell in and buried him under the rubble. You probably didn't see him."

"No, I didn't see anyone but you and…" She tailed off and looked down at her hands. She looked lost and he felt desperately sorry for her. Talking about it was helping him but he wasn't sure it was helping her and whatever level of trauma he had suffered, hers had to be greater.

"When the war ended, I left the army but I couldn't settle. After a few years I got a job at the Ministry of Defence and ended up in the Secret Intelligence Service in Berlin. MI6."

She took a sharp intake of breath. "You are a spy?"

"No, not really." He laughed, but he was pleased to see her perk up and her sudden fascination in him made him tingle with pride. *Or is it something else?* "No, I analysed coded messages and also debriefed people who escaped over the Berlin Wall. To check they weren't spies."

"But you don't do that now?"

"No. The last guy to escape got killed. They sent an assassin and he almost got me too."

"Oh my God, Harrimale, does bad luck follow you everywhere you go?" She said it with a smile but there was a serious point. Either bad luck followed him around or he brought it with him. He wasn't sure which. It made him think again about Kessler. He couldn't begin to explain to her how the "crazy German" and Bergmann's assassin were one and the same; he couldn't even explain it to himself so it would be far too much for her to take in. The fact he'd had the misfortune twice to cross paths with a pyscho like

226

Kessler was either supremely bad luck or some form of punishment meted out by a holy or unholy spirit.

"I'm not religious, but I did think someone was sending me a message and it made me to think of your family in a new way. It all seemed connected somehow, all part of my problem. I had to come back and see for myself. See what was real and what was imaginary."

"And do you now know?"

Angelo brought some bruschetta and she tucked in immediately, wiping her lips with a napkin. After the traumatic events of the day, Lucia now seemed more relaxed and he didn't want to upset her. The urge to understand Catalina's demise and see her final resting place still burned inside him, but he decided to leave any further questioning until tomorrow.

"I know a lot more now about myself."

"Do you have a wife and a family?" She sounded casual, but it caught him off guard. He would normally sidestep personal questions but somehow, in the presence of an angel, it seemed natural.

"No. My parents are both dead and… I had a girlfriend in Berlin, but she decided she didn't like my job or who I had become, so she left."

"I'm sorry, Harrimale," she said between swallows.

"You can call me Harry, you know?"

"This is the short name?"

"No. My first name is Harry and my family name is Male."

She stopped chewing and clasped a hand over her mouth in shock.

"Oh no! I thought…" And then she burst out laughing and he laughed with her.

***

One bottle of wine had been enough after all, the meal rounded off by the mandatory shot of complimentary grappa.

They strolled back to the hotel in the cool of the evening and he put his jacket around her shoulders.

"Where is your car?" she asked with sudden concern when they arrived outside the Abruzzi. The red sports car was gone and in its place sat a white Cinquecento.

"It's somewhere safe and out of sight." He saw her shoulders sag. They'd enjoyed a wonderful evening together but now, reality hit home again. He put his arm around her and pulled her close. It seemed like the natural thing to do.

"I'm going to take you for a short ride tomorrow and then we'll decide where we go next. Okay?"

"Okay."

It was after ten and he was surprised to see Fabrizio still behind the desk.

"*Ah, signore*. Here is the key to your car. Silvio has taken care of the Spyder and no one will see it." He winked, then seeing Lucia looking at a rack of leaflets by the front door, dropped his voice. "*Signore,* the *polizia* have been here. They are looking for a young woman. Signora Barone. And a man with your name. Your other name. They are asking all the hotels. I say there is no one here with those names."

"Did they have a photograph?"

"No. Just a description." He glanced at Lucia and then back at Harry.

"I'm very grateful."

"*Signore.* They say the lady is in great danger."

"She was, Fabrizio, but not now. Not with me."

The Italian looked relieved and then smiled at Lucia when she came up alongside Harry and slid an arm through his.

"We'll stay another night and leave the day after. Good night."

"*Prego, signore, signora. Buonanotte.*"

They climbed the stairs and he opened the door for her. They stood for a moment, quiet and awkward.

"The lady has the bed, the gentleman is on the sofa," he said. "Are you tired?"

"I am tired, yes. Are you sure you will be comfortable?"

"Yes, I'll be comfortable."

***

He lay on his back on the sofa, covered by a single sheet, staring at the ceiling, examining the intricate cornicing. He'd been right to use the other passport. Whatever resources Barone had at his disposal, it was far easier for him to get the police involved than try to track them down himself.

His wife had been kidnapped by an *inglese* and when her protectors, including his brother, had tried to intervene the kidnapper had killed them and sped off with her in a red sports car. The Casavento police chief was a crony so all it would take was a call from him to his colleagues in Rome, Montellano or elsewhere asking them to make enquiries. It was possible the local *polizia* were in the pocket of the other villain who'd chased Barone out of Montellano in the first place and if they made any connection, would be disinclined to help. But it was a case of murder and the fugitive was at large, so they couldn't realistically refuse. And when the suspect was caught they'd ship him back to Casavento where he'd face justice in some form or other.

Forensic checks would prove Lucia's gun was not the murder weapon, but that was a minor and inconvenient detail. He'd insulted Luigi Barone's honour and there was no greater crime, not even killing his brother. Barone would have satisfaction and it would be in the interests of his police cronies to assist in every way they could. Harry considered whether to turn himself in or even try to enlist the help of Barone's rival, but quickly dismissed both ideas. He could not rely on the impartiality of the local police and he had no idea of the relationship between Barone and Coppola; they could even be allies for all he knew and even if they weren't, these guys didn't do anything for nothing and he had nothing to offer.

He'd checked the Beretta. It was a compact Model 70 with an eight-round cartridge. Lucia had fired twice and he three times so he only had three rounds left. There was no way he could risk procuring more but he had no illusions about getting into a shoot-out with the police or anyone else. Despite that, it offered a modicum of comfort and protection, if only psychological, and he was not inclined to dispose of it until he'd worked out where they were going.

It they could stay out of sight for a few days then it was even possible it might all die down. Barone wouldn't relish the publicity of a nationwide manhunt just for the murder of two of his goons. It would put him in the public eye and all sorts of questions would be asked about him and his interests. He might just decide that the loss of his wife was not worth the effort. By all accounts, she'd been nothing more than a slave to him and there'd be plenty of others to choose from.

He swung his legs off the sofa and sat up. He couldn't sleep, but it wasn't because he was still tormented by the dark memories of the past; they'd been superseded by the sinister thoughts of the present. He glanced over at the shape curled up in the bed and saw the rise and fall of her breathing. He padded over to the door in his boxer shorts and placed a chair under the handle, cursing himself for his own carelessness. *Should have done that sooner, Harry. Sharpen up!*

CHAPTER 26

"Where are we going?" she asked as he fired up the Cinquecento and pulled out into the traffic. She wore a light, white cotton skirt with a red cashmere sweater and she'd applied some of Carla's eyeshadow and lipstick. She looked like a model from Milan. He changed up a gear and they were so close together, his hand brushed her knee.

"Sorry. It's a little cramped in this thing. I had one of these last time I was here and I thought it was great fun, but I was on my own so…" He grinned awkwardly at her and she gave him a mock reproving look in return.

"Where are we going, Harry? I thought we needed to get away as soon as possible."

"I know. But there's one thing I need to do first and I want to talk to you about it."

He found the route without going via Santa Cristina De Lago and he could sense her discomfort as it began to dawn on her where they were headed. She rested her elbow on the side window and propped her head up with one hand. There was no one around and no traffic other than a single motorcycle he'd once spotted in the rear-view mirror.

They turned off at the lane leading up to the church of San Dionisio, and Harry watched in the mirror as the same motorcycle passed by the end of the lane and carried on down the road. He caught a glimpse: big bike, Triumph Bonneville or similar, fitted with panniers, rider in black leather and crash helmet. *Long distance tourer.* It reminded him of the one he'd seen the previous day in the piazza at Monte Galliano. They weren't uncommon.

"Why have you brought me here?" she asked. The softness had gone, her manner defensive and wary. He pulled up in the same place as before and got out, then walked around to the passenger side and opened the door. She didn't move.

"Please, Lucia, there's something I need to ask you."

231

"Then ask me."

"Not here. Please. It will only take a moment."

She ignored his outstretched hand and climbed out, her expression one of anger and trepidation. She walked ahead of him along the path and then onto the soft green grass. She knew where she was going. He caught up with her standing in front of the headstone and she made the sign of the cross on her forehead and chest. He noticed tears and she made no attempt to wipe them away; she simply stared at the headstone that bore the names of her family. They stood in the silence for several minutes, each lost in their own thoughts, both remembering.

"It's a beautiful place," he said, but his voice faltered and he fought to hold back his own emotions. "You've been here before?"

She shrugged. "Maybe ten years ago. I came back once, but there is nothing for me here."

"I'm pleased to be able to share this moment with you."

"Is this why you came? What you wanted to ask?"

He paused. No, it wasn't. There was something else he needed to know.

"Lucia. Why is there no mention of the baby? Catalina. Why is she not buried with her mother?"

She turned to look at him, confused. But her eyes moved, focusing on something else, something behind him.

"A very touching scene."

Harry's heart sank. He'd been careless again and Barone had caught up with him. But he could explain everything. He turned around slowly and despite the warmth of the sunshine on his face, the chill rose from the ground beneath his feet, crept up his legs and buried itself deep in his spine like a spear made of ice.

He was older, of course – older than the film, older than that day in the farmhouse and absent the blood and soot and smoke and the crazed expression. But he still held a gun as he had on every other occasion. *Black leather jacket and trousers. Black leather boots. Jackboots.*

232

"Kessler," he whispered.

"Good day, Major Male. I am very happy to meet you again at last. *Buongiorno*, Signorina Girardi. Could this be little Lucia? My goodness, you have grown up to be a handsome woman."

Harry looked at her in confusion but she was staring at Kessler, strangely impassive. *He knows her? And she knows him? How?*

"You have no right to be here," she said, taking a step forward, apparently fearless, and Harry grabbed her arm to restrain her. She had no idea what this man was capable of.

"I have every right. Now I suggest we go into the church and perhaps we shall say a prayer together?" Kessler waved the Makarov at them, pulling Lucia's Beretta from his pocket. "Thinking about this, Major?" Harry berated himself. He'd left the gun in the car, unwilling to desecrate a churchyard. Kessler shepherded them up the path towards the door.

The church was empty and quiet. A dozen candles burned on a table next to the aisle and down one side, shafts of sunlight streamed through the stained-glass windows, a faint dust billowing in its rays.

"To the altar steps," said Kessler. They walked slowly up the aisle then stopped and turned. "Lucia, move to one side, please."

"Do it, Lucia," said Harry without taking his eyes off him.

"What do you want?" she said, her voice now laden with contempt but also the stirrings of fear.

"What do I want? I want to kill him."

"In a church?!"

"It doesn't matter where. But I think this is probably a good place, don't you think so, Major Male? You see, Lucia, this man is a criminal before God and must be punished." Harry thought Kessler must be crazed and deluded, but he appeared calm and relaxed. He was an old hand at assassination and murder. He was a Nazi after all; it was second nature to him. Harry decided he could be calm and relaxed too.

"Lucia, this is the guy, the crazy German who shot me in your house back in forty-four. He's also the assassin who killed a refugee from East Berlin along with two of my colleagues, three police officers and an innocent old woman who just got in the way. He and his Nazi pals also murdered a hundred and forty-three civilians in Santa Cristina De Lago. We have him on film."

"You forgot the two idiots in the forest yesterday," he added, smirking. Harry laughed at the irony. *Of course! The sniper.* He wasn't surprised, but he was confused.

"So why didn't you shoot me then when you had the chance?"

"Because you were too far away and I wanted to get close. I wanted to get close so you could see who was killing you. And also, you had a gun. That was inconvenient."

Harry shook his head. It still made no sense. "But you had me on the floor in my own apartment in Berlin with a gun to my head and you didn't shoot."

"I came to kill the traitor Bergmann. I didn't expect to find you there too. I confess I hesitated when I recognised you. Not good for a professional. But you could not see me! Your eyes were closed, filled with the blood and the brains of the old hag. I needed you to know. I needed you to know that I was going to kill you, just like you know now!"

"So rather than kill me there and then, you let yourself get arrested, confident you'd just escape and come after me again? Just so you could have time to explain?"

"If I had shot you, they would have shot me. That would have been a waste. The police were just a nuisance, a minor distraction. I came to visit you in your new apartment but you were not there!" Kessler ladled on the irony, he was enjoying the moment. "I did not expect you to run away to Italy. But here we are. And very soon you will die."

Harry still couldn't rationalise Kessler's behaviour, but it hardly mattered. The guy was a psychopath, he had proven that time and again and he would be the next victim. He needed to play for time and as it appeared Kessler's desire was to relish the moment, spin it out for as long as possible, that suited him too. He knew the average Nazi could be volatile and if Kessler was true to form, it might be a weapon he could use against him.

"You see, Lucia. Here's a perfect example of your typical Nazi. He's from the same mould. They kill because they enjoy it. He wants his victims to know how much he enjoys it and he likes to watch them suffer while he does it." He watched Kessler's expression. The arrogant and relaxed manner was evaporating. "He and his ilk have no respect for human life, no respect for humanity. I watched him on film, casually shooting men and boys in the head, then smiling at the camera when he'd finished."

"It is tradition to smile for the camera. Anyway, it was not my order to kill them and those who were not already dead, I simply put out of their misery. It was merciful."

"Did they teach you that stuff at school, Ernst? Did Mama and Papa pat you on the head when you came home in your little brown uniform with your right arm in the air and ask you how many Jews you'd killed?"

"The Jew had to be eliminated. The Jew was filthy and disgusting and made himself rich while we starved. The Jew was a parasite. We were superior in every way."

"See? Just like his bloody Führer: deranged, depraved, psychopathic."

"The Führer was a hero of Germany."

"He was a bloody lunatic!" Harry watched Kessler adjust his grip on the Makarov, a slight shake in the gun hand. "A short ugly little prick with a stupid haircut who killed everyone who disagreed with him because he alone had all the answers."

"He gave us back our country!" Kessler's voice was beginning to rise now, his teeth gritted.

"He lied to you. He lied to everyone. He even believed his own lies, his own self-deluded fantasies. He strutted and swaggered and shouted and convinced you Aryans were the perfect race and that everyone else was to blame for your misfortunes and you all fell for it."

"He gave us back our pride and our self-respect!"

"But he lost, didn't he?"

"He was betrayed by the cowards around him!"

"He lost because the truth finally exposed him as a fraud."

"I will not listen to the opinion of a Jew-loving Englishman. The Führer took on the whole world and it took the whole world to stop him!" He saw Kessler was on the edge, visibly shaking, foam gathering at the edges of his mouth, gun hand twitching again.

"Did you and your pals take shouting lessons at school, Ernst? I mean, why is it you Nazis are always screaming and shouting at people?"

"Because you are all fools!" he bellowed. "You cannot see what we see!"

"What do you see, Ernst? Another Tommy telling you, you were wrong back then and you're still wrong now?" The colour had risen in Kessler's neck. Harry kept going. "Are you still fighting the war, Ernst? Still trying to kill everything that gets in the way? How many more have you killed since then? Lucia, this man kills people for a living. He doesn't care who they are or what they've done; he does it because he enjoys it. Were you born a maniac Ernst or did you go to psycho school?"

Kessler looked suddenly wistful. "The war took everything from me, everything I had ever loved and believed in. Despite what you might think Major Male, I once lived a normal life. I was not the monster you think. I did my duty for my country and I will not apologise for that. I gave everything, including my soul and how was I repaid?" Harry could see Kessler winding up like a coiled spring; whipping himself up into a frenzy of vitriol. "My family was murdered and I was left to rot in a filthy Russian jail until they discovered I had a use and that use gave me a purpose;

a purpose to ensure everyone would feel the same pain that I feel.

"You!" he jabbed the gun in Harry's direction. "You and all the others like you did this to me. You made me what I am! You are responsible!" Kessler was a pressure cooker ready to burst.

"How on earth can you blame me?"

"You are responsible for the death of Ernst Kessler and his family!"

Harry looked aghast at the outpourings of a madman. There would be no reasoning with him, but about this, he was plain wrong. "What's that got to do with me?"

Ernst Kessler's rage exploded like a grenade. "You killed my wife!"

His scream echoed around the church, the reverberations eventually dissipating, leaving them stranded in the unholy silence. Jesus looked down from the cross and the Virgin Mary's eyes were lifted towards heaven, praying to God, but neither appeared moved to comment. Kessler took another deep breath. "You butchered her and then you butchered my child!"

The echoes reached into every last corner, finally subsiding, leaving Harry rooted to the spot, paralysed with confusion. He'd never been anywhere near the man's wife or his child. Kessler began to sob, but it was Lucia who tried to bring calm.

"Isabella was not your wife," she said softly, looking down at the mosaic floor.

"She would have been my wife. And we had a child."

Harry snapped out of his torpor and cast a nervous glance at Lucia. *What's happening?*

She looked him in the eye. "He is the father. Catalina was his child."

"And he killed them both!" snarled Kessler.

"No!" It was Lucia's turn to shout, to take control of the madness. "Isabella was already dead. He delivered your child," she said with passion, pointing directly at Harry.

"Liar!"

"No, Ernst. It's true. He was trying to help her when one of your German rockets hit the house. It killed my father and Isabella before the baby could be born. He cut Isabella open to save the baby. To save your daughter."

Kessler's face twitched, processing the information, preparing again to denounce the lie, unable or unwilling to accept it as truth, but also, stabbed through the heart. The sobbing started again.

"A girl? Isabella had a baby girl? We had a baby girl and this man killed her?"

"No, you fool! He saved her."

The sobbing turned again to fury within a second. "But I saw him! He had a knife! He was cutting her into pieces! I had to stop him."

Harry was back in his nightmare. He could hear the explosions outside the farmhouse, the demented German in front of him, waving the gun and screaming, shouting… *Obersturmbannführer Ernst Kessler!*… echoing in his brain, the baby wriggling upside down in one hand, bloody knife in the other. He heard himself speaking out loud.

"I had just cut the cord," he said absently, as if trying to remember the chain of events, but it was like slow motion. "She almost slipped from my hand and I caught her." He looked up at Kessler. "Then you came from nowhere. You were there in front of me. Shouting." *I am Ernst Kessler… I have come to kill you!* "The bombs fell and your gun went off and I fell backwards and you disappeared."

"I don't believe you," said Kessler, shaking his head in denial.

"The baby died in my arms. You killed her." Kessler's head shook and his eyes rolled in their sockets. "Your Nazi guns killed Isabella and you killed your own child."

"Nein!" The entire church and the ground on which it had stood for a thousand years shook at the sound of the devil in its midst. And in the deathly silence that eventually followed, an angel spoke.

"She did not die."

Lucia's voice cut through the evil resonance and both men froze. Harry turned to look at her. One of them had lost their mind but it wasn't Lucia Girardi. She was calm and composed.

"I took her from you. Catalina was alive." She switched her gaze to Kessler and Harry followed it. Ernst Kessler and Harry Male were struck dumb, but before either recovered the power of speech, they were startled by the sound of the heavy latch on the main door.

Harry lowered his head and launched himself at the German, colliding with Kessler's middle like a battering ram, wrapping his arms around his body and propelling them both into the aisle. They landed together in a heap and Kessler grunted at the force of Harry's weight falling on top of him. Harry grabbed Kessler's wrist to force the gun down and it went off with a loud explosion, sending splinters of oak pew flying as he pummelled the German's head with his right fist. But Kessler's rage made him impervious to the blows and he reached up to Harry's face with his left hand, trying to gouge his eyes. Harry lifted his head back out of reach and punched again, but it still had no effect.

And then there was a riot of noise, boots on stone, men shouting. *"Si arrenda! Stop!"* Italian voices telling someone to yield, legs and bodies on top of them, pulling at their clothes, kicking and punching, Harry being hauled off Kessler and dragged backwards, arms flailing, three *polizia* trying to restrain the German, one repeatedly hitting him with a cosh, one twisting his arm behind his back, one holding his legs, a fourth standing on a pew pointing a gun. Harry struggled and wrestled against the grip of the two *polizia* holding him but gradually ended his resistance as he watched Kessler succumb to the blows and finally go limp.

"Harry!" Lucia was in front of him, distraught.

"Vada indietro, signora!" said one of the officers, telling her to get back.

"Lo rilasci!" she said. *Let him go*.

They flipped the semi-conscious Kessler onto his front and cuffed his wrists behind his back. Then two of them lifted him up and dragged him by the arms down the aisle, feet trailing, the toes of his jackboots leaving a black streak along the ancient stone floor. Harry's breathing stabilised and he looked into Lucia's anguished eyes, feeling a sting on his cheek and a trickle of blood. A plain-clothes officer strolled up behind her.

"Signora Barone, please," he said, putting a hand on her shoulder. "Keep away from this man."

"No! You keep away," she said, pointing down the aisle. "That is the man who was threatening us. He's a killer."

He turned his attention to Harry. "My name is Commissario Fabio Bianchi. Are you Mr Harry Male?"

"Yes."

"You are wanted for the kidnap of Signora Lucia Barone and the murder of Paolo Barone and Franco Prezzi."

"I didn't murder anyone, Inspector. She's right. The chap you want is Ernst Kessler. Your men just carried him out. If you'd like to check with the Berlin police, you'll find he's wanted for the murder of seven people including three police officers. I suggest your men are very careful."

"Get off him!" Lucia shouted at the two uniformed *polizia* holding Harry and they stepped back, looking dumbly at each other. She flung her arms around Harry's chest and gripped him tightly. Inspector Bianchi cleared his throat.

"Signora Barone. Your husband has accused this man of kidnap. I must take him for questioning about this and the murders of two men."

"He's innocent, Commissario." Father Benelli was standing behind them in front of the altar. "I heard everything. The man you arrested confessed to those killings in the presence of God. He was going to kill these good people too. Here, in God's house," he said, making a sign of the cross. "He is a Nazi, a war criminal. He is guilty of terrible crimes. He participated in the massacre at Santa Cristina De Lago."

Inspector Bianchi's face darkened, trying to take in the priest's testimony.

"I think you'll find the bullets in the victims in the forest are from a Makarov," said Harry. "The one Kessler had."

Bianchi snorted and turned to Lucia. "Your husband has made a complaint," he persisted.

"My husband is a monster and a crook. I am sure you know this already. Signore Male helped me get away from him." She looked up into Harry's eyes and smiled. "Does it look like I have been kidnapped?"

Bianchi ignored the inference and continued.

"I cannot release him until he has been questioned." Inspector Fabio Bianchi was clearly a professional who knew his duty.

"Commissario," said Father Benelli. "I am sure you have more important things on your mind at the moment – your daughter Maria's wedding here on Saturday? You would not want anything to, shall we say, disrupt the proceedings."

Bianchi flushed red. Then pointed at Harry.

"Which is your hotel?" he demanded.

"The Abruzzi."

"Do not leave Montellano until I give permission!" he said irritably, then nodded to his men. "*Buongiorno*, Signora Barone."

"Girardi!" she shouted as he turned away.

Bianchi left with his remaining two officers and they heard the church door clunk behind them. Lucia released her grip and Harry put an arm around her shoulder.

"Thank you, Father."

"It is my pleasure, Signore Male. In Italy, there is a way to do business, eh?"

CHAPTER 27

They drove ten kilometres to the small town of Folluccio, where Lucia said there was a restaurant with a terrace overlooking the mountains: somewhere they could talk. He hoped they could clear their minds of the trauma of yet another day but also share their memories of 1944 and the way the events of that spring had shaped both their lives.

In the vestry, Harry had pestered her with questions while she swabbed his face and applied a sticking plaster, but she'd told him to shut up and wait. She didn't need to discuss her entire life in the presence of Father Benelli, in or out of the confessional and, to his credit, the priest had not sought to complicate matters with talk, wishing them both well as they left. Harry had thanked him for calling the police, but Benelli had maintained it was God who'd intervened to prevent sacrilege in his house and Harry had not been minded to argue the point.

"I need a drink," he said to her as they sat in the shade on the veranda. "Are you okay?"

She was rubbing her hands nervously, constantly looking around, distracted by the movement of people. "I keep expecting him to turn up and start all over again. It's eighteen years since I saw him – since I saw you. I never imagined I would ever see either of you again."

"I'm sorry—" he started to say but she interrupted, reaching out her hand.

"No. Do not be sorry. If you had not come, I would still be with that animal Luigi. I will always be grateful to you for saving me. And for what you did." Her eyes moistened again and it pierced his heart. He had fallen in love with her completely but he didn't have the courage to say so and even if he did, the analyst in him would overrule such an admission. His common sense told him the situation was unique, their emotions were running high and their judgement impaired. This was not the time to ruin everything by blurting out his feelings for her especially when he doubted very much she would feel the same.

"I will always be there for you, Lucia," he said, squeezing her hand. It was the most tentative of toes in the water, but before he got any sense of the water temperature a waiter appeared and handed them some menus. "Wine?" She nodded.

***

Italy – April 1943

Isabella Girardi was in the scullery, up to her elbows in hot soapy water, scrubbing the sweat and filth from Alfredo's shirt on a washboard. She looked out of the window to the rear of the farmhouse and saw her father hoeing the ground in preparation for planting the potatoes and the cannellini beans. The Germans had driven their tanks over the vines to flatten them, fearing they might provide cover for enemy forces in the event of attack, which, if the rumours were to be believed, would start by the end of the year. She didn't fully understand why everyone was fighting, but she knew from what her father had said the sooner that imbecile *Il Duce* was overthrown and his filthy German masters sent back to where they came from, the better all their lives would be. In the meantime, he could only grow food to eat and there wasn't much of that; for months they'd been living mainly on cabbage and the eggs from the few chickens they had left.

It had been only six weeks since one of the *bastardi* had tried to steal their goats and when her mother, Maria, had remonstrated with them, wielding a frying pan, he had shot her dead. Her little sister Lucia hadn't stopped crying and although Isabella wanted to die herself, she'd found a purpose in the role of matriarch. Her father had been very brave and she had to be brave too. Lucia had been out in the yard feeding the chickens but suddenly appeared, distressed.

"Papà! Papà!"

Isabella ran outside, wiping her hands on a towel. Alfredo had dropped the hoe and was hobbling back towards the house. Six soldiers were in the chicken run, trying to catch four panicked birds that flapped and fluttered and squawked but were soon rounded up, swiftly despatched by a twist of the neck and thrown into a sack. Alfredo put his arm around Lucia, who clung to him tightly, and Isabella watched with consternation as the soldiers approached the back door.

"Inside!" one of them said, pointing his rifle and pushing them indoors. The soldiers poked around the front room, opening cupboards and kicking over a steaming pot of water sitting on a trivet by the fireplace. They laughed and guffawed in a language none of the family could understand, and then two of them glanced at Isabella and one made a lurid gesture. They leaned their rifles against the wall and approached Isabella and Alfredo, who was still holding the terrified Lucia. The other four sat at the table and put their feet up, lighting cigarettes and grunting in their guttural foreign tongue.

One of the two grinned and held out a hand to Isabella and when she ignored him he grabbed her and pulled her towards him. She resisted but he slapped her face and she cried out. Alfredo tried to help her but he was pushed to the floor by the other one, who then grabbed Lucia. She screamed.

"Papà!"

Isabella was dragged upstairs on her back. Lucia was lifted by the waist screaming, and carried underarm like a rolled-up carpet.

"No!" Alfredo shouted, but one of the seated soldiers cocked his rifle and pointed it at him.

They reached the landing and doors were kicked open. The girls were carried into their own bedroom and flung on the bed. The soldiers laughed with each other and grunted as

244

they removed helmets and boots and then their belts and tunics and threw them to one side. Isabella and Lucia knelt on the bed, clinging to each other, Lucia in a state of panic. The soldiers came at them from each side and pulled the girls apart and Lucia screamed as Isabella fought back but she took another heavy slap and fell back on the bed. The soldiers unbuttoned their trousers and pushed them to the floor, exposing their engorged members, and held each girl down by the neck while they tore at their clothing. They heard a shout.

"Halt!" The men stopped suddenly, looked at each other and then at the door. *"Lasst die Fräuleins sofort in Ruhe!"* came the order. *Leave the girls alone! "Aus!"*

The soldiers hesitated then hastily pulled up their trousers, collected their things and scurried out of the room. Isabella held the traumatised and sobbing Lucia in her arms. She turned her head to look towards the door, terrified and wary, assuming it was merely a temporary respite and that the assault would resume at any moment. A tall officer in a clean crisp uniform and cap stood watching them, legs wide apart, leather gloves in one hand. He stared at Isabella and she stared back, stroking Lucia's head as her sister trembled. Then to her astonishment, he removed his cap, bowed gently and clicked his heels.

"Fräulein," was all he said, then replaced the cap, turned and left them alone. Isabella was afraid to move, but she heard him descend the stairs and she heard him bark orders in a language she couldn't understand and she heard the soldiers trudge out of the house and pull the door shut and she heard shouting outside the farmhouse and then she heard two shots and she gasped out loud.

***

"Kessler?" said Harry, shaken and horrified by the story but now incredulous.

Lucia nodded. "Yes."

245

"But… it doesn't seem possible. The guy was a maniac then and he's a maniac now. The idea that he possessed the tiniest speck of honour or humanity is just unbelievable."

"I know. But it is all relative, is it not?"

"Relative to what?"

"The circumstances. The times in which we lived. You do not know the background."

Harry had to agree. He'd jumped in without knowing the facts or the context. Kessler had been born an innocent baby and somewhere along the way, life turned him into a monster.

"So, then what?"

"We tried to get back to normal but we feared the same thing could happen again. Papà said he would protect us but he had no gun and even if he had it would have been no use against armed soldiers. Isabella tried to tell me I wouldn't die if I just let them do what they wanted. It would be horrible and painful at first, but it would pass, she said. We had no choice if we wanted to live."

Harry felt a wave of anger and nausea, but stifled his emotions. She was here now with him, so whatever horrors she'd experienced, they were in the past and she was safe. He felt compelled to ask even though he dreaded the response.

"Did… they come back or was that an isolated incident?"

The waiter placed two plates of pasta in front of them, although Harry had lost his appetite and Lucia looked disinterested. She picked up her fork and stabbed at her plate.

"The next day, he came back."

"Kessler?"

"He came in a black open-topped car with a driver and two guards who stood outside by the door. He carried a bunch of flowers and he took off his hat and clicked his heels and bowed, like they do, and handed the flowers to Isabella. He spoke in Italian and apologised for the behaviour of those animals and that they would not be doing

246

that again to anyone. And, he said, he had given orders the house was off-limits and he would be checking every day to make sure we were all right." Harry shook his head to dispel the image. *Kessler the gentleman?* "He came again the next day and brought more flowers for Isabella and some tins of food and fresh vegetables. My father asked him about our chickens and the next day, he came back with a truck and some men who repaired the run, put some new wire around it and restocked it with a dozen chickens.

"We could not believe our luck, although of course we did not trust any of them and we waited anxiously for another group of them to attack us. But it didn't happen. The food kept coming and Kessler kept coming and one day he even brought some chocolate 'for little Lucia' and I think I even thanked him.

"Then after a few days, he took my father to one side and they had a discussion. He wanted to talk alone with Isabella. He would do her no harm, he was just lonely and he wanted someone to talk to, someone to whom he could unburden his darkest thoughts. Papà said it was the least we could do. Kessler took Isabella upstairs and after an hour he came back down, bowed and clicked his heels and left. We watched her come down the stairs and Papà asked her if she was okay. *Yes, I am okay, Papà. We just talked. He is a very sad and lonely person.*

"He came every two or three days and every time with food, some we gave away to passing neighbours, and every time he went upstairs with Isabella until one day, he was up there for two hours. This time he looked a little more officious, embarrassed even, and Isabella came down blushing and we knew. She told Papà and he was angry but she explained she was fine and he should be realistic. He had no choice and neither did she. She could give Kessler what he wanted and they got safety, security and food in return, but if she refused him, then anything might happen. The German was gentle and kind and he would make sure we were safe."

Harry chewed on some pasta and tried to imagine the position they were in. *"Prostituta!"* had declared Rosa the cleaner. Whether or not Rosa had benefited from food handouts, he couldn't say. Either way it was an unforgiveable slur.

"We heard in the July that Sicily had been invaded by the Americans and the British and we believed it was only a matter of time before they crossed to the mainland. Kessler came less often, about once a week, but he was busy and did not stay long. Just long enough. And then, one morning in August Isabella was sick and Papà knew why and she knew why, although I didn't."

"She was pregnant."

"Yes. She told me a few days later and not to worry because being sick in the morning is normal and it would go away, but I was not to say anything to Ernst."

"Ernst? You were on first-name terms?"

"He insisted. And when a German insists, you must obey." She imparted a modest grin and seemed increasingly relaxed in the telling, perhaps relieved to be offloading the memories, just as he had been. Isabella had grown massively in his estimation and he was saddened he'd never got to know her properly, but it was clear the Girardi women were cut from the same cloth. Most of all, he was relieved Lucia had not suffered further violation.

"So when did he find out?"

"She let him continue but then she worried having sex might harm the baby, so she told him. It would have become obvious anyway."

"So she wanted to keep it?"

"It would be against God to do otherwise." There was no reproach in her answer, but he felt awkward and ignorant. She'd been brought up in the Catholic faith, there was no other, so abortion had never been considered, regardless of the circumstances. "She could not help liking him. He treated her well and he treated us well too. He protected us." *I can't believe this is the same man.* "When he found out, he

248

was even more attentive and came as often as he could, even if he had to drive himself and come without guards. Once he even brought a doctor to examine her."

"Good Lord," said Harry, "he sounds almost human."

"He loved her," she said.

It all made sense, even if he couldn't equate the chivalrous, caring father-to-be with the vile, cold-hearted assassin he knew as Ernst Kessler. It made sense of Kessler's behaviour when he'd returned to the farmhouse in the middle of an artillery bombardment and, desperate to protect his love and her unborn child, he finds an enemy soldier he thinks has already butchered one and is about to do the same to another. Nothing could excuse his criminal conduct at Santa Cristina or Berlin and probably countless other places, nor his membership of the SS, but his vendetta against Harry Male was totally understandable. Harry Male would have done the same.

"It became more and more difficult for him to visit. By January the British and Americans were getting closer, so the shelling got more and more heavy and we didn't know whether we would even survive the winter. Then in February, the Abbey of Montellano was destroyed and we thought that was the end and we would never see the Germans again. But they kept fighting and the shells kept falling all around us. It was very frightening."

Harry remembered it well. Every time they gained some ground, the Germans were easily able to counterattack because the Allies were always fighting their way uphill. The Germans had the benefit of their elevated defensive positions and in addition, the more the Allied bombing laid waste to the towns and the landscape, the more cover it provided the Germans to repel attack. Despite the Allies' overwhelming superiority in forces and firepower, the Nazis had held out for months. It had been one almighty mess from start to finish. And in all that time, families like the Girardis were caught in the middle, merely trying to stay alive.

The waiter cleared their plates and brought them coffee. Lucia looked out across the country and up to the mountains and let out a deep sigh. She looked vulnerable, yet composed, sad but not tearful. The war had done terrible things to her and her family and millions of others. He wished he could say that from now on, everything would be all right and she would never have to worry again. He hoped at least she would now find some peace and stability and he hoped she'd allow him to provide it.

"By March, Isabella was beginning to have serious pains but there was no doctor we could call. We had not seen Ernst for two weeks and we wondered whether he had been killed. You must realise, although we knew how horrible and violent the Nazis were to many people, he had only ever been good to us, so we were concerned for him and worried about Isabella."

Harry had a fair idea where Ernst Kessler had been in early March 1944. He was being driven out of Santa Cristina De Lago by Harry and his brigade along with a bunch of New Zealanders. He shivered when he thought about it. They may have shot at each other without ever realising how their lives would ultimately interconnect. He understood why Lucia's memory of the German should be so benign. Kessler may well have loved Isabella, or have had some obsession with her, even if it had not been requited. They'd used him as a shield to keep themselves safe and the arrangement had worked well, for a time. It irked Harry to think Lucia may have some sympathy for him, but as far as she knew, Kessler had done them no harm and committed no crime other than to fight for his country. Harry had evidence to the contrary but Lucia had so far heard only fragments of it and had probably not yet taken it all in. It would have been too much to comprehend for someone whose first and only impression of Kessler was of someone who'd helped them, been kind to them. She might struggle to accept Kessler was a monster just as he that Kessler had been a saint. It was a dilemma, but he would neither say nor do anything to contradict her; the risk of alienating her was one he wasn't prepared to take.

"Isabella could not climb the stairs, so Papà brought the bed down into the front room." … *Set against the far wall between the chimney breast and a second doorway was an iron bedstead...* "And Isabella lay there for a few days before the pain became unbearable and we were frantic with worry. So he went out to get help and found you."

Harry nodded wistfully. "It was the fourteenth of March. The day the Americans bombed Montellano. My platoon had retreated from Santa Cristina the day before and we were told to get well away from the town because it was going to be levelled. That's when we met your father. He pleaded with us to help him and I admit I was a bit irritated and sceptical, but I couldn't refuse."

She was smiling at him in an admiring way, her chin propped up on one elbow.

"What?"

"Nothing. I was just trying to remember you. You must have been twenty-six, maybe?"

"Twenty-four."

"Ah, twenty-four. It must have been the stubble and the filthy hair and uniform. Made you look older." She was playing with him and he loved it.

"And you kept out of sight."

"If I had been there, you would not have done what you did." It was no accusation, just a statement of fact. She was right, of course. He would have picked her up and run, at least as far as his fractured leg would allow. Saving a fourteen-year-old would have been a wonderful excuse for running away from the hideous predicament he was in. *We didn't have the luxury of retreat!* His father's voice echoed in his mind. *No, Dad, and when it came down to it, I didn't retreat from this one either.*

"I still can't understand how Kessler survived. There must have been a ton of rubble on top of him and he must

251

have still been there when they found me. Either they missed him completely or thought he was dead."

"But if I had been there, I would have been able to explain to him what you had done and maybe he would not have shot you."

"And you might have been buried under the rubble too."

It didn't bear thinking about. Whatever had happened was in the past. The most important thing was that they were together now. He decided the time was right to slay the myth of the German's sainthood.

"Lucia, the day before, Kessler and his Nazi troops machine-gunned a hundred and forty-three innocent men and boys, in Santa Cristina. I have seen the film. I saw him stroll along a pile of bodies and finish off ten or twelve who were still alive. He shot them in the head." She dropped her eyes.

"It shows sometimes you do not know people," she said quietly. He was struck and disturbed by the ambiguity in her statement. They didn't really know each other, not yet, and he didn't know whether she was being wary, reassessing her own impressions and feelings about him. But she was right. They had each formed differing views about Kessler based on their own experiences and both would struggle to come to terms with his alter ego.

"And if Father Benelli had not been there…"

"He would have shot you dead." Her eyes went moist again. "I know."

"You saved me again, Lucia."

"How?"

"You told him the truth about Isabella."

"He didn't believe me."

"And you told him about the baby."

"He didn't believe that either."

"But it bought time. Time enough for the police to arrive."

"I suppose."

Another thought suddenly struck him. Kessler had hunted him down because he believed he had murdered his wife and child and wanted retribution. From the moment Kessler had recognised him in the apartment, that had been his mission. Now he had another one. He'd discovered Catalina hadn't died, would surely do anything to find her and had aptly demonstrated how determined and resourceful he could be. He needed to see Inspector Bianchi and reiterate how dangerous Kessler was. He also needed to discuss Barone. They weren't yet out of the woods.

"C'mon. We need to go and see the police."

"Why?"

"I'll tell you on the way."

***

They asked directions to Montellano central police station and found it in a side street, three Fiat squad cars parked outside. Inspector Bianchi was in his office and a uniformed officer showed them in.

"*Prego, Signore Male e Signora Barone.*"

"Girardi," said Lucia, correcting him.

"*Sì, sì, certamente.* Please have a seat." Bianchi was clearly not expecting visitors. His shirtsleeves were rolled up, his tie loosened and a cigarette smouldered in the ashtray.

"Inspector," said Harry. "I wanted to discuss two things with you?"

"But of course."

"The man you arrested today..."

"Herr Kessler."

"I wanted you to be clear how dangerous and resourceful he is."

Bianchi sat back in his chair. "I know this, *signore*. I have spoken to the Berlin police. He fits the description of the man they are looking for" – he consulted his notes – "the murder of three officers of the West Berlin police, an elderly lady by the name of Leitner, an East German called

Bergmann... oh yes, and four workers at Hotel Regent in Kurfürstendamm… "

"What?" said Harry, casting a glance at Lucia. "I didn't know about the Regent."

"He is known there as Karl Schneider. I know he is extremely dangerous, but thank you for your advice."

"I just wanted to make sure he was locked up securely, for all our sakes."

"I can assure you, *signore*," said Bianchi, clearly beginning to find the conversation tiring "Kessler cannot escape from here. We will send him back to Berlin as soon as the paperwork has been completed."

"What about the two murders in Casavento?"

Bianchi shrugged. "We shall be pleased to be rid of him."

"And the war crime at Santa Cristina?"

Bianchi shrugged again. "Do you have evidence of this, Signore Male?"

Harry thought about it but only for a second. He knew where the evidence was but it was futile to pursue it. Even if Bianchi were an avid Nazi-hunter, he too would hit a brick wall if he tried to investigate.

"There's one other thing, Inspector."

"And what might that be, *signore*?"

"Does Barone know you found Lucia?"

Bianchi smiled with satisfaction. "It is not for the police to be involved in, shall we say, affairs of the heart," he purred. "If I tell him we have found the *signora* but she does not want to return, maybe Signore Barone will come here to, er, discuss the matter."

"That's what I'm worried about. I booked into the hotel under the name of Harper. In case he made enquiries."

Bianchi took a moment to choose his words. "Signore Barone has a reputation. He is not welcome in Montellano and it is possible that he may come into conflict with some other people who also do not want him here. It will be inconvenient for me if there is any trouble."

"What other people?"

"Oh, you know, businessmen."

"*Mafiosi*?"

"No, no!" said Bianchi in protest. "We do not have this kind of thing in Montellano. Maybe in Sicilia and Napoli. And New York!" He laughed, pleased with his own wit, but he noticed his guests were not amused. "No, *signore*, I have said nothing to Signore Barone and if he calls me, I shall say simply that you and the *signora* are not in Montellano."

"Thank you," said Harry.

"And this will be true, no? Because tomorrow you are leaving. Is that not correct, Signore Male?"

They were being told to leave Montellano. That much was clear and, in many respects, Harry was quite content to head back to Rome and get Lucia as far away from Barone, Kessler or anyone else, as soon as possible. All respects, in fact, bar one.

***

As soon as they'd gone, Commissario Bianchi lit another cigarette and slumped in his chair in exasperation. His daughter's wedding was only four days away and he cursed the Holy Father for having the temerity to threaten his arrangements. His overwhelming priority was to ensure the celebration went through without a hitch and he was certain his prospective in-laws would agree. The last thing they all needed was an imminent invasion of his town by a rabid *mafioso* and his henchmen in pursuit of a runaway wife and her *inglese* boyfriend. He was also saddled with the complication of an ex-Nazi psychopath locked up in one of his cells together with the potential arrival of Interpol, sniffing around his patch. *Maledizione!*

He picked up the phone and dialled a number from memory. It was answered within seconds.

"*Pronto.*"

"*Ciao*, Signore Coppola. Fabio Bianchi."

Mario Coppola usually had little to say, preferring to listen, but with the impending nuptials of his eldest son Francesco to Bianchi's daughter, he was in a more affable frame of mind.

"*Ciao*, Commissario Bianchi. I trust the last-minute arrangements are going well?"

Bianchi felt a shiver. Mario Coppola was well practised in the dark art of imparting menace in the most innocuous of statements.

"Yes, yes. Yes. Of course, we are all looking forward to it very much."

"So, what can I do for you?"

Bianchi cleared his throat. He very much wanted to appear helpful rather than someone in need of assistance himself.

"I have information that Luigi Barone may be planning to visit very soon." He paused, but there was no immediate response and he felt his heart beating a little faster than usual.

"Go on."

"His wife has run away. She and her boyfriend turned up here. I have ordered them to leave immediately, but it may not stop him coming to look for her."

"Keep me informed, Commissario."

CHAPTER 28

They got back to their room at the Abruzzi by four o'clock. Carla had fussed, concerned about the sticking plaster on Harry's face and he had to reassure her it was a very minor injury. Fabrizio said the police had called him to say their guest "Harper" was actually an imposter called "Male" and they were watching him carefully, but he should not be concerned. Fabrizio said he'd expressed shock and horror at the deception and promised to call them immediately the man and his girlfriend had checked out.

"I am your girlfriend now?" said Lucia with a grin, slumping on the sofa, stretching her arms and yawning.

"Does that offend you?" he asked, sitting down next to her. It had a nice ring to it and he suddenly felt like he was back at school enjoying the same rush and quiver of desire he'd had the first time he'd spotted a girl he fancied.

"No. It does not offend me." She touched the sticking plaster on his face. "Does it hurt?"

"No."

"Maybe we change it for a clean one."

"After I've had a shower. I've been rolling around in a church aisle with a madman. I can't take a lady out to dinner without smartening up."

"No you can't," she said, planting a kiss on his cheek.

Their eyes met and he placed a hand behind her neck, caressing it slowly. She made no attempt to remove it or tell him to stop, but slowly closed her eyes and twisted her head in a circular motion as if enjoying the sensation. He pulled her slowly towards him and kissed her gently on the lips. She tasted faintly of coffee and perfume. She half-opened her eyes, kept her mouth open and close to his and he could feel her breath.

"You are the most beautiful woman I have ever seen."

She smiled a big smile revealing her strong white teeth.

"The *inglese* talks like an *italiano*."

"But the *inglese* means it."

She put her hand behind his neck and pressed her mouth against his, working her lips around his, lapping gently with her tongue, then swung her leg over his lap to straddle him, her skirt riding up her thighs. He laid his hands on her legs, slid them under her skirt and along her thighs until he reached her taut slender buttocks, and then leaned forward, lifting her as he got to his feet. She wrapped her legs around his waist and clung onto his neck, snuggling her face into his shoulder as he carried her across the room and laid her down on the bed.

They held each other and kissed and caressed each other and undressed each other slowly, exploring their bodies inch by inch, examining and kissing every imperfection before slipping under the single white sheet to consummate their union. They eventually lay still, clasped together as inseparable halves of a whole, he on his back, she draped across his chest and legs with her head tucked under his chin.

"You seduced me, Harrimale," she said sleepily, squeezing him again as if she could get any closer. He kissed the top of her forehead.

"It wasn't difficult. You didn't put up much of a fight."

She tipped her head back and gave him a look of mock anger. "Are you saying I encourage you?"

"I'm saying I was in love with you the moment I saw you. It was only a matter of time before you fell for my charms."

She sniggered with delight and squeezed him again. "Let's have a shower."

She threw the sheet back and jumped out of bed and he followed her into the bathroom. They hugged and kissed each other again under the torrent of hot, steamy water and she carefully peeled away the sticking plaster from his cheek. The flesh was red and raw but the wound clean and she kissed it gently. They soaped each other to excess, laughing and giggling like teenagers and then, when the skin

258

on their fingers eventually began to wrinkle, turned off the flow and wrapped each other in large fluffy white towels.

They lay on their sides on the bed, she with her back to him, his arm around her middle, pressing himself against her like two spoons.

"Is someone going to shoot at us tomorrow?" she said quietly, sounding suddenly fatigued.

"I hope not."

"But if they do, you will look after me, yes?"

He kissed the back of her head. "We'll look after each other."

"Where shall we go, Harrimale?" She'd got back into the habit of using his full name and seemed unable to break it. He rather liked the sound.

"Don't know, but wherever we go, we go together." She gripped his arm tighter. "Hungry?"

"No."

"Well, I am."

***

They sat in the Ristorante Chimera at the same table as before, sipping glasses of cold Prosecco brought by their gregarious host Angelo.

"I give you on the house!" he'd boomed and was clearly smitten when Lucia had kissed him on both cheeks. She looked especially exotic in a black lace top and red trousers and they'd both complimented Carla for an excellent job in the procurement of Lucia's wardrobe. There would be a sizeable bill to pay and he'd have to cash in some traveller's cheques tomorrow but it didn't matter. She was worth it.

"Do you think the police will be able to keep Kessler locked up?" she asked. The German was no risk to her, of that Harry was certain, but he couldn't rule out the possibility Kessler still had a score to settle with him, even though Lucia had told him the truth.

"Difficult to say. He's shown himself to be remarkably resilient. It depends on whether he's still on a mission." He stretched a hand across the table and rested it on hers. "Lucia. I'm head over heels in love with you." She grinned sheepishly and put her other hand on his. "And I promise I'll take you somewhere no one can find us, not Kessler, nor Luigi, nor anyone else. That's, of course, assuming you want to come?"

"Yes, I want to come, Harrimale." She leaned across the table and he met her in the middle with a soft kiss.

"Prego, signore e signora!" Angelo caught them by surprise. He was holding two plates of lasagne. "I have something special for the love-birds," he announced, setting the plates down and beaming inanely at them before backing away, winking at Harry.

"I'll miss this place," he said, "but I want us to get away from Montellano as soon as possible." He was being truthful, but he knew he couldn't leave before the last piece of the jigsaw slotted into place and he wasn't sure how she was going to react. "But before I take you to some exotic place on the other side of the world, there's something I need to do first." She looked up at him, waiting for him to finish, but he hesitated. His own mission wasn't over yet and he couldn't stop now even though on recent experience, he knew it wouldn't be simple. "Lucia, you said something to Kessler that shocked and stunned both of us. You may have been making it up to distract him, but I need to know whether it was true or not."

"You mean Catalina." He nodded. She had probably been expecting it and was suddenly subdued again, her mind in possession of the facts but somehow unwilling or unable to relate them. "What I said was true. The baby did not die."

"Tell me."

***

260

What remains of the fire crackles and spits, its fuel almost gone, the only sound in an otherwise eerie silence that's descended on what's left of her home. The good soldier's eyes are closed and he looks like he has died, but she can see he's still breathing. The baby is wriggling in her arms, bloody and dusty and cold. She has to wrap her in something to keep her warm. The soldier's knife lies in his open hand. She lays Catalina on the bed between the legs of her dead mother and takes the knife and cuts a one-metre square piece from the filthy bed cover. She shakes the dust and grit to the floor but the underside is clean so she puts it over Catalina and picks her up, wrapping the heavy soft blanket around her, leaving only her face visible.

Catalina opens her eyes and purrs but then her face creases up and she starts to cry. The baby's cold and hungry. There's nothing to eat and the house is wrecked, incapable of providing shelter. She steps carefully over the rubble. She has no shoes and everywhere there are broken tiles, sharp fragments of brick and wood splinters that prick her feet and make her squeal, but she holds the baby close and the crying increases in intensity.

She picks her way towards the front of the house, now open to the elements, and out through a hole in the wall where the front door used to be. The sun is up and she can feel the warmth on her face and through her dressing gown but the ground is hard and cold and there are still patches of thin ice where puddles have formed. There's a massive hole in the front yard ten metres across and three metres deep and she can see a succession of similar craters stretching down to the road and beyond. She's wondering how she's going to get past them when she hears voices on the road. She's afraid it's the bad soldiers again so she slips around the side of the house to the back and hobbles across the field, clutching the baby to her chest, afraid they'll see her and give chase.

She stops after a hundred metres to catch her breath and crouches down, turning to look back at where her home used

261

to be. The soldiers are approaching the house which is still smouldering. They wear a brown uniform like the good soldier and two of them have red crosses on their arms. They disappear inside and haven't seen her so she runs on.

***

Angelo cleared their plates and Harry poured some more red wine.

"Must have been Marco Wilkins. He made it back after all."

"You expect him?"

"I sent him on ahead to get medical help, for Isabella. Sounds like he managed to rustle up a couple of spare medics. Pity they weren't in time to save her."

"They might have been killed too."

"Yes, there is that."

"And they were able to help you instead."

"I don't remember any of it. I must have been unconscious when they found me and I never saw them again. I never saw any of my platoon again," he said with sadness. He took a sip of his wine, holding it in his mouth for ten seconds to allow it to warm up and, when he swallowed, it filled his head with a rich velvety taste and a delicious aroma that heightened his senses. He wondered at the barefoot, bedraggled fourteen-year-old clutching a newborn baby and tried to equate the image with the goddess sitting opposite who'd just shared his bed. Angels both. But there had to be more. "So then what happened?"

"I reached a road and there were more of your soldiers there and I walked in the same direction as them but most of them ignored me. Then one of them, I think he was an officer, stopped me and said I could not walk without shoes and he offered to carry me, but I refused. He was very concerned about my feet, but he could do nothing and after a while I could not feel them anyway. He said there were many other soldiers ahead of us but they would be coming

262

back to Montellano to attack the Germans again. He said it was no place for children and we had to find a family to take me in."

"Makes sense. Did you?"

"Not at first. We came across more and more soldiers, many of them wounded and some of them on crutches, then an old man came past us with a donkey and cart and two children sitting on the back and the officer called out and stopped him. The man looked like my papà and the officer told him he should take me somewhere safe. He was not happy but after a big argument he agreed. The officer gave me a drink of water and I tried to wipe some on the lips of the baby, but it made her cry again. He lifted me into the back of the cart and waved at me as we moved off, but I could not wave back as I was holding the baby."

Harry tried to visualise the scene. While he was being loaded onto a stretcher back at the farmhouse, Lucia and Catalina were being transported to who knows where. Whoever helped her had been right. There was no way he could take children back with him and it was reasonable to assume the old Italian would look after one of his own.

"Where did he take you?"

"He turned off the road after maybe two kilometres and we went along a long rough track for maybe a half hour or so. Then he stopped the cart and told me to get off."

"What?"

"He said this was as far as he could go. He lived close by but they had no food and we could not come in. He pointed to a pathway and said there was a family called Rossetti about one kilometre away and they would take me in. And then he drove off."

"He just left you there? In your bare feet?"

She nodded.

***

Italy – March 1944

Manuela Rossetti wiped the sweat from her brow and dried her hands on a cloth she kept tucked into the ties of her apron. She put the pail of milk down on the scullery table and scooped some into a tin mug, satisfied it was still warm enough and she wouldn't need to heat it over the fire. The goats were lactating well and it was blessing they couldn't do without, not while Lorenzo and Gino were still away. She hadn't seen them for three weeks and she didn't even know if they were still alive, but there was nothing she could do about it so there was no point worrying. Anyway, her hands were full and it was as well she didn't also have two hungry men stomping around causing trouble.

She took the milk into the front room where the log fire burned fiercely in the grate. Viviana was still where she had left her, still rocking gently in the chair by the fireplace, still staring into space and, despite the warmth of the flames, she sat hunched and huddled beneath a black woollen shawl. Her daughter's eyes were dark and sunken, her skin tinged with yellow and her black hair hung in random strands like frayed rope.

"Viviana," she said but her daughter didn't even acknowledge her presence. She held the cup under her nose. "Viviana! You must eat something. This is fresh milk. It will make you feel better." Manuela sighed and placed the cup on a grate by the fire. It would stay warm for hours.

She didn't know how to make Viviana snap out of her depression. Things would be better when Gino came back. Things were always better with Gino around and of course her husband Lorenzo too, but Gino was the funny one and he loved her daughter and when they'd got married he'd promised he'd give her lots of children and they'd have a house of their own with land where they'd grow vines and olives and tomatoes. Viviana was pregnant almost immediately and Gino was thrilled and he built a cot from the wood of the eucalyptus tree and they all anxiously awaited the baby's arrival.

But God, on this occasion, had moved in one of his mysterious ways and the baby was stillborn. Gino buried his son Roberto in the back garden and tried his best to comfort his wife who was inconsolable for a month. It was God's will, but they would try again and soon they'd have a family of their own. By the summer of 1943, the men who were not already in uniform were being rounded up to defend the motherland from the invading forces. Both Lorenzo and Gino had decided Mussolini was a lunatic who had led them to disaster and that the best way of defending their country was to fight the Nazis.

They joined a partisan group and spent much of their time living wild in the countryside, attacking the Germans, disrupting their supply lines, sabotaging their vehicles and killing as many of the *bastardi* as they could. They would arrive home unexpectedly, stay for just one night and then kiss their wives and disappear again, sometimes for a month at a time. Viviana was soon pregnant again and although Gino tried to return as often as possible to make sure his wife and unborn child were doing well, they had been gone for almost two months now and the women began to fear the worst.

Manuela delivered her daughter's baby girl on 10 March 1944 but she could tell immediately there was a problem. The child had come early and was very small. Baby Giuliana died two days later in her mother's arms. Viviana cried and cried and refused to get out of bed, distraught at her loss. Manuela wrapped Giuliana in a cloth and buried her next to Roberto, fashioning a cross from the eucalyptus tree as best she could. Viviana blamed herself. She had failed again. She was a useless wife and her husband would never forgive her for losing both their babies. She would never be able to have children and Gino would leave her and she would not blame him if he did. She dreaded Gino coming back, expecting to see her and their new baby and she just wanted to die. She refused to eat anything. She would starve herself to death.

Manuela too was apprehensive about the men's return, even though she missed them terribly and still feared they had been hurt, or worse. *If Gino is the man I think he is, he will comfort his wife and make love to her again and they will have a child one day.* After four days, she finally persuaded Viviana to get out of bed. She got the tin bath down off the scullery wall and put it in front of the fire and boiled five kettles of water. She bathed her twenty-two-year-old daughter as she had done when she was a child, rubbing her skin gently with a sponge, while Viviana sat mute, staring into the water.

She dried her and dressed her and sat her in the rocking chair and implored her to eat some bread and milk, but she refused and her daughter had remained there ever since.

***

It's getting dark and cold and her feet are painful and bleeding. The baby weighs only two or three kilos but it feels like she is getting heavier and her arms are aching. She's hungry and thirsty and Catalina has had nothing in the twelve hours she's been born, so she must be hungry and thirsty too. She doesn't know where the Rossetti house is. The man who looked like Papà must have been lying. She can hear explosions in the far distance but they don't worry her any more. She has other concerns.

She hears a familiar noise nearby. Goats whinnying and chickens clucking, alert to the noise of her approach. The animals are in a five-metre square pen surrounded by a wire fence and there's a wooden shed at one end and a gate at the other secured by a rope looped over a post. She hoists the baby onto one shoulder and unfastens the loop and the chickens cluck and run to her, demanding grain. She makes her way across the pen towards the shed with the chickens following, running around her feet. The shed door is open and the smell inside is pungent and rank and two tethered goats inside bid her welcome with a plaintive cry. She lays the baby down on some straw and lies next to her and reaches for her own feet, which are cold as ice and sting at her touch. The baby whimpers. She must feed her.

She knows about goats. There's a milking pail and tin cup hanging on a hook and she crawls over and unhooks it and puts the pail under one of the nannies and lies on her front and squeezes two teats and streams of warm milk hit the pail and when she has enough she scoops it out with the cup and she drinks it and it's warm and rich and flavoursome. She takes the cup and pail over to where Catalina lies and picks her up and sits with her back to the shed wall holding the baby in one arm but she doesn't know how to feed her from the cup. She tries dipping a finger and putting it on the baby's lips and the baby responds and sucks the finger but her nails are dirty and the quantity is too small. Then she remembers.

She unfastens her dressing gown and unbuttons her filthy nightdress and clasps the baby to her skin. Her breast is small and not fully formed but the baby finds the nipple and clamps her lips around it and it tickles and she feels a strange sensation but there is no milk and the baby starts to cry. She reaches for the cup and pours a little down her chest and the milky rivulet reaches the nipple and the baby snuffles and drinks and after a while opens her eyes and she stares into the eyes of the baby and the baby stares into the eyes of the mother and she begins to weep.

***

Manuela Rossetti crossed the yard behind the house, carrying a wooden bucket full of grain under her arm. She squinted in the morning sun and her breath left a faint cloud in the crisp clear air. She looked to the west, where the sound of man-made thunder had been going on for hours but, thank God, it had never come close enough to worry her and

267

she prayed it would stay there. She reached the pen where the chickens were clucking expectantly and let herself in, tossing handfuls of grain around in a wide arc until her bucket was empty. She stepped into the goat shed to check the animals.

A young girl was curled up in a ball on the floor, a sack of manure for a pillow, her legs covered in straw. She was clutching a bundle of blankets to her chest.

"Oh my goodness gracious," she said. She knelt down beside the sleeping form and placed a hand on the girl's forehead. The waif woke with a start, terror in her eyes. *She can be no more than twelve or thirteen.* "Don't be afraid, my angel." The blankets moved and a baby cried. She drew back the blanket to reveal the tiny form inside. *"Madre Maria!"* The young girl pulled back in alarm. She offered her hand and the girl looked frightened and suspicious at first but then, after a moment, took it and tried to get to her feet. Manuela reached for the bundle to help her but she cried out.

"No!"

Despite her own misgivings, Manuela Rossetti affected her best smile. The girl looked haunted by something or someone and she was filthy, wearing only her nightclothes. She moved the straw from around the girl's feet and saw the blackened blood and blisters.

"Let me help you. Let me carry your baby and we can all go inside and have some food by the fire and I will clean your feet." She reached out for the bundle and reluctantly the girl let her take it. The baby snuffled and yawned, waving a tiny fist in front of her face. "Come with me."

She helped the girl up but she winced in pain and gripped Manuela's hand as she led her hobbling out of the shed, through the pen, and up towards the house. Manuela's mind was absorbed with one question. The girl was surely too young to have a baby. Where on earth did she get it?

"What's your name, sweetie?"

"Lucia Girardi," said the girl through gritted teeth, limping badly. Manuela had heard the name Girardi before, but she couldn't remember where. "The baby is Catalina."

"Catalina? That's an unusual name, but very beautiful. Whose baby is it?"

"She's mine!" Manuela's heart sank. Lucia had stolen the baby from somewhere and now she would have a problem working out how to get it back to its mother.

"No, sweetie. You are too young to have a baby," she said gently. "Where's her mama?"

"Her mama is dead. Her mama is my sister Isabella."

"Oh, heavens. Come on in."

Manuela felt a measure of relief, assuming the girl was being truthful, but she felt desperately sorry for her. She led her into the scullery and then into the front room. It was warm from the heat of the fire and Viviana was still in her rocking chair, staring at the flames. She sat Lucia down in an armchair by the fire.

Manuela Rossetti held the baby in her arms, swaying her from side to side and talking to her and in the warmth of the room and the faint crackle of burning logs, she felt a sudden lightness of head – a spiritual sensation, a surge of divine purity that penetrated her consciousness and filled her mind with the presence of God. She turned her eyes to the wall above the fireplace where three pictures hung. In the centre, the Lord Jesus Christ on the cross; to the left, Madonna and child; and to the right, the angel Gabriel announcing to the Virgin Mary she would have a child by the power of the Holy Spirit: *L'Annunciazione.* She looked at the baby, murmuring in her arms, and then at the young Lucia Girardi sitting by the fire, quiet and numb, filthy, hungry and bleeding, yet virtuous, virginal and profoundly beautiful. *An angel sent by God.*

"Holy Father. Holy Mother Mary. *Nel nome del padre figlio e spirit santo*," she whispered to herself, her voice quivering and her sight blurring with the tears that rolled down her face. Manuela Rossetti knew with the utmost

269

certainty what she had been instructed to do. She made the sign of the cross in the air and curtseyed in front of the picture of her Lord Jesus and passed the baby into the arms of the virtually comatose figure of her daughter.

Viviana took the bundle, looked into her mother's eyes and then down in wonder at the miracle in her arms and her own eyes filled with the tears of Christ.

"Giuliana? *La mia bambina*? Oh, Mama. This is my baby Giuliana?"

"Yes, my daughter. The angel Lucia has brought her back to you."

"An angel has come?" she said wistfully. "Praise be to God."

Viviana fumbled with her blouse and pressed the baby's mouth to her breast and Viviana's baby drank her mother's milk at last.

***

"Signora Rossetti got the tin bath out and bathed me in front of the fire. She bandaged my feet and dressed me in some of Viviana's clothes and fed me chicken and corn and potatoes and put me to bed. After a day or two I was well enough to help her with the chores around the house and farm. Viviana was besotted with Catalina and would not be parted from her. I didn't know at the time why she was so attentive and I was grateful that I didn't have to do it myself because I didn't know what to do. I was happy to have her look after the baby, but when I tried to touch her Viviana pushed me away and said Giuliana didn't need anyone other than her mother.

"I tried to explain her name was Catalina and what had happened but she was not interested and she never used the name. I had to accept that the grown-ups were in charge of looking after the children and it was for the best. Signora Rossetti treated me like one of her own and told me about

270

her husband, Lorenzo, and Viviana's husband, Gino, and that they'd be home soon and we'd all be one happy family.

"I tried to tell them about Isabella and Papà and my own mama but they didn't want to listen. It was as if I had no life before I came to them and after a while, I began to realise my old life was over and I should just fit in with the Rossettis. What else could I do? I had nowhere else to go."

"But they were kind to you?"

"Yes, in their own way, although Viviana was not so happy about me being there and never spoke to me other than to order me to do something; do some job for her and the baby. I did not mind, but I would like to have been her sister."

"So she was not like Isabella?"

"No. But then maybe Isabella would have been a different person after she had a baby."

Angelo brought them coffee and the grappa bottle with two shot glasses. Lucia declined but Harry knocked back a shot of the fiery liquid and winced as it burned his throat.

"How long did you stay with the Rossettis?

"Not long. Two or three months maybe. I heard Viviana and Signora Rossetti talking about me; Viviana saying I had to go and her mother telling her that there was nowhere for me to go and she should be more grateful to me for bringing her a baby. She said God gave her the baby and it had nothing to do with me."

"She was in denial."

"Yes, denial. That is it."

"But you did leave?"

She nodded. "After the bombing of Montellano was over, Lorenzo and Gino returned and everyone was ecstatic – the women because their men were safe and Gino because he had a baby daughter. Signora Rossetti told them she had found me wandering outside and that I had lost all my family and what could she do but take me in, and that I had been a great help to her and Viviana. The men were kind to me but they paid me little attention because everyone's mind was on the new baby girl."

"But you didn't say anything? About Catalina?"

"No. How could I? It was impossible and I thought maybe it doesn't matter. I am the only one who knows the truth. Viviana genuinely believed the child was hers and Signora Rossetti would never say otherwise."

"And Gino never suspected?"

"No, not at all. Why would he? He and Viviana were the happiest couple alive and I was very pleased for them."

"But something went wrong."

"Viviana became more and more hostile towards me. She did not want me there."

Harry could see the situation that was developing. "Because, deep down, she knew. Every time she saw you, you were a reminder that the baby was not really hers and she was terrified that one day Gino would find out and her whole world would come crashing down."

"Yes. Signora Rossetti tried to talk to her but Viviana was adamant I had to go. She believed that one day I would tell Gino and she could not let that happen and nothing Signora Rossetti said to her would persuade her otherwise."

"So what did happen?"

"Lorenzo had a cousin who lived on the other side of the mountain north-east of Montellano. His wife was dead and he had two small children and he said he needed some help. So they suggest I live with them for a while and if it does not work out then I can come back. I knew that I would never come back but I had no choice. I just had to hope the cousin was a nice man."

Harry sensed danger for the fourteen-year-old Lucia and it almost broke his heart to think about it. He couldn't bear to think that any of the men had treated her badly; she'd been vulnerable and alone and the world was still at war where normal rules didn't apply. But Lucia Girardi had proven her resilience already. This was just another chapter in her life, one of those experiences that had made her what she was, and he could not have wished for her to be any different.

"And... was he?"

"Yes." Harry breathed a sigh of relief, although there was nothing he could have done about it now. His reaction was selfish, he told himself; she didn't belong to him. Not yet. "All the Rossettis were decent people, even Viviana. I did not blame her. I am pleased she and Gino could be happy at last. Pleased that some good came out of the misfortune."

Lucia drained the last drops of red wine from her glass, dabbed her mouth with her napkin and stretched her arms.

"Are you tired?"

"Yes, a little."

Harry was reluctant to make her continue but he was engrossed in the story and if they were going to get away from Montellano he had to close the book as soon as he could.

"How long did you live with the cousin?"

"Fabio. Fabio and his children Flavia and Guido. She was ten years old and he was seven. I stayed there maybe four years and it was fine. I became one of the family, one of his daughters, and he treated me well."

But Harry was still unnerved. *Leave it alone! It's none of your business.* He was jealous of her having a life before the one they were having now. *She was fourteen, you idiot! What would you have done if you had been there – take her away and wait till she grew up?*

"So what happened after four years?"

"That's when I met Luigi." He wished he hadn't asked. The last thing he wanted was to be reminded of Luigi Barone and he was sure she felt the same. It made his flesh crawl to think about her with him. "He used to come to the house every month. He and Fabio had 'business' together but I later found out it was because Fabio owed him some money. Luigi was maybe thirty-five and he was one of those people who made a success out of the war. He had supplied the Germans and when they were driven away, he supplied the

273

Allies and when they all disappeared to Roma, he supplied the local people. He had lots of money and he lent money to people, including Fabio."

She actually smiled while she was talking and it made him angry. He realised he was clenching his fists. *Don't be irrational.* But he couldn't help himself asking.

"Did you find him attractive?"

"What? A handsome, grown-up man with nice clothes and lots of money? What is there for an eighteen-year-old girl to find attractive?" she said, grinning provocatively. She was teasing him. It was a dumb question and he tried hard to hide his irritation at his own stupidity. *Or is it jealousy?*

"I mean…" he spluttered.

"I know what you mean, Harrimale." She held out her hand and he was grateful to take it. "Luigi Barone was a charmer who could sweep any girl off her feet. He took a fancy to me and he brought me flowers. He must have had many girlfriends in Montellano but I was too stupid and naïve to know that. He asked me to marry him but I said I could not leave Fabio and the children. And anyway, I did not like him that much. I did not love him. I often thought about the handsome soldier and whether he had survived."

He squeezed her hand and she smiled longingly and he wanted more than anything to carry her back to the hotel and make love to her again. *Stay calm, Male!*

"But you did anyway?"

"Fabio said I should go with him. It was the best thing. His kids were growing up and there was not going to be a better offer than Luigi Barone and if I did not take the opportunity then it may not come along again."

"So you married Luigi with Fabio's blessing?"

She laughed wryly. "Two or three years later, when Luigi and I were having one of our big arguments, he told me that he had agreed to cancel Fabio's debt if he persuaded me to go with him. I had cost him a lot of money."

"You argued a lot?"

274

"Once I found out he had a mistress. He had more than one."

"Then why did…?" He left the rest of it hanging.

"Because he wanted children. Lots of children." Harry was suddenly struck by the thought. He had not asked her if she had any children; there had been no time and the subject hadn't come up. They'd been preoccupied with other matters. But if she had parental responsibilities, she would surely have mentioned them. She was looking at him as if expecting the question, but he didn't need to ask. "I had a miscarriage."

"I'm sorry."

"Two, in fact."

"Oh, Lucia."

"No, do not be sorry for me. How could I bring a child into the world to a father like Luigi? A criminal and a brute. I made sure I did not get pregnant again, but he lost interest in me. I know he has three sons by another woman."

"You did not divorce?"

"It is not possible in Italy."

She hadn't had much luck. But her life had been shaped by the war: the death of her mother and then her father and sister, all a consequence of the conflict. Like so many other families of the time, their lives had been ended or torn apart and she, the only survivor, had then found herself manipulated and exploited by others. *"Does bad luck follow you everywhere you go, Harrimale?"* she'd asked him. She was no stranger to bad luck and she had no reason to suppose life would be any different now. He was now more determined than ever to make sure it was.

"Lucia. Are the Rossettis still living around here?"

She pulled her hand away and crossed her arms. She looked vaguely disturbed and for a moment he thought he'd offended her in some way.

"Why do you ask?" she said, but they both knew why he was asking, why he was staring at her and why his eyes urged her to answer the question. She hesitated, but he waited patiently for her. "When I came back here ten years ago, I went to see Fabio. He still lived at home with Flavia and Guido. He told me that Lorenzo Rossetti had died and that the rest of the family had moved away and he had not heard anything from them since."

"Moved away? When?

"Nineteen fifty."

"Did he say where?"

"United States."

"They emigrated?"

She nodded.

Harry tried to take it all in. The miracle of Isabella's baby, named and delivered by a British soldier in the midst of an artillery bombardment and then rescued from the rubble by her aunt Lucia, had been alive all these years. She'd been given a new life with a new family and to this day, in all probability, remained oblivious to her true identity. She would be eighteen now and, like her mother and her aunt, she would be beautiful. He hoped she had a beautiful life. He felt a rare surge of optimism.

"We leave tomorrow."

"Where to?"

"Rome. To get you a passport."

"Where are you taking me, Harrimale?" she said, smiling at him again and it made his heart skip.

"America."

CHAPTER 29

They bid an emotional farewell to Angelo, who fondly embraced them both. He gave Harry a parting wink, which he made sure Lucia saw and, to his delight, she proceeded to slap him gently and berate him in Italian for not minding his own business. Harry asked Fabrizio to get his brother to swap the cars around for their departure the next day and then retired to bed where they made love until they were exhausted and fell asleep in each other's arms. They went shopping the next day to bolster Lucia's wardrobe and purchase a few other essentials including a small suitcase in which she could pack all her things – everything she owned in the world. Harry also visited the Banco Nazionale to cash some traveller's cheques before handing a big wad of money over to Fabrizio and Carla for their stay, the hire of the Cinquecento and the clothes Carla had bought for Lucia. Finally, Harry called Inspector Bianchi.

"Ah, Signore Male. So I hope you have a pleasant journey. Do you mind to tell me where you are going?"

"I'd rather not, Inspector."

"The information will be safe with me, Signore Male. But I must insist. It is possible I may have to contact you again."

"All I can tell you is that I am going to Rome. I am not sure where we'll be staying."

"The hotel will keep a record and inform the relevant authority, but if you telephone me when you arrive that would be helpful." Harry couldn't see how he'd be needed. The Italians were not prosecuting Kessler ahead of his extradition to Germany so he was no use to them as a witness to the murder of Barone's goons, and the less they knew about Lucia's location the better. They'd been satisfied she was not acting under duress, they had no incentive to help Barone and every incentive to keep him away from Montellano to avoid the possibility of another turf war. On balance, he decided Bianchi wasn't really interested and was just going through the motions.

"I will do that, Inspector. May I ask if your prisoner is still secure? I cannot stress enough how dangerous he is. He has demonstrated his murderous talents many times before."

"Signore Male. I shall be pleased if you will leave police matters to the professionals. Herr Kessler cannot escape from here and I expect within two weeks, when the paperwork is completed, he will be taken by armed guard to Berlin."

Somehow, Bianchi's confidence and reassurance did nothing to assuage Harry's fears that, given half a chance, Kessler would kill anyone who got in the way of his escape. But he clung to the notion that Kessler's psychopathic feelings towards him might have been tempered by discovering the truth about Isabella and the baby – assuming, of course, he believed Lucia's story.

"I hope the wedding goes well, Inspector."

"Grazie mille, signore," Bianchi said graciously although Harry thought he could detect irony in his tone.

With arrangements complete and hugs and best wishes for the future exchanged with their hosts, they climbed into the Spyder and set off for the three-hour drive to Rome. Within ten minutes they'd reached the main north-south highway, the sign for Rome pointing to the right. He turned left.

"Where are we going? Rome is this way," said Lucia in her confusion. "This is the road to Napoli."

"I know that. Trust me. I thought we could go and have one of their famous pizzas first."

***

"What are you thinking?" he said after a long spell of silence. He was still in a state of semi-euphoria, cruising along in the Italian sunshine in an open-topped sports car with a ravishing auburn-haired beauty by his side, embarking

278

on the next stage of his adventure, yet still taking nothing for granted. Their circumstances were unique and it was understandable their common history and shared experiences would bind them together, but he had to consider that the dangers they'd faced, together with the inherent uncertainty of the future, might have coloured their judgement and distorted their feelings for one another.

Harry Male challenged his own thinking in the same way he always did. He stepped outside the emotional bubble and assessed their nascent relationship as objectively as he could, adopted the role of proxy, a third-party as far as he was able, there to identify and alert him to the fatal flaw in his otherwise muddled thoughts. There was no doubt in the mind of the professional interrogator, the trained psychologist, the cynical evaluator and well-practised dissembler of fact from fiction, all of which he was. No doubt at all there could be but one conclusion. He was in love, utterly, completely, unconditionally and irretrievably under the spell of the woman next to him. The angel of Solano.

Harry felt invincible for the first time in his life. While she was with him, there was nothing he feared, nothing he wanted, nothing he couldn't do and nothing he wouldn't do for her. His only purpose was to protect and serve her for as long as she wanted him to and for as long as she stayed by his side.

"I was thinking, Harrimale," she eventually replied. He wondered whether her use of the concatenation reflected some change in her feelings towards him. It was either a device to slow the acceleration of their relationship to a controllable pace, or further evidence of her being at ease with him. He thought again of the previous day and night together in bed and tried to reassure himself it was the latter.

"Three days ago, I got up and did my housework as usual and then went to the restaurant to do my lunchtime shift, expecting to go home to do some washing and ironing and then cook my husband's dinner before he went to spend the night with one of his whores. Three days later I am here. And in that time, I have relived the most terrible days of my childhood; I have been pursued and shot at by madmen; I have lost what little I ever owned and all my possessions are contained in one small suitcase. And I have slept with a ghost from the past, who is taking me across the world to somewhere I don't know and to a future I cannot imagine."

He should not be surprised; it was all too much for anyone to take in. Events had spiralled out of control from the moment he'd decided he had to go back in time and discover the truth. However miserable and objectionable her life had been before, it had been roundly trashed, turned upside down and shaken to the core by his reappearance, and if she was now anxious and regretful, he was the cause. He pulled the car off the road into a layby and turned off the engine.

"I know how hard it must be for you," he said. "I didn't mean to cause you any distress. I just needed to understand what happened, whether I had been imagining things all this time, or whether it was all true. I never imagined you were real."

She leaned over, put a hand behind his neck and pulled herself towards him, pressed her open mouth on his and kissed him hard with an energy that took him aback. He slipped his arm around her waist and pulled her body as close as the confined space would allow. After a few seconds, she relaxed and pulled back, grinning like a guilty teenager.

"You are my ghost and I am your angel," she said, pressing her body against him again. A blast of a car horn made them jump and they watched as a big Lancia roared by, its male occupants shouting, cheering and whistling out of the open windows.

***

They reached the outskirts of the city by four, and twenty minutes later, the Naples branch of the car hire company whose address Harry had found on the back of the paperwork. He told them his plans had changed and he was flying out from Naples instead of Rome and asked if he could leave the Spyder there. The receptionist had a brief telephone conversation with her Rome office, inspected the Spyder carefully and declared everything to be in order.

"Are you able to recommend a good hotel?" he asked her as they were leaving.

"*Sì, signore.* The Hotel Vesuvio is very fine. It is five minutes in a taxi."

Outside, he flagged down a taxi and opened the rear door for Lucia, who still appeared confused and mildly irritated by his behaviour.

"Train station, please."

"Napoli Centrale, *signore? Prego.*"

"Where are we going, Harrimale?" she demanded. He was beginning to learn that her use of his full name was sometimes a term of endearment but could be, as on this occasion, when she was annoyed with him. He loved her either way and kissed her.

"Be patient, my love. I'm taking you to your hotel.

*****

The express train from Naples to Rome left an hour later. He'd bought first-class tickets and was pleased to find they had a compartment to themselves. He stashed their cases on the racks above and pulled the sliding door shut. She sat down heavily opposite him, crossing her legs and arms.

"Why do we not just drive to Roma?" she asked him, irritated, but in her own lovable way. "We would be there by now."

"Then let me tell you, my darling Lucia." He stretched across and put a hand on her knee. She fixed him with a steely stare, trying not to smile. "Assuming Luigi and his

281

goons are in pursuit, they'd have had to choose between Rome and Montellano, just as we did. The fact that he didn't turn up in Montellano yesterday suggests he went to Rome, probably expecting to catch us up along the way. When he didn't, he'd go straight to the car hire company and find out whether we'd returned the car. He'd draw a blank and guess we went to Montellano instead, so if we'd driven direct to Rome from Montellano today we would have passed him on the road and they'd have spotted the Spyder immediately. When he doesn't find us in Montellano, he'll call the hire company again; they'll tell him the car's in Naples and we're at the Hotel Vesuvio." He grinned at her, proud of his own analysis, and she shook her head in dismay. "What?"

"How do you know all this?"

"It's called laying a false trail. Sending them on a wild goose chase."

"I do not know what goes on in your head, Harrimale, you crazy *inglese*. What mind thinks of a wild goose?"

"It's what I do." He frowned, disappointed at her lack of enthusiasm for his brilliant analysis, his devious strategy and flawless execution. "I suppose intelligence types are a weird and suspicious bunch. It's just the way we're made."

"Then I shall have to teach you how to be a normal person," she said, but she broke into a grin, leaned over and kissed him.

***

It was seven thirty when they arrived in Rome and took a taxi to a hotel in a side street off the Piazza Navona. "*Benvenuti a* Hotel Amalfi, Signore Bristow," said the *portiere* as he handed back the passport. "I hope you and your wife have a pleasant stay." He snapped his fingers and the bellboy who'd been standing to attention behind them burst into action, bowing formally and picking up their cases.

"Please, follow me, Signore and Signora Bristow."

282

He showed them into their superior room, pointed out all the facilities and Harry slipped him a thousand-lire note. *"Grazie."*

"Grazie mille, signore. Prego."

Lucia stood with her hands on her hips, looking puzzled and not a little severely at him but it just made her even more lovable.

"So, I am now your wife?"

"Sì, la mia amore," he said in his best Italian, grinning wickedly at her.

"And my name is Bristow?"

"Yes, well, my old job did have a few perks."

"You have two passports?" she said, still uncomprehending.

"Three actually. I'm sure my old mate Johnny wouldn't mind if I use his name for a while." He stepped forward and put a hand on each of her arms, looking into her eyes, kindly but serious. "We're going to be here for a few days and I want to make sure Luigi can't find us. And I don't need Inspector Bianchi or anyone connected to him to be able to contact me either."

"Harry, do you think Kessler might be able to escape?" The fear in her voice was evident. He pulled her close and she gripped him tightly.

"I don't know. I don't think so, but he's done it before. I don't want to take any chances."

"But he knows now you did not harm Isabella and the baby."

"I know. I'm a good judge of character and I'm trained in psychology and the more bizarre aspects of human behaviour. But you've got to remember, he's an unfathomable psychopath. I have no idea what goes on in his mind."

"So what do we do now?"

"We go and have a nice dinner somewhere and find out where the passport office is. Then tomorrow we'll go and apply for one. I guess it'll take a week before it comes through."

"Which name do I use?"

It was a question he'd already considered, but hadn't yet formed a judgement. "Which name would you like?"

She pulled back and looked up at him. He was being deliberately provocative and she knew it. She kissed him softly.

"I am already married, Harrimale," she said, batting the question back into his court. She was no pushover and he loved her all the more for it.

***

They ate in the Ristorante Umberto where Harry's Italian adventure had started less than a week ago. The Piazza Navona was still teeming with tourists and locals and the crowds would have provided more than adequate cover for two people wishing to remain incognito, but the evenings were getting cooler, so they chose a table inside.

"What are we going to do while we wait for the passport to come through?" she asked.

"Well, we could just be tourists, provided we keep a low profile. We'll also have to go to the US Embassy and arrange a visa, but we can't do that until you get your passport, so that will all take a little more time."

"This is costing a lot of money."

"It's no problem."

She looked down at her hands and he guessed what was bothering her. It was another reminder she was totally reliant on him. She had burned her bridges and there was no going back. She had placed her trust in him because she had no other choice and he knew, however much she liked him, how unnerving it must be for her. She had no money, no family, no power or ability to do anything except attach herself to a crazy *inglese* she'd known for only a few days. *But we've known each other for eighteen years.*

It was easy for him. For the foreseeable future, he could go anywhere he wanted, do anything he wanted and make any long-term plans as and when he chose to. At the moment, he was still on a mission and when that mission had been accomplished, he was sure the future for him would become clear. He desperately hoped that future would involve Lucia Girardi, but he couldn't rule out the possibility that, in time, she might think differently. He reached across the table and she took his hand. He rubbed his thumb over the back of hers; it was small, delicate and cold.

"I feel like I have known you all my life," he said. "It may sound irrational, but I know now you're the reason I came back. For the last eighteen years, I've been stuck like a record playing the same tune over and over again, unable to move on from that day in your father's house. Constantly tormented about what happened, forever blaming myself and desperately sorry it had all been in vain. I thought Catalina had died and you were an angel from heaven." He laughed. "Strange thing for someone who's not religious. But Catalina didn't die. You and I saved her and you saved me too. And now I'm going to save you."

"I am no angel, Harry. You do not know who I am. What I have done." He heard regret in her voice but it was also a warning, a thinly veiled attempt to deter him. Perhaps she was simply not ready to put her trust in him.

"And you don't know anything about me either."

"Then tell me."

He told her about growing up in Coventry with a loving but subservient mother and a domineering disciplinarian of a father, something he later discovered had to be a reaction to shellshock from the trenches. He told her about school, about history and English lessons and about losing his virginity to the form master's wife, at which Lucia laughed out loud; about playing rugby and following in his father's footsteps by joining the army in 1938 aged eighteen, being shipped across the channel with the British Expeditionary Force and then beating a hasty and humbling retreat in June 1940 from

285

Dunkirk. Being a lieutenant at twenty-two and fighting in North Africa before the invasion of Sicily and reaching the end of the road at Solano.

He told her about sitting out the remainder of the war pushing paper and then going back to civilian life and working for the post office and he told her how introspective he'd been, how he'd been unable to form relationships with men or women and why, presumably, he'd never married. He told her that not a day had gone by when he hadn't thought of Alfredo and Isabella and Catalina and the angel who took them all and he could never understand why time had not healed the wounds. He told her how, in a futile attempt to escape the painful memories, he'd joined the ministry of defence and ultimately MI6, living in the shadows, in a world so far removed from normal life.

He told her about his work in Berlin and about Petra and how, so preoccupied with his demons, he'd failed to demonstrate how much he loved her and it drove her away. He told her terrible stories about the Wall and about life in the East and about living in the shadows with the constant danger that the war would start again at any time. He told her how he'd succeeded in getting away from normal life at the price of becoming a complete stranger, even to himself – putting himself in danger, because he was, after all, immortal. Yet whoever had decided he should live at Solano had doomed him to relive the events day after day.

"And you say you are not religious?" she said.

"God or the devil. Is that the only choice?"

"Maybe God was trying to tell you something and all you could see was the devil?"

"If God had decided I should live because I'd done something good, then why did he torture me all those years?"

"Perhaps he wanted you to see for yourself that you had done something good. Perhaps you were just looking for the bad."

Her words hit home but he fought the urge to accept them without challenge. There was no God, of that he was certain. He'd never needed it nor wanted it and rebelled against the notion that he should subordinate his soul to a higher being. There were just too many things God had got wrong to make him worthy of acknowledgement.

"Are you telling me God is the reason I'm here?"

"Why are you here?"

"I told you. I needed to revisit the scene of my nightmares to see if they were really as awful as I imagined."

"To find out whether it was all true, what you thought you did. You must have had doubts otherwise you would not be here. And you found out that what you did was brave and good and better than anyone could have done. Did God make you do that or did you do it yourself?"

He shook his head in despair. "I don't know. What's the difference?"

"There is none. I believe there is a reason for everything we do and the things we cannot explain are because of God. You have no answer for things you cannot explain, and so you think the worst and blame yourself."

"Maybe I do," he said.

"And why do you want to keep going?"

"What do you mean?"

"Why do you want to go to America?"

"You know why. To find Catalina."

"Is it not enough to know she lived? Can you not leave it alone and move on now?"

He didn't want to discuss it. He didn't want to discuss it because he knew she was right. He didn't know what was driving him on and he'd suppressed the nagging doubts he'd already had. But he knew if he didn't, he would always wonder and he feared the thoughts and questions would never leave him. He had to finish the story and close the book.

"I just need to see her. Then we can move on."

"We?"

287

"I love you, Lucia Girardi."

She beamed. "No one said that to me before."

***

"Harry, my boy. How the devil are you?" Arthur Rowland's voice boomed down the telephone line as clear as if he were standing next to him. Harry guessed the elderly lawyer felt he had to shout to cover the distance.

"Very well, Arthur, thank you."

"Are you still in Bella Italia?"

"Yes, but I'm planning a trip to America, soon."

"Oh, my word, you are a globetrotting jetsetter. I'm very jealous. What can I do for you, young man?"

"Two things, Arthur. Can you transfer some money to me at the Banco Nazionale in Rome? About five hundred should do it. I'll get the hotel to telex you all the details."

"Will do. It should be there in two or three days. Anything else?"

"Yes. I need to track down a family that emigrated from Italy to the US in 1950. They must have immigration records but I don't know where. Can you find out where I go and the procedure I need to follow?" There was a pause on the line and Harry could hear Arthur Rowland's pen scribbling furiously.

"We have connections to a London firm which has an office in New York. I'll ask them to find out. What's the name?"

"Rossetti." He felt Lucia tugging his arm. "Manuela, Viviana, Gino and Catalina." She was looking at him and mouthing something unintelligible. "Arthur, please hold the line for a moment," he said, putting a hand over the mouthpiece. "What?"

"Viviana and Gino were married so they have a different name. And they called the baby Giuliana."

"Good point. What is it?"

"What is what?"

"Their surname?"

"I don't know."

***

They'd been waiting in the corridor of the passport office for over an hour for their turn until her name was called by an officious-looking man in a uniform and she got up, clutching her application form.

"Shall I come with you?" asked Harry, getting up with her.

"No, it might just complicate things." She kissed him and followed the official down the corridor. They turned left and disappeared and he felt a rush of alarm. She'd barely been out of his sight for a moment since the day in the forest and he felt suddenly fearful for her safety. He knew it was irrational but he couldn't help it. *I should have gone with her, complications or not! Don't be an arse! It's the bloody passport office! You're in love, that's your problem. You just can't bear to be apart. That's what love does to you.*

He sat down again and fidgeted, rubbing sweaty palms together, watching other people being called and wondering how long it would take. They'd decided they would use her married name, Barone. It was probably unnecessary and certainly too risky to lie as it was a verifiable fact. On the other hand neither of them knew what checks would be carried out, so there was always the danger Luigi might somehow be alerted.

There were risks either way and Harry convinced her the truth was usually the best option, especially when dealing with authorities. She had never had a passport before, so it was a new application and she had filled out the form using her home address in Casavento, naming Luigi as her husband. If pressed, she would say that she wanted to visit family in America but that her husband could not go with her because of his business interests. Disingenuous, but basically

289

true. She was back in ten minutes and he looked at her anxiously.

"It's fine. They took my picture and stamped the form. The say it will be ready in two days."

***

They did some more shopping and bought bigger suitcases. He couldn't judge how long they would be in America because he had no idea how long it would take to find Manuela Rossetti and her family. He was also unsure of the weather they'd encounter so they bought shoes and clothes for a range of conditions.

They visited the usual attractions to kill time but wore hats and sunglasses wherever they went, constantly nervous someone would spot them and continuously scanning faces in the crowd for anyone appearing to show an unusual interest. There was no logic to it, Harry knew. They'd done nothing wrong and had only villains and maniacs to worry about, as if that wasn't enough, but it would have taken more resources than Barone and Kessler could muster to find them in Rome, of that he was confident.

They ate in restaurants, drank cappuccino in cafés, held hands wherever they went and when the heavens opened and torrential rain cleared the streets, they went back to their hotel and made love.

"How do you like being Mrs Bristow?" he said, hugging her naked body in bed at four in the afternoon as rain lashed the windows.

"I forget sometimes who I am." She giggled. "Who is your friend?"

"Bristow? Oh he's not a friend really. Just someone I worked with. Heavy smoker, loves cricket."

"He eats cricket?"

He laughed. "No, no. It's an English sport. Difficult to describe. It's a game where men dressed in white hit a ball with a wooden bat around a field for five days and then call it a draw."

"You *inglese* are all crazy. You do not smoke?"

"I used to. Gave it up. Petra hated it and used to nag me about it. Used to tell me this little rhyme.

> *Tobacco is a filthy weed,*
> *That from the devil doth proceed.*
> *It drains your purse, it burns your clothes,*
> *And makes a chimney of your nose."*

"Ha!" she said. "That is funny. She was a clever lady?"

"Oh yes. She spoke several languages and was, is, a lecturer in philosophy at the University of Berlin."

"Wow. I am not clever like that." He kissed her head and she sat up to face him. "Do you miss her?"

"She was very beautiful and very clever and I hope we can still be friends. She was right to walk away. Petra wanted something else. Something I couldn't give her."

"What was that?"

"A normal life, with a husband and children."

"Do you not want that also?"

"I never thought about it before." He put a hand on her cheek, caressed it gently then slid it around her neck and pulled her towards him, kissing her open mouth with his, massaging her lips with his, and not stopping until they needed to breathe again.

"Oh, Harrimale," she said, inhaling deeply. "I hope you can have a normal life."

"So do I, Lucia."

***

The next day they went back to the passport office and after an agonising wait, she eventually emerged, waving her new passport in the air in triumph.

"Now I can go anywhere in the world!" she announced with glee, throwing her arms around him and kissing him. "Of course, only if someone is paying the fare."

"Stick with me, sweetheart," he said in a terrible American accent, winking at her. "C'mon. Next stop, US Embassy."

***

When they got back to the hotel, there was a message waiting for him to call Arthur Rowland in England. Harry looked at his watch. It was five fifteen in Rome, an hour earlier in Coventry, so he asked the *portiere* to arrange the connection and put it though to his room.

"Prego, signore."

The bedroom phone rang five minutes later.

"Arthur?"

"Hello, young man. We've had confirmation the money's been received at the Banco Nazionale."

"Thank you."

"And I have some information. I'll put it on the telex. It's a law firm in New York who specialise in immigration and in particular finding out where all the migrants went. The name is Greenberg Travis Morgan and the chap you want is Martin Kopelsky. I've had a chat with him and told him who you're looking for and I've agreed to underwrite their fees and have the bill sent to me."

"Thanks, Arthur. I'm very grateful. I expect we'll be flying out in couple of days or so."

"We?" Arthur may have been a staid old English lawyer, but he didn't miss much.

"Ah yes. I met an old friend out here. She's going with me." He winked at Lucia, who was leafing through a magazine.

"I see. Well, have a safe trip, young man, and by all means call me if you need anything else."

"So I'm just an old friend now?" she said after he hung up.

"Get over here, Mrs Bristow!"

CHAPTER 30

The *capostazione* was surprised to see three black Mercedes 220Sb saloons pull into the taxi rank outside Montellano central train station. As stationmaster he was responsible for everything that went on there: the tracks, the platforms, the station buildings and the cars outside. The Mercs had no taxi permits and had ignored signs that forbade unlicensed vehicles to take up spaces in the taxi rank, so he would have to move them to the car park opposite.

A group of ten men in black suits had decamped from their vehicles and hung around smoking, chatting and gesticulating at each other while being berated by a portly moustachioed fellow who, from the quality of his shoes and the glint of gold, looked like he was in charge. Capostazione Amato straightened his peaked cap and strolled over to the group, deciding pleasantries would be skipped in favour of authority.

"Move those cars," he shouted as he approached, waving his hands in the air. "Taxis only!" None of the men appeared to have heard him so he repeated the order. "I said—!" he tried to continue but was stopped by the corpulent boss-man who held up a palm without even showing him the respect of looking in his direction. His outrage was complete. "Oi! You lot. Move! Now!"

Luigi Barone gave a tired shrug, reached behind his back and pulled out a Beretta. He pointed it at Amato's head and Amato instinctively held up two hands in surrender.

"Vaffanculo! Imbecille!" snarled Barone.

"What are you doing?" blustered Amato, suddenly terrified.

"I told you to piss off, you moron. I won't tell you again, so get back in there and play with your trains. We'll go when we're ready. *Capisce?*"

The gun twitched and Amato went into reverse, walking backwards with his hands still in the air as taxi drivers

294

around him hastily climbed into their cabs and drove off. He backed up until his heels touched the bottom of the steps and he felt brave enough to turn around and scurry back inside. He went straight to his office to call Commissario Bianchi.

***

Luigi Barone was more irritated than usual. Precious time had been lost because that fat idiot Bruno had been certain the bitch and her boyfriend were heading towards Rome. It was clear they weren't there. Even with a thirty-minute head start they should have overtaken them on the road, but they'd checked the car hire company, all the major hotels and done the rounds of the bars and restaurants in the city centre before he and the boys had dinner in a backstreet trattoria. He gave them a wad of cash and told them to go find somewhere to stay.

He'd got drunk alone in a seedy bar where he'd picked up a whore and taken her to his room at the Hotel Grand Duce. There, he spent twenty thousand lire to be tied to the bed, having his corpulent frame pinched, punched, slapped and generally abused by a heavily made-up, raven-haired vixen who, when naked, he judged to be many years older than she had first appeared.

He and his men piled into the Mercs the next morning, leaving two of them behind to watch the car hire firm, just in case. Apart from the hundreds of tiny villages in the region, Montellano was the only other option and the more he thought about it, the more likely it was they'd come back here. The *inglese* said he'd been recently and also during the war and the bitch came from here too. It had been his old stomping ground, until that *bastardo* Coppola had muscled in on his little empire. Well, his return was long overdue. It would be good to find out who now pulled the strings in his old town and whether perhaps he could expand his empire out of Casavento.

He'd split the town into three sections – east, west and centre – and given his men their orders. Check the hotels, check the restaurants, keep a lookout for a red Spyder and report any sighting through the in-car walkie-talkies. If possible, shoot the *inglese* and grab the bitch. He looked at his Rolex: one fifteen.

"We meet at the Piazza Vittoria at the north end of town in two hours. *Avanti!*"

***

Ernst Kessler was spending his second day in captivity in the high-security cell in Montellano central police station. He lay on a metal-framed cot on top of a thin mattress, one hand shackled to a rail on the wall. This allowed him movement across the length of the three-metre cell from the toilet bucket in the corner to the barred door at the front. His wrist and arm were aching again and as he had done repeatedly in the last twelve hours, he sat up to adjust his position and ease the pain. He'd been there thirty-six hours and had had no contact with anyone other than the pig who brought food and water on a tray and slid it under the barred door and who'd obviously been told not to engage with the prisoner under any circumstances.

Kessler had felt no urgency about talking his way out of the cell; his opportunity would come in due course. They would have to move him sometime and as soon as they did, he was confident there would be an opening he could exploit. It was tiresome, but temporary, and he was nothing if not patient. He had waited eighteen years after all.

The bucket stank even before he began using it and now it was worse. It had been the ultimate indignity taking a dump in plain view of anyone who cared to watch, but he'd experienced worse and he wondered how they were going to empty it without entering the cell, or if indeed they were going to empty it at all. As far as he could tell, he was now the only occupant of the four-cell block, the drunk who'd

296

spent the night in the one alongside thrown out that morning. He could see the two cells opposite were empty and there was no sound from the one next to him. All he ever heard was the general noise of people moving around the station, the opening and shutting of doors, the constant ringing of telephones and the endless jabbering in Italian.

He lay down again and turned on his side. He couldn't stop thinking about what Lucia had said. She'd said his daughter was alive and if she were telling the truth, then she was probably still living in the area. Why else would they come back to Montellano? But he'd seen it with his own eyes and the memory had never left him: the English butcher with his bloody knife and his crazed expression of violent lust. He still had the urge to kill Male and be done with it and wouldn't hesitate if given the chance, but if it were true and the baby had survived, then the Englishman might be useful to him now. He could always kill him later, one more for the fatherland.

Lucia would be useful to him too. She reminded him of Isabella: the same strong feisty character, a typical Italian woman. He had a new mission now, probably the most important of his life, and he revelled in it. He would never be defeated.

His thought process was interrupted. Something was wrong. There had been some frantic activity earlier, but he noticed the ambient sound gradually being sucked out of the building and now, an eerie silence had descended – silence apart from telephones that rang and were not answered. He got up and approached the bars, stretching as far as the chain would allow, straining his neck for a view down the corridor. It sounded as if everyone had gone.

***

By three thirty, and a kilometre away from Kessler's cell, Luigi Barone was getting angrier by the minute and taking out his frustration on his useless troops.

"Are you sure? How do you know they are not lying? How do you know, eh? They must know something? It is not possible to hide a car like that!"

He and his hoods had barged into and terrorised the owners of every hotel, bar, restaurant, café and shop in the centre of Montellano to no avail. They had not heard of anyone called Male, Barone or Girardi, or seen anyone fitting their description, nor noticed a red Fiat Spyder, even when threatened.

"Maybe they are in Roma," ventured Bruno helpfully but all it earned him was a slap on the face.

"Imbecille!" screamed Barone, pacing up and down on the pavement while his men stood around smoking and looking every bit as useless as they were. He stopped and looked around the Piazza Vittoria until he spotted what he wanted. A phone box. "Salvatore! Go telephone Vito in Roma and ask him if there is anything from the car hire company." Salvatore stubbed out his cigarette and lazily climbed off the bonnet of his Merc. *"Avanti!"* screamed Barone, kicking his backside, and Salvatore broke into a trot across the road towards the telephone box. He was back in five minutes.

"Capo! Sono a Napoli!" Vito has been waiting for you to call him. The car has been returned to Napoli and they are at the Hotel Vesuvio."

"Napoli?" said Barone, frowning, then suddenly pointed at the three cars. *"Andiamo!"* They turned to face their vehicles and then froze. Two black Mercs similar to their own raced across the piazza towards them, spinning sideways and screeching to a halt, puffs of smoke billowing from the tyres. Eight guys in black suits and sunglasses got out and arranged themselves in a line twenty feet away. They stood with legs apart, each with one hand in a trouser pocket, the other inside his jacket. Barone and his men circled their cars and casually stepped into the piazza, assuming similar positions.

Another black Merc arrived and pulled up behind the others. The driver jumped out and opened the door for an elderly man with slicked-back silver hair. He wore a fur-trimmed brown camel coat over his shoulders and stepped forward, removing his sunglasses. Luigi nodded and relaxed, hands on hips.

"Mario Coppola. *Come stai?*"

"*Bene*. And you?"

"*Molto bene, grazie.*" Barone affected a small bow and waved an arm with a flourish.

"What brings you to Montellano, Signore Barone?"

Barone could see that the piazza had miraculously cleared itself of people and that only a few pigeons remained.

"It's a personal matter," he offered, grinning. He was not about to explain nor embarrass himself in front of his erstwhile rival.

"Perhaps your wife would rather live in my town than in yours?"

Barone bristled at the insult but managed to maintain a rictus grin. The disrespect had persisted even after all these years; the war was never over.

"We were just leaving for Napoli. So I will bid you good day."

The encounter might have ended there and then. Both sets of men would have got back into their cars, driven off and got on with their business without incident. But they were distracted by rapidly approaching police sirens and half of Barone's men turned to see four squad cars screech to a halt behind them, doors opening to allow a dozen armed *polizia* to leap out. Barone held up a hand to calm the situation, but he was too late. One of his men instinctively pulled a gun and started waving it around, whereupon one of Coppola's men did the same and the situation spiralled out of control.

It was not clear who fired the first shot but within seconds all three groups of men were shooting at each other from behind cars which took the brunt of the fire, showering them all with fragments of shattered glass before gradually settling down on punctured tyres. Three of Barone's men fell along with two of Coppola's and four *polizia* amidst shouts by all concerned to drop weapons and surrender.

***

The sound of continuous gunfire peppered the silence in the police station and echoed down the empty corridor to Kessler's cell. It sounded to him like World War Three had broken out in Montellano and it excited him, reminding him of the good old days. He rattled the bars with his free hand and shouted.

"Hey, *Scheiß-Itaker!*" he called out, deliberately using a highly insulting term they'd had for Italians during the war. If there was anyone there, they would surely respond. He heard a sound and saw a pig he recognised appear at the end of the corridor. "Hey, what's happening? Where is everybody?"

"Shut it, Adolf," the pig called back.

"Too young to play with the big boys, eh?"

"I said shut it!"

"Hey, my bucket's full. Needs emptying."

"Tough."

"If you don't empty it, I'm going to piss in your corridor." He heard a muttered curse followed by the sound of footsteps. He went to the back of the cell and picked up the enamel bucket that was half full of liquid excrement and sodden toilet paper.

"Show me," said the young police officer, standing by the bars. Kessler walked forward and tipped the bucket forward to reveal the contents. "That's not even half… " he started, but didn't finish the sentence.

Kessler flung the contents into the man's face, his open mouth ready and able to receive a sizeable quantity of the putrid, semi-liquid substance that drenched his head and upper torso. He convulsed in shock, trying to expel the raw sewage that coated his teeth and tongue and dripped down

300

his face. Kessler dropped the bucket and reached out through the bars, grabbing the young man's wet and slimy tunic, yanking him forward so his face collided with the metal bars, emitting a loud clang. He screamed, spraying a mixture of blood and sewage into the face of Kessler, who, unmoved, yanked again and again until the screaming and the clanging stopped. The man went limp and his body slid down the bars and onto the floor.

Kessler reached for the cop's holster and took out the Beretta, pulling the slide and then shooting once to sever the chain holding his tethered arm to the rail. He fumbled with the groaning cop's tunic trying to find any keys, but then noticed a bunch on the floor across the corridor out of reach. He shook the cop awake and he coughed and spluttered and groaned again. Kessler held his face close to the bars and pressed the gun against the cop's brown-smeared cheek.

"Listen, my friend. Let me out of here and I promise you won't come to any harm. Your keys are behind you."

The cop's tongue was working overtime trying to eradicate the filth and stench from his mouth and he spat some of the mixture at Kessler in defiance. Kessler moved the gun away from his cheek and shot him in the thigh. His body twisted, his face creased in anguish and he bellowed in pain.

"The keys, pig. You have seven rounds to go."

The cop whimpered and moaned and turned his head. Kessler released his tunic but held on to his belt as the cop stretched a hand across the floor and retrieved the bunch of keys. Kessler dragged him backwards and helped him up to a kneeling position in front of the door. His trouser leg glistened red and wet and blood smeared the corridor floor. Kessler rammed the gun in the cop's mouth.

"Now, just unlock the door and everything's going to be fine and you'll be able to get that leg fixed. *Capisce?*" The guy couldn't speak with the gun in his mouth but, nodding furiously, fumbled with the keys. "Quickly. I won't shoot you again if you help me," said Kessler, trying to sound soothing and supportive, but he was in a hurry. The shooting across town had stopped and could only mean at some point soon, the other *polizia* would be back. The key was found and inserted, the lock sprung and the door moved outwards. "Thank you," he said and pulled the trigger.

The cop flew backwards into the corridor and his head hit the bars opposite, where he lay dead, eyes open wide. Kessler found another key to unlock the cuff, then strode down the corridor, ready to shoot anyone that appeared, but he was alone. He heard car sirens howling by outside, or maybe ambulances, but he had to get out. He stopped by a closed door, the glass in the upper half etched with a name: *Commissario F. Bianchi.*

He pushed it open and swung the gun around. No one. He went over to the desk. It bore several piles of papers and two manila folders: one with a white label marked *H. Male*; another, *Kessler/Schneider/Radler*. He picked them up, then rifled through the drawers on each side of the desk. He found a grey metal tin with a security lock, key left in place. It contained some receipts and bundles of lire notes in various denominations. He grabbed a handful, stuffed them in his trouser pocket and left.

Out in the street, people were standing and gossiping, all looking optimistically in the direction of something they couldn't see but then another ambulance flashed by, sirens wailing, and all eyes swung to follow its progress up the hill towards Piazza Vittoria. He pocketed the gun and walked briskly in the opposite direction, heading for the train station. He was there in ten minutes just as a train came in and he glanced at the departure board. Rome.

He flipped open one of the manila files, scanning the front page. It had a range of scribbled notes, yesterday's date, the names of Harry Male and Lucia Barone and a place: *Roma!* He rushed to the ticket office.

"Biglietto per Roma." The uniformed ticket master looked at him in disdain. The tramp before him had brown

streaks on his face and in his hair and he stank of drains. He guessed the customer was foreign from his accent.

"You have luggage?"

"*Nein!* No luggage. Quick! *Presto! Schnell!*"

Kessler dumped a handful of notes on the stainless-steel counter and the official slid a ticket across in return. Without waiting for change, he sprinted onto the platform and over the footbridge and ran, as fast as his aching legs would allow, hoisting himself onto the already moving train bound for Rome.

CHAPTER 31

Their US visas were granted. They could visit as tourists for a period of ninety days and were prohibited from doing any paid work, but if they wanted to apply for permanent residence and become US citizens they could apply to the Department of Immigration in Washington, D.C.

They went to the Banco Nazionale and, after showing Harry's passport, withdrew the cash Arthur Rowland had sent. They found the Alitalia office in the Via del Corso. There were no direct flights from Italy to the US but they could fly to London and get a PanAm flight to New York. He bought two tickets for London on the next day's flight and then took Lucia to lunch in a restaurant at the foot of the Spanish Steps.

"I have never been away from Italy," she said wistfully. "What is London like? I hear it is very exciting."

"We won't get a chance to see it this time; we'll just be passing through the airport, but I promise to take you round the London sights when we get back."

"That will be nice." She raised her wine glass and beamed at him. "And New York! Wow! I can't wait."

"It's my first time too." They were sitting outside in the shade of an umbrella, but when she leaned back and the sun caught her hair, it glowed with a rich, intense colour that filled his heart with love. He leaned forward and took her hand. "I'm not sure you will be able to come home for a while," he said, worried the thought might upset her.

"This is my country, but it is not my home. There is nothing for me here," she said, shaking her head as if in regret. He cast his mind back to the farmhouse in Solano, convinced she was thinking the same. She suddenly brightened. "Maybe we can emigrate to America?" It took him aback. It was something he hadn't considered because he was focused on just one thing: finding Catalina. And once that was done, he assumed the future would naturally drop

304

into place. But Italy was ruled out for now if not forever, he had no desire to return to Berlin and had long since ceased to regard England as his natural home. Maybe America was the place to start a new life? It remained the land of opportunity and the land of the free. But what struck him most of all was that she had said "we". He had never felt so liberated and confident as he did at this precise moment and he knew the reason. He had met the love of his life.

"We can do anything we want, Lucia. You can do anything you want, you just have to name it."

She took a sip of wine and he hoped it wasn't just the alcohol making her grin coquettishly at him. "I want to be with you, Harrimale."

He pulled her towards him and they kissed across the table.

"Buongiorno, signore e signora! Questo è amore!" said the waiter, startling them as he placed two menus on the table and they laughed out loud.

***

The recently opened Leonardo da Vinci–Fiumicino Airport was teeming with passengers, porters, handsome airline pilots and beautiful air hostesses as well as a number of armed *polizia*. Harry carried a suitcase in each hand as he strode across the marble-floored concourse with Lucia gripping his arm and looking around nervously.

"Don't worry. No one's interested in us," he said, trying to put her mind at ease.

"Then why do I think I have done something wrong?"

"You haven't."

"I have run away from my husband and now I'm leaving the country with a handsome *inglese*. This is a crime in Italy!"

"I don't think so."

"Where do we go?" she said, still flustered, gripping her passport in her spare hand.

"We have to drop our bags off. They have porters who'll take them to the plane. And you can put your passport away; you won't need it."

"Then why did you make me get one?" she said, sounding disappointed.

"You'll need to show it in London and New York, but you don't need it for leaving. We just show our tickets."

They reached the luggage conveyor and Harry handed over the suitcases to a man in an Alitalia uniform, who wrote out two tags and tied them to the handles. Within seconds their bags were gone. He turned round. Lucia was standing by a kiosk, looking at a rack of newspapers. She was frozen to the spot.

"C'mon," he said, "they're boarding the plane," but she didn't hear him. Her eyes were fixed on the newspaper in front of her, her arms crossed tightly around her chest, and she was shivering. "What is it?" He caught the headline in massive print. *"Morte a Montellano!"*

Two photos dominated the front page of *Il Tempo.* The one on the left was of a body lying on the ground, white shirt open but stained black, a pool of black on the ground by his head. Despite the fuzzy picture, he recognised the gold medallion and the Rolex. He could also understand the words under the headline: *mafioso*, *morto* and the name under the picture *Luigi Barone.*

Next to him, in a separate story, a police mug shot below a banner that included the words *Assassino*, *fuga* and *Interpol*, and the name below: *Ernst Kessler.* Lucia was shaking uncontrollably and he pulled her away.

"Harry. Oh Harry, my God!"

He plucked the paper out of the stand and handed the seller a hundred lire, then grabbed her arm.

"Come away, we've got to get on the plane."

He marched her across the concourse to the departures hall and found the gate, showed their tickets to a hostess at the desk and stepped outside onto the apron where their

306

plane was waiting. He half-dragged, half-carried the numb Lucia up the stairs and they found two seats near the back.

"Is the *signora* not well?" asked an attractive, slim stewardess in a crisp uniform.

"My wife is on her first flight. She's a bit worried," he said.

"Then all she needs is a glass of Prosecco. I shall bring."

"I am your wife now," said Lucia after a moment, staring into space.

"It just came out. Sorry."

She looked into his eyes and gave him a weak smile. "I am your wife now."

***

The flight to Heathrow took four hours. Lucia downed her Prosecco in two gulps and promptly went to sleep despite the terrific noise on take-off and the constant drone of four propellers. He held her hand throughout and only disturbed her when views of London appeared through the circular window.

He'd tried to sleep himself, but his mind had been racing again. The newspaper report said Barone was dead, killed in a gang-war shoot-out and Kessler was on the loose having murdered a *polizia*. Barone would never bother them again, but Harry could not quash the lingering fear that Kessler might still come after him even though he could have no idea where they were going and was himself the subject of an international manhunt. By any reasonable measure, it was the last they would see of him, yet something still nagged at the back of his mind. He'd impressed on Bianchi how dangerous the German was and it gave him no satisfaction to find out he'd been right. He knew that when it came to Ernst Kessler, he couldn't afford to take anything for granted.

He'd watched her sleeping peacefully and resolved to protect her at any cost. He and Lucia were together now, for as long as they wanted to be together and nothing could tear them apart.

CHAPTER 32

Colonel Lance Travers had had a good day already and he was looking forward to an excellent evening at the opera. Ambassador and Lady Haywood had invited him and Antonia to join them for a performance of *Die Fledermaus* at the Reich Opera followed by a champagne dinner at the Hotel Regent. The hotel had an excellent reputation for the finest dining and despite the unfortunate events of a couple of weeks ago, when, it had been reported, a fight had broken out between right wing extremists and immigrants in the basement, resulting in the death of four, its popularity had not been affected.

He'd had a good lunch with his opposite number from the American Embassy but had eschewed his regular visit to the Kolonial Kavalier Klub. He missed young Kristof and his hyperactive tongue and it gave him a tingle in his groin just thinking about it, but he still suffered mild anxiety whenever he thought of the place and that hideous animal Kessler. He took some comfort from the fact that the bastard had gone to Italy and, as a wanted man, it was unlikely he'd show his face in Berlin again. He put his feet up on the desk and yawned. It was only just after four; he would leave early and have a long bath at home before dressing to go out.

The intercom buzzed.

"Yes, Charlotte."

"Sorry to bother you, sir, but there's a gentleman to see you. Says it's urgent."

"Who is it?" He sniffed. He didn't see anyone without an appointment and his PA knew it.

"His name is Heinrich Radler, sir."

"Radler? Never heard of him."

"Yes, sir. I've checked his passport. He looks terribly worried. He says he has important information regarding a meeting between Mrs Travers and her fitness instructor, Mr Kessler."

Travers felt a wave of nausea rising up like a tsunami. It was not possible.

"What does he look like?" He tried to keep his voice calm and measured but he was on the verge of panic. Charlotte lowered her voice to a whisper, her hand obviously shrouding the mouthpiece. Radler, or whoever he was, must be within earshot.

"He's bald, sir, with a long beard and he looks frail. His passport picture must be quite old, but it's definitely him."

The description bore no resemblance to anyone he knew but the mere mention of Kessler's name was enough. "Has he been through security?"

"Yes, sir, Robert frisked him at the front desk."

"All right. Show him in."

Travers checked the right-hand drawer of his desk although he knew for certain what was in it. His Walther PPK hadn't moved in the three years he'd been there. It was a souvenir and he'd never fired it, but it gave him piece of mind.

The door opened and a bald elderly chap shuffled in, head down, hands fingering his homburg, turning to Travers' young PA and muttering obsequiously. *"Danke. Dankeschön. Danke sehr."*

Travers was not minded to waste time. He put on his most officious tone. "What can I do for you, Mr Radler?"

The man shuffled forward and Travers hesitated. He didn't want to offend the chap, but he was getting a bit too close. He glanced nervously at the desk drawer as his guest lifted his head and then his body to its full height. Travers recognised him immediately. "You!" He went for the drawer handle in a panic, made two attempts to open it, then accidentally pulled it out of its runners and the contents clattered to the floor. He dropped to his knees to retrieve the gun, all the while wondering why Kessler hadn't attacked him or tried to stop him and finally managed to point it at him with a shaky hand. Kessler was regarding him with a mixture of bemusement and contempt.

310

"My dear Colonel, do not get overexcited. It is not good for the heart."

"What are you doing here?" he hissed, keeping his voice low even though he knew his office was soundproof. "Are you mad?"

"I am sure you could find a doctor to certify my insanity, but I can assure you I know exactly what I am doing."

"You have to leave now," spat Travers. "I'll call security."

"You won't do that, Colonel. You have much more to lose than I do. You are a traitor and a homosexual. Do you know, I am not sure which is worse?" Travers found Kessler's sarcasm intolerable and frightening in equal measure.

"Then I'll just shoot you right here!" he blustered, then suddenly remembered to flick off the safety catch.

"No, you won't do that either. Please sit down."

Travers watched in fascination as Kessler pulled up a chair and sat down. He crossed his legs and gestured him to sit as if he owned the office and Travers was the guest. Travers sat down slowly and his gun hand relaxed but remained pointed at Kessler.

"You bloody maniac! You... you took me up the bloody arse!"

"Oh, I'm sorry. I thought you enjoyed that sort of thing? Not enough foreplay perhaps? I'll ask permission next time."

"There won't be a next time."

"There could be," said Kessler, toying with him.

"Not if I shoot you first!"

"Put the gun away, Colonel. Anyway, I won't take up too much of your time. I have to go soon. I have to meet my friend Rudi in" – he looked at his watch – "thirty minutes. To stop him delivering a package to the *Polizei*." Travers was tempted to ask but feared he knew what Kessler was telling him and he felt the sweat forming under his shirt. "Photos of you and that schoolboy Kristof in the sauna, photos of you in a backstreet brothel snorting cocaine off the belly of a whore, a record of all the assignments you passed over to me, the manner and source of their transmission and copy statements of your bank account in Zurich, which contains rather more money than a military attaché can earn in a lifetime. And, oh yes, I almost forgot. Your commendation from the GRU for services to the motherland."

"What do you want?"

"I only want your assistance. One last time. Then I shall disappear forever. You will never see me again."

"If you go anywhere near my family…"

"Colonel. Please stay calm. I have no interest in your family. That was just a crude threat made in the heat of the moment. I apologise. I am a different person now." Kessler smiled warmly at him, but Travers was not convinced. The guy terrified him and had the power to have him hanged. He had to be silenced but now was not the time and here was certainly not the place. Travers would get a message through, tell them Kessler had gone rogue and they'd have to deal with it or else all hell would break loose. If Kessler could play the double game then so could he. He put the Walther back in the drawer.

"What do you want?"

***

The Boeing 707 landed at New York International Airport seven hours and ten minutes after its departure from London Heathrow. The flight had been quieter, smoother and far more luxurious than the one from Rome to London and they'd enjoyed champagne, fine food, comfortable reclining seats and a standard of service appropriate to the needs and demands of the most discerning international traveller. Lucia had shown no fear of flying, but remained subdued throughout, as she had since they'd left Rome. Harry was not surprised, and assumed her mind was preoccupied with events that had changed so quickly.

312

They checked into the Hilton on 5th Avenue, overlooking Central Park, and were shown into a room on the thirtieth floor from which they had a magnificent view west across the Hudson River to New Jersey. Harry placed a call direct from his room to Arthur Rowland, calculating the time in Coventry to be around midday.

"Nothing yet, I'm afraid," said Arthur over a line that crackled and had a short delay in transmission. "Martin Kopelsky is expecting you at two thirty tomorrow, if that's convenient? I'm sure he'll be able to bring you up to date then."

"Thanks, Arthur, and thank your secretary for arranging the flights from London; I had no idea they'd be so expensive."

"You seem to be burning through your inheritance at an alarming rate, young man." Despite Arthur's light-hearted demeanour, Harry knew there was a serious point behind it.

"I know, Arthur, but this is something I need to do."

"Would you like to tell me about it?"

"It's a long story. I promise you a full debrief once I'm back in England. In the meantime, I need some more cash. Can you wire it across to one of the big banks here? Another thousand?"

"I think Western Union is a better option. Where are you staying?"

"The Hilton on 5th Avenue."

"I'll set it up."

Lucia was standing by the window, taking in the view. Harry walked over and wrapped his arms around her and she tilted her head back on his chest.

"You've been very quiet."

She spun around and kissed him. "Make love to me, then take me to a burger joint!"

***

313

They'd walked all the way down 5th Avenue, past the astonishing Empire State and the iconic Flatiron Building to Lower Manhattan where they were literally dazzled by the lights on Broadway. Neither of them had ever seen so many people and the traffic in Rome seemed as nothing compared to the relentless volume of huge automobiles and yellow taxis that honked and rumbled their way, nose to tail, along every street.

The autumn air was cold and crisp and clouds of steam mixed with pungent exhaust fumes billowed around them as they navigated their way through the human maelstrom arm in arm, wrapped up in their long overcoats. Amongst the flashing neon beckoned *Henry's Diner.*

Just like the streets outside, the restaurant was laid out in a grid system and was so packed with diners they had to shout to be heard above the noise. They were led to a simple melamine table for two and sat down bewildered by the frenetic activity around them.

Uniformed waitresses in short skirts and impossibly tight blouses with tiny white side caps perched on their heads raced around the restaurant floor, holding aloft trays laden with huge plates of food and extra-large glasses of beer and Coca-Cola, barking orders to colleagues and customers alike. The open kitchen was manned by a dozen uniformed chefs sporting side caps and bow-ties who darted from one position to the next, bellowing unintelligible instructions to no one in particular while flames, steam and smoke leapt from their griddles to be swallowed up in the extractor vents above their heads.

"What canna getcha, folks!" said a gum-chewing, heavily made-up blonde with a notepad and pencil whom Harry believed was the spitting image of Jayne Mansfield until he felt a kick on his shin and realised he'd been gawping. They ordered cheeseburgers and French fries and beer and ice cream sundaes and coffee and staggered outside exhausted and replete into the cacophony and madness of another evening in downtown New York City.

They found a cocktail bar in a side street. It was dark, smoky, and mercifully quiet, dreamy jazz emanating from a shiny grand piano set on a low stage in the corner played by a black man in dinner jacket. They sat at the bar on tall stools that had red leather seats and chrome legs and at the recommendation of the barman ordered Manhattans, the only cocktail, he insisted, to drink in this part of the world.

Around them couples sat at low tables lit by candles: wealthy white New Yorkers sipping iced drinks from crystal glasses, engaged in subdued conversation while music wafted around the room. He took her hand and kissed it and she gave him a loving smile, but he could tell she was still unsettled. She'd been that way since they'd left Rome.

"Tell me," he said. "You're thinking about home?"

"No," she said quickly. "I told you. Home is where you are, Harrimale."

"Then what's troubling you? Is it about Luigi?"

"No. Luigi created the world he lived in and he paid the price. No one is going to be upset about the death of Luigi Barone. There were times when I wished it but I did not really mean it. But I am not sorry. I am happy I am no longer married to him."

"Then what? Kessler?"

She nodded and her eyes went moist. "Luigi was evil in his own way, but I have never seen anything like…" She broke off, searching for the words. "I knew Kessler as a lovestruck soldier who would do anything for Isabella. I knew the Germans were dangerous; they murdered my mother, but he protected us and his men protected us. I don't understand why he became such a monster. How could he murder innocent people like that and then bring flowers to my sister?"

"I told you. I've met many strange and twisted people in my time but I haven't yet got into the mind of a psychopath like Ernst Kessler."

"But are we all capable of such kindness and such cruelty at the same time? I don't understand."

He touched her cheek with the back of his hand. It was a valid point. He was in love with her and as far as he could tell, she with him, even though she had fallen short of actually saying it. Maybe she still had doubts, harboured irrational fears that, deep down, Harry might be the same. He too had shown extraordinary kindness to her family and had then committed a barbarous act on the body of her dead sister, a heinous crime on the sanctity of the deceased, the sole justification being to give life to an unborn child. Or so he had said. Maybe, deep down, she thought he was just as capable of evil as Kessler. Each had been subjected to and damaged by the horrors of war; who knows what that did to people?

"Lucia, you and I will never forget what happened to your father and Isabella. We experienced that horror together and we can't just forget about it. Once we see Catalina has grown up and is safe with a loving family and a normal life, we will know that what we did was right. Then we can wish her well and get on with our lives. Together."

"Together? Do you really mean that?"

"Yes. I really mean that. I told you I would look after you and I will. We will forget all about Ernst Kessler."

She shook her head, as if unable to accept what he was saying. What did he need to do to convince her?

"Harry. You said Kessler murdered that man in Berlin."

"Yes, the escapee from the East plus a load of others who got in the way."

"And that was where he recognised you. You met by chance?"

"Yes, although I didn't know it was him at the time."

"But how did he find you in Italy? In Casavento? How did he just turn up in the forest and start shooting? He said he'd found your new apartment in Berlin but you had already gone. How did he do that?"

It was something that had nagged at his subconscious for a while but he'd refused to apply any serious thought to it, put it to the back of his mind because he was always

316

concentrating on his own next move. He had called Kessler resourceful but that didn't explain it. From the moment he and Bergmann had escaped from the safe house, he knew the assassin had had inside information. The department had also assumed there was a mole somewhere and it went high up the chain of command. Kessler had probably followed him from the safe house to his apartment. That was plausible, but after Kessler had escaped from arrest, how did he know where to look?

"Kessler was a trained assassin and the speed and the accuracy with which he acted could only mean he had inside knowledge. When, finally, he recognised who I was, he flipped, and made it his mission to exact revenge in as brutal and violent a way as possible."

"But how did he know you had gone to Italy?"

"I don't know. I left the keys in the apartment along with a note that said '*Arrivederci*'." He was being flippant. He knew that alone would not possibly direct Kessler to Italy, let alone Casavento, but it was all he could think of.

"Why?"

"I was just having a joke with my ex-employers. Not a very good one, I admit."

"And you told no one where you were going? Petra maybe?"

"No. She'd already left before I decided to come here. And I never talked about my war experience so she had no idea where I'd been or what I'd done. She didn't even know for certain what I did for a living although she must have guessed." Lucia had never known Petra so it was an easy question for her to ask. He couldn't bear to think Petra may have been involved even though the professional in him knew that in Berlin, anything was possible. *She was vetted, Harry, and anyway, you would have known. Wouldn't you?*

"You never discussed it with her?" she said, interrupting his train of thought. She was clearly sceptical. "You kept it all to yourself?"

"I worked for the secret service. She didn't need to know that; she wasn't cleared to know that."

"No, I mean about Italy. About Solano."

For a moment, he failed to see the relevance of the question. He had never discussed Dunkirk, North Africa, the invasion of Sicily and the battle for Montellano, the deaths of many of his comrades nor any of the hideous recollections of war and, in that, he was no different from many others who'd taken part. He'd been able to put such memories aside, as if they'd never happened, because the war had never really ended. And in Berlin, they were still fighting it.

But Solano was something final. It had ended with his own death and the deaths of the innocent people he'd been trying to protect, until he woke up in a hospital and discovered he hadn't died after all. He alone, the most unworthy, had survived and the price of his survival had been to relive Solano every day by way of punishment. He had never been brave enough to reveal to Petra something so intensely personal and all consuming.

"It was too difficult and too painful. I just wanted to forget but it wouldn't go away. She always knew there was something I kept hidden and she pleaded with me to let go. But I didn't."

"What have you hidden from me, Harry?" She wasn't smiling now. He'd made her suspicious, shown her a side of his character she didn't like, or was at least nervous about. She was right. He couldn't make the same mistake again.

"Lucia. I'm forty-two. I have forty-two years' life experience and if I could tell you every last second of it I would, if it would help you judge who I am. The reason I'm here is to find out who I am, because I never really knew."

The piano tinkled and the musician started singing Nat King Cole's "When I Fall in Love". Harry cast him a glance and he was certain the gleaming white smile was for them.

"Petra was a clever lady. It must have hurt you both, but I'm glad she left you." It stung, but only for a second, because her face softened and she gripped his hand in both of hers. "Because you would not have found me and I would not have found you."

**

The Mercedes-Benz pulled over to the pavement and Travers leapt out. The psychopath may have ruined his day but he still had time enough to do what he needed to do and get back home for a quick shower and change before the opera. He checked his watch: five thirty.

"Half an hour at the most," he said to his chauffeur through the open window and then strode fifty yards along the street before turning left and then left again, stopping in front of a door to an apartment block. He looked left then right and let himself in with a key, climbing two floors to a door that bore a white card with a handwritten name: "R. Simpson". He selected another key and opened the door.

The apartment was empty. He checked his watch again. If he weren't here in the next ten minutes, he'd leave a note telling him to make sure he was tomorrow. The psycho would just have to wait another twenty-four hours. He'd told him getting a Swedish passport in the name of "Sven Johanssen" was simple and would only take a day or two, but finding the whereabouts of a former MI6 officer was a more complicated task, especially since he'd left both their employ and the country.

But that was just to buy him some time. He knew exactly how to find out; he just didn't know whether it would be useful and whether it would satisfy Kessler. He sat down nervously on the sofa. He wanted to get the current crisis over with as soon as possible, then he could alert his masters and Kessler could be dealt with permanently. He couldn't carry on like this and anyway, Kessler seemed to be on a private mission and that was unacceptable. He was also a wanted man and had to be silenced before he could be caught. He checked his watch for the fourth time. There was a noise at the door and he stood up in anticipation.

A young man with tousled hair in a striped sleeveless pullover and brown corduroys sauntered in, carrying a leather satchel. He stopped abruptly.

"Lance!" said the young man, bursting into a wide grin. "What a nice surprise."

"Look, Roger. I haven't got much time."

"Oh, you're not staying?" said Roger, pursing his lips and affecting disappointment. "I've missed you."

Travers felt a familiar and involuntary tingle. He'd missed Roger too even though it had only been a week.

"I need to know where Harry Male is. Are you chaps still monitoring him?"

"As far as I know. I'd need to pull the transcriptions. When do you need it by?"

"Tomorrow."

"Okay, should be doable. Depends on how much material there is. I take it this is official?"

"Of course it's official!" said Travers with irritation. "Male's got himself into something deep and we have to stop him. It's a matter of national security."

"Wow," said Roger. "I didn't take to the guy. Tore me off a strip for no reason."

"It's gone way past the DIPD, so not a word to Webb or anyone else. Okay?"

"Gotcha!"

"Good man," said Travers, putting a hand on Roger's shoulder, and Roger covered it with his own, which only intensified the throb in his trousers. "Do you like the flat?"

Roger beamed. "Of course, who wouldn't? I couldn't afford anything like this on my wages. I'm very grateful, you know."

Down below, Travers felt the blood pulsating and the pressure building like an over-inflated tyre.

"It's my way of showing appreciation for everything you do." He pulled the young man closer and kissed him roughly, ramming his tongue into his mouth.

Roger pulled back and his eyes lit up. "I thought you didn't have time?"

"Should only take you five minutes," said Travers, placing his hand on the young man's head and pressing him down to his knees. "Time to pay the rent."

CHAPTER 33

The offices of Greenberg Travis Morgan were a short walk from their hotel, on the forty-fifth floor of the Chrysler Building on 42nd Street. Martin Kopelsky met them in reception; it was ultra-modern, with acres of smoked glass and chrome and highly stylised furniture in primary colours reflecting the dawn of the space age. He took them to a meeting room, the windows on two sides affording a view of Lower Manhattan to the south and Long Island to the east.

"Great news, Harry," said Kopelsky, opening a manila folder. Harry was struck by the familiarity of the American – on first name terms immediately. "Our guys down in D.C. thought this was going to be a tough one, but they stuck at it."

"Washington?" asked Harry.

"National Archives. They have records of everyone who ever was in the US. Who's born, who dies, who came, who went. We have a team based down there. Turns out your family came in fifty-one, not fifty."

"Lucia's family," he said, squeezing her hand.

"Excuse me. Manuela Rossetti arrived at Ellis Island on the *Conte Biancamano* on April 15, 1951. She was the only Rossetti amongst the fifteen hundred or so passengers but when we searched on first names we found also Eugenio, Viviana and Giuliana Monti."

"Eugenio?"

"Gino is short for Eugenio," said Lucia.

"Do you know where the Montis went after that, where they are now?"

"No, but we soon will. All immigrants have what's called an A-File. It starts with an alien registration form everyone needs to complete if they want naturalisation in the US and contains other relevant documentation such as driver's license, misdemeanours, etcetera. One of the conditions is they report any change of address to the Immigration Service."

"So how do we see the A-File?"

"We simply request it from the Immigration Service. Takes four or five days to come through."

"Okay, thanks. We're staying at the Hilton on 5th Avenue."

"Yeah, I briefed Arthur this morning and he told me. I'll get a message to you as soon as we get a response."

***

They had time to kill, so they became tourists again although, unlike Rome, they were less worried about their appearance. They were thousands of miles away in a city with a population of almost eight million – needles in the proverbial haystack. Even so, Harry was impatient to hear news. He had come a long way, both mentally and physically and the end was within sight, but despite the frenetic atmosphere of a world-famous city and all its attractions, neither of them could settle. A cloud still hung over them, the spectre of evil threatening to reappear at any time.

And at the heart of it all, betrayal. There was no other word for it and in the absence of a rational explanation, irrational ones took root and grew. They were having dinner when her interrogation started again and in the considered opinion of Harry the professional, she was good at it.

"What about the people at your office? Did you tell them what you were doing?"

"No. I resigned and was immediately marched off the premises. I stayed in a government apartment for a couple of weeks but it was only meant to be temporary and I had to leave at the end of the month. They had no idea I was planning to leave the country."

"Maybe they just followed you?"

"Well, they did in Berlin, but only while I was still on notice. They were easy to spot and made no attempt to stay out of sight. I even bought one of them a drink! I guess they were still suspicious I had something to do with Bergmann's death."

"That you were the mouse?"

He laughed. "Mole."

"Ah yes. *La talpa* not *il topo.*"

"My knowledge of Italian is improving by the day."

"And so is my knowledge of spies and assassins, but that is not such a good thing."

He laughed again, charmed by her innocence, overwhelmed by her beauty and looking forward to getting her undressed. But something had just occurred to him.

"But Kessler said he found my new apartment, even though it took some time." He sat up, his interest suddenly piqued. "I was never a target in the operation to kill Bergmann any more than the two service personnel. We weren't on the bad guys' hit list. We were just in the way. But as soon as he recognised me, I was on Kessler's personal hit list, precisely because of Solano."

"I don't understand," she said, shaking her head.

"Bergmann was not only a big noise in the East German government, he also had explosive evidence of a Nazi war crime. Kessler had inside knowledge of where to find him, and that knowledge could only have come from a source high up in the intelligence service. But that same source didn't send him to kill me. Not even his own masters, whoever they were, sent him to kill me; that was his idea. And he didn't even know my name."

"So?"

"So he had to find me himself and although we both know how clever and determined Kessler is, he's not that clever."

"So the information came from your own office? Your own friends? What about Johnny Bristow?"

Harry shook his head in frustration. He was tantalisingly close but the answer remained elusive. He ran over it again. It was much easier to articulate thoughts when he had a sounding board.

"The department obviously knew me and knew where I lived and they sent a low-level flunkey to follow me because they were still looking for the mole. Maybe because I'd resigned they still thought I had some involvement, but it's likely they were just going through the motions. They didn't question me again and put no restrictions on my movements."

"They knew you were innocent."

"Exactly. Which is why they didn't follow me to Italy."

"That still does not explain how Kessler found you."

It was the key question, he had to agree. Kessler didn't just know which country he'd gone to; he knew exactly where to look. That was not guesswork. He went over it again in his mind and he saw her watching him, still anxious. She said what he was already thinking.

"If he could find us there, he can find us here. He'll either still try to kill you, or if he doesn't, we will lead him to Catalina. We can't let that happen."

He had already thought of that. It was why he needed to solve the riddle. It wasn't enough to protect Lucia or indeed himself; he couldn't expose Catalina to the nightmare.

"Someone knew, Harry. Someone you trusted."

The cogs turned and the wheels aligned and the pointer pointed, illuminated by the light of logic.

"Arthur Rowland," he heard himself say and she frowned at him, uncomprehending.

"Your lawyer?"

"Arthur was the only one who knew. He needed to be able to contact me about my father's estate and I needed him to send me money. I told him my new apartment address and I told him I was leaving Berlin and then I called him from Montellano. I also mentioned Casavento." It all fitted. It was

325

blindingly obvious, yet at the same time utterly inconceivable.

"Are you saying your lawyer has been telling Kessler where you are?"

"It's not possible. I won't believe it. He was my father's lawyer for at least thirty years. As young men they fought together. They were at Ypres together and they met up again between the wars. There is no one I trust more. But the fact is, he was the only one."

"I have heard it said, the people you trust the most are the ones most likely to let you down."

Harry's head was beginning to throb. He still refused to accept it but the fact remained, only Arthur had known where he was at any point in time and only Arthur now knew he and his "old friend" were in New York and why. It was becoming horribly clear. He was now certain Kessler was still on their trail and at any time, he would show up.

**

Harry hadn't slept much. He'd been awake most of the night thinking about Arthur Rowland, trying to rationalise how he could possibly be connected to Kessler and coming to the same conclusion each time. It was not conceivable an elderly partner from a sleepy provincial legal practice could be involved in cold war espionage. He knew that many Nazis had gone to ground after the war, fleeing to the far-flung corners of the world either to escape justice or perhaps, hoping to continue the fight another day – Rio or Buenos Aires perhaps, but Coventry?

Rowland was the quintessential English gent; he'd fought in the first war and had been a friend of his family for as long as Harry could remember. But Rowland's character and history aside, Harry's connection to Kessler was a private matter known only to them and had nothing to do with his old career in the intelligence service, so it could be of no interest to anyone other than Kessler. That meant Rowland

and Kessler had to be linked somehow and his mind went round the same interminable loop until daylight began to seep through the curtains. He threw the covers back and went to the window, looking out over Manhattan and the New Jersey skyline.

He heard the rustle of bedclothes and he felt Lucia come up behind him, wrapping her arms around his middle. It reminded him of where it had all started: the Berlin apartment, Bergmann's escape, Petra's horror at the drama and the violence. But it hadn't really started there. That was just a chapter in a story that had started eighteen years ago in Solano with this angel next to him and having deluded himself into thinking the story would soon end happily, now he was not so sure. His career had taught him to trust no one and for a while since he'd left, he'd felt liberated from the dark forces that inhabited his old world, reinvigorated and fascinated by the opportunities of the new. Now, the doubts had returned, his new world undermined and tarnished by the evils of the old. He turned in her arms, pulling her warm body against his.

"Good morning," he said, kissing her gently

"*Buongiorno.*"

"How did you sleep?"

"Better than you."

He knew that whatever challenges lay in wait, he would overcome them as long as he had his angel; he just wished he knew what those challenges were.

"I used to do this for a living," he said, musing over his erstwhile career. *Harry Male the psychoanalyst, the expert solver of riddles, the master spotter of bullshit and the genius who disentangled fact from fiction.*

"Hold naked young women in a bear-hug?"

He laughed and she laughed with him.

"We have to move on from here and not tell anyone where we're going."

"We can't hide forever, Harry."

"No. But we trust no one."

327

"No one but us."

***

Kopelsky slid a single sheet across the desk. "This is Manuela Rossetti." And then a second. "And this is Gino Monti."

Harry scanned the sheets. In both cases their first address was in New Jersey, but in June 1959, the entire family moved to Belleview, near St Louis, Missouri. He showed them to Lucia but she didn't react; she just looked strangely apprehensive. Harry decided to follow Kopelsky's lead and use his first name.

"Martin. I'd be grateful if you didn't share this with anyone. I mean not even Arthur Rowland."

Kopelsky's satisfied grin quickly vanished and he shifted in his seat, looking uncomfortable.

"Arthur's your attorney, isn't he?"

"Yes, but… He doesn't need to know this yet."

"Er, Harry. I'm afraid he already does. I called him this morning with the news before they closed up for the day." Harry's face said it all as Kopelsky went on. "I'm sorry if this inconveniences you, but you gotta understand; Rowland, Jarvis & Stroud is my client. They signed the engagement letter and gave us the brief. They're the ones paying the tab. Arthur just asked me to meet you and present in person because it'll take a few days for the paperwork to reach him."

"I'm actually paying the 'tab'," said Harry, trying not to appear truculent.

"I don't know about your arrangement with Arthur Rowland; that's client confidential," said Kopelsky stiffly.

Harry glanced at Lucia but her head was down, clearly thinking as he was. It wasn't Kopelsky's fault. He had played it by the book and even if he had reason to suspect there was some lack of trust between a lawyer and his client, it was none of his business and he would never allow it to compromise his conduct or professionalism. The irony was that, until last night, Arthur Rowland's honesty and integrity had been unassailable. He'd been vital in helping Harry in his quest and he owed him a lot. Yet based on fear, supposition and a potentially flawed hypothesis, he'd become an imaginary enemy. Kopelsky broke the awkward silence.

"Harry, these are public records and this is public knowledge. It's not confidential to anyone who takes the time to look." He was right of course, but it didn't help. Arthur Rowland knew where the Montis lived and now, so did Ernst Kessler.

***

They switched hotels. They checked out of the Hilton and into the Marriott on Lexington Avenue. Harry had no idea where Kessler might be, but he couldn't take the chance. He had to work on the assumption that whatever Arthur knew, Kessler knew too, but if he was already in the US, then he would have only two objectives: track down Harry Male and kill him, or else go straight to St Louis in search of someone he believed was his daughter. If he'd been alone, he'd have taken his chances on the former, but he had Lucia to worry about. There was no reason for Kessler to harm her but if he was anything, he was unpredictable and if he came after Harry, Lucia, like many of his other victims, might simply get in the way.

But there was now a new dimension. The Montis had never heard of Ernst Kessler and until now, he'd never heard of them. That one night they might get a knock on the door from an ex-Nazi psycho like Kessler was simply unthinkable. Whatever personal motivations Harry still had, he had a moral responsibility to protect them, and especially Catalina. Unwittingly, he had placed them all in danger. He'd placed everyone in danger. The doubts and fears and nightmares returned and he woke in a fever, thrashing around on the bed.

"Harry!" cried Lucia, trying to restrain his arms while dodging his flailing fists. "Harry!" She slapped his face and he went still, staring up at her in fear. She rolled on top of him and kissed him and he wrapped his arms around her.

"Angel to the rescue," he whispered in her ear once his breathing had subsided.

"You were having a nightmare again? The same one?"

"No. This is new." He held her face in his hands. "I've made a terrible mistake." He saw her sudden look of alarm and he kissed her. "Not you, Lucia. Not you." She sighed and rested her head on his chest. "I've put Catalina and Viviana and Gino in danger and they don't know it. My damned stupidity and self-indulgence…"

"Ssh. Be quiet. You were not to know."

"And I've put you at risk too. At risk from that madman."

"Everyone is at risk from a madman. That's why they are called mad."

He couldn't fault her logic but nor could he escape the burden of guilt. *Think, Harry, and stop feeling sorry for yourself! What are you going to do about it? You don't have the luxury of retreat.*

***

They sat in the hotel restaurant having breakfast. Harry kept glancing nervously around the room, expecting at any moment Kessler would burst in, screaming and foaming at the mouth, spraying everyone and everything with machine-gun bullets and proclaiming the invincibility of the Third Reich.

"We've got to go to St Louis immediately. Before he gets there," he said between mouthfuls of fried egg and hash browns.

"Kessler is wanted in Italy and West Germany for murder of police and civilians and your British friends have a film of

330

him committing a war crime," she said to him, calmly. "He is public enemy number one and he needs a passport and a visa to get into America. That is not an easy thing even for someone like Kessler."

"He must have people helping him."

"You might think so, but he is a lost soul. He will kill anything and anyone he chooses. A man like that does not have friends. He does not have an organisation around him. Anyway, this is personal. Whoever employed him before, when he killed that man Bergmann, they are not interested in his personal hang-ups. You said so. They would not approve or pay for him to chase you around the world just so he can take revenge. And they would not help him find a long-lost daughter either. So he has to do this alone and that will be very hard."

He'd picked a smart one for sure and it filled his heart. "He has Arthur Rowland."

She took a bite of blueberry muffin and shook her head. "No. You are wrong about that," she said, waving the bun at him provocatively. "You think Arthur Rowland has been a Nazi in the closet or else maybe a communist spy for the last thirty years and no one ever found out? You think he has spent his life just waiting for the chance to punish you for something and now he has been sending messages to his Nazi psycho friend so he can finally do it? You are not stupid, Harrimale. You would know before now."

"All the evidence suggests that whenever I tell Arthur where I am, Kessler turns up. There is no one else."

"What possible connection can there be between Kessler and your lawyer? None!"

"But Arthur is the only one who knows."

She popped the last morsel of muffin into her mouth and licked her finger. "Someone else knows."

***

331

Colonel Lance Travers was pleased with himself and pleased with young Roger. The young man was lying on his back on the bed with his knees hooked over Travers' shoulders, one arm stretched across a face that contorted rhythmically and synchronously with each thrust. Travers' concentration was focused on drawing out the experience for as long as possible without causing the lad too much discomfort, which in itself would heighten his pleasure, but his loins told him they were getting close to the point of no return and so he welcomed any mental distraction, however distasteful.

Roger had again retrieved not only the transcripts, but also the file containing the edited version: the extracts relating to the target, Harry Male. He'd read them but he hadn't wasted any time trying to understand what any of it meant or why it was any business of Kessler's, but it didn't matter. The maniac had said all he wanted was a Swedish passport and to know where Male was. It had taken a day to get the passport and two to get the most up-to-date transcripts, but he had parcelled them up in a brown envelope and made sure they were deposited at Rudi's kiosk yesterday as instructed.

He was relieved the job was done and, providing Kessler was true to his word, he'd never see him again. He had already alerted his handlers, told them Kessler was out of control and had to be eliminated before his reckless behaviour compromised the network.

"Hurry up, Lance," Roger gasped between short breaths, "my... arse... is... burning."

"Just... another... minute," puffed Travers, his concentration returning to the task at hand. But the message from down below was clear: the car had hauled its way steadily up the slope, was approaching the summit of the rollercoaster and would, at any second, plunge him headlong into the gorge of pleasure. At this seminal moment, the weird sensation of cold steel against the back of his neck was incongruous and heart-stopping.

"Yes, hurry up, Colonel. I need to talk to you."

"Jesus! What the bloody…?"

"Oh my God, Lance," shrieked Roger in panic. "He's got a gun!"

"I know he's got a bloody gun, you stupid tart."

"Have you finished?" said Kessler; his boredom threshold was low and had already been reached. "Or do you need another big push?"

Travers disentangled Roger's legs and extracted himself roughly.

"Ow!" screamed the young man, rolling onto his side, clutching his buttocks in pain.

Travers shifted his kneeling position so he could see Kessler and instinctively covered his rapidly receding member with both hands. Kessler's head was still smooth and clean-shaven but the long beard had gone.

"What do you want, Kessler?"

"Kessler?" Roger was suddenly alert. "He's the guy…"

"Shut up!" shouted Travers. "I'll deal with this." Travers knew that naked with both hands over his private parts, kneeling on a bed in front of a madman with a silenced weapon, left him little room to deal with anything, but he pressed on regardless. "What is it now? I gave you what you wanted."

Kessler pointed the Makarov at Travers' forehead and waved a sheaf of papers in his face.

"What is this?"

"It's what you asked for!"

"It's bullshit!" shouted Kessler, flinging the papers at Travers, who flinched as they fluttered onto the bed cover. "Male is in Italy with his girlfriend!"

Travers jerked his head towards the young man, who was sitting up, quivering, knees pulled up to his chest. "Roger?"

"No. He's in the US. He's gone to the US."

"Where do you get this *Scheiße*?"

"His lawyer."

Kessler swung the gun towards Roger, who whimpered in terror and put a hand over his eyes. "Explain!"

333

Roger peeked through his fingers and wasted no time. "Major Male resigned from the service, after the incident with Bergmann. They knew you, er, I mean, the assassin must have had inside knowledge and they thought Major Male might be in on it. We picked up a letter in his apartment. It was from his lawyer telling him his father had died and because Major Male had left the country and we wanted to know where he went, we got onto MI5 and they put a tap on his phone. The lawyer's, that is. We knew he'd gone to Italy, but we didn't know why. Then he flew back to London and on to New York. It's all in there!" He waved at the scattered pages on the bed.

"How do I know you have not made this up?" hissed Kessler, but Travers could see his uncertainty and hesitation and took it as a good sign. It revealed how reliant he was on them. He and Roger were his only source of intel and that meant Kessler had to engage. *Calm things down.*

"Make it up? What for?"

"So you can send me off to the other side of the world, Colonel."

Travers felt his heartbeat slow, but just a little. The psycho knew nothing and therefore still needed them. He decided a touch of familiarity might help.

"Look, Ernst. The intel we gave you about Male's new apartment and going to Italy came from the same source. It's rock solid. Anyway, I know you. You'd be bloody upset if I misled you and you've made abundantly clear what you would do. I'm not stupid." Kessler had no answer to that. They both knew it was true. Retribution would be absolute. "I don't even know what you're up to or why you're so obsessed with Male? Why didn't you shoot him when you had the chance? I wouldn't care if you didn't keep losing him." Roger looked at Travers and if he'd had eyes in the back of his head, Travers would have seen from the young man's expression that an awful truth was beginning to dawn on him. "There's no possible merit in our making this up.

334

The DIPD is on a wild goose chase with Male. He's a loser. He's off chasing ghosts."

"Lance?" said Roger nervously. "How do you two know each other?"

"Shut up, Roger," said Travers without turning around.

"You said Male was a threat to national security but you're dealing with this guy?"

Travers turned and put on his darkest expression. "I said shut up. It's way over your head." Roger glared at him and his lip quivered. "Kessler, look at the notes, man!" He gestured to the paper, keeping one hand over his genitals, aware that, in the interests of self-preservation they'd unilaterally shrunk to a fraction of their normal size. "He's got American lawyers looking for Italian immigrants. That's where he is. Now I have no idea why or what that's got to do with you and frankly, I don't care. But you asked me for information and I've provided it, now go away!" Travers had to use all his nerve to stay calm, to make his point forcefully without unduly aggravating a volatile serial killer, but Kessler didn't respond and the gun was still on Roger.

Eventually, he spoke. "I don't know these names. Find out who they are and where they are."

"Now wait a minute, old chap!" The gun swung back to Travers and he had to use all his willpower to keep calm and carry on. "You said all you wanted was a passport and to know where Male was and then you'd leave me alone. I've done my bit!"

"You have not finished. I will say when you have finished. Your boyfriend here will find out the information and you will get Sven Johanssen a plane ticket to New York and a visa for America. The three of us will meet here in twenty-four hours."

CHAPTER 34

They checked out of the Marriott and got a cab to the Greyhound bus station. There were only two flights a week to St Louis and they decided it would be better to get on their way rather than stay in New York for another three days. Taking the bus would get them to St Louis a day sooner even after a stopover in Cleveland. It was the quickest way to get there.

In Cleveland, they booked into a simple motel adjoining the bus station and went shopping in a local mall. There were no questions asked, and no identification or paperwork required in the land of the free. Harry Male left Cleveland with a shoulder holster and a Colt M1911 nestling under his linen jacket and box of twenty forty-five calibre rounds.

"It's America," he'd said when Lucia challenged him. "Everybody's got one." But he could see she wasn't convinced.

"You are going to have a shoot-out with Kessler? This is crazy, Harry."

"I know. But if he turns up he's bound to be armed and we can't go without some protection."

"Why don't we just call the police?"

"And tell them what, precisely? They'll either throw me in jail, lock me up in a mental institution or simply kick me out of the country."

"It frightens me, Harry."

He'd hugged her and tried to reassure her. "It's now more important than ever we find the Montis. We have to assume Kessler has the same information as us. Even if he's lost interest in me, he's bound to try to contact them. We have to warn them."

"And tell them what, precisely?" She parodied his own words, but unlike him, hers were rooted in fear.

He wanted to say "the truth" but he knew it was not that simple. "That there's a possibility a crazy German believes their daughter Catalina…"

"Giuliana."

"… Giuliana is actually his daughter and he's likely to turn up at any time. He's highly dangerous, he's wanted for several murders in Europe and they should warn the police and the FBI. Interpol will have already circulated the details and they can check the case back to Berlin and Rome."

"And why can't we do that?"

"Do what?"

"Tell the FBI."

"I told you, they'd think we're lunatics. You know the Montis and they know you, or at least they'll remember you. They'll believe you and if we can convince them, then together we have a better chance of convincing the police. They're US citizens; we're not. The police will have to act on a threat to their own people."

Harry had already come to the conclusion that Kessler had to be apprehended or killed. It was the only way the Montis could be safe and the only way he could keep Lucia safe. None of them could hope for a safe and secure future while Kessler was on the loose.

He hated himself for putting Lucia and the Montis in danger; that had never been his intention. But in pursuing his reckless quest, his foolish attempt to vanquish his own imaginary demons and bring closure to the nightmare of Solano, he'd opened a Pandora's box. The only glimmer of hope he could draw from the whole sorry mess was that the knowledge Kessler now had would bring him out into the open and, finally, he could face justice. Harry had unwittingly set the shark bait. He now had responsibility to ensure the shark couldn't bite.

***

The Greyhound had pulled into St Louis bus station at ten minutes past eight the previous night and a cab had taken them, at the driver's recommendation, to the Chase Park Plaza Hotel overlooking Forest Park. The bus ride had been long and tedious, but it had given them both time to think and they'd shared their thoughts over a late dinner and drinks in the hotel.

It was Lucia's idea and they'd debated it at length. Harry was reluctant to make any further contact with Arthur Rowland, but Lucia had eventually persuaded him. He was still profoundly disturbed at the notion the old lawyer was conspiring against him and although he knew the evidence was purely circumstantial, it remained, in the absence of any alternative, the most likely explanation. His instinct was to remain incommunicado but he knew he couldn't stay like that for long, not least because Arthur Rowland still controlled the distribution of his father's estate. There was no escaping the fact; he would have to be confronted eventually.

But for the moment, the balance of advantage was with them. If Arthur was indeed one of the enemy, avoiding contact might create suspicion and be counter productive, whereas keeping in touch might even prove useful to them. He called Arthur the next morning straight after breakfast.

"I wondered where you'd got to, young man," he said. "I tried to leave you a message at the Hilton but they said you'd checked out." Harry tried to spot the duplicity and deceit in the voice of Arthur Rowland but the old boy sounded just the same as normal. He was either an expert in mendacity or had been unduly and unwittingly maligned. For his part, Harry had to make his own words and tone of voice sound casual, which he found difficult, knowing what he knew; or thought he knew.

"Sorry Arthur, we did a bit of sightseeing around New York and then jumped on a bus to St Louis."

"And why not?" he said in his typically avuncular fashion. *He's good, is Arthur.* "How did you get on with the Montis?"

It was the first question he'd been waiting for and they'd already worked out the answer. "They're not in Belleview any more."

"Really? I don't understand. Martin Kopelsky had it in black and white."

"They moved three months ago. We've been there and spoken to the neighbours. They've gone to Las Vegas."

"Nevada?"

"Yes. Gino got a job out there, apparently."

"Well then, I shall get on to Kopelsky and make a complaint."

"I'd leave it, Arthur. It could simply be Gino hasn't got round to reporting in to the immigration authorities. We don't want to rack up any more fees." Harry put his hand over the mouthpiece and whispered to Lucia, "This'll clinch it."

"Do you have an address?" said Arthur. Harry nodded at Lucia in satisfaction. It was the obvious next question and they were ready for that too.

"Yes. 1545 Paradise Road." They'd seen a tourist leaflet in the foyer advertising trips to Vegas and its attractions. The address was a Mexican restaurant. "We're heading there now. It's a four-hour flight."

"Goodness, you are covering the miles. Make sure you let me know when you get there."

Harry looked at Lucia and raised his eyebrows. "Of course."

"Oh, by the way, Harry. There's a chap trying to get in touch with you. Name of Johnny Bristow. Says he's an old colleague."

Harry was suddenly thrown. He thought he'd been in control of the conversation and now Arthur had deliberately, or otherwise, lobbed in a grenade. He had to think quickly.

"Did you tell him?" he said, suddenly guarded.

"Of course not!" Arthur sounded a little indignant and with good reason. "Client confidential, my boy, even if I knew, which I didn't. Unless, of course, you'd like me to?"

"Did he leave a number?"

***

Harry steered the Ford Falcon off Memorial Drive, onto Eads Bridge and across the Mississippi River into the state of Illinois. Lucia sat beside him, tracking their progress on the map provided by the hire company and issuing Harry directions as they navigated their way out of the city of St Louis. He was confident their strategy to steer Arthur away from Belleview had worked and, if they were right, the message would get to Kessler and send him on a wild goose chase to Las Vegas. The German would never give up, but it would buy them some time. But he was totally perplexed by the message from Johnny.

"So now we have another spy to worry about," said Lucia, her bronzed arm resting on the open window, catching the evening sun. "Is he really a friend or is he working with Arthur?"

"He was a sort of friend. We were never bosom buddies, but we got on okay."

"He is the one who likes the grasshopper."

"Grasshopper?"

"That stupid game the *inglese* play."

"Cricket."

"Sì! Cricket!"

They crossed the bridge into Illinois. It was only twenty miles or so to Belleview but it was after five and the commuter traffic was heavy, so progress was slow along the three-lane freeway. The news bulletin on the car radio featured reports of tensions building between the two superpowers as the Russians continued to build missile bases on Cuba. It made Harry think immediately of West Berlin.

340

"He is the other man," said Lucia, breaking his concentration.

"What other man?"

"I still do not believe your lawyer is a criminal. I said there was someone else."

"And I don't believe it either, but…"

"The cricket man, Johnny Bristow is the someone else. He works in the same place where you worked. He is a spy like you were a spy and he has lost you and is trying to find you. Arthur does not know him or he would not have mentioned his name."

"Arthur may not know Johnny, but how does Johnny know Arthur?"

"I don't know everything!" she said in frustration. He loved it when she got a little wound up. It was pure Italian, a passion for everything – something he could learn from. Eventually they reached Belleview and pulled over to ask directions from a passer-by.

"Take this here road out of town for about a mile heading east towards Scott Air Force Base and you take a left into Cedar."

Cedar Boulevard turned out to be a pleasant tree-lined avenue with an array of timber-clad houses arranged on each side, all situated in generous grounds with block-stone driveways and double garages. Harry pulled the Falcon over under a tall cedar tree and switched off the engine.

"This is it. Four-seven-five. Are you ready?"

"I feel sick, Harry. I am not sure this is right."

Harry felt a wave of apprehension. He was uncomfortable too but he knew they had no choice. "Would you like to stay in the car?"

She shook her head and grabbed the door handle.

He took her hand and led her up the driveway towards an impressive bungalow with a well-kept lawn and white picket fence. Gino Monti had done well for himself, he thought. But the house seemed quiet. There was no car on the drive and no sign of activity. He pressed the doorbell, hearing it ring inside and they both stepped back, hearts beating in their ears. He tried again, but there was no reply. No one was home.

"Can I help you folks?"

They turned together, feeling instantly guilty, as if caught doing something wrong, which in a way they were. The man was six-four or six-five, late forties with a shock of silvery dark hair greying at the temples and a white bushy moustache. He wore a heavy checked shirt with rolled-up sleeves, faded blue jeans fastened by a thick leather belt with a bronze buckle in the shape of an eagle and, on his feet, tan cowboy boots that looked like a size twelve. He stood on the lawn twenty feet away, legs apart with his hands on his hips, eyeing them closely, like a cowboy ready to draw.

"Evening," said Harry, trying to sound cheerful, but the cowboy's face was unsmiling. "We were looking for Mr and Mrs Monti."

"And who might you be?"

"We're family," he said, but he sounded flustered and unconvincing. "Well, Lucia here is family, and I'm a friend." It sounded lame although loosely based on truth.

"They know you were comin'?"

"No. It was supposed to be a surprise."

"Is that so?" The cowboy was clearly not impressed. "Folks ain't here. On vacation."

"Ah, I see. Do you know when they'll be back?"

"Yep."

They waited a moment for clarification that clearly wasn't on offer and Lucia tugged his arm. "Harry, I think we should go."

"You Italian?" said the tall guy and she nodded nervously. He looked at Harry. "You Italian too… Harry?"

"No, English."

"Don't get many limeys round here."

"No. I imagine not. Look, we're sorry to trouble you."

"Who shall I say called?"

Harry was suddenly nervous about giving the guy their full names but wary it might make him even more suspicious if he refused.

"Just say Harry and Lucia." The guy nodded but didn't respond. "And you are?"

"Just bein' neighbourly. Looking after the place while the folks are away. I'll say Harry and Lucia came by. Maybe next time you should call 'em first and tell 'em you're comin'?"

"Thanks."

Lucia grabbed Harry's hand and led him back down the drive.

"What do we do now?"

"I don't know."

***

The next morning after breakfast, Harry dialled the number Arthur had given him. He recognised it and the code for West Berlin and after a lot of hissing, popping and crackling he heard the ringtone. It was answered in three.

"Department for International Policy Development, how may I be of assistance?"

Harry could visualise the switchboard, all four girls with headphones and banks of connections and plugs, pulling them here and there. He thought he recognised the voice, but decided to skip pleasantries. Lucia sat with him on the bed, watching and listening intently.

"Johnny Bristow, please."

"May I ask who's calling?"

"Arthur Rowland."

"And may I ask what is the nature of your call?"

"Mr Bristow left a message for me to call him. I'm calling from Coventry."

"One moment please, Mr Rowland."

The line clicked, leaving only a background hiss to indicate he was still connected. Harry began to get nervous;

the longer the delay, the more suspicious he would get. He looked at his watch. He'd give her thirty seconds before he hung up. She was back in twenty.

"Mr Rowland, so sorry to have kept you. Mr Bristow is in a meeting and asks if he may call you back? He says he has your number."

"No. I'm leaving the office," said Harry, saying the first thing that came into his head. "I'll call again in one hour."

"As you wish."

"He's busy," he said to Lucia as he replaced the handset.

"Do you think they are playing games?"

"Possible."

"Did you used to play games like that?"

"All the time."

"Then what would you do?"

"She says he has Arthur's number so that means they've spoken; that much is true. And if he thought it was urgent, he'd have broken off his meeting. So it's too relaxed to be a trick. Maybe he just wants to be sure who he's talking to."

"What do we do about the Montis?"

"We keep driving back to Belleview every day until we see a car parked in the drive or some signs of life. Trouble is, the cowboy will eventually call the police if we keep snooping around. But we can't waste any time."

"If you are right about Arthur, then Kessler is on his way to Las Vegas."

They both knew what would happen if he was wrong. If Arthur wasn't the source of Kessler's information, then somehow, he would turn up in Belleview, Illinois. The irony was not lost on him; he now needed Arthur to be the enemy in order to stay in control. He looked at his watch and made a quick calculation.

"It's nine thirty. That makes it four thirty in Berlin. If I know Johnny he'll knock off soon so I can't wait an hour if I'm going to speak to him today."

"What is 'knock off'?" she said, looking genuinely puzzled. He laughed and put his hand behind her neck, pulling her towards him.

"I love you, Lucia Girardi," he said, kissing her and dragging her backwards onto the bed. He started to unbutton her blouse from the bottom up and she wriggled under him.

"What is 'knock off'?" She giggled as his hand tickled her flesh but then suddenly, he stopped. He sat up and lifted the handset. He dialled the number again and waited. This time, he skipped the preamble.

"I have important information regarding Major Harry Male." It took fifteen seconds.

"Transferring you to a secure line," said the operator.

Another pop and crackle and then a familiar voice.

"Arthur! Good to hear from you. What news?"

"It's Harry." There was a pause on the line while it sank in.

"Harry? Is that you? Where the hell are you?"

"Never mind that, Johnny, why are you trying to trace me?"

"I'm not trying to trace you, old man, just wanted to give you some news, that's all."

Johnny sounded like his old self and Harry desperately wanted to believe he was still a friend, still on his side and not another one of the enemy. That would be too much to bear.

"How do you know Arthur Rowland?" he said, brusque and detached. There was another pause. *Johnny trying to think up a lie?*

"Well, that's part of the news. I don't really know him, but I have spoken to him."

"Do you know him or don't you?"

"Harry, listen. You know the last day you were here, just before the suits interrogated you and then put you in jail?"

"Go on."

"There was a letter on your desk." *The letter from Arthur about his father.* "They'd already read it and copied it.

345

They'd been through all your stuff. They'd already come to the conclusion you weren't involved in the Bergmann thing but then you resigned suddenly and they thought they'd better keep an eye on you, just in case." Harry said nothing, his mind whirling with possibilities. "They got the spooks in London to tap Arthur Rowland's phone, so they knew where you were all the time. We have transcripts of all your calls and loads more besides."

His mind went into overdrive. Arthur's phone had been tapped, all his calls recorded and put down on paper. They'd been read, reviewed, discussed and assessed, all presumably, in interests of national security. Discussed with whom?

"Who read them, Johnny?"

"Er, I did."

"And who did you tell?"

"No one!"

"Come off it!" Harry felt the heat rising in his neck.

"No. No, honest to God, Harry. I didn't tell anyone because there was nothing to tell. It was all routine stuff. The suits weren't really interested and I reported to Webb that you were just on holiday, which was the truth. They just got filed and forgotten." Johnny sounded peeved he had to defend himself. *If only you knew.*

Harry exploded. "Well, someone knew, Johnny, because while you morons over there had your heads up your arse playing with your phone taps pretending you were looking for a mole, I was being pursued by a fucking psychopath who knew where I was every step of the way!"

"What psychopath?"

"Kessler, dammit!"

"What? The bloke who killed Bergmann?"

"Yes!"

"Kessler's trying to rub you out?"

"Charmingly put, Johnny. Yes, Ernst Kessler has already tried once and he's likely to try again! So who's giving him the gen?"

346

"That's why I'm trying to get hold of you. To tell you you're in the clear. We found the mole, Harry. We got him!"

Harry Male would have punched Johnny Bristow if he hadn't been four thousand miles away. His erstwhile friend and colleague sounded more enthusiastic about finding the mole than he was about Harry's safety.

"Who?"

"Military attaché at the embassy. Stuffed shirt called Travers." Harry knew him vaguely. Travers was on the JIC and they'd met twice, once at an embassy function and again at an official briefing a couple of years ago. Pompous. Arrogant. But it still made no sense.

"So how did Travers get the intel about Bergmann and me?"

"Well, he knew all about Bergmann through the JIC, but he got the rest through Roger Simpson."

"Who the bloody hell is Roger Simpson?" Harry was losing it but he felt Lucia's arms around his waist and it calmed him.

"Spotty kid. In the tech section. Stripy tank top." *Roger. The young man who'd showed him the film.* "He was just the courier. The stooge. Travers was the main man. He was a double for years, we now think."

"Was?"

"They're dead, Harry. Assassinated. Bullets in the brain, naked in Roger's flat. Coitus-not-quite-interruptus if you get my drift."

"They were homosexuals?"

"Faggots. Yes indeed. Roger was feeding Travers the stuff about you. We found a sheaf of your transcripts covered in blood and, er, you know what, together with a dossier on Travers, photos of his indiscretions, details of his Swiss bank and the codes for his handlers. It's been a big, big win."

"Well, bully for you, Johnny. I couldn't be more pleased." Harry was fuming but he was also worried. How much of the transcripts had they found? "When did this happen?"

"Yesterday."

"So you got straight on the phone just to tell me I was being monitored but now I was in the clear?"

"Not just that, old chap."

"Then what?"

"Webb wants you back."

"Say again?" Harry couldn't believe what he was hearing.

"Webb. He wants you back. He said he always knew you were innocent and a valuable member of the department. He's cleared it with the suits and he wants you to have your old job back. Thought it would sound better coming from me."

Harry had to fight hard to suppress his anger. "Tell him I'm a bit busy at the moment, old chap. Ernst Kessler just assassinated Travers and Simpson and thanks to you bloody idiots, he's coming after me."

***

They sat in a restaurant that had a veranda overlooking the Mississippi River, picking at their food and sipping their Budweisers.

"What is this they call pizza? It has everything on it at the same time. Not made by Italians. It should be thin and crispy at the edge with tomato sauce and mozzarella and maybe a little herbs," she said, picking off lumps of ham, green pepper and mushrooms and eating them separately. "They have given me two meals on the same plate!"

"The Americans try to make everything bigger and better."

"Not better!" she said, outraged at the suggestion anyone could improve on Italian pizza. Passionate as ever. "When do we go to Belleview?"

"We go straight after lunch. If they're travelling back from somewhere they won't arrive till later in the day. We can have a couple of runs past and if they're not there by seven we can come back and try again tomorrow."

"What if the big cowboy is there?"

It was a risk, he knew. If their neighbour saw them again he'd probably call the police and Harry would be forced to explain what they were doing there. He'd wanted to speak to the Montis first but the sands were shifting again and he wasn't certain in which direction. He had already made an assessment and there could be no doubt.

"I last spoke to Arthur yesterday afternoon their time. The recordings wouldn't have reached Berlin until yesterday evening and transcribed this morning at the earliest. Travers and Simpson were already dead by then so there is no way Kessler could have got our fake intel that the Montis are in Las Vegas. As far as he's concerned, they're still here in Belleview. So if he got a flight to New York today and another to St Louis tomorrow, he could be here in a couple of days."

"Waiting with us for the Montis to come back from their vacation," she said, chewing on a thick lump of pizza dough.

"Which means we may have to go to the police sooner rather than later."

"Are you going back to your job?" she said casually, but she'd averted her eyes and he could tell she was worried. He reached out a hand and squeezed it.

"Not a chance in hell. That's over. My new life started with you. There's no going back for either of us."

She smiled weakly and he knew why. The final chapter was about to be played out and he had no idea how it would end.

CHAPTER 35

The skies had been grey over Cedar Boulevard and it had added to the gloom and anxiety they felt as they cruised slowly past the Montis' house for the second time that day. There had been no activity at mid-afternoon and there had still been no activity at seven-fifteen – no lights on and no car in the drive. On the plus side, there'd been no sign of the cowboy either, so they'd avoided another confrontation and the risk of him raising the alarm. But he had to assume that at some point, other neighbours might get suspicious if they saw a strange car driven by the same strangers day after day. They'd driven back to St Louis and tried again the next day with the same result. Time was running out for them to warn the family; Kessler might never come, but if he did, it could be at any time.

"He will come," she said over dinner. "He has nothing left to live for. Unless he is caught, he will do anything to reclaim what he thinks is his."

"And does Catalina belong to him?"

"She is his blood. He did not give permission for her adoption. And I have seen a side to him you have not seen."

"That's true, but you'll forgive me if I say I just can't imagine Ernst Kessler's sensitive side."

"He has committed terrible crimes but he is still human."

"I can't feel sorry for him, Lucia."

"I'm not asking you to feel sorry for him. I just say that his human side will dictate what he does next. He will not kill you and he will not kill me. Maybe, like you, he just wants to see his daughter."

"Catalina is not my daughter," he said. He felt regret in saying it and she recognised it immediately.

"But you behave as if she was your daughter, now you know what happened in Solano. You saved her and gave her life and now she lives a good life in a nice house in a rich country with loving parents. What else does she need?"

"She needs to be protected from a monster like Kessler. He'll either hang or die in a hail of police bullets and until that happens, he has to be kept away from her."

"Then you have to tell the police. You can't protect Catalina yourself. Not with that pistol. He will kill anyone and anything that gets in his way."

***

"Johnny, tell Admiral Webb I'd be delighted to come back, if he'll have me."

"I'm sure he would, old chap. What changed your mind?"

"Sorry about yesterday, I was just a bit overwrought. But I never left the service really; it's in my blood. In fact, I'm in a unique position to help with the Kessler case. I'm in the US at the moment."

"Yes, I know – Las Vegas," said Johnny with aplomb, confident with the latest intelligence.

"No, moved on from there. I'm in St Louis, Missouri and Kessler's on his way here too."

"How do you know?"

"Believe me, I know. He's been following me around Europe ever since he killed Bergmann."

"Why?"

"It's a long story. I'll tell you over a beer one day, but for now, just accept my word; he's after me and he's seen the same transcripts as you. Now I'm happy to be the bait but you must mobilise the US authorities. Get onto Interpol and the FBI and tell them they've got a Nazi war criminal turned commie assassin turning up on their doorstep and you have an agent already in St Louis waiting to brief them."

"Harry, mate, they'll go berserk if they think we put an MI6 man on their patch without permission."

"Tell them I've been chasing him across the world, Johnny. Tell them I'm just trying to help. Special relationship and all that."

"Okay. Where can I contact you?"

"You can't. I don't know who's listening."

"Cheeky sod."

"Whatever. Do it now and I'll call you tomorrow at the same time."

***

They did the Belleview run again without success. A neighbour was mowing his lawn in front of the house directly opposite and he gave the Falcon a long hard look as they drifted by. They were running out of time.

***

"The wheels are in motion, Harry," said Johnny Bristow the next day. "There's not much else I can do."

"What the hell does that mean?"

"It means I've informed the relevant authorities and they're taking it up from here."

Harry saw red. The "relevant authorities" meant nothing was happening and nothing would happen. He'd lost patience.

"Get me Webb!"

"Er, I can't do that, Harry."

"Now!"

The line went quiet and he thought he'd been cut off but after two minutes another familiar voice came on the line, pompous and lugubrious in equal measure.

"Admiral Webb speaking." *Jesus!*

"Harry Male, Admiral."

"Ah yes, Male, I hear you're in a spot of bother." Harry was almost apoplectic with rage. *I'm in a spot of bother?*

"Admiral. Listen carefully before I do something we'll all regret. I'm in the United States of America on the trail of a notorious international assassin who has, so far, been able to elude justice in West Germany and Italy. He's wanted for war crimes, a string of political assassinations, the murders

352

of several policemen and civilians and he's been able to do most of this with the help of the British Secret Services."

"Now wait just a minute, Male…"

"I have evidence that his arrival in St Louis, Missouri is imminent. He's armed and extremely dangerous and if the Yanks want to grab him before he kills any of their own people, now's the time to do it."

"Look here!" blustered Webb.

"Shut up! So you get on the blower now to either the foreign secretary, Harold flaming MacMillan, J. Edgar bloody Hoover or the goddam president of the United States, whoever it takes, and you make sure they get a message to the St Louis police to alert them to an imminent threat and that they can expect a detailed brief from an MI6 officer in the next twenty-four hours."

"You're in no position to—"

"Or my next call will be to *The Times*. Do you understand… sir?"

"You'll pay for this, Male."

"Someone will, sir, that's for sure."

***

The afternoon traffic on the road to Belleview was light and the trip took less than half an hour. Harry steered the Falcon into Cedar Boulevard and past the Monti residence. Neither cowboy nor lawnmower man were in evidence, but then neither were the Montis. He drove to the end of the road and pulled into a car park that overlooked football fields.

Harry and Lucia stood in the sunshine, leaning against the front wing of the car watching a few dozen young men, all kitted out in helmets and padded American football gear, running around in circles throwing a ball and colliding with each other for no apparent reason. A rumble overhead distracted them all.

Five enormous bombers with impossibly long wingspans cruised by at low altitude, their eight whistling, whining jet engines throttled back, their flaps down and undercarriage lowered for landing. Even so, the noise was deafening.

"B-52s. Must be landing at Scott Air Force base," said Harry but Lucia had her hands over her ears and her eyes closed. He put an arm around her and she clung on tightly.

"I can still hear the bombs," she said, "as if it was yesterday."

"I know."

"What are they for, Harry? These planes are made to kill people."

"They are made to deter people from killing other people."

"Maybe one day, we won't need them any more."

The noise subsided and the college boys resumed their training session.

"C'mon, I'll buy you a weak milky coffee and a Dunkin' Donut," he said, planting a kiss on her forehead.

"Yuck! I'd rather have espresso and cannoli."

"When in Rome…"

"But we are not in Rome?"

**

They decided to make one last pass of the house. It was six thirty; they were tired and subdued and had no expectations of seeing anything other than an empty drive and a dark house. The Montis could be on vacation for another week or more. They had no way of knowing. Lucia suddenly sat forward in her seat and gripped the dashboard.

"Harry! There is somebody there!" she gasped, and he felt his heartbeat quicken.

A large station wagon was parked in the drive: a twenty-foot long monster in two-tone brown and cream with faux-wood panelling along the sides and rails on the roof. The light was on in the porch, the curtains drawn. Harry drove the Falcon to the end of the road, turned round and pulled the car up fifty yards away from the house. He switched off the engine.

"I'm frightened, Harry."

"I know. I'm nervous myself."

"Maybe we should leave it until tomorrow. Then maybe the police will get the call and they can come too?"

Harry had already tried to think through the next steps but in the absence of the family, it had all seemed unreal, a perverse fantasy. He'd tried to rehearse what he would say to Gino and Viviana Monti and how he would feel when eventually he saw Catalina, what she would look like, how tall she'd be, how slim she'd be, how long her hair would be and whether she would be as beautiful as her mother. And her aunt.

He saw the baby again, pink and dusty and stained with Isabella's blood, kicking and crying, clinging on to life when all around her there was only death, and he could not equate her to or imagine the eighteen-year-old woman in the house up ahead. He'd come this far. He could not bear to wait another day.

"No. We have to do this now."

"Think, Harry!" she whispered and he sensed the urgency and fear in her voice. "If you go there now, what are you going to say?"

"I'm going to tell them the truth."

"What truth?"

"The truth. There is only one truth."

"No, there is the truth that you know and the truth they know. You know what you know because I told you. You were not there. You did not see it for yourself."

"Are you saying it wasn't true?" It filled him with dread to think she may have misled him in some way. *No, please, God. Not you too, Lucia. What's it got to do with God, Harry?* "All those things you told me about Kessler and Isabella and the baby and Viviana. They were not true?"

"Of course they were true!" She burst into tears and covered her eyes with both hands.

355

"Then I don't understand. Come here." She fell into his arms and sobbed and he stroked her head and held her and after a while, she pulled a small handkerchief from her sleeve and wiped her face.

"Let me explain," she said with a final sniff and he turned in his seat to watch her. "Viviana thought the baby was hers. She thought God had brought her baby back from the dead or maybe had given her a new baby in its place. She would not let me near her. It was her baby. She had suffered for it and it was rightfully hers. And I remember the look on Gino's face when he came home and his wife presented him with their child. *Their child.* Viviana could not explain even if she wanted to. It was too late for her by then. She had accepted her own version of the truth and Gino did not know otherwise. His wife was pregnant when he went away and when he came home, he was a father. You cannot now tell them it is not true. And you cannot tell Catalina or Giuliana that Gino and Viviana are not her parents. She will not believe you."

"But Viviana must know. At some time in the last eighteen years, the reality must have dawned on her."

"Yes, maybe. And if so, she has kept a terrible secret and she has paid the price for it, worrying every day that someone will come along and betray her. You cannot tell them it is a lie and that Viviana has known all this time. It will destroy them. It will destroy their family. You cannot do that, Harry. Why would you do that?"

Harry felt overcome with sadness. She was right. What exactly was he trying to achieve now and what price would have to be paid? It wouldn't be he who suffered. It would be the Montis and they would be made to suffer for no reason other than to satisfy his own pathetic insecurities. He would get to meet the young lady whose life he'd saved and he'd be able to tell her how it all happened and who her mother really was and who her grandfather really was. And then, she would hate him forever. It may as well be a lie because it would never, ever take the place of the truth as they knew it.

"I wouldn't. I wouldn't upset them for anything and I wouldn't upset you either, Lucia. It breaks my heart to think of it. The sad fact is, though, it's too late."

"Why? Why is it too late?"

"Because someone else knows the truth, our truth, and he won't hesitate to use it to get what he wants. If I don't do something, Kessler will cause pain and suffering beyond anyone's worst nightmare. I have seen it. I know him. I have to stop him and that means speaking to the Montis and warning them."

"Wait for the police, Harry."

"I can't be sure Webb did anything or if he did whether they took him seriously or even if they did, how long it will take for them to react. The Montis are here now and Kessler will be here soon and I can't afford to wait. I caused this mess and I have to clear it up. I owe it to them." She turned to look at him and he affected a weak smile. "Damned if I do and damned if I don't."

She leaned over and kissed him hard on the lips. "*We* owe it to them, Harrimale."

"We?"

"I told Kessler the baby lived, not you. You didn't know. I'm the reason he's coming after her. It's my problem too."

"Well then," he sighed. "What do we do?"

***

Lucia rang the doorbell and stepped back. Harry stayed one or two steps behind. They'd decided she would lead the conversation, gauge the reaction and then they might be able to steer the conversation towards the threat. Gino had been a partisan; he'd killed Germans; he was on a list; there was a crazy Nazi hell-bent on revenge; they were here to warn him. It was flimsy, but it was better than nothing.

Harry looked around; there was nothing untoward. Nobody watching or driving by; just a typically quiet evening in Cedar Boulevard. He heard the door latch and he faced forward again. A man in his forties, paunchy, thinning hair and black moustache, appeared in the open doorway. He looked questioningly at the two strangers outside his house, as if waiting for one of them to explain their presence. Lucia opened the pleasantries.

"Gino?" she said extending her hands and it was clear she recognised him. "It's Lucia. Lucia Girardi?"

Gino Monti opened his mouth to speak but was interrupted by a shriek from behind him and he turned. A woman appeared at his side, a hand over her mouth, a look of shock and terror on her face.

"Lucia?" she whispered, barely able to pronounce her name. Harry's heart filled with an icy dread. This was all going wrong before it had even started. The box was open and the demons ready to escape. There was no going back. "Is it you?" continued Viviana Monti. "Oh my God! Gino, it's Lucia!"

Then to Harry's astonishment, Viviana stepped through the porch, rushed forward and threw her arms around Lucia and squeezed her so hard he thought Lucia might suffocate. The two women held each other, weeping uncontrollably, while Gino looked non-plussed and embarrassed and shrugged at Harry, who gave him a rueful smile.

"Madre Maria. Dio abbia pietà di lei!" God have mercy on her. *"Nel nome del padre."* Viviana launched into her mantra and Gino stepped forward and put a hand on her shoulder. She released Lucia and kissed her forehead and made the sign of the cross in the air between them. Then, grabbing Lucia's hand, she pulled her inside the house. Gino shrugged again and gestured Harry to follow.

The hallway was wide and long and opened into a large open-plan sitting room. Harry could see a dining table and chairs at the far end and, beyond that, floor to ceiling windows that looked out onto a wide expanse of lawn. The women were hugging each other again and talking animatedly in Italian and Harry couldn't keep up. He extended a hand to Gino.

"Harry Male."

"Eugenio Monti. Welcome to my home. Ladies! Hey! Please speak English or Harry will think you are talking about him." It broke the ice and they all laughed.

The two couples sat opposite each other on sofas separated by a glass-topped coffee table and Gino served them white wine and olives. Harry felt inadequate trying to compete with three excitable Italians, even if they were speaking his language.

"How did you find us?" said Gino. It sounded an innocent enough question but to Harry it signalled the start of the interrogation. He decided it was time he made a contribution.

"Immigration records from the National Archives. Even in the land of the free, they keep track of who's coming and going."

"You are English?" asked Viviana.

"Yes, for my sins."

"And how do you know Lucia?"

"We met a long time ago. I was in Italy during the war. In Solano. We met briefly then and I was lucky enough to find her again after all this time." He tried to make it sound innocuous, but as with all half-truths, it simply spawned more questions.

"And what brings you here, to Belleview?" said Gino, looking first at Harry and then Lucia, who jumped in.

"I wanted to see you again."

Gino nodded sagely. "You wanted to see us?" He was inviting her to continue, to say what she really meant, lest he had to spell it out.

Lucia kept smiling but sounded anxious. "How's Giuliana? She must be a beautiful young woman by now?"

Viviana and Gino looked at each other and she took his hand.

"Gino knows, Lucia. He knows we are not Giuliana's parents. He knows we adopted her from you." She turned her eyes on Lucia and they were kindly and warm. "We will be forever grateful to you for bringing Giuliana into our lives and I will be forever sorry that I sent you away."

Harry watched the scene unfold as if he were in a dream. It had never once occurred to him their meeting would be so wonderfully benign and emotional. He'd assumed they'd encounter denial, rage and rejection; their meeting would turn out to be destructive and hideously awful with nothing to be gained other than, potentially, the capture of Ernst Kessler. Kessler's evil had pervaded his thoughts, rendering him incapable of seeing the good. Well, he was seeing the good now and his relief was palpable. He tried to lighten the mood.

"I'm pleased you sent her away. Otherwise I may not have found her." He took Lucia's hand and winked at her.

"Are you two married?" asked Viviana.

"No!" they said simultaneously.

"Not yet," said Lucia. She took a deep breath. "Harry delivered your baby."

Their eyes said it all. They could not have expected it.

"You are a doctor?" asked Gino, but before Harry could answer Lucia jumped in.

"No, he's just a soldier. But he's a brave soldier. Giuliana was born of my sister Isabella. There was an explosion which destroyed our house and killed Isabella and my papà. She was killed giving birth and Harry was trying to help but he was injured too. He cut open her dead body to get Giuliana out. I saw it myself and then he collapsed and I thought he would die too, so I took the baby and ran and then eventually I turned up at your house."

They sat quietly for a while, sombre, in prayer for the dead.

Viviana wiped away a tear. "I must have had my baby at the same time. But God took her. And then the angel brought one to me and I pretended I had given birth to a healthy child. I lied to Gino and I was afraid you would say something and spoil it for me. I am sorry. For five years, I kept a terrible secret. And then, Giuliana became ill and no

360

one knew what was wrong with her and we decided to bring her to America. The doctors said she needed a blood transfusion and we said we will give ours. We will give all of ours!" She gave a hollow laugh. "I am type O blood and Gino is type B, but Giuliana is type A. This is not possible." Gino squeezed his wife's hand. "He forgave me. He said, 'It does not matter, Viviana. We have a child.' But I always wondered what happened to you, Lucia."

"We have to thank you both," said Gino, "for our beautiful daughter. Giuliana knows too. We told her when she was twelve."

But the girl they were all talking about was nowhere to be seen and Harry could wait no longer.

"Is Giuliana here? May we see her?"

"She has gone out with her boyfriend, Brad. We have been away for two weeks and she has not seen him. You know how these young folks are. She will be back soon."

The doorbell rang. Gino got to his feet and went to the window. He turned with a look of consternation.

"It's the sheriff," he announced and went out into the hallway.

Harry jumped to his feet, a brief wave of optimism and relief washing over him. He hoped the arrival of the sheriff was the advance party, the precursor to the cavalry. But his professional instinct told him there was something wrong. He rushed to the window and looked down the drive. A brown sedan was parked on the road. It had lights on the roof and a six-point star motif on the door. Even from the distance of fifty feet, he could see the driver's window was wound down and through it, the crazed pattern on the windscreen, like a spider's web. He followed Gino, pulling the Colt from the holster and yanking back the slide.

"Gino! No!"

But he was too late. Gino's frame was blocking the door and his view to the outside. His hands were in the air and he was shuffling backwards.

"Drop the weapon, Harry," said the hidden voice. "Or you know I will kill this man without hesitation."

Lucia came up behind him and Viviana screamed. "Gino!"

"Back inside," said Harry, fingering the trigger.

"What's happening?" said Lucia. "Oh God."

"I said drop the weapon."

Harry reluctantly lowered the Colt to the floor and they all retreated into the sitting room. A tall man with a shaven head appeared from behind Gino, holding a Makarov. He wore an ill-fitting, crumpled sheriff's uniform with bloodstains on the collar. He picked up the Colt and slid it into his pocket.

"Please, everyone, sit. I shall not take long and then I shall leave you."

"Who is this guy?" said Gino, holding his distraught wife tightly.

"His name is Ernst Kessler," said Lucia.

"What do you want?" gasped Viviana.

"Where is my daughter?"

The Montis looked at each other in shock, but it was Lucia who answered. "He's Giuliana's father."

"Signora Lucia, how nice to see you again. Lucia is my sister-in-law. Please. Sit. Now!" He waved the gun to emphasise his point.

"You know this man?" said Viviana as they lowered themselves onto the sofas as if in a daze.

"He was in love with my sister."

"Isabella was in love with me too," countered Kessler.

Harry blinked. He'd sensed a flicker of emotion, the faintest whiff of humanity from the mouth of the monster.

"She had no choice," continued Lucia calmly.

"She had a choice!" the monster roared, snuffing out the human in a split second.

"But he is German. He was a Nazi?" said Gino as the terrible truth dawned on him.

"I'm afraid so," said Harry. "The worst sort. We came here to warn you, but we were too late."

"Enough!" barked Kessler. "Where is my Eva?"

"Eva?" Viviana's confusion was complete.

"I named my daughter Eva."

"Her name is Giuliana!" shouted Gino.

"That name is not valid."

"She's not here, Ernst," said Harry, "and the cops will be here soon so I suggest you make a break for it while you can."

"I will wait," said Kessler. "I have waited so long."

Viviana began to weep and Gino tried to comfort her. Harry stood up and faced him.

"Sit down, Harry, I don't want to shoot you again."

"Well, you've already had two tries and missed both times, Ernst. Don't you know an angel was looking after me?" He knew the risk. Kessler would shoot them all in the blink of an eye. But he felt an unnatural sense of empowerment, an invulnerability that belied the facts of their situation. "I don't know what you're trying to achieve here but whatever you want, it's not possible."

"I want my daughter back!" he snapped. "It is not complicated." But then, he seemed to relax and his voice took on a courteous note. "I did not thank you, Harry, for saving her and I am sorry I tried to kill you. It was just a misunderstanding. And I thank you, Lucia, for finding these nice people to care for Eva in my absence. Signore and Signora Monti, I thank you for bringing her up on my behalf. I trust she was not a difficult child?" He grinned at his quip but then turned serious. "So, I thank you all for your help and sacrifice, but I have come back now and I no longer need your services. Eva will come with me and we shall live as father and daughter together."

"No!" wept Viviana.

"You will have to kill me first," snarled Gino.

"That is no problem and can be arranged."

Harry gestured to Gino to stay calm. He mimicked Kessler's tone, courteous but sympathetic.

"Ernst. Eva doesn't know who you are. This is her home and these are her parents. There is no way she can be happy with you."

"Nein!"

"Why do you chaps always have to shout? Can't we just have a grown-up conversation without you frothing at the mouth and bellowing orders? The trouble with you lot is you always think you're right."

"But I am right. Eva belongs to me. She is my flesh and blood!"

"We know that, Ernst." Harry was determined to stay on first-name terms, like a hostage situation where language and names were designed to placate the aggressor; calm things down. But somehow it seemed appropriate for another reason. He knew Ernst Kessler. They had a shared history and a shared trauma. Harry wished they had met before the war. Maybe he had once been normal? Maybe they could have been friends? "But you're a man on the run. You're wanted in Germany and Italy; you're wanted by our side and your own side…"

"I do not have a side!"

"… and soon, you'll be wanted in America. Where are you going to run to next, Ernst? Where are you going to hide with Giuliana?"

"Eva!"

"You have no place to go. You have no country, no home, no friends. Only enemies. The whole world is against you."

"The whole world was always against me!" he shouted. "The whole world was against us all. All we wanted was to make a better world for everyone!"

Harry forced a laugh. "Really? You mean everyone apart from the Jews. And the Slavs. Oh, let's see." Harry made a show of scratching his head. "Then there's Communists, blacks, homosexuals – although you had one or two of your

364

own, didn't you? Let's skip over that one. Gypsies, er, anyone with a disability, an IQ under a hundred. I could go on."

"The trouble with you English is you think the same as we do but you say something else. We asked you to join us. Together we could have conquered the world, be rid of the filth and the retards, but you wanted it all for yourself. And now look. The world is a mess and you created it."

"You lost Ernst. Get over it!"

"We have not finished."

"You won't be finished until you've killed everyone. How many have you killed, Ernst? Did you keep score or have you lost count?"

"Sometimes it is necessary."

"Are you going to kill us all too?"

"It should not be necessary, unless you try to stop me or get in my way."

Kessler's anger was building steadily, but Harry still felt calm. He could hear ancient explosions in the distance – the storm brewing – but despite that he would carry on. Carry on where he'd left off.

"She'll hate you for taking her away from her parents. Are you prepared to take the risk your daughter will hate you?"

"I will explain to her. When she understands I can give her a better life, she will be happy."

The sound of the front door latch made all of them jump.

"Giuliana!" screamed her mother. "Run away! Run away!" But it was futile. Kessler stepped back to the window as a curious teenager walked in, confused and disturbed by the cry. Lucia stood next to Harry and gripped his arm. The girl was eighteen with long blonde hair and blue eyes; she was slim and beautiful and belonged in another world, a product of a different race and a different time. *Catalina.*

"Why's the sheriff here?"

"Eva!" Kessler grabbed her arm and pulled her towards him and she shrieked in fright. Gino leapt to his feet but

Kessler swung the gun and shot him in the thigh and he fell back on the sofa. Viviana started screaming and Giuliana joined her.

"Daddy!"

"I am your father, Eva," snarled Kessler, "not this retard!"

"Ernst, for Christ's sake!" shouted Harry. He wanted to throw himself at the German, but the gun was still pointing at them and he was ten feet away, too far to leap and too close to dodge a bullet.

"How beautiful you are, my Eva," cooed the monster that was Ernst Kessler. "Come with me now. Everything will be all right."

Gino Monti grimaced and clutched a leg that was bleeding all over the carpet and Viviana was on her knees beside him, shaking and weeping. Kessler dragged Giuliana towards the hallway and she struggled and screamed but his grip was like a vice.

"Goodbye, Harry," he heard Kessler shout. Harry raced to the door in pursuit, watching Kessler drag Giuliana down the lawn towards the car like a dog on a leash. She dug her heels in but he was too strong. Harry leapt out of the porch and called after them.

"Kessler! I won't let you take her."

Kessler stopped and pulled Giuliana towards him, left arm around her waist, right arm extended, the Makarov aimed at Harry. Giuliana had stopped struggling and was now sobbing uncontrollably. They were twenty feet apart.

"Then I will kill you, Harry Male."

"You can't kill me, Ernst. You and I are already dead. We died in that farmhouse." Harry watched Kessler's face turn from sneering self-confidence to confusion and doubt. "You and I are the same, Ernst."

"We are not the same!" he shouted as Harry took three steps forward. "I will kill you!"

"Giuliana?" Harry said gently, taking another step. "This man is your father. His name is Ernst Kessler." The girl turned her eyes towards him and he sensed Kessler's gun hand shaking, but he took another step and gave her a warm smile. "My name is Harry. I knew your mother, Isabella. I'm sorry to say she died before she was able to look at you and see how beautiful you were. I was the first person to see you and hold you in my arms and I haven't seen you since the day you were born." He gestured towards Kessler, whose whole body was beginning to shake. "Ernst is your biological father. He believed I was trying to hurt you and he shot me. He thought he was doing the right thing, protecting his child and to be honest, if I'd been him, I'd have done the same. But I was just trying to keep you alive." He stepped forward again. He heard police sirens in the distance and he saw Kessler flinch and cast a nervous glance over his shoulder. "We both wanted the same thing. We both wanted to protect you. Isn't that right, Ernst? Don't we want the same thing?" He waited but Kessler offered no response.

"And here we are, Ernst, trying to do the same thing all over again. Keep your daughter safe. Giuliana? Your biological father wants to take you away from your real mum and your real dad. He wants you to go with him."

"No, please," she said, the fear almost overflowing. "Please let me go."

The sirens were getting louder and Kessler was beginning to crumble. Harry stepped forward.

"Ernst, the cops will be here any minute. If you don't let her go they'll start shooting. You know how trigger-happy the Yanks are. Giuliana may get hurt. You don't want that."

"She comes with me!"

"No. If you try that you'll kill her, just as if you killed her yourself."

"I am not a monster!" he bellowed. "I am a human being!"

"I know, Ernst. You're like me. You died trying to protect her and you've been dead ever since. Just like me. Why don't we just let her go back to her family and let her have a nice life?"

A voice behind him, urgent, pleading. *Lucia.*

"Harry, please stop! Harry! He will kill you."

He kept walking. "No he can't, angel. He's already done that."

Kessler fired and Harry felt a piercing stab from a white-hot knife that cut into his flesh, burning deep inside his shoulder. He twisted involuntarily from the force of the bullet.

"Harry!" screamed Lucia, and Giuliana screamed with her, writhing and struggling to escape Kessler's grip.

"Get back, Lucia," he gasped, the pain searing and intense. He was twelve feet away. He felt wetness on his shirt, then his upper body went numb and he felt light-headed as his heart lowered his blood pressure to reduce the flow. He'd been here before so he knew what it was like. He'd died once before and it wasn't so bad. He had his angel, after all. He raised his left arm because his right hung limp, no longer connected to his brain. "Giuliana. Come to me. Come on. Let her come, Ernst."

Kessler's face creased with agony, his eyes filling with tears. He slowly relaxed his grip but it was enough and Giuliana wrestled herself free. She ran past Harry and into the arms of her mother and they gripped each other, sobbing. Kessler raised the shaking Makarov and pointed it at Harry's head.

"Drop the gun, fella." The voice boomed with uncompromising authority and they both slowly turned their heads towards it. Six-four, shock of silvery dark hair, bushy white moustache, checked shirt, faded jeans, cowboy boots, leather belt with the American eagle for a buckle. And in his hands, a shotgun, its long slender barrels pointed at Kessler. Out in the road, four black and white police cars and two unmarked sedans, sirens wailing and blue lights flashing, screeched to a halt. A dozen men leapt out, and squatted down around their cars, guns drawn and pointed. "Won't tell you again," said the cowboy.

Kessler's frame shrunk visibly and the gun swung slowly downwards, pointing to the ground. He shrugged.

"Well, Harry Male. It seems you have won again."

"We both won, Ernst. We saved Catalina."

Kessler erupted like a volcano, throwing back his head and screaming at the sky like a howling wolf, his body and arms shaking in rage.

"Heil... Hitler!" Then with careful deliberation, swung his gun slowly towards the cowboy.

Both barrels exploded with the sound of thunder and as if attached to an invisible rope, Kessler was yanked into the air, flying backwards to land on the lawn ten feet distant. The police raced up the garden and four of them stood over the body, legs apart, pistols extended and steadied in two hands. One of them kneeled down.

"He's dead, Lieutenant," he announced to a suit in a brown overcoat and a fedora. The suit walked over to the cowboy, who snapped the shotgun open and the cartridges flew out, the breech exuding a cloud of white smoke.

"What kept ya, Joe?" said the cowboy. "This man needs a doctor." The suit cast Harry a glance. The blood had seeped through his jacket and he lowered himself onto the grass. Lucia threw her arms around him.

"Harry! You crazy *inglese!*"

"Ow!" He grimaced. "Watch out, that hurts. Same bloody shoulder!"

"I hope it hurts. It will teach you not to be so crazy."

"Rossi," shouted Joe, the suit. "Get this man an ambulance. Fast!"

"There's another injured man inside," Harry shouted after him, but he felt weak and it sapped his strength. He looked into Lucia's eyes.

"Hello, angel," he whispered. "Are you going to take me away from here?"

"Yes, Harrimale. I will look after you."

The cowboy sauntered, languorous and bow-legged, to where they were sitting, Lucia cradling his head in her shoulder.

"You okay, mister?"

"I'll live. Thanks, by the way."

"You're welcome. Who was that guy?"

"Oh, just a Nazi with a bad attitude."

"Nazi? I hate Nazis. Do y'all know him?"

"Yes. Italy. 1944. We were on opposite sides, of course."

"Hey! You don't say! I was in Italy in forty-four. Flew B-17s over Montellano. Still get nightmares though," he said, looking pensive.

"Really?" Harry held out his left hand. "Harry Male."

"Pleasure to meet you, Harry," he said, taking the hand with his left. "Mitchell McLennan. Friends call me Mitch."

CHAPTER 36

West Berlin – March 1963

Lucia pulled her coat collar up and fastened the button at her throat. The snow was falling steadily, coating the pavements and roads with an ever-deepening layer of frozen white candy floss: typical weather for the time of year. She stomped feet encased in fur-lined boots and slid her arm through his.

"It's freezing, Harrimale!" she squealed. "Can we not go somewhere warmer?"

"Of course we can. *Kaffeeshop mit Sachertorte*, or hotel room with, er… bratwurst. Which would you prefer?"

"I meant a warmer country, *stupido*."

"Like England?"

"England must be warmer than this?"

"A little, I suppose. How are you with rain?"

"I can make do. If you are there with me."

"We'll be back in a couple of days. I just wanted you to see the Wall."

They stood in the Straße des 17 Juni, looking east at the twelve-foot high concrete structure and, behind it, the iconic Brandenburg Gate topped with the Quadriga that, incongruously, faced east over the city.

"Up until 17 June 1953, this street used to be called the Charlottenburger Chaussee. It was renamed after an uprising against the communists but was brutally suppressed by the East German police. Eventually they built the Wall. They said it was to keep us westerners out." He laughed at the irony.

"It's terrible," she said. "Do you think it will ever come down?"

371

"Can't see it. Not in our lifetime. But the US has a strong young president, in contrast to those dinosaurs in the Soviet Union. Maybe he'll make a difference."

He swung her around and they took a path through the Tiergarten, its snow-laden trees giving it the appearance of an enchanted forest. A young couple pushing a pram approached from the opposite direction and they all stopped.

"Hello, Petra."

"Hello, Harry. How nice to see you." The greeting was warm and genuine.

"It's very nice to see you too. This is Lucia."

"Hello, Petra," said Lucia. "Harry told me all about you."

"This is my husband, Walther," she said, and a tall bearded young man with glasses extended a hand which Harry shook. He peered into the pram.

"And who do we have here?"

"This is Marie," she gushed. "She is just a few weeks old. I thought work was hard but this is much harder. How have you been, Harry? Are you still working for the government?"

"No. I left all that nonsense behind. I have you to thank for that. I gave up the cigarettes too."

"Tobacco is a filthy weed…" she started and they both laughed.

"That's enough, thank you!"

"When is the baby due?" asked Petra. Lucia had instinctively placed a hand on her own swollen figure.

"June."

"Lucia and I live in England now," said Harry. "I just came back to show her one or two of my old haunts."

"And are you still haunted by the dark?"

"No." He put his arm around his wife. "An angel showed me the light."

Author's footnote

My wife's late father, Major Colin Keartland Mole, was a twenty-three-year-old second lieutenant with the Manchester Regiment when he served in Italy in September 1944 at the Battle of Montegridolfo, in the Province of Rimini.

Despite having no medical training, he helped deliver twins to a local family during an artillery bombardment and in return, was given the honour of naming one of them after his mother, Kathleen.

After the war, he briefly took up a civilian career before joining military intelligence in West Berlin. He was there when the Berlin Wall was constructed and conducted de-briefings of escapees from the East.

This much is true.

Everything else is from the author's imagination.

Acknowledgements

I am grateful to a number of people who helped me in writing this story.

Graeme Douglas, author of the Haynes Owners' Workshop Manual on the Boeing B-17 Flying Fortress, who provided invaluable advice on the technical aspects of the aircraft and gave me a private tour of the *Sallie B,* currently on display at the Imperial War Museum, Duxford;

Loredana Harley and Volker Bertram, who helped me with the Italian and German phrases;

Kristin Bryant for the cover design (www.coroflot.com/kristinbryant)

Becca Allen for the copyediting (www.beccaalleneditorial.co.uk)

Jean France for proofreading and,

my darling wife Nicky, who planted the story worm in my head and encouraged me to write in the first place.

Printed in Great Britain
by Amazon